VIVA

Also by Alice Nunn

Illicit Passage

Stella's Stripes

Sail On

Going Down Gordon Brown

VIVA

Alice Nunn

ASHWOOD
PUBLISHING

ISBN paperback: 978-1-7636921-9-0
ISBN epub: 978-1-7641254-0-6

Published by Ashwood Publishing, Cradoc, Tasmania.
ashwoodpublishing.com.au
info@ashwoodpublishing.com.au

This is a work of fiction, and the persons, events, and locations depicted herein are either fictitious or, in the case of real locations, persons, or organisations, are used fictitiously.

The work of Ashwood Publishing is nurtured by the beautiful country of the Melukerdee people in the Huon Valley in southern Lutruwita/Tasmania. We acknowledge and pay respect to the traditional owners and continuing custodians of this place.

A catalogue record for this work is available from the National Library of Australia

Dedicated to my father

Author's Note

Some of the details of the trip to Salamanca are derived from the diary entries of my father, who made this journey in 1970. Some of the wartime reminiscences are also derived from his letters to my mother. However, all of the characters in the novel are purely imaginary, and their backgrounds and the stories they tell are fictional.

A.N.

I

Pilgrimage to Salamanca

One

'Is this normal?'

The words had a strange echoing muffled quality in the wide stone spaces. Or was it my hearing failing to adjust?

Whatever the cause, I felt a surge of irritation at my son's question. What was a teenager doing criticising? As a late addition to the trip, as someone there on sufferance, an inconvenient extra, it was not his place to be questioning such things. I was going to say something along these lines, a rebuke.

But I was too slow. Bob Campbell replied instead. 'What? The Mass?'

'Yes. Walking into someone else's church and having your own service. I can't imagine anyone doing that in Dad's church.'

'Well, Father Gregory is ordained. And well … I think different rules apply.'

The words I was going to say somehow got lost in this unexpected response, unexpected because of the doubt also being expressed. Even though it was respectful doubt. Bob was a Presbyterian, a faith not much given to candles and gilt images. Yes, I supposed different rules did apply in the Catholic church. One God, many religions – uncountable possibilities beyond the ken of the ordinary person.

Jack nodded as if satisfied, and Bob took his arm. 'Come on, we'd better go and join in, what are friends for otherwise?'

I hung there a moment. The conversation was over and Jack was walking with Bob over to the chapel – they'd resolved it in their own minds and were now ready to accept whatever transpired. But I'd been somehow shocked and now I thought about it, maybe it was the church that affected me. Coutances Cathedral. One of the most beautiful places I'd ever been; coming out of a grey misty morning into this extraordinary space had somehow knocked me off balance.

Perhaps Gregory had been the same. He'd taken one look and said, 'Oh, this is wonderful – let's say Mass.' Was that normal?

Of late I'd been avoiding any examination of what normal was. So my son's question at first seemed impudent, imprudent, one or the other. My head felt slightly dizzy – too little sleep, too much stress, someone else would have to drive the next leg. And I felt rather overwhelmed by everything. It was so long since I'd been out of England and I was only used to a watered-down version of Gothic – minus the exuberance of the interior around me, the braided luminous theatricality of it.

I certainly couldn't imagine anyone walking into my church, St Margaret and St Chad's, and requesting to run their own service. Why would they – the sheer ordinariness of the place, rebuilt in 1886 to a template popularised by Pugin, was in startling counterpoint to this. Although I have to say that one of the other churches in my parish, a tiny eighth-century minster, was sometimes the object of strange requests from people wanting to dress up in long robes and chase moonbeams and ghosts through ancient archways and flit among the illegible gravestones to the sound of tabor and reed pipes. But requests of that sort were firmly refused by the parish council, who didn't want hippies or Druids or whoever chanting solstice weirdness in their pre-mediaeval gem.

As I walked over slowly to join the others, reflecting on all of this, another thing struck me – something which had often happened of late. In adjusting to the question Jack had asked, instead of immediately leaping to Gregory's defence, I was momentarily held back by the architecture of an internal dam wall which I seemed to have erected to stop words spilling over the edge before due consideration had been given to them. Cautiousness. It was often a good thing, made life run more smoothly and prevented things being said that would cause ruptures, fissures, ruin of dreams and happiness. But on the other hand it acted as a mute. I was becoming increasingly unhappy with this muted middle age. I wanted my life to be more – I cast around for the word – more vivid.

Meanwhile, Gregory had been preparing for the service with the help of the priest on duty. Bob, Jack and I were, to start with, his only congregation. After the first strangeness wore off, I became quite comfortable with this. But then I felt a slight flicker of alarm: a French woman had come along and had sat down next to Jack. I assumed she was French because she was straining forward slightly to catch the words and she was dressed in an indefinably continental fashion, in which even though her clothes were rundown they had clearly once been smart, even stylish, and of a sort that in England only the rich could ever aspire to.

Bob went up to read the Epistle and I went up for the Gospel, and as I did so I saw out of the corner of my eye that Jack was murmuring to the woman, perhaps translating. I suddenly realised that his French was much better than any of the rest of ours – I had known it theoretically but had no previous experience of it in practice.

The Mass continued, everything in English except for 'le Corps du Christ'. At this point the French lady came forward and received it.

So that was a small experience in the Chapel of St George. I was somewhat calmed by the orderliness of the proceedings. I could see that we were helping Gregory to do what he was called to do and felt happy that our presence and goodwill were of use in our friend's religious observances.

Afterwards the three of us walked around the cathedral and I was enraptured by the encaustic floor tiles in their asymmetrical running bond, and then the exquisite vaulting, the expanse of space, the extent and delicacy of design. Up there was old air last breathed by mediaeval masons working with precision for the greater glory of God.

Of course Bob, whose approach to these matters verged at times on Marxist, didn't hold with the view that these giant structures were constructed for the greater glory of God. He believed they were constructed to induce calm in the populace. 'Lot of things to worry about in the eleven hundreds – pestilence, war, witchcraft. You come in here and your blood pressure immediately goes down. Much easier for the high-ups to keep the underclasses docile.'

I was always amused by Bob's world view, and Gregory was too buoyant after his Mass to argue. We started heading towards the door and I signalled to Jack, who was still sitting quietly talking to the French woman, that we were off to get lunch provisions.

———

When we emerged from the church, the previous drizzle had turned into light rain. We went shopping for a picnic lunch – bread and two sorts of cooked meat, some camembert and four sticky buns. Meanwhile Jack stood in the shelter of the cathedral doorway. I suddenly wondered, with concern and irritation, whether he'd brought a raincoat. For heaven's sake! The boy was sixteen, nearly seventeen. Surely by that age his father didn't have to pack for him. But then, perhaps I should have taken more notice, been more help, given more guidance? The trouble was … Well, I didn't want to start thinking about what the trouble was. The final phone call with my wife the night before I left had rattled me and I didn't really know why – perhaps because its businesslike tone seemed to be hiding something else, some sort of tension, some excitability lurking below the surface. And of course the complete absence of blessings or bon voyage. I'd become used to those sorts of disappointments but still … Perhaps that was the reason I hadn't turned my mind to Jack. Or perhaps it was because my son was much more used to travelling than I was, although now I came to think of it, his was travelling of a different sort, to destinations where any number of raincoats could be pulled out of a cupboard if needed.

Then, to my surprise, I saw the French lady come back and hand my son something, a largish package of some sort. There was more conversation between the two of them and the lady was pointing, clearly some instruction written on the outside, as if explaining. She had a hurried, nervous manner and when she left I noticed she walked in a bent sort of way, as if curved in to the right.

'What's that she gave you?' I asked as we went back to the car.

'She has a sister who lives in Ligugé,' Jack said. 'She asked if I could deliver this.'

I sighed, somewhat irritated. The car was packed to the roof. Even stowing the lunch materials in the boot was difficult, and what she had given him was a largish box. But Jack seemed happy to hold it on his knee and so I said nothing.

Bob was now driving, with me beside him as navigator. Gregory got in the back with Jack and he too asked what he was carrying. Jack explained, 'I said we were driving through France to a religious conference in Spain, and when she asked me where we were staying en route, I said in monasteries. I said that tonight we were staying at Ligugé, and she threw up her hands and said she knew the monastery there and that her sister's family lived quite near to it. So she went off to get this and asked me if I could take it to her family.'

Gregory exclaimed at the coincidence. How many other people on the face of the planet were driving through France on their way to an ecumenical knees-up in Salamanca and had stopped to celebrate Mass at the very moment when she was in the cathedral and they could be of use to her? How wonderful were the workings of God! He was clearly very pleased about how things had turned out and said what a wonderful start this was to the trip.

That put me in my place. I was relieved, in the light of Gregory's enthusiasm, that I had held back from voicing disapproval of my son's actions. Relieved yes, because despite my increasing impatience with my own discretion, it was nevertheless a good trait to have when travelling in company.

Gregory was young, or youngish, and had fairly recently taken his vows. He seemed to see the world as somewhere shiny and bright, freshly scrubbed clean by God to bring joy to his people and to encourage and console them. I envied him his happy belief and wished I still held that view.

Gregory continued to enthuse because he had now remembered that it was almost five years to the day that he had joined his order, and this was yet another sign of God's blessing. That, of course, started a conversation about 'callings' and what had prompted him to become a monk, had something strange and amazing happened to give him that feeling?

He said, 'I always thought I might have a calling but there's a lot going on when you're young, possibilities which you need to explore, so I went to university, which was expected, and got caught up in all sorts of things. I started teaching at a Catholic school after university, and it's hard to put a finger on when exactly I decided – it was gradual, a building up of need. And then I went to a retreat at the monastery one Easter and it immediately felt like home. It didn't seem like much of a step at all when I left the secular world and joined the community. The boys I started teaching there were the same sort of boys as my previous school, but I felt different in myself, more centred and relaxed.'

'But why a monk?' asked Bob. 'You could have been a priest.'

'No, I wanted to keep teaching and I had no calling for the cure of souls, only for a more deliberate relationship with God and a contemplative life in which to examine it. And I have to say, the kind of life where people will call me Gregory and not Greg. Greg to me sounds like some bumbling second-division football player who can barely dribble the ball. I could never get my family to stop calling me that until I entered holy orders. It was a second coming to some extent.'

'Oh well, that lets me out,' said Jack. 'I'm quite happy with my name.'

Jumping Jack Flash. Jack of all trades. Yes, they all agreed, names were important. And the shorter the name the less likely it was to be desecrated, turned into some one-syllable approximation.

'Like me,' said Bob. 'Robert married Barbara and we became Bob and Barb, like characters from children's television.'

My sister used to call me Marty. It wasn't really a shortening, more of a family softening. I remembered suddenly her calling to me down the lane, but I shut that thought down pretty quickly.

The conversation had moved on to nicknames.

'Of course I used to get Ginger,' said Gregory. 'And even now, behind my back, Father Gingery. It's a cross I'll have to bear all my life.'

'Don't worry,' I said. 'At some point you'll probably start going grey like me.'

No, responded Gregory gloomily, his father was in his sixties and still resolutely ginger.

'Maybe you need a big fright,' said Jack. 'I've heard that can turn people's hair white.'

Ah well that might be a problem, due to him taking up a life almost devoid of shock. Perhaps his family could provide it, could one of them be persuaded to turn Protestant? Or more shocking still, Jehovah's Witness? And what was wrong with the colour of his hair anyway, hadn't one of his sisters become a model?

Yes, his sister Ann had taken her bright orange hair all the way to the cover of Vogue. She was now based in Milan and had changed her name to Madellena. But it was different for girls, said Gregory.

Madellena. Nice, now she even sounded like a model. 'I suppose some people change their names completely when they take their vows,' said Bob. 'You don't hear of any of the religious with modern names, you know like Father Ringo or Father Elvis.'

'Oh yes, people do change their names, but I didn't have to or want to. Saint Gregory was a spiritual leader and missionary. I'm quite happy to bear his name. In full of course.'

We were driving through an attractive rural landscape and a contemplative mood hit the car. Jack was asleep again, slumped against the pile of luggage in the middle seat. Gregory commented on it. 'Catnapping. Some of the elderly in my community find it very hard to stay awake after lunch. At Midday Prayer you can see them gently nodding. I know they're mortified that they do it.'

'I wish I could sleep like that now,' said Bob. 'A few years ago Barb and I went round America on a Greyhound bus. Ninety-nine days for ninety-nine dollars and we slept every second night on the bus to save money.'

'Ninety-nine days!' exclaimed Gregory. 'That's a long time.'

'It's a big country and pretty well all of it is inhabited. It amazes me to think how you can go on and on and there are towns and small hamlets and farms and so on everywhere you look. But they don't do deals like that anymore, I've been told that nowadays it's ninety-nine dollars for thirty days. I don't think I could do it again anyway, once you get out of the habit. Nowadays I need to be pretty well flat before I can go to sleep at all.'

'Jack can sleep anywhere,' I said. 'Plus he was up half the night talking to those girls on the ferry.'

'That's the thing about travelling,' said Bob. 'Suddenly you end up having all these conversations with people you don't know and will never meet again. When we got back, we felt a bit flat for a while. It was supposed to be the holiday of a lifetime before we settled down, but there's something about travelling like that which is inherently unsettling, so it was a couple of years before we decided we were ready to start a family. Then of course the problems began.'

Ah. Gregory and I delicately refrained from inquiring into his problems. Even though it was now 1970 and so many things had advanced, such things were still somehow off-limits. I had my own problems anyway, of a different sort. Perhaps Gregory had problems too, who could tell.

———

It was raining steadily when we drew up outside the great fortress-like monastery at Solesmes. We had planned only for a short stop, so as to listen to the monks chanting their nones. Solesmes – one of the biggest communities in France – had a special way of chanting.

Afterwards it was still raining and Gregory, who had been greeted with hospitable warmth, organised for us to eat our lunch in a guest room on the second floor. We spread the food on the table and sat quietly watching the rain fall among the silver birches within the mediaeval garden walls. There was something about the place, a solemnity, which seemed to discourage talking.

Once back in the car, we discussed the chanting. I have to

say I was not much impressed by it, although of course I was impressed by all that practice and devotion. But to me it was like listening to a man who was putting great effort into telling you a joke which you didn't in the end find funny. In other words, I didn't get it.

Bob turned to Jack and asked, 'What did you think?'

'It was like they were embroidering with silk on the air and offering up the patterns to God,' Jack responded.

Now that slayed me every time, the realisation that my son didn't see things in the same way I did. I always wondered how that could be; for a son who was flesh of my flesh, surely I could expect similarity, solidarity, compatibility. But on the other hand maybe it was me that got it wrong, maybe I was listening to the music in the wrong way, categorising the 'patterns' as manufactured and I don't know, unnecessarily complex. Bob was right, travelling was unsettling.

Gregory found it hilarious that Jack had bought one of the 'miracle medals' for sale in the foyer at Solesmes despite being neither devout nor Catholic.

'Why? Do they only work if you're a Catholic?' Jack asked with a look of innocent disappointment.

Gregory explained that they were to bolster the faith of those who already had some.

'It's a bit of a con though isn't it?' said Bob doubtfully. Gregory didn't defend the practice.

Jack, however, was not put off. 'I'm going to take it in with me to the next calculus exam. And if I scrape through, I'll have faith then. It will be a true miracle, and I will carry it with me into every difficult situation and breeze through unscathed.' He was dangling the medal in front of him as he said this. 'Am I supposed to kiss it as well?'

Kissing holy objects, was that a con too? The conversation

returned to miracles. Jack said, 'Dad's religion doesn't really do them.'

'Oh I don't know about that,' I said. 'As a largely Protestant country, in conjunction with America as a largely Protestant country, we've come up with some things which fifty years ago would definitely have been miracles.'

I cited the example of penicillin. 'If I'd been wounded during the First World War, the result would likely have been one of two things. The most likely would have been that the wound would have got infected and I would have died. The second most likely would be that they would have cut my leg off using basic anaesthetics and I might have survived. I don't know what the survival rate was for heroic surgery then. But the Americans started producing penicillin large-scale just before the Second World War and when I was wounded – like Lazarus I rose from the dead, or the potential dead. Not only did I not die but took up my bed and *walked*. Isn't that a miracle?'

My companions rose to the challenge, and there was much discussion on the definition of a miracle, which didn't reach any satisfactory conclusion before someone noticed that the rain had stopped.

We brewed up afternoon tea beneath a walnut tree in a side road not far from Tours. Bob, who owned the red Vauxhall Viva we were travelling in, brought out three fold-down seats from the boot and a small table to put the fuel stove on. Jack, being a late addition, wasn't catered for with a chair but got out the groundsheet and sat quite comfortably cross-legged on it. 'Were you near here during the war, Dad?' he asked.

'No, further back, in Normandy. Although I was never quite sure where we were.'

'So you don't know where your Road to Damascus moment happened.'

'No, not exactly. But we would have passed it a while ago, it was much closer to the coast.'

I had gone into the army in August 1939 having just finished my articles, at which point I was an officially qualified solicitor with a piece of paper in scrolled copperplate to prove it. Were they wasted years? All that studying I did and then, when I came out of the army, I threw it all in to take orders and become a vicar in the Church of England.

It was on a long, straight road past a chateau that I changed my mind about my future. My platoon had crossed a river on foot the previous night – it was pitch black and we had had a long trudge in the dark. Then we rested for a while and it began to get light. There were no signs of fighting at that point and we all breathed a sigh of relief, putting off the evil moment.

It was to be an early morning attack. The general scheme was to break out of the Normandy bridgehead, and the battalion had been given a village as an objective with a line of advance to it. My company were to be in support, following up behind another company.

In the dawn we were told to get ready. And suddenly as the light strengthened came hundreds of heavy bombers overhead and thudded down their loads. Anti-aircraft from the German side put up their shells and then part of our artillery took on the German anti-aircraft batteries. It was now fully light and the whole countryside seemed to be on the move. Down every hedgerow, along every road, came infantry and tanks. All our artillery was blazing away and one could hardly think for the racket. My men formed up and waited for the moment to set off and go. Two of the men wanted to 'go sick' with diarrhoea but of course they had to come along with us – war is different to peace, you don't get time off, you don't get to be sick, you either survive or not.

We started to move.

We had been walking for about an hour, firstly along a narrow road with friendly hedges and, I noted, even more friendly looking ditches. The noise was intensifying all the time. We came to the end of this shelter and the road now ran through open fields towards a chateau. The sky was dark with machines and smoke and explosions, up ahead trees were on fire, clouds of smoke puffed into the air like a steam train. The noise. And the smell. No film, no photograph, no book, could convey the terrifying smell of all-out combat.

It was then I saw the man. He was from the leading company and had been left behind, all by himself, with his hands over his ears like in that painting …

The Scream.

What a war picture that was if you filled the background with yellow and purple smoke and filled the airways with the howl of ordnance. The man's eyes fixed on me for some reason as if I could save him, looking at me pathetically, like a rabbit in the jaw of a greyhound.

Was that the first test? Leaving him there?

I never really got over that, although in theory it should have been all the dead bodies, the metal smell of blood and rancid death. But it was this that was the most upsetting, the image that has startled me awake at night time after time. How long did the man keep standing there? After we left, did he have the sense to at least find somewhere safer to stand? Or was he cut down, a stationary target?

My platoon kept going but at some point we paused, perhaps we were waiting for those ahead of us to move. I remember being beside a German field dressing station which was in a dugout, and outside, stretcher after stretcher lay in a long line each with a soldier on it, nearly all of them dead. One man was still groaning, he appeared to be missing an arm and what was left of his sleeve was soaked in blood. One of my men offered him a cigarette but the man only wanted to groan, softly and relentlessly.

For some reason my memory kept fixating on individuals, ones that were still alive, to blot out … I had seen corpses the previous day in the position we had moved into. There was nothing really horrible about them. I did not see anything very horrifying in death – nor did the corpses look particularly horrific, for they mostly had quite composed faces. I thought that after our artillery barrage the last moments of a German soldier's life, when consciousness was slipping away, must have been peaceful almost. Their faces and hands were pale and like waxworks. I touched one to move him and the body was already stiff; not like a poker but like a tailor's dummy where perhaps you could move an arm to a different angle if you applied a little force. I didn't try.

No, it wasn't the memory of those bodies that came to me the most vividly, it was that poor frightened man quivering beside the road, that was the first test. The one I kept coming back to.

Beyond the chateau, the land opened out, a park with no shelter and the German artillery was onto us. The earth bubbled where shells exploded but we just had to go on. I had always been a believer, had always had faith but now I prayed extra hard, please God give me strength. A shower of earth from the side and my shoulder felt warm for a moment as if something had pressed against it, had I been hit? No but the warmth remained and spread, I got strength, I felt it suffuse me bodily, Oh Christ Who Wast With Me in Normandy. I was possessed with gratitude, I wanted to go back and help the man I had left, breathe some of my belief into him, help those around me to cope through this strong visceral connection I now had to another, greater Being.

I thought this feeling would dissipate when the immediate danger was over, having been brought out in extremis. But it didn't – it even grew if that was possible.

I felt immense sadness for the dead. I looked through a dead German's photograph wallet, showing him and his family. They were mostly in uniform, youngsters in the Hitler Youth movement. A wedding – was it *his*, I wondered? Posed groups, everyone smiling.

A bitter viewing.

Bitter because there was no such thing as a 'just' war, there was just bloody awful war, with women sitting dishevelled on their front steps weeping over telegrams, children's arms poking out from underneath bombed buildings, lines of the dead waiting to be processed. All this collateral damage caused by the people at the top, the ranters and demagogues who swept the small fry up and sent them clamorously into attack. There was no fairness, no justice.

And because of this, I felt I should try and do something, I didn't know what. This feeling stayed with me as we pressed forward, that I should be doing something, something more useful than walking along carrying a rifle. But I walked on anyway, my platoon around me, walking through the valley of death as bombs and artillery went off everywhere, walking on because that's what you did in a war.

That night my platoon slept on a bank. In the morning, we realised we'd been sleeping on dead bodies that someone had piled rocks on top of. My men reacted with horror but it didn't matter to me, death was now a comfortable place with no terrors.

Strangely enough, one memory was still vivid although I don't really know why. My sergeant and I went down into an officer's dugout. Battle-scarred and filthy, we were astonished by the range of cosmetics we found there – hair oil and aftershave and other unguents in pots and bottles. I looked around pretty sharply to see if there was any soap but that's the one thing he didn't seem to have. Or someone else had found it first and nicked it.

Maybe the reason I retained that scene was because of the

intimate accounting it gave of other people's lives, presumably lives lived under the same duress as mine.

Anyway, those were the memories which sometimes resurfaced, and originally they had bolstered my commitment. But of late I noticed that's all they were, just memories.

I was wounded a couple of weeks later, I didn't know exactly when – shrapnel in the leg and grazing my head, very possibly from friendly fire. I had no recollection at all of how it happened – I was knocked off my feet and lay unconscious for a while and found when I eventually woke up that I didn't know how I got where I was and didn't remember anything that had happened in the previous twenty-four hours.

And that was the end of the war for me but not the end of that feeling of being inhabited by something wonderful, something beyond me who for one short moment had laid His hand on my shoulder.

———

We packed up and drove on to Ligugé. The monastery stood in a smallish village, near to a railway station on the Paris to Bordeaux line. Vespers had already begun but Gregory nevertheless went in to do his duty.

Jack proposed to deliver the package and Bob said he would go with him. I wasn't keen; there was something I'd spotted in the French woman in the cathedral which made me think her not quite normal, some over-quick gestures and excitable phrases which I hadn't understood although Jack seemed to. I didn't want to get caught up if her family was equally odd, so I followed Gregory inside and sat peaceably watching the service.

Afterwards we were welcomed by Père François in charge of the guests. Jack and Bob had not come back but he showed us to our rooms in quite a modern building; four plain cells but with hot showers and toilets across the landing. I was pleasantly surprised. Running water and all mod cons seemed more comfortable than I was expecting, and I wondered if this was even a little more comfortable than St Benedict may have had in mind. My room was furnished with an iron bedstead, a table, a chair and a reading lamp. A jug and ewer were found in a shelved cupboard together with a shaving mirror. Everything was scrubbed clean and smelled of incense and bread pudding … Allspice? Nutmeg?

We were then gathered up by Père François and taken downstairs where we had a peep at part of the ancient subterranean stonework. At that moment the Abbot passed by, and Gregory performed an act of fealty by kneeling and kissing his ring. I was somewhat taken aback by this sudden excitable gesture and reflected that if this had been required in my own religion, I would have had to have carried some sort of kneeling frame so I could get back up again, my war injury being increasingly unkind in middle age.

I was surprised and disturbed to find when we returned to the cloisters that the other two had not yet reappeared. It was just before dinner, and we were lining up with half a dozen other guests. What should we do, I wondered to Gregory but Gregory, ever practical, had stowed extra provisions in the car in case we arrived at a monastery that was fasting. So if they missed the meal there was at least something for them.

I turned to go in with a sigh. I should have taken more of a hand in the matter when that Frenchwoman extracted a kindness from my son who, I noticed, seemed particularly likely to be taken advantage of. Kindness of that sort, I thought, should be rationed to particular occasions and not when such acts would inconvenience others.

On entering the refectory we found the Abbot standing beside a beautiful and ancient bowl of silver with scripture in Latin engraved around the rim. In this he washed the hands of each guest and dried them on a beautiful linen towel. I was immensely touched, and my previous thoughts seemed tawdry and unchristian after such a welcome – it was a reminder that a kind act, an act of charity, an act of humble generosity, is a precious and golden gift.

The guests were placed around a long table in the centre of the refectory while the monks lined the walls, facing us at a slightly higher level. I realised this was to see that the food was circulated without any traffic hold-ups. Thus a monk (in particular Père François) would interrupt his own meal to see that the soup didn't give up too soon – it was in large bowls with ladles for each guest to help himself – or to top up a wine glass if need be.

The clink of cutlery and glass accompanied a reading in French for our mental sustenance. Probably only Jack was sufficiently fluent to have followed it, but he wasn't there, and I stopped being irritated and started being concerned.

After the soup, there was cold meat of the sausage family, salad, a kind of ravioli with tomato sauce, stewed fruit, then cheese. It was pleasant without being overly tasty and there was sufficient without profusion. I knew that Gregory, being a young man, found the quantity and quality of the food at his own monastery wearisomely inadequate, no doubt because it came out of the kitchens that also provided for the school. I had on occasions eaten there as a guest and had to rigorously discipline myself not to go home afterwards and have grilled cheese on toast.

So over the last couple of years I had sometimes, on a weekday night when only Jack and I were at home, killed the fatted calf and invited Gregory for dinner. Roast beef when I could afford it, Yorkshire pudding, roast potatoes, carrots and parsnips, peas if they were in season or braised cabbage, and a huge jug of gravy. And then a pudding with lashings of custard. Comfort food. And for further spiritual comfort, I would usually invite Jack Halstead, a

Methodist minister and widower, who was witty and disputatious and occasionally irreverent. Two Jacks at one table, one cheerful and gregarious and the other quiet but hospitable, helping out with the preparation, handing things round and urging Gregory to have a third helping. Then my son would withdraw and leave us men to sort out the pressing concerns of the world.

This meal wasn't on that level, although quite agreeable. It also wasn't particularly French, except for the cheese.

Afterwards, Gregory and I attended Compline in the abbey church. I had an impression of elderly men maintaining a tradition. They all had character, those men, if faces and bearing were anything to go by, but I did think that young enthusiastic monks like Gregory must be gold coin to these ageing communities.

After that there was a conducted tour for the visitors – kind Père François again – of the ancient ruins, unearthed but not removed from beneath the floor of the neighbouring parish church. To my relief, Bob and Jack joined us from somewhere and Gregory introduced them to the guest master. I could hear Jack saying they were fine thank you, so it appeared they had been fed elsewhere.

Père François turned back to the tour – a church had been founded there in the fourth century. Layer after layer of subsequent accretions had been discovered – ruin upon ruin, as war after war had done their worst, particularly by the English. Bob made a joke, at some point in Père François's explanation, by saying, 'Moi, je suis Ecossais', but it was clear that everyone (except maybe the war profiteers who had raided the place for building materials) had long been forgiven.

Afterwards, Bob and Jack were allocated their rooms. 'We delivered the parcel, and they absolutely insisted on us coming in and having dinner with them.' They'd had soup and chunks of bread and a great platter of fried aubergine plus some green beans in tomato sauce. 'The meat,' Jack confided to me, 'I'm pretty sure was horse but I didn't tell Bob, I'm not sure how he would've felt about it.'

I wasn't sure what I would've felt about it either and was glad I hadn't gone. There was nothing to object to about the meal we'd had at the monastery.

Everyone was very tired, so further descriptions were put aside till later on and I retired to my austere bedroom.

I had made a pledge to myself to keep a diary, which normally I would have done in bed, but the way the room was set up made this impossible. There was no bedside table or lamp near the bed, and the overhead light was too dim to write by anyway. My only option was to sit at the desk near the window and use the small desk lamp there. The notebook I'd brought was blank and I'd been intending to write descriptions of our travels, how far we went on each day, sights we had stopped to take in. But as I sat there, I looked out of the window to the darkened trees and the faint bulk of the abbey walls.

I wrote:

> I have been looking out of the window for several minutes, my mind absolutely blank. Do the monks here have windows and views that they can gaze on? I'm wondering if gazing and having absolutely nothing in your mind is allowed? I know eastern religions want you to empty your mind to meditate but I suspect the Christian religions want you to fill your mind up with thoughts – of God of course – to the exclusion of everything else. Although now I remember, I think the Buddhists have to chant a word internally? I suppose with Christians, focusing on prayers and inspirational thoughts is the same. So words, all words, man-made constructs, have been keeping the

ineffable and unimaginable at bay. It's nice to stop and think of nothing.

I suddenly felt immensely weary and gave up. Changing into my pyjamas, I looked at the thin mat beside the bed. Apologising to all the other guests who had knelt on it, I folded it double. Shrapnel, I told them as, clutching the bed frame, I lowered myself onto my knees.

There was a time early on in my ministry when my bedside prayers had taken in the good of all mankind, praying for peace and no more war, praying during famine and pestilence for the multitudes affected, and as an afterthought praying for the assorted ills of my congregation. Now I just prayed for my family. Was that bad? Had I travelled so far down the road from my previous expansive liberality as to end up in some metaphorical ditch, trying to save the few rather than the many?

I prayed for my eldest son, whom I hadn't heard from in months, prayed that his studies were going well and that he was using his summer vacation productively. I prayed for my daughter, who was staying with my brother-in-law while I was away. Mainly I prayed that my brother-in-law was coping. And finally I prayed for my wife Joan. This was the hard part. The easy part was to pray that her summer diploma course at Oxford University was going well. And because I was tired, I left it at that.

I switched off the light and climbed into my creaking single bed. It was usually my habit to collect my thoughts in the dark, what the following day would bring and so on. Instead the dark blotted me out and I was instantly asleep.

Two

I was woken by Gregory moving around in the room next door and was surprised to see light streaming in through the window. A very good night's rest; I felt refreshed and invigorated. I got up, dressed quickly and went down with Gregory to attend Mass in the abbey church.

When I returned to my room, I wondered about shaving. There had been no time the previous morning because despite the ferry advertising that disembarkation could be delayed till 7 a.m., this was not the reality. The ferry crew was keen to get us all off the ship as soon as possible and as a result we had had time neither for breakfast nor for anything else. There had been periods during the war when shaving was equally difficult, and going bearded was something I quite enjoyed. But Joan didn't like it and so for the last twenty years I had been clean-shaven. But Joan was elsewhere, grimly pursuing her own agenda. And this realisation brought a sense of peace, even release – I too could go my own way.

I went to rouse Jack, who was completely dead to the world. Breakfast was in the guestroom and again conversation was discouraged apart from essentials. I noted however the variety of things that Frenchmen could do with bread, butter, a cup of coffee and a spoonful or two of conserve. I watched Jack enthusiastically plunging his bread and jam into his café au lait and he was copied, after some experimenting, by both Gregory and Bob. Only one other man seemed willing to do one thing at a time, and he turned out of course not to be French but a wandering student from Harvard.

Before leaving, we looked at the enamel work produced by the monks. Bob thought of buying a beautifully coloured 'abstract' mounted in a picture frame for his wife, but in the end baulked at spending up big so early with the car was piled high – no, he was sure he would be able to find something suitable on the return journey.

Off we went again, through pleasant rolling countryside. Gregory was driving this time, with me again in the front seat navigating. After some passing remark regarding the previous evening, Bob asked Jack how he came to speak such good French. 'My own French,' he said, 'is of the heavily Anglo variety which the people of France sometimes refuse to recognise as being French at all.'

Jack told him that he liked doing languages and because his older brother, Pete, was already involved in the French exchange system at school, he had been allowed to join earlier than the others and was originally supposed to 'exchange' with the cousin of Pete's student. But as luck would have it that boy's family had had to pull out and instead he'd got Antoine.

I reflected that there was a great deal of luck involved in such transactions. Pete and his exchange student had gone their separate ways, but Jack and Antoine had bonded and become great friends. Jack was only twelve when he went over the first time but had already shown a facility with languages; his quick grasp of French had surprised his teacher. Even so I had been worried that he was too young, but at least Pete was over there too. Pete had come back not particularly overwhelmed by the experience. 'It was okay,' he said, and proceeded to scrape through O level in French. That was it as far as he was concerned. But Jack had obviously had a much better time.

Possibly the reason for this was that Antoine lived on a farm, as did Jack's best friend, Tony Barker, who was only a mile down the road from us. From an early age, Jack had been engaged in farm work, helping Tony with the lighter tasks when they were younger, feeding the animals and so on and then graduating over time to driving tractors and other farm machinery. When he had arrived in France to stay with a pupil his own age on an isolated farm, it was somewhat to the concern of the school authorities who were organising the exchange. Would he feel cut off? Would he be happy there, some distance from his brother and the other exchange students?

Their fears were unfounded. On the second day he got behind the wheel of a French tractor and never looked back. He was endlessly curious about the different ways they had of doing things. His letters home were full of farming details and country life. He spent the following year writing to his exchange student, describing the rural calendar of events around him in England.

Antoine came to stay with us the following summer. He was a rather shy boy, perhaps because he lived quite some distance from the nearest town and had a long bus ride to get to school, similar to Jack. He was a small and dark-haired with anxious eyes; also, perhaps, a little young three years ago for an exchange lasting a month. I had always thought of Jack as shy too, but realised as time went on that he was merely quiet and watchful.

Nevertheless the two boys got on very well, and Jack took great care of him, making sure he didn't get too distressed with home-sickness. Within a couple of hours of his arrival they were down at the Tony's farm to see a Clydesdale foal newly born two nights previously and to admire their weird-looking Polish bantams.

The summer Antoine came had been a rather hectic one. One of my wife's brothers had arrived from Australia with his family for a few weeks and was staying with another brother, Don, in

Woking. Joan had wanted them all to come up to the vicarage but even with a hire car it would have been quite difficult, especially with teenage children, to have entertained them all with such poor public transport. Woking, with its easy access to London, was a much more tempting base for them. They *had* come up for a couple of days, and everyone was easily accommodated at the vicarage, but afterwards Joan had decreed that we would all go back south with her brother. Jack had taken me aside quietly and said he thought Antoine was a bit overwhelmed by the numbers of people and the noise, and instead of going down south with them, Mrs Barker, Tony's mother, had invited them to stay down the road on their farm. So that's how it was arranged.

I myself had gone south for a few days but was glad of the excuse to come back to look after the boys. I chauffeured them around, taking them to Scarborough for a day on the beach at a typical seaside resort. We had gone up onto the moors and picked bilberries, to Castle Howard with its peacocks, to the Kirby Misperton zoo, plus to some social events organised by the school for the visiting French pupils.

That summer in England seemed to have consolidated the friendship between the two boys, and Jack couldn't wait to go to France the following year. His host family had then made an interesting suggestion. Instead of coming just for the summer, why didn't he come over after Christmas and spend the second half of the school year there, attending school with Antoine?

This was the reason, he told Bob, that his French was so good. Nothing beats immersing yourself in the culture for several months. Also, he said, going in the summer with organised activities was just basically a holiday. Living day-to-day, getting up in the dark to catch the bus to school, dealing with children his own age in a foreign language, helping around the house and the farm – there was no end of words you would never normally learn. The names of herbs, the different breeds of pigs and ducks, the rhetoric of political parties, even some of the concepts in the schoolwork were different. He came back with a vocabulary hugely greater than his schoolmates and even his French teacher.

One casualty of the arrangement had been the concept of an exchange. Last year they had asked him to come to them again because Mme Berger's father's health was poor and they felt that he didn't have long to live, and Antoine wanted to be in easy distance if he deteriorated.

I rather worried that Jack's willingness to engage in farm work might have been a factor in these invitations, but as Jack so clearly enjoyed it I saw no reason to demur. The old man had rallied, but this year the arrangement was still that Jack should go to France. He should've been there even as we spoke but the grandfather, who lived in Switzerland, had died a few days previously. Antoine and the whole family had gone there for the funeral and to sort out the bureaucratic details of death. Which was the reason Jack was a last-minute addition to this trip.

'Had you met the grandfather?' asked Bob.

'Yes, Mme Berger was always popping over the border. I stayed there a few times. Nice old chap.'

'I've always thought I'd like to visit Switzerland,' said Gregory.

'It's very orderly. Even the French-speaking part is Calvinistic. There is a whole list of things you can't do on Sunday. Hanging out washing and things like that. Driving a car.'

'Driving a car!'

'Yes, well in the part he lived anyway. Anything that could be thought of as work-related.'

'How did you get to church?'

'Walk. Or go by bicycle.'

I mused that it was only in the last dozen or so years that ordinary people would have had a car. Before the war nearly everyone had to walk to church. My own parish, with four churches, would have required a number of curates for Sunday services. Now I had a car provided by the parish and of course all the farmers had at least one vehicle, including some which were only for Sunday best.

Yes, Jack told them of one rich farming family with an Austin Princess which was mainly kept in their garage during the week while they zipped around in the farm van. However, during the Suez crisis they wouldn't have got a petrol ration for it just to go visiting and to church, so the lady of the house had insisted it be registered as a farm vehicle so they could get fuel.

'Mrs Wills-Lester had a motherless lamb that she had raised by bottle, and it thought it was a dog,' said Jack. 'She was training her poodle, sit, lie down, come here, and she noticed the lamb had started to sit and lie down on command as well. So it went everywhere in the car with her until rationing finished.'

I laughed. 'So she could point to it and say look, farm animal.'

'What happened to it then?' asked Bob. 'I hope it didn't end up as cutlets.'

'Oh no,' said Jack, horrified. 'You wouldn't waste a friendly sheep like that. It's out in the flock and when you call for it, it comes, and all the others follow.'

———

We arrived at Angoulême and went to look at the cathedral. The general design was quite pleasing and I admired the brickwork, especially around the organ, but thought there was also something slightly off key about it, perhaps as a result of the internal seating arrangements.

Bob agreed. He'd seen genteel churches in Scotland like this with the pulpit at one side of the nave, enabling the preacher to hurl declamations at the pews facing him. Fire-and-brimstone was always slightly off key, but those who were looking to shut their eyes in contemplation could sit out of range so an agreeable balance was reached. Whereas in America, churches were designed so the whole congregation was under observation and the preacher would move around lest anyone even for a moment thought of having a nap. Architecture and design, according to Bob, were crucial aspects in the control of religion.

'What about Jesus though,' I objected. 'He preached in the open air, people could arrange themselves before him as they saw fit.'

'Unless he had an extremely powerful voice, they'd be right in front of him. Outdoor acoustics dictate the design of the service.'

'Do you think he had a powerful voice?' wondered Jack. 'They always paint him as a slight figure.'

'I'm sure Father Gregory here could preach to a field-full without any difficulty and he's as thin as a rake.'

Gregory grinned. 'I've had lessons in how to project. HOW NOW BROWN COW.' The words, slowly spoken, slipped from the dome down the hemispherical vaulting, each one a golden plum of clarity.

People turned to look at us and we scurried out of the cathedral like naughty schoolboys.

In the pleasant grassy park outside, I said, 'My sergeant major didn't so much project as fire projectiles. Words like grenades packed with shrapnel. Blessed Are The Meek You Horrid Little Men,' I demonstrated. 'He could have preached to thousands who would have heard every word, but I doubt if they would have got the message, love and peace.'

By the time we got back to the car it was raining. 'Oh no,' cried Jack. 'Retribution. For your blasphemy.'

'No, no,' said Bob. 'Barb assures me that God has a sense of humour, otherwise he wouldn't have designed women's bodies in the way he did.'

'Joan would agree with her,' I said, getting in the driver's seat.

Jack pondered this as we drove along. 'Mrs Colbeck, my history teacher in third form, used to go into gory detail about the number of women who had died in childbirth over the ages. All the girls got terribly upset and said no way were they ever getting married, they were all going to be nuns. But not the nunnery down the road which is a bit austere. No, they wanted nice food, French cooking for instance. And to be able to go to the cinema and see musicals.'

'Sounds like bliss. Oh for French cooking!' cried Gregory.

'That was because we had a French teacher's aide at the time, on exchange, who was showing them how to put wine into stew. Anyway, one of the parents complained to Mrs Colbeck, so she gave a whole lesson on the history of advances in gynaecology, which if you ask me was even more gross. But I read in Reader's Digest that women are biologically triggered by huge hulking men and have huge hulking babies as a result.'

'Well you're hulking up a bit.' Bob was sitting next to him in the back and reached over to give his upper arm a tweak. 'I'm sure they'll come flocking now.'

'I know lots of nice girls,' replied Jack with a grin. 'But how do you choose one over another? How did you choose Barb?'

That assumed that Bob got to choose.

They'd met at university. Barb came from England and was much more sophisticated than him, he didn't think he had any chance there. But he'd had a girlfriend during high school and his girlfriend and his sisters were learning all the latest dances and so he learned to jive. 'I was pretty good at it, but my girlfriend dumped me for somebody who was even better! So I went to a first-year university dance on my own and I started dancing with one of Barb's friends and boy did we burn up the floor. And when we went back to where Barb was standing she just put out her hand and grabbed me. And that was it.' He laughed. 'Sometimes you have no say in it. What about you, Martin?'

Pretty much the same thing although very different times. I belonged to my church's youth group, which organised weekly tennis parties, and during 1938 I'd had a regular doubles partner – we were pretty good, she had a great backhand and I had an unbeatable slice, a particular kind of spin which I'd developed after long practice. So although I was not romantically inclined towards my partner, I did enjoy winning, and in the euphoria of Chamberlain's 'peace in our time' I thought we would keep on winning. In 1939 when tennis started again it was a whole different ball game, excuse the pun. For a start, I found that someone had decided that everyone should change partners. And the partner I had drawn was Joan. I wasn't sure where the decision came from, but I suspected Joan had had a hand in it. Anyway that was it for me too. Once I started playing with her, I found I wasn't nearly as interested in winning as before and by July 1939 the international landscape barely impinged; all I thought about was the next tennis party and seeing Joan.

'There you are,' Gregory told Jack. 'Just take up some activity that women like and you'll be partnered up before you know where you are.'

'Did you ever have a girlfriend?' Jack asked him.

I felt myself sort of freeze, it didn't seem the kind of question you should ask a monk. But to my surprise Gregory immediately said, 'Oh yes, Rosemary, a lovely girl. I went out with her for years, in the summer holidays and then later at university. Her family were what you'd call 'County', very upper crust and with that sort of ancestral Catholicism that's more of a badge than a faith. Whereas my family were just common farming folk. So right from the beginning it obviously wasn't going to go anywhere but I don't think either of us thought about that. We were too absorbed in each other to think about the realities.' He'd met her first in the Young Farmers, they were both in the theatrical group and both of them in love with religion and acting and anything else requiring total teenage intensity. Rosemary had once been to confession in a black lace veil and black lace gloves, head to toe in the whole theatrical get-up and then realised that, in the process of turning herself into the most humble of penitents, she'd somehow forgotten to do anything wrong.

They loved everything to do with the theatre. Together they went to acting workshops, voice lessons, dance classes. Yes, we heard him right, dance classes. 'Not social dancing like Bob, but theatre dance, the sort you do on a stage. And very useful it's been too. Any time a maths class is dragging on with everybody getting fractious, losing concentration, I get them all up and make them stand against the wall and do some basic dance steps, left hand right hand, left leg right leg, shake it all about. And then I'll ask them questions and those that get it right get to go back to their desks. Otherwise they have to keep on dancing!'

'Really!' said Jack, entranced. 'I can't imagine our maths teacher doing that.'

'Does that make you wildly popular or wildly unpopular?' asked Bob.

Gregory wasn't sure, but he got results. He said boys don't mind dancing in a chorus line when they're all doing it, all being silly together, but none of them wanted to end up dancing on their own at the end. So they all worked just a little bit harder.

Acting had stood him in good stead as well in other ways. He taught drama and occasionally English literature, mainly to the younger classes at school. And he was usually either director or assistant director of the school play. 'It's always fun to get boys to play girls,' he said. 'Boys who have sisters can be hilarious if they're any good at mimicry. I was casting last year for Adriana in *The Comedy of Errors*, it's a pivotal role if the play is going to be funny. We'd chosen a boy and the voice and everything was right but he was a bit stiff. I asked him if he couldn't walk more like a girl, his sister for instance. And he said his sister didn't walk, she jumped, flounced, flourished and fidgeted and he gave this hilarious imitation of her coming in with a rush and going on about her rabbit, who'd moved the rabbit food, why do people keep moving stuff, it's all very very annoying honestly really honestly didn't anyone care about her rabbit she'd been searching high and low and why did she always have to do everything?' Gregory tried to demonstrate from the front passenger seat to our great amusement. He continued, 'The rhythms in it were fantastic and as some of Adriana's speeches are a bit long and obscure, I got him to do one of them exactly like his sister. It was brilliant.'

The conversation, in the way such wandering conversations did, turned to rabbits. I remembered during the war being in the front of a troop carrier, a converted truck with a canvas cover at the back which, because the weather was warm, was rolled up. We were on our way to exercises in Wales and had been travelling through rural countryside. There was a bang on the partition, so my driver stopped and my corporal appeared at the window and begged me to accommodate Private Smith in the front with us as he was driving them all mad at the back. I was surprised, because he was a quiet young recruit who'd only just arrived. But to please my platoon I made room for him in the front. We'd barely gone a few yards when the young man piped up, 'Look sir, rabbits!' Yes, there they were, rabbits in the field. Well spotted. Two minutes later, 'Look sir, rabbits!' Yes, more rabbits. Then two minutes later, 'Look sir, rabbits!' This went on for twenty minutes, by which time my driver offered to throttle the young man.

So how had I dealt with that, asked the others.

I'd made the men pull down the sides of the canvas and stuck

Smith right at the back where he couldn't see the bloody things. It was not a popular move because of the heat but at least we all arrived at our destination with some degree of sanity intact.

They wondered what happened to Smith but I didn't know, he'd been offloaded elsewhere pretty smartly. The army during wartime had to accept a lot of misfits, men who would spend the entire war cleaning latrines or peeling potatoes. My own company had one such bumbler who couldn't ordinarily march in step to save himself, but someone discovered that if you gave him a trombone he could march precisely to the beat of whatever he was playing. Unfortunately though, you couldn't offload every useless soldier into a military entertainment unit.

'Trombones are hard to play,' said Jack.

'There's a lot of difficult things in civilian life which people learn to do through long practice and perseverance such as trombone playing … and conveyancing … and theology … But they're all completely useless in the army. In the infantry, apart from learning how to fire a gun there is only one other skill required, and that is to march in a disciplined way towards the enemy.'

———

We'd been thinking of lunch for some time, but it kept raining on and off and we were nearly at Libourne. We turned up a quiet country lane and got out the chairs and spread out the groundsheet at the corner of a vineyard. It had stopped raining and the sun had come out and was drying the ground, but the air was fresh still and there was the occasional drip of raindrops from the vine leaves.

We debated whether to say grace at alfresco lunches and came to the conclusion that yes, it might be a good thing to inveigle our way back into the good graces of the Lord. Try as we might, our conversations often drifted towards the boundaries of the heretical.

We also wondered about prayer for a safe journey but decided not. Jack said that he would rather that we didn't keep on reminding God about it and Bob laughed and said, 'My thoughts exactly.'

Back in the car, I was still driving and it had started raining again, this time blotting out the landscape. Excellent timing as far as lunch was concerned. Jack returned to a previous conversation. 'Did your girlfriend go on be an actress, Father Gregory?'

'Her family wasn't at all keen on her taking it up as a career. I don't think they were keen on her having a career at all, or even if the truth be told going to university. Except of course Durham was a lovely mediaeval-looking place – definitely not a redbrick university. It had class and a very good drama club and we were both in *The Merry Wives of Windsor*, which of course is Shakespeare and therefore class, and Rosemary played Nell Quickly as a strumpet which was okay because it's a Shakespearean strumpet. But unbeknownst to them an agent saw her and the next thing she's a saloon girl in *Carry On Cowboy*. Everyone in our district was terribly excited about it but her family were appalled, so vulgar! And they blamed me. Rosemary told them I'd encouraged her to do it.'

And had he?

No, he hadn't.

Oooh. Treachery. Betrayed by your true love.

Gregory laughed. He'd always encouraged her to keep on acting but by the time the film came out he was already teaching and the two of them had … Well, they'd had a rift. When university finished he needed to make some money to pay off debts, and finding a well-paid job in theatre wasn't a likely outcome in the short term. She couldn't bear the thought of him giving up acting and being a teacher even if it was only for a couple of years – in her mind nothing could be duller. She'd written him a letter saying if he was going to move to ordinary-land, as she put it, their relationship was over. And shortly after she met someone else, who she eventually married. And then, as far as he knew, *she* gave up acting.

There was a pause and that seemed to be the end of the subject. But then Jack asked, 'Do you miss that, not having a girlfriend?'

At that moment there was a hold-up in the traffic and I had to concentrate, but I hung there in agony, distressed that my son should ask such an inappropriate question. Gregory was frowning, but I was having to focus on the road and didn't know how to intervene.

Eventually Gregory sighed. 'I haven't thought about this for a while, perhaps it was something I was trying to forget.' Rosemary had come to see him after he became a novice and asked if it was because of her that he was becoming a monk. He had to explain that it wasn't like running away to join the Foreign Legion and that it had always been a possible choice. And then she asked what the other choices were and he'd said, well of course being a world-famous thespian at the Old Vic, on Broadway, possibly getting into films like her. With a wife? she'd asked. Scads of them, he'd said. But it went without saying that there was nothing he could have done, however great or rich or famous he became, which would have ever persuaded Rosemary's family that he was good enough for her. So he didn't say it, she didn't say it, they let it pass. Instead they got sentimental, they reminisced about some of the lovely times they'd had together. Remember, she said, the time when they were sitting in the Buttery cheek to cheek drinking one ice cream soda through two straws and when they got down to the ice cream fighting each other for their share and giggling so much that fizz came out of their noses. Yes, back when they were young and silly. And deliriously happy. They had to be grateful for that but then, things change and one has to make do with ordinary life. And that was it, she left, having achieved absolution or whatever it was she came for. Here's looking at you kid. They would always have Durham.

'That's rather sad,' said Jack.

'It's sad and not sad. It's just moving on to another stage. Becoming an adult is complicated. There are always trade-offs, some happinesses are forgone in order to achieve other benefits. But I do know that I wouldn't trade what I have at the moment for anything in the world.' And then he added, 'It's strange how you move from one version of normality to another and looking back each pod seems quite distinct. How do we cross the boundary and barely notice? It's a mystery.'

Yes, it was a mystery, and it was a mystery I was much preoccupied with at that time. Even at a simple level, moving from a parent supervising his child's behaviour to a parent realising his child now had autonomy, and such supervision was neither required nor appropriate.

———

From Libourne, we made our way cross-country. Traffic was fairly heavy, one obstruction being numerous brightly coloured gypsy motor caravans, some with television aerials. There was something lumbering about this progress that was frustrating and started to fill me with dark, hostile feelings towards gypsies.

But then Gregory said to Bob, 'Travelling in the States for so long, you must have felt at times like gypsies.'

'Oh yes, it seemed to me you could just go on and on, no responsibilities, stop when you felt like it. It was just a matter of money. Stopping is a lot harder than setting off, I found.'

'So, what would make you stop somewhere? What would you look for?'

'Sometimes it wasn't the place, just the necessity. Wash our clothes mainly. If you found a nice hostel, or sometimes not even a nice hostel but a hostel with nice people in it, you'd stay a few days, wash your clothes, have showers, talk to people about the road and what there was worth seeing ahead, play cards, go to the bank and change traveller's cheques, swap books, all that kind of thing. Days could go by, and then suddenly everybody was up and off again. And instead of just the two of you, there might be a whole party by then. And then that group would slowly dissipate and you would be at some other hostel, washing your clothes again, having showers again, forming groups again. That's what I mean, the gypsy life can be pretty communal. Coming home and settling down can be a bit like coming off a drug – you see a long-distance bus go by and all your addiction floods to the surface again.'

'You must have met some strange people, travelling around like that.'

'Yes, strange and sometimes wonderful.' He told us of one of their most memorable experiences, which started in Baton Rouge in one of those chains of events that began with a casual recommendation and ended up in something you could never have imagined. They had visited the citizens advice bureau near the bus station and found there was no hostel in Baton Rouge, but a lady there had given them an address of a house where they were told the owner, Becky, rented out rooms. The house, however, turned out to be more like a full-scale mansion. 'The adventure would have stopped right there the moment I saw it,' Bob said, 'if it had been up to me. No way were we going to be able to afford a room in such a place. And I was right. Becky didn't rent rooms, instead she had guests. Captains of industry, important personages.' But his qualms had no influence on Barb, she was made of stronger stuff so in she bowled, with Bob in tow, to find Becky and the whole household in a crisis. Nothing daunted, Barb had said, 'Linda Golding told us to come here to see if we could rent a room.' To which this very elegant lady responded, 'Have you ever waited on table?' Barb said, 'Of course, we've just finished being students, how else could we save for such a trip? And Bob here worked in a bar.' Then Becky said, 'I didn't used to love Linda Golding that much but now I love her more than I love my own mother.' The upper echelons of Baton Rouge were arriving there for a dinner party that night and the hired help had been in a car accident.

So Bob had served the drinks and Barb took round the finger food and then the two of them served dinner to about twenty people and they got a free room and free food in return. But then things got a bit weirder. 'This old lady came up to me at the bar early on and asked for something non-alcoholic. She commented on my accent, where was I from? Because her family was originally Scottish. We didn't really have time to talk because there were so many people milling around, but I made her up a non-alcoholic cocktail which the old ladies in the pub where I worked used to like. Basically it's just soda water, lime juice, Angostura bitters and sugar and then you plonk fruit in it. Sort of like a non-alcoholic Tom Collins. She mustn't have ever had it before.

'Anyway the next day we were helping tidy up and Becky invited us to stay a couple more days, which we were quite happy to do because why wouldn't you want to observe how the other half live. And then the old lady rang and invited us to her cousin's place to have afternoon tea and a chat and to "get the recipe for that nice drink".

'So off we went with Becky to another mansion, where the afternoon tea was spread over three tables, and eight society ladies elegantly picked at strawberry tarts while Barb and I made total pigs of ourselves! Well the old lady was also a Campbell but I doubt we were related. Her grandfather had had a lot to do with the Caledonian railways before he emigrated, and I told her that I'd grown up living in a railway station.

'She assumed it was a disused one but I said no, one train a day used to go straight past our sitting room window. And I told her the story of the lost Paisley–Barrhead line and she was hugely interested because she thought her grandfather had been involved with that. She said her brother in New York was the family historian and made us promise to call on him when we got there. Of course we solemnly agreed that we would, those promises you make when you're travelling with every intention of keeping except when reality gets in the way.

'Then she asked us what we were going to do for the rest of our stay in Baton Rouge, so we said that it being Sunday the next day, we would try and take in as many church services as we could, as we liked going to different denominations. That created great interest in the party, as the eight ladies went to several different churches and were most intent that we went to theirs. Nothing like a bit of healthy competition I always say!'

'Did you go to church a lot while you were there?'

'Oh, my yes!' Sundays were fantastic. Often they would go twice or three times a day, more if they could manage, to different churches. They loved all the evangelical ones, happy clapping, singing along, but they also went to mainstream ones, Catholic, Episcopalian and so on. Although sometimes they'd get funny looks when they went to the black churches. Funny looks from both sides. 'We always looked very benign, we kept special clothes just for church, always clean and pressed. And we'd sit in the back, so as not to be a spectacle. But the sad thing is, there's a different God depending on your race apparently.'

Gregory was highly enthusiastic about such a trip. 'I'd love to do that,' he said.

I thought that maybe he'd committed a little early and wondered aloud whether the religious should be made to go out into the world, in the same way as I'd heard the Amish made their children take a year's breather before committing to the religion. We were discussing this as we entered Dax, where a fair was in full swing.

'Ooh, let's stop,' cried Jack, but I was driving and I wasn't having that. It wasn't a holiday. But when Bob also added his voice I was forced to reconsider, Oh, on second thoughts it *was* a holiday. And with a convenient parking spot suddenly becoming available, I pulled in and we spent a happy hour immersed in the French version of holiday fun.

'It's good, isn't it,' said Bob, 'to remind ourselves that not all of the French are chic and not all of their food is cordon bleu.'

We were tossing up between toffee apples, ice cream and fried crinkly donuts when Jack came up with a large bag of some sort of confectionery. 'What have you bought?' I asked.

'I won it.' Jack pointed to one of the booths where you fired darts out of a pink rifle.

There was an immediate spirit of competitiveness that required us all to have a go, but without success and it was time we were back on our way. We were already running late.

Bob was now driving. The steady crunch of Jack's pralines put paid to any conversation, and in any case Gregory was concentrating on the map – the Belloc monastery was not signposted in any way, and the nearest village only appeared on maps of the largest scale. But with only one wrong turning, he was pretty sure we had struck the track leading to the monastery. However, when we pulled up beside a fine-looking building, he gave out a pious ejaculation of dismay when a nun appeared. It was a Benedictine nunnery!

The Benedictine monastery was half a mile away and with new instructions we finally arrived. As usual we were given a warm welcome and although the evening meal was finished, we were taken to the refectory where places were laid for us. Despite having spent the last hour or so working our way through a large bag of caramel-covered nuts, we tucked in. Soup, followed by a sort of Spam and pasta, salad and stewed plums. Plus home-made red wine. Pretty similar to the meal we'd had the previous night, apart from the wine, which I thought superior.

Gregory gave the impression of meeting old friends of the family when in conversation with the two monks looking after us. He spoke slightly better French than me but still had to fall back on Jack's help from time to time. The chat was about friends and acquaintances in distant monasteries and spiced with family-type gossip.

We were shown the abbey church and for once Bob, whose appreciation of ecclesiastical architecture tended towards the critical, expressed real enthusiasm. Instead of hankering after some half-forgotten Gothic dream, the designer had taken a simple shape, like a truncated wedge of cheese, and had thought how to make it into a place of worship. With a risen Christ, represented by a plain square Holy Table and an empty cross with the nails still there, it appealed to Bob's more austere aesthetic.

Later that evening, the three of us attended Vigil, mainly psalms (in French) which Bob and I could follow fairly easily with Gregory's psalter, and two readings which were beyond us. I noticed the monks were a comparatively youthful lot, which was good to see.

Jack was already in bed and we now followed, in plainly furnished rooms overlooking a wooded valley. I had looked out on the view earlier, but looking out now into the moonlight from the quiet of the stone, I once more found my thoughts blotted out.

I got out my diary and wrote:

It's good to come to a full stop. To empty your mind after a day spent in conversations and adventure. I suppose travelling through a landscape quietly would be restful, although from the road it doesn't amount to much more than fields and trees and hedgerows and pretty villages and ugly villages. Pleasant prospects of rolling hills followed by petrol stations and grey metal factories. But how much faster the journey flies when you have companionship and laughter and stories.

I meant to start writing down those stories, but leaves started fluttering over my eyes and my jaw stretched into an enormous yawn. I knelt and prayed that my family be kept safe, that was the best I could do. Sometimes praying that they all be happy was beyond me. I turned out the light and was instantly asleep.

Three

BREAKFAST AT BELLOC WAS AT eight and consisted of bread, cheese, confiture and coffee. Coffee was served in bowls the size of a medium Christmas-pudding basin. It all went down a treat even though I found I had to concentrate in holding the handle-less cup. Again Jack in particular, and now the other two as well, merrily dipped their bread.

After breakfast, we met the Abbot and learnt something of the history of the place. Then Père Bernard, a youngish monk, showed us round the establishment. As we were going round, Gregory and Père Bernard discussed the future of the community. They were talking of another religious house which, having given up its school, seemed to be falling apart. The small school run by the Belloc monastery was then under review, and Gregory was urging them to keep it going. I could understand why Gregory would advocate this, because the school attached to his own monastery was highly regarded and had many very good lay teachers as well as casting a strong pull for intelligent younger converts to do something in the world. But my own preference was for schools as secular entities, in other words schools run by Catholics or other church groups but outside in the wider world.

We set off – a bit late of course – still discussing the place of schools run by religious bodies and our own experiences of education. I went to a state primary school first and then won a scholarship to a fee-paying Church of England high school. I had enjoyed the high Anglican nature of the religious observances there but didn't think it was particularly inspiring academically. Gregory had gone to all Catholic schools and reported that in the senior school most of his teachers were good and some very good but one of them was a complete misfit, a sadistically brutal man whose only pleasure seemed to be in beating boys. Fortunately, some of the parents had banded together in protest and he was removed. After that, Gregory had enjoyed his time at school, and it had shaped his views on how a school should be run.

'As for me,' said Jack, 'state school every step of the way.'

'You could have gone to a Quaker school in York like Sally.' My daughter went to a girls' boarding school and there was a similar one for boys.

'I don't think you could afford two of us.'

I reminded him there was a trust fund for him and Pete.

But he didn't think he'd like an all-boys school. His friend Tony's cousin went to Sally's school and said the food was awful. 'So I choose, or more likely suffer, our local grammar school, even though it's really a comprehensive. And even though it's well over an hour by bicycle and bus to get there.'

'Over an hour!' exclaimed Bob.

Longer still if Jack went in the minibus. That left at half past seven but most days, unless there was deep snow, torrential rain or blizzards, he and Tony preferred to set off later and ride their bikes to the local town to catch the school bus, rather than trickle round all the other villages first. He said there were kids up in the wilds of the North York Moors who had even further to travel. And in winter they often couldn't come at all, snowed in nice and snug, lucky them. 'But I wouldn't miss any of it for a moment. Our headmaster, who always wears an agonised expression, currently teaches Religious Instruction because our regular teacher went batty and is locked up in an asylum. And he told us in the second-last class before the holidays, that in the final class, for a treat, he would prove to us conclusively that God exists. So, we all held our breath in anticipation, a week has never gone so slowly.' He stopped, looking mischievous.

I gave a grunt of laughter. I knew what was coming, but the other two cried out, 'Come on, tell us!'

'So we turned up on tenterhooks. Sharpened our pencils and set out our biros in preparation for taking voluminous notes, Dad was particularly keen on that. Sat expectantly at our desks. Five minutes went by. Ten minutes went by. No headmaster. We started to riot, wouldn't you, with such a promise dangled in front of you? But then another teacher came in and told us to shut up and if we didn't have anything better to do we should all go to the library. So that was it for the big reveal. Eternal disappointment.'

'I'm still envious,' said Bob. 'At least you had that promise to look forward to for a week. Most of us live out our lives without ever even getting such an offer.'

Bob had gone to a state primary school in Paisley, a rapidly expanding outer suburb of Glasgow. It was an ordinary grey school with a grey wall surrounding a grey playground and inside, everyone sat in desks two by two and did times tables and endlessly practised their letters in exercise books. 'I don't think you would have got any different education at that stage if you'd gone to a private school. There were plenty of teaching materials, musical instruments for making horrible noises on, lots of paints, a school library with Enid Blytons and children's classics. It wasn't a dreary place. Everyone thinks that the whole population of Glasgow lives in slums, which isn't true.'

His father was then assistant station master at Paisley Gilmour Street and his family lived in a station on the Paisley–Barrhead line. 'As I was saying yesterday, people have funny reactions to that, being told that I lived in a railway station. It was one of those bizarre situations where someone had built a railway from somewhere in Paisley to somewhere else in Paisley and by the time they'd finished it, trams had been introduced and it was never used except for coal trains – they had to run one train a day to meet the terms of some long-ago lease and in the meantime they rented out the stations as houses. It was a pretty cool place to live. We used to grow vegetables on the platform and we walked to school down the railway line, just a hop step and a jump that way instead of going round by road.' His mother worked at night in a bakery nearby and would come in from work at about eight o'clock in the morning with bags of broken bits. 'What a ragamuffin I was in my boots and short trousers and an old railway cap stuck on the side of my head, walking down the railway line eating warm butteries and slightly burnt bridies and broken scotch pie out of a paper bag all mixed in together. That's a breakfast I could eat every day of my life. And I also discovered that if I kept some of the better bits back and shared them round at school with my friends, I could pretty well avoid any of the bullying going on. Lesson number one, always be part of a gang. Lesson number two, if the other members of your gang don't stand up for you, their chance of getting any more bits of millionaire's shortbread or Dundee cake is zero.'

Bob had no idea how he got to go to the boys' grammar school, which was a fee-paying Presbyterian school then. His elder brother had gone there too, and it must've been a stretch even on two wages. 'But it's a funny thing, the railways. It's not exactly working-class. You'd think it would be, but it isn't. I certainly wasn't the only kid from a railway background that went to the grammar school.'

'So how did you end up studying law?' I asked.

'Pure chance. The school was bursting at the seams, there were a lot of temporary buildings which had been temporary for nearly forty years and everything had a down-at-heel look to it – parents were complaining this wasn't an education they thought they should be paying for. So when a new headmaster arrived he was expected to be a new broom.

'I was doing Religious Studies for my sixth-year certificate and was constantly arguing with the teacher. In the end he got his knickers in a knot and sent me to the headmaster who said, I hear you're a troublemaker. So I told him what a troublemaker Jesus Christ was and St Paul, and I was moving on to Martin Luther when he put up his hands in defeat. So then he asked me what I planned to do after school, and I told him my father wanted me to get a job in a bank. As far as my parents were concerned, a job in a bank was a ticket to a life of ease and prosperity. But the headmaster gave me a look and said no, that wouldn't do for me at all, and he was going to get me into university to study law. And that was it. I went home and told my parents I was going to study law and they looked at me like I'd done a loop up to Mars on the way home. How on earth were they going to afford that? But then it turned out they didn't have to. The headmaster had done some deep digging into the school's finances and found a whole heap of money salted away in various old trust accounts and whatever. So this big building boom started at the school and as well as that, he decided there should be two scholarships to the University of Glasgow every year and I was one of the inaugural recipients.'

It was funny that in life's lottery of luck you just needed one person. Bob wouldn't have been happy in a bank, he had very little interest in either numbers or money and no patience with bureaucracy. And his headmaster had recognised that and saved him from a dreary future. Just one person, not a whole school-full, just one was all you needed.

'For me, it's my French teacher,' said Jack. 'Miss Linden makes me feel like I'm capable of anything. You're good at languages, she says, here do German, here do Spanish. Had I thought of doing Russian? She could organise it. She wants me to go to one of the top British universities to do languages and when I told her I was thinking of going to France and doing the baccalaureate, her enthusiasm reached new heights – of course I must do my baccalaureate, then I must go to the Sorbonne.'

'Studying Russian!' exclaimed Bob. 'She was going to get you to study Russian in Ryedale! Well, for trouble-making you beat me hands down.'

———

We arrived at the French–Spanish border. Père Bernard had advised against the San Sebastian route into Spain where, he warned us, there would be long queues of cars at the frontier post – at Dancharia there would be no delay, he said.

It was true there weren't long queues, but maybe the customs officers had a problem with this because what could be slacker than a customs post where everyone sails straight through? It could look as if the officials were not doing their job. The man on duty wasn't going to let that false impression take hold. He decided to go through everything. So the bulk of the luggage was opened up. A customs officer must be able to tell an awful lot about people just from looking in their luggage. Gregory's neat hold-all was precisely packed with everything just so, his habit carefully folded, his spare black tunics and trousers arranged; even his underpants looked as if they had been ironed. Bob's backpack, by contrast, unleashed a riot of colourful shirts, khaki cargo pants and a mixture of bright cotton underpants and more traditional white Aertex Y-fronts. My own small, battered suitcase looked quite conservative by contrast and although my clothes were still clean, they nevertheless appeared rather grimy, especially my vests and underpants.

I was pleased to note, however, that Jack's small bag, which seemed to consist mainly of T-shirts, short-sleeved shirts and brightly coloured cotton underpants, looked sensible enough, and saw that my son had in fact packed a light rain jacket. He also had a pair of bathing trunks, even though I couldn't think of any location where they might be used. I felt rather bad about this because after all, the boy was on holiday.

I had never given much thought to underwear before, but it appeared Bob's underpants were of the same ilk as Jack's – somewhat similar to the brief beachwear men were now sporting. However, the addition of a few Y-fronts seemed to indicate that this rather radical new fashion was fading in Bob's case as he headed towards middle age and comfort.

Spanish Customs, after rootling around among our general luggage, now demanded to look in Gregory's briefcase, which held mainly religious books and papers. My companion was looking rather sour about this intrusion, but I myself felt nothing par-ticular when they focused on some Russian Orthodox literature I was carrying. I was interested in Orthodoxy in a general way and so, in a general way, I wasn't bothered if the customs official was also interested in it.

Eventually, when everything had been prodded, we got waved through.

'For heaven's sake,' Gregory exploded, and expressed his dismay for the next half an hour.

'Your problem, or rather your church's problem, is that you gave up Latin,' said Jack. 'Back when things were in Latin, priests were priests and it would have been like blasphemy for them to go trawling through religious works like that.'

'Back when things were in Latin,' said Bob, 'border officials probably couldn't read. They'd only be on the lookout for illicit liquor and other goods that needed to be taxed.'

'Well, we are importing two priests in mufti into Holy Spain,' said Jack. 'Perhaps that's taxable.'

Gregory laughed, a surprised braying sort of laugh that came out in a spurt. I laughed too, and our good humour restored we proceeded up the Pyrenees.

We had lunch near the road's summit with a magnificent view over the tips of fir trees to the blue distance of the French foothills. We found a group of convenient logs which saved the effort of getting the foldable chairs out of the car; we were running late. It was a pity because the view almost demanded that we stand forever entranced.

But sooner than we wanted, we were zigzagging our way downwards. Almost immediately the weather changed as if someone had flicked a switch. Bob was now driving, and I was in the back with my son. I looked at the mountains shrouded in watery clouds and said, 'This is like that holiday in the Lake District, the scenery and the rain, don't you think?'

'I can't really remember the first visit that much,' said Jack. 'Did it rain?'

'All the time. Don't you remember having to wear a mac and sou'wester, wellingtons?'

Jack shook his head.

'No, you were probably too young. I think you were only seven or eight.' A heavy shower blotted the landscape for a few minutes when nothing was visible. 'It was just like this. A holiday from hell.'

'I've heard you talk about it like that, but I don't remember it as being awful, in fact what I *can* remember was great.'

'Oh yes, all you kids loved it.'

'I remember huge rhododendron bushes we used to hide in. And I remember Cousin Katy squatting to do a weewee in one of them and shouting out she'd done a big job instead, which we all found immensely funny. And I remember the house had wide banisters which we slid down on a piece of rubber matting and if you gripped with your knees you could make a lovely rude noise.'

The simple pleasures of an eight-year-old.

'It had been some sort of mansion,' I recollected, 'but the gardens were unkempt and the inside was almost derelict. Your mother was only there three minutes and wanted to go home.'

'Did she! Why did we stay then?' said Jack.

'Why indeed. Uncle Peter, who Pete is named after, was the only one in the family who was ever rich. He made paint,' I explained to the car. 'Not any old paint. He specialised in paint for metal, powder coating for cars and so on. He was well off enough before the war but then suddenly they're producing the stuff day and night, green and grey and khaki to disguise any tank so it looked like a hillock. He made a packet and after the war, too. In the last twenty years, everyone has wanted a car. So, he's our only rich uncle and he'd bought the place to give to … I forget who now, some charity. Or maybe it was the Youth Hostel Association. Anyway he invited all his relatives to be the first ones to stay there.'

'Still doesn't explain why you stayed, if you hated it.'

'*I* didn't hate it. And, like I said, he's our rich uncle. That's what happens when your only seriously rich relative invites you for a two-week free holiday at their expense. Except for the expense of getting a family of five there with five new sleeping bags and the expense of your time in cooking the food and cleaning up after the kids and cleaning up generally. Joan went on strike after a few days and said she hadn't come on holiday to do all the same things that she was doing at home. She got a rucksack from somewhere and she went off walking for a day. Just set off one morning without saying goodbye to you kids.'

'I don't suppose we … Oh wait! Sally – I do remember now. Sally wailing at the top of her voice.'

I sighed.

'Didn't she run away? I seem to remember that she ran away, saying she was going to find Mum. Oh yes, now I do remember the rain that day, it was coming down in sheets.'

'We found her,' I muttered. 'Everyone got soaked.'

A nightmare holiday, one of many subsequent ones. Sally out somewhere screaming down the road and the other kids forming a Lord-of-the-Flies band with spears and sticks to hunt her. The first indication that pleasant and reasonably restful holidays were over and that just finding somewhere with a sandy beach where the two boys would make sandcastles and run happily about with other children, all that was gone.

But I remembered again carrying my poor wet distraught little daughter back to the house. The first time I had been really angry with Joan. We had had tiffs before but nothing serious and nothing that hadn't been resolved almost immediately by talking it through. Now she wasn't there to talk it through with and in actual fact I had no idea why she had gone or where. Did I ever truly resolve it in myself?

'You told us a story about cake,' Jack remembered.

'It was Hansel and Gretel, it was supposed to be a cautionary tale about going out and getting lost in the wild woods and falling in with a witch.'

After I changed Sally into dry clothes I put her in a sleeping bag for a bit because I was worried she was still cold. I lay down next to her and started telling her the fairy tale and explaining that a witch could look just like an ordinary woman, and in fact when I was describing her in my particular story she started to look a fair lot like Aunt Winnie. We came to a stop when Sally asked me what gingerbread was. Ah. Not much good warning about getting lured into a gingerbread house if you didn't know what gingerbread was. So instead I made the roof of the house out of cake covered by pink icing, the walls were made of chocolate crackles, chocolate fingers lined the doors and windows and so on. And inside the floor was chocolate shortie, a particularly favourite cake in our household made of biscuit crumbs, cocoa, flour, sugar and lard, cooked in two separate tins and then sandwiched together with chocolate butter icing.

By that time all the children were gathered round Sally's bed listening and I realised I had turned a cautionary tale into a description instead of a child's paradise where any of them would throw caution to the winds if given the chance.

That afternoon I made gingerbread men with Sally so if I got to tell the tale again, we wouldn't get sidetracked into a smorgasbord of sweet treats. As it was still raining most of the other kids joined in and the kitchen was full of chatter, and calm reigned.

'And then Mum came back,' said Jack.

Yes.

—◆—

The rain thudded against the windscreen and added to the deceleration imposed by the tight hairpin bends and the badly surfaced mountain roads. So when we reached Loyola for lunch, it was almost four o'clock and we were still barely halfway to our destination.

I thought we should press on, but Gregory was determined to look at the basilica and the adjoining house. The church was overwhelmingly magnificent, and the main altar magnificent far beyond even grotesque. A painter interested in the subject could have spent a whole day on his back, looking at the pictures on the ceiling. Everything was carved and coloured regardless of expense. And regardless of taste, I thought uneasily to myself.

It was the same, on a smaller scale, in the sixteenth-century house next door, formerly the home of Saint Ignatius. Without the same expanse to fill, the artists and craftsmen had gone to town making every room into a chapel. If there was any other room that was actually lived in, it must have been hidden behind the panelling and not available for public viewing. I fantasised that somewhere behind all this extravagance in St Ignatius's day, there would have been at the very least an unmade bed or a plate covered with crumbs. I was reminded of the baroque churches shown in TV documentaries dealing with poverty and exploitation in South America. Was the history of the church (and not just the Roman Catholic Church) a history of misdirected energies, I wondered. All those resources poured into huge and useless buildings while around them people had barely a roof over their heads. Perhaps Bob was right, it was the showiness of the endeavour which was the point. Nowadays governments did the same, but instead of huge churches to corral the faithful, they built stadiums for the same reason. The pointlessness of it.

Shortly after leaving Loyola, we merged onto the main San Sebastian–Santander Highway. This wasn't too bad into Bilboa. From Bilboa westwards it was appalling. Our average speed was barely twenty miles an hour, mainly behind great lorries toiling up twisting roads.

As the sun was setting, there were still a hundred miles to go. We stopped to fill up at a service station and when I came out of the lavatory I saw Gregory and Jack with their heads together over a public telephone. We drove on, with Gregory somewhat relieved at being able to get through to our hosts for the night but even so a certain tension invaded the car. Up until then we had felt no particular discomfort in the Viva but now it felt squashed, hot and confining. But it was impossible to go any faster so all we could do was sit and silently endure. At last we turned off the main road and now Gregory was trying to follow the hand-written instructions and sketch map with a small pocket torch. His navigation was spot on and at the end of a very long, bumpy farm track, in total Spanish darkness, we reached our destination. It was a newly constructed seaside villa belonging to one of Gregory's relatives. We had made it, though it was now 11 p.m.

Thank God for Spain and Spanish hours. At least it's not 'late' here, I thought. I couldn't imagine turning up to someone's house in England at this hour and receiving the same beautiful welcome as we received now from the Robson family.

We were all ravenous and fell with enthusiasm on the meal offered. Cold roast chicken and Palma ham, hot refried potatoes and many different sorts of salad. Home-made gelato, a cheese board, a white wine tasting of gooseberries, and coffee. The family had eaten earlier to accommodate their daughters, but the parents joined us at the table for supper and to talk. Liberated simultaneously from the car, the last few hours of glum endurance, and our hunger, we were all suddenly in high spirits and conversation became animated. For some reason, in discussing the local preference for the Virgin Mary ahead of all other religious symbolism, we became immersed in the interesting theory that wisdom was predominantly a female characteristic. This indeed was my view of the world, as the bulwark of my early life was my maternal grandmother who, in my eyes, had a goddess-like relationship with the natural world. She used to scour the hedgerows for simples to make potions for all our earthly ills and would probably, a few centuries before, have been called a witch. Our hostess and Bob immediately joined forces to suggest that the Church's fear of witches was fear of this sort of wisdom – it was the kind of talk which could have gone on all night, but someone pointed out that it was after 1 a.m.

Jack, who had been chatting with the eldest daughter, who was about his age, said he would sleep on the couch (they had only been expecting three) and as this was arranged with very little fuss, I went off to the twin room facing the sea that Bob and I shared. I gave no thought to my diary or to throwing out prayers into the ethos, in fact I had no idea who even turned out the light because I was asleep when my head hit the pillow.

Four

WHEN I WOKE UP, I looked out on a very attractive sandy bay near Comillas. I could hear the sound of waves and the cries of young people. When I dressed and went out onto the patio, I could see that the young people consisted of Jack, wearing his bathing trunks, and three girls also wearing bathing costumes. They were running up the beach laughing, having clearly been for a swim. As they clattered sandily onto the patio I identified the three girls as the Robsons' two daughters and a third girl who looked slightly familiar.

'Dad, this is Amanda, she was on the ferry with us. She's staying up the road with her parents. Isn't this a coincidence!'

'Well, well!' I said in surprise. 'So when did you get here?'

'Thursday morning. I came by train to Santander, nothing as exciting as what you've been doing. Monastery hopping. I didn't even know you could do that.'

She was an attractive girl about Jack's age with a wide toothy smile and already, with two days' start, the beginnings of a tan.

'How on earth did you know we were here?'

'Danielle rang me. She worked it out last night. Isn't it amazing!'

Yes, it was amazing. Young people chattering and making connections, the communal way of travelling that Bob had talked about. I wondered if Jack would get bored, not having access to those group dynamics on this trip, but he didn't seem bored. In fact Jack hardly ever seemed bored.

We had breakfast with the family, glorious croissants! And as we were waved off, I noticed the girls were blowing kisses to Jack and Jack was grinning and waving back. I suddenly wondered about possible girlfriends, a thought which had never crossed my mind before. My son was sixteen and he'd said the previous day that he knew a lot of nice girls and was wondering how to choose. Possibly when you were sixteen you didn't have to choose one for the rest of your life, that came later when the qualities you were looking for solidified into one particular girl you couldn't move on from. With myself it had been Joan, but I had gone out with other girls before that. Was this the kind of thing a modern parent discussed with his son? In addition to the birds and bees?

I remembered my embarrassing attempt at a fatherly talk with Pete when my eldest was fifteen and Pete saying, 'Oh Lord, Dad, I know all that!' But when I had tried the same talk with Jack, my second son had listened respectfully to what I had to say. No wonder his teachers went the extra mile to help him, I thought, with this respectful attitude. Jack's French teacher must be putting in hours of extra work, in the absence of a German teacher, to get him through A-level German, because Jack would express gratitude for the assistance and work hard to please her. If I talked to him about girls he would listen just as respectfully and take on board what I was saying, but was I really the one to be giving him advice? My only experience of sex had been within marriage and from what I could gather this was not the expectation now of an average teenage boy.

I was driving and looked at Jack in the rearview mirror. Clearly he was attractive to the three young girls, and I wondered what the current fashion in male 'handsomeness' was. Jack certainly didn't fit the bill for Mr Atlas, as he was small featured and slightly built – although I had noticed that his chest was starting to fill out, no doubt as a result of physical labour on the farm. I doubted that girls now looked for muscle men – their enthusiasm seemed to be directed at pop singers who were all quite skinny and slight like my son. My parishioners had always referred to Jack as 'angelic', no doubt because of his hair, which in winter was a light brown but which in summer, especially under the stronger suns of France, would turn almost golden. It was curly and fairly long as was the current fashion.

It was a mystery to me, the workings of the modern world. Maybe I should pay more attention, I thought. At the moment I needed all my attention on the road.

We were following a cross-country route recommended by the Robsons. Slow, we were told, but not so slow or so frustrating as the main road south from Santander. But they hadn't warned us that it was a road which would encourage dawdling.

It led up and up through the Sierra Cantabria with lovely views at every turn. I stopped once or twice just to take it all in. At the top of the pass we stopped again just to enjoy the scenery, the autumn crocuses in profusion, the Siamese-cat-coloured cattle complete with cowbells, and the wonderful air. Gregory got out a trowel to collect some plants for the garden at his monastery – three or four blue-leaved thistles and some lilac-tinged crocuses – while Jack crouched holding out a collecting bag.

Back in the car, Jack asked, 'Do you all have to take a turn at gardening?'

'Just those who want to. I find it relaxing after teaching all day. Trying to force geometry and algebra into boys with restless hormones and the attention span of a bluebottle would be a thankless task without some recreation to take my mind off it.'

'My maths teacher does marathon running.'

'Well yes, I think that would do rather nicely. I had thought of doing something like that, so long as it wasn't a team effort.'

So what would he wear? Was there some monastic version of a track suit?

Gregory laughed. 'Shorts and a T-shirt I suppose. Something sensible. That's what Father William wears when he takes the boys for rugby, and he's fiendishly good at it I've heard. I'm sure there's sporty clothing in the store and if there isn't they would get it for me.'

'So, you just go down and take things?'

'Yes of course, if you need them. Everything is on the basis of need.'

'So what happens after? Do you have to put things back?'

'Well, the Abbot likes us to spend a day maybe every year, going through all our things and deciding what's superfluous. So, how many pairs of socks you need, that kind of thing. It's a great discipline, I'd recommend it for everyone. Well, for adults anyway. I don't suppose you have much to sort through.'

'No,' said Jack. 'I don't keep anything much in my room, nothing that I value particularly.'

That hung like fire in my mind for a while, even in my chest. The conversation turned to other things.

Now we were down on the plains, and it was fairly fast motoring across a parched landscape. Lunch in Palencia at a small café – we thought we might save time by not buying provisions and stopping for a picnic later. Then by a good road to Valladolid and finally Salamanca, the venue for the 1970 Congress of the International Ecumenical Fellowship, an event which the three of us had been planning for and looking forward to all year.

We arrived a bit late, just as the briefing session ended. However, a kindly Anglican parson told us that we hadn't missed much and accompanied us back to the conference headquarters, where we collected hand-outs and other literature. Then we went to sort ourselves out at the residential college, half a kilometre away. Getting there meant bumping over the most atrocious urban potholes I've ever experienced. I saw that Salamanca was a mixture of ancient and modern and that tower blocks of flats were shooting up but there were still streets virtually unpaved, lined by wretched hovels with sagging shutters, rusty doors and peeling paint. The people, however, didn't look at all wretched and seemed to be going in and out of those houses completely unconscious of their awful state.

I was worried about the accommodation, as Jack was such a late addition to the party, but everything was sorted out quite well; Jack and I had adjoining rooms on the fourth floor and Gregory and Bob were on the second floor. The rooms, as everywhere we had stayed apart from the Robson household, were quite austere, holding little more than a single bed, a chair and desk and a small wardrobe. But it was all quite modern, though the water was 'non-potable'.

The bathroom facilities were a bit odd, however. Only one of the WC cubicles had a door that locked. I made use of a pedestal that rocked gently, and when the flushing process took place, a dribble of water appeared on the tiled floor. If I had taken a fancy to that particular pedestal I could have taken it back to England, as it was not bolted to the floor in any way. When I pointed this out to Jack, my son laughed and wondered whether it was a Protestant thing – being so plumbing conscious.

Jack had spent a lot of time in France, which of course gave him experience of continental plumbing. Maybe the young don't care, I thought. How liberating. The last time I had been to France, during the war, we had earth latrines if we had anything at all. Plus grass and leaves and a few precious pieces of toilet paper.

When we had freshened up, we joined the other two downstairs and walked back to the conference centre and to the grand opening ceremony, where a camera from Spanish TV swept slowly through the audience. I immediately became self-conscious and tried to put on a thoughtful, ecumenical, broadminded, intelligent expression as the camera panned by – we were listening to a speech in Spanish at the time and I spoke no Spanish, but I felt I ought to *look* interested as the occasion demanded it. However, it also struck me that anyone watching would probably be more interested in my son – what on earth was a young person doing there? What on earth indeed. And now we were here, how was this going to work? I turned to look at Jack and suddenly realised that he seemed to be *actually* listening. Oh yes, of course, he had just done a year of Spanish, I remembered textbooks lying around. Not that one year would necessarily give much fluency to an ordinary person, but Jack did seem particularly good at languages.

'Did you catch any of it?' I asked after the speech was over.

'Oh, it was just general welcome to this magnificent country, we're all going to have a magnificent time, and the magnificent WCs are on the left and the dining room is behind us where we will no doubt have magnificent meals. And other stuff but it's all in the program.'

Dinner was at 9:30 p.m. – all hours seemed to be late in Spain. I noticed in the program that lunch was at 1:30 p.m. A long stretch in between, I remarked. Jack said that we needed to stock up on bread rolls and chocolate, apparently that's what people had about five o'clock, after their siesta.

Dinner was a pleasant enough meal although, as Gregory pointed out, we had now moved on to the Spanish version of Spam. There was a tempranillo with the meal, a dark full-bodied wine that I was rather taken with. I noted that Jack invariably diluted his wine with water and wished I had done the same as we walked back towards the accommodation, as I felt slightly muzzy and remembered there was no potable water. However, my son had already thought of that and had secreted a couple of bottles of water from the table in the conference bag he was carrying, and gladly gave me one.

I wrote in my diary,

> Now we are settled for a while, which I am glad of. Sometimes I find the constantly passing parade drains my energy and new places and new things start blending with each other – everything begins to look the same. I seem to have turned into a rather dull homebody, that is if I was ever anything else. My early life was safe and predictable and when I got older, I never wanted to rush off elsewhere like some, I would have been quite happy pottering along locked in place like peasants of old. Then one day I found myself loading men onto a troop carrier, temporarily promoted to captain, and as we got underway I knew that nothing would ever be the same again. Changes succeeding changes, helter-skelter, all certainties gone.

I stopped writing. All certainties gone. It was happening again, and I had no more control than previously. Panic seized me for a moment. I didn't kneel by the bed this time, I bowed my head at the desk and prayed for myself, help me. Help me, Lord. Then I felt ashamed, this was not what prayer should be about, pushing your way to the front and demanding service. It wasn't a sweet shop. Or if it was, it was one where you should be praying that others got the good things, like little Anne Ellis who'd had polio and walked with a caliper on her leg; *she* deserved the chocolate creams. Help her, Lord, help her to keep on smiling through and making the best of it and being an inspiration to those who felt like giving up and lying down and moaning.

I got into bed intending to have a quiet moan but maybe God had heard me, because I fell asleep before I could even get started.

2

At Salamanca

Five

I slept well despite heavy traffic on the cobbled main highway below, and in the morning I looked out west across the city to a beautiful skyline of towers and spires and roughly tiled red roofs. It struck me that the more dilapidated a place was, the more picturesque it appeared to those who didn't have to live there.

I went down into the basement of the college where breakfast was a do-it-yourself affair, pretty much the same as we had become used to in the monasteries. The only addition was orange juice, yoghurt and some sort of mixed cereal in small packets.

Jack was leafing through a rather battered Spanish guidebook in which Salamanca took up a slim chapter, and I asked him what he intended to do for the day.

Jack replied, 'I thought I'd tag along with you to start with, as nothing seems to open till ten o'clock.'

I wasn't at all sure that what I had planned would appeal to my son; nevertheless we went off to attend a unity service held in the Purisima Church. The idea of a unity service was that conference attendees could attend the services of other faiths, and the one that morning featured the Orthodox rite.

When I saw the venue, I had an uneasy intuition it was not going to go well. La Purisima was a baroque basilica like the Loyola one and featured paintings and gilt and candles in profusion to the glory of God and the mystification of his creatures.

The sermon by the Orthodox Archbishop was inaudible. The service went on and on and a lady worshipper gave up and left, leaving our pew otherwise empty, and when the local Catholics came in for their own Mass we were joined by four Salamancan girls, the eldest of whom was about Jack's age. Jack smiled at them and they smiled back. The girls then crossed themselves and seemed quite willing to sit it out. Most of the congregation knew not whether to stand or sit, but generally stood up to be blessed, which seemed to happen every five minutes. I kept seated on account of my war-wounded leg, which made me think of Saint Ignatius Loyola, who also had a poorly leg.

At some point the locals also gave up and retired for their own Mass in a side chapel, so the four young girls got up to go too and smiled again at Jack, who got up and followed them. Leaving me all alone. Finally, I too had had enough and retreated to have a comforting cup of coffee before the rest of the congregation were dismissed. I was dismayed by the service; I was sure that worship was never meant to be incomprehensible to someone of goodwill and average intelligence.

I then returned to the conference, and we sorted ourselves into discussion groups. Mine included a learned American monk, a lady Salvationist from Swindon and a Lutheran pastor from Holland, among others.

After lunch, I took an unintended siesta. I had planned to go shopping but at two o'clock I left the main building to find – *whump* – the heat bursting all around me. So instead I went back to the accommodation and lay down for a couple of hours.

I left my door open and Jack, who I hadn't seen at lunch, came past for a siesta. 'What have you been up to?' I asked.

'Those girls took me home after the service. They only live a couple of streets away – their dad's got a tobacconist and gift shop on the square. He had to go out, so they were going to help in the shop and I said I'd help too, to improve my Spanish. Mainly I've been teaching them the English names for things. It's been fun. I'm going back at five o'clock.'

After my siesta, I attended a talk on discipline and freedom. I was much interested by it, as I had been thinking along the same lines in relation to my own personal circumstances. The question was whether following duty or what you saw as your duty was for the public or personal good if you did not freely wish to engage in those actions. The answer, as far as I could make sense of it with it being translated from Spanish in small dribs, was that if you were following your duty out of love, then the discipline required would create no internal stress. If your duty gave you no pleasure, so that you resented the actions you felt compelled to carry out, then this was a perverse discipline, which could bring no good either to you or those around you.

There were other talks afterwards, but I found I was so troubled by the one on discipline that I couldn't move my thoughts on to anything else. I slipped away and went back to my room to find somewhere quiet, and started a letter to my wife. I'd always felt that Joan should be a sounding board for these matters. Lately, and for some time in fact, she hadn't, but nevertheless I often found myself composing letters to her as if this might solve the dilemma. Of course I would never send them, but it was a discipline in itself to set out the problem and to clarify my thoughts.

I took up the notebook where I had been writing my desultory scribbles, knowing any notes put down on that afternoon's talk would be equally haphazard.

I started thinking again about that holiday in the Lake District. Uncle Peter had turned up with a very much younger woman in tow, which had caused much lip-compressing in my aunts. Which I had thought hypocritical in the extreme, as the one problem with Uncle Peter was that none of his relatives could stand his wife. Amelia (she was actually christened Amy) was a social climber and a snob and was aiming to be the world record-holder in rudeness. Uncle Peter's new companion, Dotty, was the opposite. She was gregarious, slightly mad as her name suggested (the kids loved her), and unfailingly kind.

For some reason Joan took an instant dislike to her. Although if the truth be told she had taken a dislike to all my relatives, so I probably shouldn't have been so surprised when one morning she confronted me as I was getting out of my bunk and told me she was going walking for the day. On her own. To get away from 'all these people'. She was standing with her walking boots on and a backpack when she told me this, and turned and went without any further discussion.

Why was I so dismayed when she went away for the day? It had been brewing from the moment we got there. When we had all arrived and stood gazing in horror at the derelict interior of the place, Auntie Winnie had taken charge. Auntie Winnie was my mother's sister-in-law and even though she rarely raised her voice and appeared on the surface to be nothing more than a normal housewife, she had a steely edge, the result of raising a large and disciplined brood. I watched her transition into the role of implacable tyrant at first with amusement and later with concern. Under her command the women got busy in the kitchen and the men were sent out to fix everything else. This was fine for the first couple of days because survival was everything. But after that, when the war was over as it were, resentments began to appear. I had tried to point out to my aunt that this division of labour did not happen in every household, and it was time maybe for the men to take a hand in the kitchen. My gentle remonstrance fell on deaf ears and in fact it was my mother, when she arrived, who put an end to it. My mother was not accustomed to being instructed what to do and when she rebelled, everyone rebelled with her. I was thereafter pleasantly cocooned in the kitchen making bread for a dozen or more adults and an uncounted tribe of children.

But maybe by that time it was too late.

Joan had endured Auntie Winnie's regime with increasing rage. It was as if her acceptance of the cook-and-bottle-washer role had finally come to an end, as if the duties traditionally associated with being a wife and mother had transformed into the heavy stone of Sisyphus, constantly being pushed uselessly with no end in sight.

I wrote in the notebook:

> Today I heard a talk on duty and how unbearable it was when duty was carried out without joy. Has there been any joy between us in the last 10 years or has it all been duty?

I thought again of my Uncle Peter who had managed, in the teeth of his first wife's objections, to get a divorce. Now, married to Dotty, he had joy in abundance and two new children. That was the advantage of being rich, I realised – money could overcome any social or moral barriers; yes, that afternoon's talk had no relevance to those with the money and the determination to be free. A disconcerting and rather depressing insight.

When I returned to the conference later in the evening, I slipped into the back of a prayer meeting and found a little consolation, which soothed my rather stressed and tumbling thoughts.

People were by then circulating, waiting to be let into the dining room, and I saw Bob sitting chatting with several others. They had been to a talk on the use of 'fire and damnation' rhetoric.

'I've been to a few sermons like that,' Bob said. 'Barb and I were in the south of the States, and we went to a church where a charismatic preacher took us down the road towards doom. It was electric. You could smell the hellfire, and everyone was shaking in terror and I was shaking and Barb was clutching my arm. Hell was opening up before us, we were poised on the brink until in the nick of time the preacher reeled us back in. "Not today," he cried, but that was the future if we didn't reform and mend our ways and come to God as little children. Heavens, it was powerful. The relief walking out. But then you see, you almost immediately want to do it again. All that adrenaline, all that release, I love that kind of thing. It would be like jumping out of an aeroplane and waiting till you've nearly hit the ground before opening your parachute.'

A free way for someone to dangle over the fiery pit without getting actually burnt. Though not exactly free, according to Bob, because the more frightened you were, the more you put in the collection plate.

But apparently all was not well among the torturers in hell, and now they'd entered the 1970s they were in danger of becoming a laughing stock if they continued to use those images. A pity. The need to be rational these days. And noncontroversial.

'And boring,' suggested a Lutheran pastor.

At dinner that night we were randomly allocated numbers so that we sat next to new people, and I sat next to a newly arrived young American couple from Arizona. Spain, it seemed, reminded them of home. This similarity did not extend to the food and, being American, they discussed its shortcomings rather loudly. I didn't think it was very appetising either but I was too polite to say so. I looked around for an escape and saw that Jack had been allocated to a very noisy table which appeared to be made up entirely of nuns. Jack was making a fair amount of noise himself, in fact to my surprise and concern, he was talking over the top of everyone else. Jack was usually quiet and well-mannered, which was why it seemed so out of character. However, when I went over to join him I found out why – he was doing simultaneous translation between some American and French nuns. I stood and listened along with several others and got great enjoyment from it.

Afterwards I was introduced to the American nuns, Sister Angela and Sister Carol, and Sister Angela said to me, 'My goodness, we must borrow your son again. This has been the best brawl I've been in for a long time.'

Jack said, as we walked home under a starry sky, 'This has been a fun day. I'm so glad I came.'

Six

WHEN I WOKE IN THE morning I got up intending to make up for lost time in my failing diary project, but when I read the short paragraph I had written the day before I started thinking again about that Lake District holiday. Eventually I took up my pen and wrote:

> Socrates was right about the unexamined life. For some reason things are surfacing on this trip which should have been dealt with a long time ago. We have been telling each other stories and each time I tell a story I get a jolt. The war was horrible. My early marriage was wonderful. These stories emerge like floor tiles fitting together. But then in the last few years nothing has fitted. How do I make sense of it?

I stopped writing.

There had been a time at the beginning of our marriage when Joan would come into my study to listen to the points I was making in my sermon and make suggestions. I would look up as she went past and she would enquire if she could be of any help and it was to her, as audience, that many of my early sermons were directed. But that hadn't happened for a long time. I wondered when she had stopped being there for me as a muse. And when the slightly derogatory comments had started about my sermons, about how they were all about me. 'Yes,' I had agreed, 'they are all about me and Jesus, me and God. What else would they be about?'

Had I ever thought of looking at things from a woman's perspective? she'd asked. A woman's perspective. She meant herself, I presumed.

A week or so previously when I'd been in my study, she'd come in to discuss something that needed doing while I was away. After I'd agreed to take charge of the matter, she'd looked around her with dissatisfaction. 'How nice you have a bolthole like this,' she said. 'I have to do my lesson plans on the dining room table.'

'It's set up for a vicar,' I answered, reasonably I thought. 'It's the reason we get this house.'

'This house. This house, this everything, it's all set up to you.' She got up and left and I didn't know what to say. I just had the uneasy feeling, which I'd had for some time, that there was something I needed to fix, something major about my life.

After breakfast we all went to another unity service, this time the Reformed Church. Bob noted that it was St Bartholomew's Day. 'It's rather like having a unity service for Catholics and Protestants on Bonfire Night,' he joked.

Not a bad idea, I thought. How much more distressing for Guy Fawkes to look down and see everyone peaceably getting along, much better than burning him in effigy.

Fortunately, the service had to be short because we were all going out for the day. With the other conference attendees, we duly climbed onto buses and went to Alba de Tormes, where Saint Theresa had lived and died. There was a meditation in her church, led by an Anglican and listened to by unseen nuns through what looked like a barbed wire mattress. As the congregation was otherwise mixed, including a number of nuns, there were mutterings about whether this arrangement was to keep the nuns in or the terrible outside world out. Some of the American nuns wore skirts that came just below the knee, and I wondered to myself if the sight of such shocking modern freedom might otherwise tempt these holy women to come rushing out of seclusion. The only signs the American nuns used to denote their religious status were a rather casual wimple and a cross worn round their necks. And sometimes not even that.

The meditation, interrupted by translation into Spanish, was trying and therefore not meditative. The priest stood with raised voice at the microphone and was too loud and distorted as a result, whereas the young monk translating stood to one side without a microphone and his sentences, spoken in a low, level voice, came through as clear as crystal. It would all have been much better if the priest had not bothered with the mike (or learnt how to use it). And because I was thinking about how poorly it was delivered, I couldn't afterwards remember what it was about. I made a mental note to check with Jack who perhaps got more out of it listening to the Spanish.

Lunch was taken in two sittings at the local hotel. We missed the first sitting and Jack was almost immediately scooped up by the nuns. I felt slightly deflated at being abandoned. I am not naturally gregarious, and I knew that I probably didn't put enough effort into being sociable as I should. If Joan was here, I thought, she'd immediately begin talking to the person next to her. Jack seemed to have inherited that tendency – it was a skill I wished I had but it was not something you could acquire easily, and at that moment I was not in the mood to practise.

Not seeing anyone in the crowd around me that I knew, I moved over towards the corner where there appeared to have been some sort of recent celebration. Two stands were set up with many photographs on them, and I puzzled for some time about what they meant. It was some clerical happening and featured various groups of people with a priest standing in their midst. I concluded that the youth of the priest in each case, and the smiling faces of the people around, meant it was probably the celebration of ordinations. Was there a theological college nearby? One young man in a clerical outfit had two young women on either side of him kissing his cheek. Relatives? Sisters? Girlfriends he was about to leave behind?

I had a similar photo of when I myself was ordained. In my case, as well as my mother, grandmother and other well-wishers, the main one kissing me was Joan. But Joan had never been keen on my change of career; in fact when I told her, lying on a hospital bed, that when I came out of the army I was going to take orders in the Church of England rather than pursuing my career as a solicitor, she had at first refused to take me seriously and for some time thereafter maintained that it was the blow to the head which had scrambled my thoughts and led to this decision.

But the months went by and I continued to be determined to follow where I was called. It wasn't just Joan – my mother and grandmother, who had supported me while I did my articles, were not keen either, and Joan's side of the family found the whole thing slightly comic and a bit embarrassing. Eventually Joan agreed, when she saw I was determined, but only on the proviso that she would not be required to become a 'vicar's wife'. 'I married a solicitor; I'm quite happy to be a "solicitor's wife". But a vicar's wife, no. I will merely be the woman he happens to be married to.'

When I was interviewed for my current parish, I was asked about my wife's views on my change of career. I was honest about it: she hadn't been keen. I added, 'She has promised, however, not to dance on the tables in the pub in her knickers and embarrass me!' And just so that nobody got the wrong impression about the future, I also added that she would probably want to go back to teaching at some point.

The archdeacon was elderly, and I wasn't expecting that my honesty would gain me any brownie points, but to my surprise the man was highly critical of the Department of Education and the government generally. He said, 'It will be just like it was after the First World War – after they'd opened the box and let women out to run the place and then found it very hard to shoehorn them back in the box afterwards. And why would you want to be put back in your box when you've been shown to be competent and reliable?' He added, 'And here's something to watch for. A few years after the last war hems shot up, probably in protest. And you know what, it'll probably happen again. Maybe not so soon this time because we were all affected, women and men, by this last war and I think everyone just wants to settle down and make the most of peace. But if hems start going up again, you can be sure that's the tipping point.'

He'd also said, with a sigh of frustration, that it wouldn't be long before the Education Department was round banging on the doors of ex-teachers, begging them to come back. Everyone would be churning out children and he would bet all the tea in China that in ten years' time the bureaucrats would wake up one day and notice to their surprise that there were far more children than there were school places or teachers.

Despite, or maybe because of, my honesty, I was appointed to the parish. Over the next twelve years, as we produced three children, Joan took to the domestic sphere, spending her spare time in baking and bottling and winemaking, becoming a leading light of the Women's Institute and joining the Conservative Women's Lunch Club (even though I suspect she has never voted Conservative). This was good for my parish work because Joan liked to entertain, so we were always inviting and being invited to dinner parties, cocktail parties, afternoon teas and so on. As a result of this, I no longer had to worry about sociability; I knew pretty well everyone in the district.

And then, almost exactly as the archdeacon had said, the postwar baby-boomers reached high school. And of course they didn't have nearly enough teachers, and of course they started trying to round up the married teachers they had so blithely discarded. Even before Sally started school, Joan was preparing to go back to work. In fact, I realised with the shock of sudden enlightenment, she'd started organising herself almost from the moment that we got back from the Lake District holiday. If Sally had been a normal child, I have no doubt that Joan would have found someone to look after her and started teaching that year. But Sally was not a normal child …

The following year, when Sally turned five, Joan had arranged to start teaching at the local comprehensive. I thought this was overly optimistic and I was right. Sally was not ready to go to school, she was not ready to cease being the golden queen bee in her own special hive and to share the attention of a teacher with a couple of dozen other children. It was a dreadful few weeks, witnessed by the whole neighbourhood, but somehow we prevailed.

A year later, a position came up for a high school in York with subjects more in line with Joan's preference and she jumped at it, even though it meant a forty-minute commute. Five years had passed now and it hadn't worked out too badly, although the entertaining had reduced as a result. Or maybe that wasn't the reason …

———

I was aware as I mused on these things that someone had joined me. To cover up for my apparent lack of sociability, I turned to the man and asked, 'Do you remember when you got ordained?'

'Too young!' the man cried, pointing at one of the photos.

'I had to wait till the end of the war,' I said. 'I was nearly twenty-nine when I had my photo taken like this.'

'Yes, same here, I was over thirty. Probably ten more years of life experience than these boys here. And gruelling years they were too. But let's not talk of the war.'

He was an English member of a French order and over a cool beer, we discussed the Baptists in measured tones which, if overheard, would not give the impression that we were in fact slagging them off. The man had also travelled extensively in Eastern Europe, coming into frequent contact with the Orthodox faith, which I was interested in, and we both agreed it was stagnant, too submissive, and unwilling to listen to reason. This was, in my view, justified criticism, although I continue to have quite a fondness for their unreconstructed ways.

Much refreshed by this discussion, I headed into lunch and sat next to the head of an Anglican community and found we had several common acquaintances, as a result of which a certain amount of gossip ensued which was very pleasant. However, we also discussed the problems of an ageing community, without any likely lads, or novices. It was a common trope, and he had no answers as to how you attracted young people to a life of discipline and contemplation.

'Nowadays, there is such an overload of information and activity demanding attention, how do you get the young to even sit still?'

'But they go off to India,' said the father. 'And wear orange and sit cross legged at the feet of some guru and get diarrhoea and other nasty diseases. You would think with a nice clean monastery right on their doorstep, they would want to come and do chanting and wear loose robes with us.'

'Fashion,' I said.

The father leaned in conspiratorially. 'Perhaps we should change the colour of our robes, maybe that's the problem.' We had an ecclesiastical chortle.

I would have liked to have continued this discussion, but someone was coming round with a little bell and we were all being herded back onto the buses.

We went on to the gaudy but unpretentious village church at Valdejimina. Prayers were offered by a Dutch pastor, which served to remind us that the local bigwig, the Duke of Alba, had not been all that popular four centuries back. (I wondered if they could ever persuade an Irish delegation to hold a prayer meeting at William of Orange's burial place.) Afterwards I noticed the Madonna much in evidence, she having appeared to a local hermit, and it seemed some of the congregation were going upstairs to kiss her statue. I very much hoped that Jack wasn't being inveigled by his nun friends into doing anything quite so unhygienic.

We then all went outside to watch an exhibition of Spanish country dancing in the bullring beside the church. It was, I noted, pretty much like every other form of country dancing, being designed for the capabilities of the lowest common denominator. Of which I was probably one. Then there was a certain amount of flamenco, which oozed sensuousness and probably took time and practice to perfect, but most of it was holding hands and jigging around although with slightly different music to what I was used to. I enjoyed the display.

Then a picnic supper was laid out for us. While I was filling a plate, one of the nuns I remembered meeting before came up and re-introduced herself. Sister Carol. She said, 'Jack tells me that you started a men's group.'

I was startled – a men's group? Then I thought, okay, I suppose it is a men's group.

I sat down beside Sister Carol on one of the foldout chairs and balanced my plate on my knee. 'It didn't start as a men's group;

it didn't start as anything. It started because I was cleaning some bricks to make some steps and a path down to my vegetable garden.' It was one of those projects with no timeline; cleaning the bricks seemed to take years. Every Saturday when there were no weddings or christenings I would sit with these old bricks under a covered area near the garage, patiently chipping away at the mortar and adding them to the cleaned pile. It was a form of therapy, meditative and undemanding, and often parishioners would arrive during the process and stand talking to me. Then my verger, Bill Wilson, arrived one day to talk about some aspect of parish affairs and he was dressed in overalls and carrying his own mallet and stonemason's chisel. So after that there was my pile and then what I liked to call the visitors' pile. Bill had been in the war, and we often sat talking about what had happened to us. Gradually some of my other parishioners became regulars and it became a communal activity where gossip was exchanged and village affairs were discussed as well as the politics of the day – usually the latest strike. But often it came back to the two world wars, and I came to think that there was a thread of trauma through many of our lives that had no other outlet. It was as if someone had said, the war is over, shut the door, don't look back and just get on with it. The men who returned couldn't talk about it after a certain point with their families. 'They just don't get it,' said one. 'You try to talk about it but it's like, we heard that before, don't go on about it. But how can I not go on about it, it's all I think of.'

Things progressed in this comfortable unstructured way until the doctor's wife, Valerie Boyes, secretary to the local WI and prominent personage in the district, came round one Saturday to see Joan and found us all there. By then there were enough bricks and we had started on making the steps down to the vegetable patch.

'What's all this, some sort of club?' she asked sharply. Any move on the part of men to escape their duty as husbands and providers by slipping off and joining groups was viewed with suspicion by many of their womenfolk in the village. Long years of getting by on their own during the war had made them intolerant of extra-curricular activities by the men, who should be home 'doing their share'.

But Bill, who was a bit of a wag, said yes it was, and we called ourselves Men and Bricks.

'I see,' said Valerie. 'And this is all just to do up the vicarage?'

'No,' I said. 'Mainly we get together to talk.'

'What about?' asked Mrs Boyes with deep suspicion.

'The war, the things that happened to us.'

'Why do you want to keep talking about that? It's unhealthy, it's been over for nearly four years.'

I said, 'Yes but … I think it helps. You don't forget this stuff, even in four years.' I told her that many of us who had served in the war had nightmares, and even the older men who got back from the front thirty years ago still had terrifying dreams. And sometimes we were just seeking reassurance from each other. One of the group, now a father himself, had said that as his platoon was advancing through a village in Normandy, they had seen beside the road a woman with her head blown off by some sort of missile and beside her was something which they thought at first was a doll. It had a pink dress on but when they came up to it, they saw it was a baby girl, her face still and pretty like wax.

'Oh lord,' Valerie Boyes said, putting her hand to her cheek in horror.

The men were under fire and had to keep moving but now the man woke in the night with that image and was terrified for his own baby and whether he could protect it, whether he was going to be a good enough father.

'But surely he can talk to his wife about it.'

His wife was pregnant again and got upset by the image he was describing. So no, he couldn't talk to her about the effect it was having on him in the present. She wouldn't understand, only those who had gone through the same experiences would understand. Soldiers advancing, they didn't have the chance to process these things. They had to keep going, living on adrenaline and corned beef, because in five minutes they might be dead. But now, in peacetime, they needed to let it out, among people who would listen and console.

Mrs Boyes stood for a minute, considering the matter, and then nodded her head. Clearly a decision had been reached. She then supposed that when we had finished at the vicarage we could go and help old Miss Downey whose new glass porch was surrounded by mud and builders' rubble.

The group considered this. It was an outrage to the village, to every working man, to manhood itself, that those blokes could come all the way from York and then leave without clearing up after themselves.

'Yes,' said Bill, 'we could help. But does she have her own bricks?'

One minute we had been a loose confederation gathering for a chat, and then suddenly the women were involved and we were a regular group, approved and certified. We moved from my carport to a donated Nissen hut on the old aerodrome, where truckloads of old bricks appeared from time to time. Years had gone by and paths and patios, courtyards and garden-surrounds had spread far and wide throughout the parish and beyond. New members found us and the talk continued, as we gradually became the masters of herringbone, basketweave, running bond, stack bond, pinwheel and interlock. Men and Bricks also extended its range to take in carpentry, metalworking, plumbing, plastering and even, after evening classes, glazing. We drew the line at roofing; old men, or even middle-aged men, up ladders made some of the women nervous.

Sister Carol seemed to enjoy this description and strangely, in some way, find it helpful. 'So the fact that you are doing things with your hands, things that men would normally do, gives you permission to talk I suppose.'

'Are you interested in men's groups?' I asked.

In therapeutic groups, yes. Not necessarily for men. She wondered whether the knitting circle could make a comeback for women but there might be problems in that cheap machine-knitted garments were now available. Also, knitting socks and scarves and beanies during the war for men at the front had been a worthy patriotic cause. They could be sent off in virtuous parcels with no thought as to how they would be washed or how long they would take to dry. But today, needy families might prefer garments they could take to the laundromat. 'I'm envious,' she said. 'Cleaning bricks for making paths and so on as part of a charitable project, that would be perfect. And while you clean the bricks, it's something to concentrate on while you talk.'

I felt strangely buoyed, as if I'd somehow arrived at a really good idea without even being aware of it.

After supper, it was off back to Salamanca in the gathering darkness. On the way, there was much singing. Our bus had a good proportion of Spanish and Portuguese and much of the singing of popular songs was led by a nun who had the kind of voice which could have seen a career for herself in cabaret.

Overall, a very pleasant and quite entertaining day. I got off the bus still humming some of the tunes I'd heard.

As we were walking back to our accommodation, Jack asked

if I would like to detour into an adjoining square to say hello to his friends Manuel and family. I was dog tired, having missed my siesta, and after a day of relentless communality, couldn't have felt less like meeting new people. However, it was clear that Jack intended to go, and I wasn't keen on him walking around in the dark on his own. So I agreed, but just for a short time. Bob and Gregory, who seemed to have more energy than me, also agreed to come, which I was pleased about as that meant I didn't have to stay long and could leave Jack with them.

The square Jack led us to was rather down at heel and as a result, immensely picturesque, with peeling painted verandas and shabby striped umbrellas outside tiny cafés and shops. As soon as we entered, a shout went out from one of the little cafés: 'Jacques!'

My son led us over and a small, stout man with a moustache greeted us all enthusiastically. The teenage girls I had seen in the church also stood up and there were smiles and exclamations all round. A waiter hovered.

'I don't suppose they've got tea, have they?' I asked. It was a forlorn hope I thought, but suddenly that was what I really wanted.

Jack turned back from the waiter. 'What sort would you like?' was the heartening response.

I sat in the square among the chatter and felt peaceful and at ease. Jack was clearly translating the day for the family and translating back their exclamations. Gregory's vocation as a Benedictine monk also seemed to hugely impress them. The tea when it came was in a strange contraption, but this too was amusing, as was my adding milk to it which was clearly not a thing much done in Spain. 'Delicious,' I said. And it was.

Seven

The next morning, after a very good night's sleep, I was enjoying breakfast when the concierge came over and started talking to Jack. Apparently someone had rung the day before, a woman or a boy, for one of us. But the person ringing didn't speak Spanish and the concierge didn't speak English. So all he got was, they were looking for someone called Nixon.

'Could it have been one of your American nuns, wanting you to go and translate?'

'No, it was while we were all away together. And it wouldn't be Antoine because he would have been speaking in French.'

It was true that Antoine was the most likely to have rung. He was still keen for Jack to go over there. He couldn't speak Spanish so he might have tried English.

'Oh. And it might've been Mrs Robson,' Jack suddenly said. 'She asked me if I wanted to stay with them and said if I got bored in Salamanca to get on the train and come back and stay in their villa.'

'She would speak a bit of Spanish though, wouldn't she?'

'She might not, but now I come to think of it, Danielle would.'

A mystery. I would go to the conference centre later and see if they could shed any light on it. I was now off to the daily unity service in the Purisima Church. Jack thought he would give it a miss. 'The service is always a bit of a muddle. I think I'll go and help out in the shop again instead.'

Yes, I thought as I set out, the morning service was the most disappointing, or embarrassing, feature of the conference so far. That day it was the Episcopalians (the churches in communion with Canterbury and Utrecht) and they made as big a muddle as the Orthodox and the Reformed. To say 'bigger' muddle would be to draw distinctions – I can only say that it was uninspiring, and only the input of a most efficient Catholic monk who was involved in the scheduling and organisation of these events relieved it from disaster.

I was carrying a notebook and pencil, and during a period of unrelieved tedium I wrote the following:

> To any bishop or cardinal seeking my advice on such matters, I give a few rules for a successful international interdenominational religious service.
>
> 1. Choose a barn, tent, cinema, warehouse – anything other than a baroque basilica.
> 2. Print leaflets for each service to avoid maddening uncertainties.
> 3. Shoot all press men.
> 4. Search all Americans for flashlight cameras.
> 5. Place a bomb near the communion table, due to explode in 60 minutes, to get some urgency into the proceedings.

Coming back to the conference centre, I was running a little late and went straight to my discussion group. This was now much more promising and enjoyable. Several new recruits had joined: two other Anglicans, two RCs, an Old Catholic from Switzerland, another Lutheran from Sweden, an Orthodox (originally Russian) from Ireland and a Baptist from Detroit. We discussed the nature of the ministry and it was all rather satisfactory.

After lunch I went to the conference centre, but they had no record of anyone trying to contact me. I'd seen no sign of Jack at lunch so I presumed the family was feeding him, but I was just settling down for my siesta when my son came by on the way to his own room.

'You don't think it was Mum?' he said.

For some reason it had never entered my head that it might be Joan, and the thought filled me with cold panic. 'I can't imagine why she would ring.' Ringing long distance, at her own expense – it just wasn't likely. You could either call Joan thrifty or a penny pincher, so even though she now had her own money, she was definitely not one to splash it around. 'If it *was* her, I presume she'll send a telegram.'

I privately thought that if she had anything to communicate, she would have sent the telegram first. Got me to ring her. It was much more in character. I wondered if that thought was uncharitable. I had to be on guard against thinking uncharitable thoughts about my wife.

'Uncle Don's probably got sick of Sally,' said Jack.

That was the nightmare that I was afraid of right from the beginning. But I was here in Spain, the complete escape, and whatever problems were taking place in England, they were for once not *my* problem.

So I drifted into a doze without giving it much more thought.

The afternoon was spent with more discussion on the concept of ministry, of a very useful though slightly anxiety-inducing sort. Do I still have a vocation? I wondered. Or had it been dissipated in the day-to-day trials of the world, bringing up two normal sons and a very difficult daughter. Had I even done the right thing to start with by giving up my original profession to take orders? Might not my relationship with Joan have been less prickly if I had continued along the path that I had originally intended when I married her? If I did no longer have a vocation, was it too late now to bail out in midlife and either go back to my original qualifications or even to take up a completely new career? These were the thoughts running through my head when, after dinner, I thought I would take a stroll into the centre of the town with my son.

It would've been nice to go alone, by which I meant just with Jack, but it seemed that any outing with Jack by its very nature now included a largish cohort of hangers-on plus greetings from a surprising number of locals.

We went down to a colonnaded shopping centre where I noted an extraordinary number of shoe shops. There was a huge square with plenty of cafés for evening drinks, and we sat down at one of the tables and ordered. I tried again, successfully, for tea. Jack disappeared for a while and came back with some of the young girls, and there was a lot of laughter and chattering up their end of the table.

I was sitting next to Sister Angela, one of the American nuns. She was a vivacious dark-haired woman of about my own age, and although she wore a cross around her neck, she didn't bother with the short wimple the others wore. 'You don't have to advertise your status as a nun when you get to my age,' she said. 'Every woman over fifty is a nun.'

I wasn't sure if that was true, because I found her really quite attractive, but it definitely wasn't a situation where such a compliment could be paid.

She asked me about my ministry.

I told her I was a vicar of an obscure but extensive parish in the North Riding of Yorkshire. It had once been a rich living in the days when clerics were entitled to all the income from their parish; its church lands had been filched from a great mediaeval monastery nearby which had been sacked by Cromwell, and instead of it being controlled by some aristocratic landowner, it had always been within the gift of the Archbishop of York. My parish contained no fewer than four churches: one was eighth century and required constant maintenance, and three others, in three separate small villages, all had Gothic spires puncturing the almost flat farmlands in which they nestled like ballerinas doing arabesques, one elegant limb pointing to heaven and the body in graceful counterpoint.

'You're kept busy then?'

Not that busy pastorally, as the farmers were prosperous and had been investing in mechanisation, as a result of which the working rural poor had migrated north to the factories of Middlesbrough or south to the steelworks of Sheffield. But the farmers, who were not poor whatever they told you, did tend to be superstitious; science could only get them so far and then it rained and rained and ruined the hay, or it didn't rain at all and ruined the wheat. Much better to have God on your side, so there were always good congregations on Sundays, a meeting point for gossip, maybe a shot of whiskey at the pub before going home for Sunday dinner.

So what do you do with your working day, I was asked.

I spent the morning doing the parish accounts (which were complex). I had discovered very quickly why, as a complete novice, I had been given such a large and asset-rich parish. Without a legal background, it would have been very hard to understand the complexities of the landholdings and the various trusts and leases which came with those assets, and a less qualified minister might have thrown his hands in the air and given up, which is apparently what my predecessor had done. These matters necessitated frequent trips into York to consult with the archdiocesan lawyers, represented originally by an elderly and very knowledgeable solicitor. By the time the man retired, I knew almost as much as he did and a good deal more than his replacement.

As well as keeping on top of the paperwork, I would catch up on my correspondence, which was large, eclectic and constant. I had been inveigled by Bob onto a charitable trust for an Orthodox community. It was perhaps a strange thing for an Anglican minister to be involved in, but Bob had thought that with my understanding of such trusts and the fact I was an outsider I might, with gravitas and patience, be able to find a way through the dysfunctional infighting; something which Bob himself had been unable to do. Well I hadn't really done much better in that regard; instead I received correspondence from all corners of England and Europe complaining about other members of the community. But there were benefits, which included an Orthodox priest who had given up in disgust and gone back to Greece and who every few weeks wrote me the most interesting and amusing letters about his doings under the Colonels' regime.

I also spent the morning editing the monthly parish newsletter and thinking about and writing my sermons.

How did I choose a subject for my sermon? Sister Angela was interested.

I suddenly didn't know what to say. Or how much to say. For my evening service I tended to work over readings from my extensive library. But for my morning service they were always original, and the topics didn't always come to me straight away. Sometimes the idea came because … Well, because I was under the impression that God talked to me.

'Well of course He talks to you,' said Sister Angela.

Oh. For a moment, I was lost for words. For some reason I had thought that this was some mental aberration in myself, believing that God would find the time from all His other millions and millions of duties to say a few words. I had never admitted it before in case people thought I was mad. It had never entered my head that God might talk to other people. Or that having a 'calling' meant exactly that, that God called or spoke to you. I wasn't sure how I felt about that. I had thought that even if it meant I was mad, it also meant that I was special.

Anyway, in relation to the sermon, if I really couldn't think of anything what I would do was go down on the bare floor on my knees and ask God to help me and then empty my mind as far as possible, although the throbbing in my war-wounded leg when I knelt would make that difficult. And I would wait for a word. They were always two syllables, and I wondered if it was a word from God or whether the brain was reacting to the throbbing. But every word I had ever received in this way resulted in an excellent subject for a sermon, so I continued to believe that they *were* words from God.

'How fascinating!' said Sister Angela. 'Give me an example of a word and how you turned it into sermon.'

A month or so previously I'd had a busy week and realised that Sunday was fast approaching, and I'd given no thought to my sermon. So I'd gone down on my knees and, as usual, apologised to God for bothering him but could he give me an idea. I had then emptied my mind, trying to drive out the pins and needles in my thigh and the soft wailing pain of my kneecap and the screech of my pulsing blood. And the word came. And the word was, kitchen.

'Kitchen!' exclaimed Sister Angela. How extraordinary. So how did I go about finding something uplifting and morally instructive about a kitchen?

I went and sat in my own kitchen and looked around, wondering the very same thing. We were having a few coolish days in a row and I had lit the Rayburn, so it was warm and safe and quiet. And I remembered, possibly because I had been focused on this trip, another kitchen in Normandy during the war. Bombs were raining down from the skies, aimed at the enemy positions a few miles in front but bouncing in among our own troops as well. Trees hung wearily in black tatters or pointed shattered trunks to the sky in despair. Everywhere was in ruins, smoke hung in the air and there was an awful pungent smell like a rubbish heap burning underground. The villages and towns we tramped through were destroyed; I felt so sorry for the inhabitants and for the dead killed by friends coming to liberate them. Even worse were the bodies of our own soldiers flung down beside the road, many from my own company, some that I knew or recognised.

We had stopped for the night next to one of the ruined houses and we were not in great shape. We had been for days without proper sleep and eating terrible food and moving forward over the bodies of the dead, including horses and farm animals. The house where we stopped gaped open at the front, but my sergeant and another man went to reconnoitre and returned excitedly to tell me that the kitchen was still intact round the back. When the platoon went to investigate it was true – despite the floor being covered with glass, the back annexe of the house seemed to have escaped damage. There was a fuel stove still connected to its chimney, and various pieces of kitchen equipment lying around. The problem from my point of view was that my men were all looking to me and I had no idea how any of it worked.

While doing my articles I had lived at home and had hardly ever been into the kitchen, where the daily help and my grandmother held sway. When I was called up I spent four years eating army food. Now, with our cans of disgusting mush, we had for the space of a few hours the possibility of cooking something. And I had no idea at all what to do.

I wondered whether to bluff it out, but as I stood there indecisively, one of my men, Evans – who up until that point I had always looked out for because he was older and of slight build – put down his pack, gave some part of the stove a good strong shake and looked in the firebox. Evans then picked up the coke scuttle and organised his comrades to help him pull debris off what he deduced was the coal cellar.

The next moment there was a sharp 'Sir!' and I went over quickly to find two terrified children and an old woman holding a whimpering baby – they had been trapped while hiding down inside and I, as the only one who spoke French, was able to make myself useful. The water pump in the yard had been damaged and when the fire was got going, my corporal (another practical man) managed to fix the pump with some hot metal wire and a hammer. Now, with both water and a blazing stove, we got the kettle on to boil and rations into a pot to stew. Private Teasdale, who had a couple of kids himself, set about looking for baby paraphernalia in and among the wreckage and was going to strip everyone of their powdered milk until he managed to fight his way through piles of rubble to what was clearly a pantry, where he found several tins of evaporated milk. A short while later the baby, who had been given a pretty good scrubbing under the pump, was wrapped in a tablecloth, and Teasdale was bottle feeding it sitting on a stool.

The other two children, who had also been given a good scrub, were ensconced in a large, sagging armchair with bowls of army slop which they were eating as if their lives depended on it. The old woman, who had at first seemed shocked and dazed and use-less, came out of her coma and suddenly appeared with a couple of chickens dangling from her hands, which she proceeded to pluck. Those went into the oven, and she reappeared with carrots and potatoes which were scraped at the pump and went into the pan with the chicken. She gathered herbs and green vegetables and meanwhile my men had cleared away the shattered glass, mended the shutters, fixed the door and found kerosene for the lamp. Some time later, with an audible sigh of contentment, we all sat down to eat.

The subject of my sermon was Proverbs 11:2. When pride comes, then comes disgrace, but with humility comes wisdom.

And the message of my sermon was the necessity for everyone from the highest to the lowest to be equipped with the skills necessary for survival. No one should turn up their nose at any chore, however humble, because who knew when they might need to know how to do it? Almost the only thing that schoolchildren knew about King Alfred was that he burnt the cakes. He didn't have to make them, he just had to watch them: how humiliating not even to be able to do that!

I had been made a sub-lieutenant, a leader of my platoon, for my skills in being able to pass exams for subjects which were completely useless in a time of crisis. I had set forth in pride, carrying a gun, pips on my shoulders, the flower of the British Army, and yet when it came to the crunch I had to trust my men for the most basic skills of everyday living. I described to my congregation how I had stood beside the old woman in Normandy, watching her as she made the gravy and how she made it. What a meal that was. Not only roast chicken and vegetables, but gravy. As a result of that experience in France I had resolved never again to be caught in such a situation; never again would I walk into a kitchen and not know how to use everything in it. I didn't need to become an expert, just competent, and I had kept my goals modest. Over time I had become more confident but had to be careful that I didn't spruik my expertise in anything, knowing that there would always be someone better at it than myself. All of this so that when I got to the Pearly Gates and St Peter asked me how I thought I'd gone in the world, I could reply that I hoped I'd found a way to be kind and to care for the people I came into contact with, to lift up the fallen, to commiserate with the bereaved, to hold hands with those in search of truth and to make a halfway decent gravy.

Sister Angela was amused. 'And did your congregation enjoy that sermon?'

Oh yes – I tried to be modest, but my congregation enjoyed most of my sermons. 'I don't make them deep and meaningful, but I try to make them at least meaningful to them. Shallow and meaningful I suppose you'd call them.' I hastened to add, however, that I didn't let them off the hook morally, socially or even environmentally. They often came out of church buzzing like outraged bees. Once I gave a sermon based on Rachel Carson's *Silent Spring* that had the whole district in an uproar, and when Sunday came I thought I'd have an empty church but there they all were as usual.

'Waiting to be outraged again,' cried Sister Angela with a laugh. 'No wonder you have a good turnout on Sunday. And I'll bet all those farmers went home determined to outdo you in the gravy stakes.'

'It's a pity men are so competitive, isn't it.'

She laughed again, a merry, engaging laugh which lit up the air around her. Then she said, 'I love that story, the humanity on so many levels. The private with the baby in the crook of his arm, and your men fixing the pump, fixing the shutters and the door. All of you working as a team, doing what needed to be done, making a safe space for this poor little remnant of a family so hopefully they survived the war. So many good things happening in this kitchen which had nothing to do with cooking.'

I was pleased she liked it. Cups of praise had been in short supply of late and I was happy to drink every drop going.

Sister Angela told me she lived in New York with a number of other nuns who were mainly teaching at a Catholic university, plus some like Sister Carol who had started out teaching but were now doing other things.

She taught during the week, and her evenings were spent

in marking and keeping up to date with reading. On Sunday everything came to a halt. She spent the day fasting and in going to Mass, in prayer and in meditation, expunging all thoughts of the week from her mind. As a result, on Monday morning she was up like Rice Krispies, snap crackling and popping, ready for the week ahead.

'Sounds wonderful,' I said.

'Yes, but since being here and listening to the pastoral work that others do, often in difficult situations, I'm wondering if it isn't self-indulgent.' Anyway, she and the other nuns lived together in a substantial house provided by the church. When they had taken it over, the ground floor had been a commercial business and the basement had had a small restaurant. The ground floor space had been redeveloped for use by Sister Carol as her practice rooms. The basement had been turned into their kitchen and communal dining area, and the upper three floors were bedrooms, bathrooms and a small chapel. And yes, when I asked, it had central heating and all mod cons, a lift, secure parking area – very desirable in other words.

When the house had been acquired, it was in a rundown part of Brooklyn with a lot of problems, but in the last few years cashed-up professionals were moving into the area. So she was beginning to wonder what would happen when somebody in charge of the moneybags realised that their valuable asset was only being used by no-account nuns. The attitudes of those higher up in the church to a group of nuns living outside their community would not be that different to how they viewed a coven of lesbians.

I looked shocked. She laughed. New York was a pretty sophisticated place. A coven of lesbians added more to the cachet of the area than a group of nuns. Although with Carol's latest innovations the city was getting both. She let out another of her merry laughs.

She turned away to respond to her other neighbour and I

thought about my friend Oliver who had lived above the village in an ancient manor house. Nobody could accuse *our* village of being sophisticated, but nevertheless Oliver had managed to live for decades with his boyfriend without any eyebrows being raised. Bachelors, two bachelors one of whom was a man servant, each with their own bedroom, nothing to see here. Although of course there were strange eccentricities which should have been clues. Such as the arguments. According to their daily help, who also came to do the vicarage two afternoons a week, the two of them bickered all the time. Far from being a self-effacing, endlessly efficient persona like Jeeves, Oliver's companion contested instead for his share of being Bertie Wooster.

But that was accepted by the village. Oliver was a baronet, and so, if he shouted at his gardener that he couldn't find something and his gardener shouted back, had he tried actually looking, well that was your other half for you. Different lives of the rich and titled.

The previous year, Oliver had said to me that everyone was only a short step away from fame and once upon a time it used to be a nine-day wonder, but now he'd just read of an American artist who had reduced it to fifteen minutes. That fame was nearly always not of a good sort – and the more respected and socially luminous you were, the more likely you were to encounter disaster.

'Yes, my dear,' he'd cried, 'we are all poised on the edge of scandal. Take me. I've always had a taste for forbidden fruit, and one night I couldn't control it and went into a public lavatory in Leicester Square. I knew the moment I saw him that my name was going to be all over the newspapers, but he looked familiar and I have a very good memory, especially for young men. I asked him back to my place and that's when I nearly got arrested. The young man I had accosted turned out to be a police officer. Fortunately my memory delivered, and I remembered where I'd seen him – he'd come with his father, who was an electrician, to add some amenities to a friend's stately home. I said I had been going to give him a cup of tea and some fatherly advice about hanging about in common toilets, how upset his father would be et cetera. They had to let me go, saved from a terrible scandal, a jail sentence perhaps. And just then my uncle conveniently died so I scuttled up here to the country as fast as I could, and I knew the moment I arrived that I was going to be happy. Because the first thing I saw was Ben pruning the roses. Hello, I said, I'm the new Lord of the Manor. Hello, he said, I'm the new gardener. And we looked at each other, and smiled, and fell in love. And we lived and loved for forty years with no scandal. Until he sadly passed on.' Oliver looked at me. 'Are you shocked?'

'No.' And I truly wasn't. The army had tried to inculcate in me the idea that of all crimes, sodomy was the worst. I liked to think that was because when it came to light it was usually in connection with blackmail. Or suicide. But I suspected the power structure within the army had other motives for turning it into some dirty heinous crime committed by monsters. However, my experiences of war wiped clean my moral compass of judgement when it came to what people did peacefully in private.

Plus, faithfulness was a wonderful thing in all of God's creatures, as was love, and the two together, however obtained, should be nurtured. I would only be scandalised, I told Oliver, when faithfulness and love were dragged in the mud and viciousness reigned.

I looked around at those merrily chatting at the surroundings tables. To come to such a conference must indicate a greater level of tolerance in general than I suppose was often found in religious adherents. But how far would that toleration extend? Would it extend to the proposition 'I respect how you choose to worship and who you choose to love and live with'? Mmm. No, the second part, dealing with sex, was the problem. Sex in all its iterations was a difficult topic of conversation, and that was a situation which attending unity services was not going to alter.

I wondered how Sister Angela, whose passing mention of lesbians had set off this train of recollection, would go on the subject. I suspected because she had raised it so cheerfully that it was probably not off-limits, an impression which seemed justified when she turned back and told me of the innovations introduced by Sister Carol.

Carol was a psychologist who focused on the problems of women in the workforce and had recently decided that as she wasn't using the ground floor in the way it was originally intended, she would reconfigure it so it was of more use. She had gone round tapping a few wealthy women for funds and had come back with a substantial war chest. This allowed her to turn part of the space into a usable conference and training room for the training group she'd set up, and the rest into office space for a part-time lawyer for assisting women in employment situations. 'A free legal service. Only for women. How radical is that! As you know,' said Sister Angela, 'any practical help just for women, outside of their core business of having babies, well it's an outrageous proposition … Why would you do that? It can only emanate from a radical bra-burning feminist mentality. From lesbians in other words. Because what normal woman would even think of doing such a thing!'

The powers that be in the church were not happy at all with the new arrangement, but now they had a headache if they wanted to stop it, because they were up against rich women philanthropists who, for reasons completely obscure to these men in cassocks, were committed to the enterprise. Angela gave another laugh, 'Ah, religion and money. That's my subject, I'm writing a book about it and what could be more delightful than to be right there in the thick of it where you can see the whites of everyone's eyes.'

As for their long-term future at that address, it didn't matter to her. If they had to move, they had to move, and she was not going to spill tears about having to relocate to somewhere not so palatial.

I agreed with this sentiment, thinking about the vicarage. 'When we moved in, we thought we were the luckiest people alive, and we certainly were lucky after the war to have a completely furnished house. But as time goes on, as you get older, the winters feel colder, the amount of cleaning to be done seems to get bigger, and the inconvenience of living so far out in the country gets greater.' Time for a change.

A drink Sister Angela had ordered appeared and during the pause I became aware of a conversation going on at the other end of the table. 'Is Jack translating German now?'

She listened for a moment. 'Yes and no. They're nuns from a Swiss order and I understand some of them speak Swiss German as well as French. But they seem to be discussing Durkheim and his ideas on gemeinschaft and gesellschaft. Theories of community. I think Jack is quite interested in such concepts.'

I wondered whether to admit my ignorance, but she seemed happy to give me a lecture without even being asked. Eventually, having drunk my tea, I got up to go, as it had been considerably less restful than the previous evening. My head was bursting with sociology and vaguely dissatisfied ideas about my own place in the scheme of things.

Jack walked back with me and said, 'Sister Angela teaches sociology and Sister Carol, I think she practises psychology. I didn't even know there were such subjects you could do. How can you choose what to do at university if you don't know what some of the subjects *are*? Sister Angela told me of all the courses available at her university. Political science. What's that? Economics. Apparently that's what you study if you want to be a politician, not political science. Then there's journalism, or some universities call it media studies. And all sorts of other things.'

'Have you any idea what you want to do, after the baccalaureate?'

'I thought I did but now I'm not sure.'

'Would you do the same subjects for the baccalaureate as you're doing now for A level?'

Yes, but because he didn't think it would take much effort to reconfigure his current subjects into French, he was thinking he would add something new. Perhaps one of the subjects he'd been hearing about if it was possible, something his current school didn't offer. But as for his subjects at university he didn't know. 'Pete will have finished his geology degree by then and is hoping to have a job lined up in Australia. He wants me to go out once he's settled and maybe go to university there.'

I stopped in shock. 'Pete's going to Australia?'

'Didn't you know? I didn't know if he'd told you.'

I had heard nothing from him since Christmas.

'No. Me neither. Then he wrote a few weeks ago care of Tony.'

'He wouldn't even write to you at home!' I took his arm, and we walked on for a while in silence. 'Where is he at the moment?'

He was in Scotland doing a summer job as a surveyor's assistant and they were on the move pretty well every day. He was going to send an address when they got to Inverness.

Jack said after another pause, 'I didn't know about when Mum visited him at the university.'

I stopped again. 'She told me she'd gone to Sheffield for work and called on him to try and persuade him to come home occasionally. But she said the timing was wrong because he was going to a lecture and said he couldn't talk.'

'Pete wrote that she was waiting outside the lecture theatre when he came out and she had Sally in the car. She was angry, she said you were both angry, because of what happened at Christmas and she wanted it to be resolved. She'd said, "We can't keep financially supporting you unless that happens." And she wanted him to go and apologise to Sally.'

I groaned 'Oh God,' and we started walking again. I didn't need to ask what Pete's reaction had been to this suggestion. After a while I said, 'Sometimes I feel like I'm living in a parallel universe. She said that *I* was angry! That I was going to stop the payments … I knew nothing … Why would I do that? But I've been writing letters regularly to him, care of the university, hoping he'll respond. I suppose if he thought if I was in agreement with your mother …' I left the sentence unfinished.

Pete had always been the leader, the one with a gang behind him ready to fight pirates in the wood, making pea-shooters and slingshots and home-made bows and arrows, and dashing here and there on his bike and making lots of noise. He was eight years older than Sally, and by the time she went to primary school he was already in high school. He had always pushed back angrily against any attempted incursion by her into his possessions and activities, and the older Sally got, the more of these incursions there were and the more angry shouting resulted. It seemed to be a circular sort of situation. The more Sally tried to push into his life, the more Pete rejected her, and the more provocative Sally became as a result. This had muted in the last few years, since Pete went to university and was living his life elsewhere. At times their relationship now seemed almost cordial.

In fact peace of a sort descended the moment Pete left home, but I knew that this was not because Sally's behaviour had improved but because Jack was a different boy: he didn't push back, he simply absented himself.

That was no solution, but I didn't really know what the solution was. But I now saw with horror that a solution was necessary, otherwise I was going to lose both of my sons.

Back at the hall of residence, I attempted a bath. The bath had two taps (both cold) and a plughole (no plug). It only worked because the waste pipe was half blocked. Nevertheless I thought the cold water would refresh me and wash away the sticky feeling of being swamped. I returned to my room and was thinking on the symbolism of the blocked plughole when Jack knocked on my door. And handed me a telegram.

It was from my wife, telling me to ring urgently.

Joan was doing a summer program at Oxford University in the hope that it would enhance her career as a teacher and increase her chances of obtaining a job as an assistant headmistress. The opportunity had come up suddenly when someone she knew had to withdraw from the course through ill-health. She didn't hesitate; she enrolled and paid the fees and then assumed, I was aggrieved to find out, that I would stay home to look after Sally even though right from the beginning she had assured me she would be available to look after our daughter when I went to Spain and even though I had been planning this trip for months.

I made it clear that was not going to happen, that I also had enrolled – many months before her – and I had also paid fees, and that I was committed to the trip, and reminded her of her promise that she would look after Sally. She then suggested that I took Sally with me. I'd said I had a better idea, which was that she take Sally with her to the university where, instead of sitting for days in a car complaining she was bored and generally whingeing about going into churches which she hated, she could instead sit beside her in class and disrupt her day instead. I also pointed out that at least Sally would have a bed, because Joan's college of residence accepted females whereas, as she seemed to have forgotten, we were staying at monasteries and I couldn't see that Sally would enjoy sleeping in the car.

For a while we were barely speaking to each other as Joan harangued me on my lack of commitment to her career, even though she had had to fit in with mine. This irritated me because it wasn't my fault she had had to give up teaching. 'I've always supported your career,' I pointed out. 'The Department of Education made you stop, not me!' And I became increasingly angry that she seemed to be giving no weight to her promise to look after Sally and what was the point of a promise if it wasn't going to be kept when something better came along?

In the end she managed to persuade her brother Don to take Sally for the fortnight when I was going to be away and, because Don's house in Woking was not that far from the university, she had taken Sally down with her a couple of days before I was due to leave.

The following day, as if one problem gets solved and another raises its head, Antoine had rung to tell Jack about his grandfather's death and that they were going to Switzerland for what Jack translated as 'a family battle over the spoils'. It was clearly not something Antoine thought Jack would want to be part of. Or indeed anyone for that matter.

So suddenly Jack was at home too. He was old enough to be left behind, I supposed, even though his friend Tony was away for the holidays. But a curate I didn't know was going to run the parish and might be staying odd days at the vicarage and everything was suddenly complicated. It was Bob's idea that Jack come too, and Gregory had no objection, so that's what happened.

All of this went through my mind when I noticed with surprise and some alarm that the number I was being asked to call was that for the flat in York that Joan had been renting four days a week for the last couple of years. Why was she there and not at Oxford?

I had long been acclimatised to the fact that any telegram presaged bad news. It might be one of our elderly relatives who had chosen that moment to slip off their mortal coil. My own mother was dead, but I still had aunts and uncles as did Joan. And there was always the possibility that it was a younger relative, which would be tragic. Even if that was the case, there was no way that I could get back to the UK before the time we had planned for. I had paid into the kitty for the petrol for the car, the ferry, the food for our picnics and the accommodation plus, at the last minute, for Jack's share. Apart from that, I saw any extra as just pocket money, for occasional drinks, maybe a couple of postcards, presents to take back, and at that point I had less than £20 to my name. This had seemed when I set off quite adequate, even luxurious. But not at all adequate in emergencies, and there was something about the urgency of the demand that filled me with a sense of foreboding.

It was after eleven, but I rang anyway with Jack's help; reverse charges because the phone at our accommodation was not a payphone. I suddenly felt pleased that I was ringing Joan's flat in York and that she would have to pay, not me. I wasn't sure where that mean thought came from.

I heard the discussion at the other end: 'Reverse charges!' in Joan's least congenial voice.

I was going to explain but I didn't get a word in edgeways. Instead, Joan barked at me, 'Sally has run off. You'll have to come back.'

The words, and the way they were said, gave me a shock. There was something raw in the voice and something peremptory in the tone which made me feel I was not talking to my wife but somebody different. Plus, she said these words as if I would comprehend them immediately. I didn't, I couldn't comprehend them at all. Run off. What did she mean?

Apparently our daughter had disappeared the day before. Don

was a teacher like his sister and during the summer holidays also undertook marking for O-level Latin. He had found his niece restless and disruptive, so for the past week he had laid the marking aside to entertain her, taking her to the local swimming pool, cinemas, clock golf course and so on. The time was ticking on and eventually he had to get down to work, doing an all-night session which broke the back of it. When he got up about eleven o'clock in the morning, she was gone. He knew straight away something was wrong. He went into her room and found that her stuff was gone too, so he immediately sent a telegram to his sister and rang the police. Since then, they'd heard nothing.

Joan said Sally wouldn't have gone back to the vicarage because she knew a stranger was there. Anyway, Joan had rung the diocesan office, who got hold of the locum, who had only been using the study and not staying there but he hadn't seen her. 'So I thought she might have come back to the flat. It's easier here with a phone anyway, the only phone I could use at the university was a payphone down in the common room.' She then repeated that I would have to come back.

I was concentrating, however, on where Sally might be. Was there a boy, was she even old enough for there to be a boy? Had something happened while she was at Don's? What about friends, would she have gone to stay with friends?

All of which my wife impatiently gave short shrift to. Sally would've told her, she told her everything. She didn't know what had gone wrong at Don's, clearly something he had done. But anyway, I must come home at once.

'That isn't possible.'

'Somebody has to be here, and I have to get back to Oxford as soon as I can.'

'Well that someone can't be me, it's just not possible.'

'Don't you care where she is?'

'That's a ridiculous thing to say. I care as much as you do. More, obviously, if you're so dead set on getting straight back to the university.'

Joan wasn't even listening. 'So you don't care. I thought as much. She could be anywhere. Here or on the continent.'

'How could she be on the continent? She doesn't have a passport for one thing.'

'Yes of course she's got a passport.'

'What!' I was astounded. 'No, she can't have. How could she have a passport? I would have to sign for it.'

'You did sign for it.'

'I have never signed for it. I never agreed for her to have a passport. I never agreed for her to be part of an exchange. She's not mature enough.'

'It's for the Belgian trip.'

'What Belgian trip?'

'With the school. She told you about it.'

'No she didn't. I haven't agreed to any trip.'

'I don't know what you're talking about. She said you'd signed the form, and she sent it off herself and got her passport a couple of weeks ago.'

The realisation sunk in. 'So she forged my signature.'

There was a slight intake of breath. 'If she's done that … That's beside the point. What are you going to do?'

I had no idea what I was going to do and stood there for a moment at a loss. Jack was behind me and had obviously picked up what was going on. He said quietly, 'Ask her if Sally knew that I was coming to Spain.'

Joan said, 'Who's that with you?'

When I answered that it was Jack, she said, 'Why are you talking to Jack Halstead about it?'

'What! What are you talking about? Jack. Jack. Our son.'

I could feel her doing a double take at the end of the phone even as I myself realised the implications of what she'd just said.

She'd rung me the night before I left, a fairly brief conversation during which she'd asked me how my preparations were going and then described her accommodation in an old college building, a bedroom to herself but sharing a largish sitting room with another woman – the room having a view of an ancient quadrangle although she would have little time to sit and look at it. She told me that if there were any emergencies I would have to send a telegram as there wasn't any phone number for contacting students doing summer courses. At that point I had passed on to her the information that Jack was no longer going to France and would be coming with us. She had just said 'So there'll be four of you,' which now I came to think of it was a slightly odd remark, but she was clearly in a hurry, she had to go, the evening meal was about to start in the refectory.

Now I connected with what she'd just said. When I said Jack was coming, she had heard, not our son, but a Methodist minister, Jack Halstead, whom I was friendly with and occasionally invited to meals with Gregory. I found this revelation shocking, deeply disturbing. But, clearly this meant she hadn't told Sally that Jack was coming to Spain.

In any case Joan said she hadn't even spoken to Sally since she went to stay with her brother. 'I haven't had time. This course is very demanding. Look this is costing a fortune. I just want to know what you're going to do. I really want you to come back, I can't cope with this on my own.'

I struggled to keep my tone even, though I was fighting down panic. 'I can't come back. I am travelling in someone else's car, I have less than twenty quid and I have Jack here with me. You are there on the spot with no one to look after so you will have to deal with it. I'm sorry.'

'Then I need to know where Pete is. Perhaps he can help, seeing as you won't.'

My shoulders slumped. 'I don't know where Pete is. From what Jack tells me, he's currently in Scotland doing a summer job. After what happened at Christmas, he's hardly likely to come back for this.'

'They are both so selfish. I can't believe I had such selfish sons. Okay I am hanging up now. The pips are going.'

'Wait.' Jack was talking in my ear. 'Jack thinks if she's got a passport, she's gone to France, to the Bergers' farm. She's been asking him how to get there.'

'No, that's ridiculous.' She was decisive. 'I was only saying the continent in a general way. In that it was possible, theoretically. How would she get the money to travel right over there?'

Yes, that was true, I admitted it to myself. 'I'll ring you tomorrow then, shall I?'

'I won't *be* here, I keep telling you.' The line went dead.

I stood there for a moment shocked into stillness and then turned with an effort to my son. 'Why did you want me to ask about you coming to Spain? Sally never showed any interest in my plans to come to Spain.'

'No, I don't think she's interested in Spain. It's rather whether she knows I'm not in France.'

'You don't think … Isn't it possible that she might have gone to a friend?'

'I don't think she has any friends, Dad. I don't think she knows how. Friends are people who fit in with what you want to do and then you fit in with them. They share things with you, and you share your stuff with them. Sally never got the hang of the second part of that.'

Give and take. I remembered one of Joan's recent outbursts, 'Give give give, that's all I ever do!' Was the mantra of the new woman to be, take take take? I could see how difficult it would be to make friends on that basis. But maybe things were different elsewhere, away from home. 'Perhaps at school she might have made friends.'

But I suddenly found that Jack knew a great deal more about Sally's life at the boarding school she attended than I did. Things Joan hadn't told me, that no one had thought to tell me. After some incidents, which Jack didn't elaborate on, the school had intimated to Joan that Sally was not settling, not fitting in, and that Joan needed to start making alternative arrangements. Joan had apparently extracted a reprieve from them. But it seemed that Sally's continuation at the school was precarious, and her fellow classmates would rejoice if she went. All of this hit me over the head like a hammer. I had no idea … It all felt like a dream, no, more like a nightmare.

'So where … You really think she's gone to France?'

'I'd be pretty certain of it. She's been going on about it. And then, when Mum decided to do this course, she didn't say things like, 'Why does Jack get to go to France and I have to go to Uncle Don's?' Nothing like that.'

Yes of course. I could see it now. The passport obtained behind my back, the miraculous absence of complaint … If Jack was right, she'd been planning this.

When Jack had gone to France for eight months a couple of years previously, what dreary months they had turned into. Pete had just started at university and Sally was in the last year of primary school. I had thought that the two boys being elsewhere would be something she would prefer. With no need to share with anyone and with no activities going on that she was excluded from, she would become more content. To start with it was fine and I don't know what changed it, but suddenly Sally started whining and grizzling almost constantly, she wanted to go to France, why couldn't she go to France, when was Jack coming back from France. It went on day after day, nearly drove me mad. And obviously Joan too because, I still couldn't believe this, she told me she was going to write to Jack and order him to come back. Absolutely not! We both knew he was getting an educational opportunity not open to many children and one which, if only Sally could become better at making friends, perhaps in a few years might be open to her too. Why on earth should he be made to come back? He was four years older than Sally, they'd never been companions. Pete had left already. Jack would leave soon. That's what children did.

By that point I could see clearly that Joan was not dampening down Sally's gathering momentum but almost inflaming it. She said she would go over at Easter with Sally to visit him. I said I couldn't stop her going but Sally definitely wasn't going, because I wasn't going to agree to a passport – she was too difficult a child to land on an unsuspecting French family without being invited. I suggested that instead of encouraging Sally in her nagging, she needed to coach Sally in the realities of life, that you don't always get what you want.

Joan said that she would go to France on her own then, which was fine with me. By that time we were nearly always taking separate holidays, and I had arranged with Pete to go to Cumberland after the Easter services to stay with Uncle Peter and his family. My uncle had retained the lodge of the mansion we had stayed in years before and used it as a holiday house. Taking Sally would be a bit of a risk, but she seemed quite happy to be going with us and when Pete said he would pick her up on Good Friday and go up ahead of me, this suddenly was all she talked about. Jack was forgotten as she became increasingly excited about going up north in Pete's sportscar.

This was well in train when we got a letter from Jack saying the Berger family were all going to Switzerland for Easter to stay with Mme Berger's father and that he and Antoine would be sleeping in a tent as there wasn't room for everyone in the house. He was hoping there would be snow, as he had never camped in the snow before.

So that was the end of Joan's trip to France. As she had fallen out with Uncle Peter and his wife, she went to stay with her brother Don for a few days instead.

The week in Cumberland went surprisingly well, with wonderful spring weather, and while Pete and Sally and other members of my extended family were tramping the hills, boating, canoeing and going on picnics, my uncle and I went flyfishing. Five days of deeply relaxing contemplation and several large trout.

For some reason, when we got back Joan was in a resentful mood. She seemed to get even more resentful as Sally and Pete said what a good time they'd had, and all this made me uneasy. Then to my horror, when Pete left to go back to university, it all started up again. The whingeing and whining. Sally wanting to go to France, bemoaning the fact I wouldn't let her go to France. How unfair it was. Jack was allowed to go, I'd given him money to go. Why couldn't she go to France too …

In the end, and I don't like remembering this, I flew into a rage and shouted at Sally that she wasn't going to France, Jack wasn't coming back from France, and that if she mentioned France again I would to go up to her room, take one of her things and throw it on the bonfire. And then if she howled and carried on about that, I would go back up to her room, take another of her things, and throw that on the bonfire. And so on.

Interestingly, there was immediately peace after that but of a sort that was indistinguishable from cold hostility, from both Sally and Joan. But I had learnt something. Uncontrolled anger could achieve things which reason and argument sometimes couldn't.

Which took me back to the present, where it was clear that despite that, or because of that, the problem had not gone away; instead it seemed to have magnified exponentially. Now the problem was that Jack was not in France. And neither was his friend Antoine or Antoine's family.

Had she even met Antoine?

Yes, Jack reminded me, for the week or so during the visit of Uncle Roy and family from Australia.

Hardly enough to make an impression, and although thinking back I was sure that Antoine had enjoyed his stay, it did strike me in retrospect that he had had very little exposure to Sally and I wondered now if Jack's intervention, in remaining with Antoine in Yorkshire, was actually for that purpose. 'She's barely met him. Why would she try and go there?'

'Any time she comes into my room she's always looking at the map on the wall. I'd shown her where their farm was, and the railway station. I saw her, a week or so ago, looking closely at it again. And she's been wanting to write to Antoine's sister remember, even though his sister isn't learning English yet.'

Oh yes. That constant nagging from Sally and her mother joining in, it wouldn't hurt for Sally to write to her and Joan would post it. So off it went a few months previously in basic second-year French. A couple of weeks later there came back, in French on squared paper, a polite hand-written letter which Sally was unable to read. Jack translated it. Antoine's sister thanked Sally for her letter, sent respectful greetings to her parents and said she was looking forward to seeing Jack in the summer again and hoping he'd had a nice time with her cousins in Germany at Easter.

Nothing else.

Sally was not discouraged, despite the general tenor of the letter being one of complete disinterest. She beavered away on another massive missive that her mother sent off. But the weeks went by and no response was received. Now the nagging turned to whether it had got lost, and more worryingly, whether Jack had written to Antoine about 'the accident' over Sally's birthday present.

Accident!

Apparently that's what they were calling it now. But no, Jack hadn't mentioned it and in any case he was by then preparing to leave for France. He merely said that he would ask whether Sally's letter had been received when he got there.

'So you think it might have something to do with that letter?'

'Well the thing is,' said Jack, 'the address it was sent to is no longer where they are now. They sold that farm quite suddenly and moved around Easter while I was in Germany. They'd been talking for some time of moving somewhere less isolated before Brigitte went to high school, and an opportunity came up and they took it. I didn't realise, until Sally started whingeing about it, that the second letter had already been sent. But I didn't say anything because I know for a fact that Brigitte isn't interested in an English pen pal at the moment.'

'They moved! Where to?'

'Only about twenty miles away I think, I haven't seen it yet. They were going to pick me up from Besancon rather than Pontarlier.'

'And Sally wouldn't know that.'

'No. I've only got a general post restante address – even I wouldn't know how to get there.'

I thought about it. She had managed to keep the passport secret from me, although what amazed me was that Joan knew but hadn't mentioned it, even though I had always made it crystal clear over the last couple of years that I would not be signing for a passport. But then, I'd just found out that there were a whole lot of other things Joan hadn't mentioned of late – what else had she been doing without consulting me?

I had been pleased at the time that my daughter was cheery and happy about going down to stay with her Uncle Don. But now looking back, well yes, what Jack was suggesting seemed plausible; it was possibly all playacting with the endgame being to follow Jack to France while I was away and out of action. An adventure but a safe adventure where she would end up in a family that she knew of, even though she didn't know them.

If Jack was right … I was at a loss. 'What should I do?'

'I'm going to ring Antoine tomorrow morning to see how he's going in Switzerland. I'll ask him to contact some of his father's relatives and get the police to look out for her. I don't think the new owners have even moved in yet; it's possible an agent is running the place so there may be no one there. If she's wandering around, she should be pretty easy to spot – she only speaks very basic French.'

I felt that somehow, subtly, the burden had been shifted although I didn't really want that to happen. Still, what Jack suggested was sensible. I sighed and absentmindedly put my hand on his shoulder as we went back up to our rooms. 'I'll send Joan a telegram in the morning reinforcing your belief that she's in France.'

Deep in my heart I wasn't totally convinced. It was a huge undertaking for a thirteen-year-old, and I thought it much more likely that she would pop up at one or other of our relatives' places in England. Or Scotland. Could she have got hold of Pete's summer address? For some reason, and I couldn't put my finger on why, I thought that was by far the more likely place for her to have gone. It also struck me, which was another odd thought, that despite what had happened at Christmas, he would probably be perfectly okay with it if she did turn up.

I lay on my hard narrow bed. I'd managed to snaffle an extra pillow and so was able to prop myself up somewhat, which was good during the siestas because I didn't want to fall into a deep sleep where I would wake up groggy and hot. Siesta time, I considered, was a time for dozing, that rather delightful half-sleep where your eyes were closed but the outside world still impinged on the edges of consciousness.

This propped-up position was also useful if I wanted to read. I'd brought a book, a life of Kipling which I had thought I might like, but unfortunately I had found it to be rather lumpen, with a gratingly dry style and too many footnotes. As a boy I had enjoyed listening to my uncle read aloud from a book of Kipling's stories set in India. Called *Soldiers Three*, it told of men who were like the Three Musketeers. I had thought Uncle Ken made up the Irish dialect, but when I later came to read them myself I realised that's how they were written.

I found when I embarked on the parenting journey that the books from my youth did not satisfy or engage my own children. I thought for a while that Sally might be different, but I vividly remember early one Saturday morning when I was reading to her in bed. Usually I didn't read from books but made up stories instead about Edmund, our cat at the time. Edmund had two positions – prone or eating. But in the past, I told Sally, he had lived an adventurous life including time working in the circus, where he lived in a caravan with three other circus cats, Snowy, Chalky and Pom-pom. They were a quarrelsome lot but banded together to defeat the machinations of Regina the evil lioness, while being outmanoeuvred on every occasion by Pretoria, the head of the band of performing rats. Sally was entranced by Edmund's antics but when I tried 'The Cat that Walked by Himself', no, things did not go well. It was my favourite Kipling story, and I made my voice sonorous and portentous so as to milk the story for all it was worth. But just then a door suddenly shut and there were voices outside, the boys pushing out their bicycles. Sally sprang up in the middle of the story and was out of bed and rushing to the window to look out; she then rushed out the bedroom door before I had a chance to get my wits together. To be fair, I don't think it was Kipling. I doubt Edmund balanced on a unicycle going across a high wire would have helped at that moment. The boys were going off to play with their friends and Sally was not welcome. Of course she was not welcome, Jack was seven and Pete eleven as I recall, and the games they played required a great deal of rushing around on bicycles. Sally had a small tricycle suitable for her age and that was the limit of her mobility. But I remember the set, mutinous look that clamped her jaw when she realised she was being abandoned once again. That look on her face, a mixture of jealous rage and determination as she made for the door before I could stop her … Trying to stop Sally! How old was she? Maybe three years old, possibly four. Whenever I saw that look on her face after that, and it happened many times, many many times, I knew there was going to be shouting, screaming, temper tantrums, things being broken.

Was there a parenting guide for children like that? If there was I never found it. It was only after she was sent away to school that that look seemed to disappear and the ones that replaced it … they seemed increasingly desperate. It worried me, those looks, as if I should know how to respond but didn't. And now she had taken off somewhere, possibly France, possibly with one or other of those expressions.

I lay there looking at the book on my bedside table but not making any attempt to pick it up. Kipling had had a dreadful childhood – sent from India to England to be cared for by a woman who beat and abused him. That must have been traumatic. Had Sally been subject to something that had tipped her off the rails? I couldn't think of anything. On paper her childhood should have been ideal. A large country house where she could have her own bedroom, a big garden full of nooks and crannies, a good primary school with an energetic headmistress, two doting parents. I didn't know what the missing factor was, the factor that was making her so discontented and unhappy. And difficult.

Sally was difficult. This was my view of things even if it wasn't Joan's. For a long time I had tried to accept Joan's take on the situation, but by the time Sally was eleven, warning bells were clanging. Whatever explanation Joan had of Sally's early behaviour, it no longer made sense to me as she got older. She was difficult and things were not getting any better.

No one goes into family life expecting a difficult child. Children are hard enough to raise anyway; adults have to make concessions in their own behaviour and expectations. So when a child comes along who is acknowledged, by one parent at least, as difficult, basically what it means is impossible.

Our sons had not been more than usually demanding I suppose. They were active and tussled and argued. But Pete would hold Jack's hand on the way to school and would stand up for him if he got teased or bullied. In return, Jack was usually Pete's uncomplaining lieutenant.

I had assumed that that was how things would be with Sally. Unfortunately the small village school had closed by the time Sally started, and a new one had been built for the whole district nearly three miles away. Jack rode his bike there in company with his friend Tony and various other classmates. Joan would not at first let Sally ride to school; she had decided it was too dangerous when she was so young, and I agreed with her over that one. A young child had been knocked over while riding his bike some months before – the number of vehicles on the road was increasing all the time. So every morning I would drive her there. And every morning there would be a tempest of screaming and sobbing when Jack departed on his bike and she was relegated to being driven.

Oh heavens, I got sick of that. That first year. On and on, day after day and it was only a matter of time before I lost my temper.

Joan wanted to take the easy way out and have me drive Jack to and from school instead of him going on his bike, but I wouldn't agree. 'Whichever way you organise it, you're going to have at least one resentful child.' I thought it would eventually dissipate, especially when Jack joined Pete at the grammar school – I thought that Sally would wear herself out with her constant lamentations and maybe make her own friends and, now she was allowed to ride her bike, start living a more independent life.

But that was not the reality. She never really seemed to settle, and I was constantly being called to the school as one behavioural issue succeeded another. And it was even worse at home. For an hour or two after school everything would be peaceful. We would go down to the shop together and she would put her hand through my arm and do little skips as I told her what Edmund had got up to during the day, and when we got back she would try to get him to jump through a hoop but I'd tell her poor Edmund was tuckered out, he had been doing cart wheels all morning. She would think this hugely funny and then help me with preparing the evening meal, harmony between the two of us. But the moment Pete and Jack crashed through the door it was on for young and old.

Years and years like that – disruption, chaos, grim battle.

Her ups and downs at primary school had seeped into the public sphere and her behaviour at home had also become known locally. My parishioners sympathised with me, but professionally it had affected Joan more when she started teaching at the local secondary modern. Having a child who was out of control was not a great advertisement for discipline. Perhaps that was part of the reason that she took the job in York, well outside the district.

Sally passed the eleven-plus, somewhat to my surprise, so she could have gone to the grammar school where Jack was starting fourth form. But Joan had already decided that she should go to a boarding school in York, a school with a very good reputation academically and also the resources to deal with children who had challenging behaviours. It was almost a fait accompli, and she decided this when we not on particularly good terms, a couple of weeks after I had lost my temper with Sally. Joan thought getting Sally away from the area would provide a 're-set', but I wondered if Joan's insistence was really to get Sally away from *me*. I did agree eventually, if reluctantly, because I was worried about the reputational baggage she was already carrying and thought maybe a new start *would* be the answer.

Sally had no say in the matter and, predictably, went into meltdown. Far from wanting to get away from me, she clung to me desperately and cried most piteously.

I remember that with anguish. And I also now remembered Jack coming back from eight months away in France into this maelstrom, just as his sister was being carted away in tears, complete with uniforms and accessories. What had he thought about it? It had never entered my head to ask. Was he relieved? And what did he think when Joan decided to share a flat part-time in York with another teacher, to be on hand, she'd said, to deal with the problems which inevitably arose at Sally's school? She was now absent Monday to Friday; what had Jack thought about that?

Whatever Jack had thought, whatever I had thought, the end result was an approximate sort of peace. Calm descended on the household during the week, with Pete at university and just me and Jack at home. At the weekends Jack had a part-time job collating and packing for a local print works, and I would potter with some of the local men on Saturdays while Joan worked on her lesson plans.

Even when Sally and Pete were at home for weekends or on holiday, those days too were now reasonably peaceful. Sally would often sit handing tools to Pete as he crawled about under his car, and would go with him on test drives, both their heads bent listening to the engine. The dynamic would somehow shift when Jack was there, I wasn't sure why, but that wasn't often, as he was usually on the continent during the holidays, or working at the weekend to raise money to go there.

Whole days would go by with nothing but civilised conversation, and sometimes a week could pass with no angry outbursts or shouting.

There were disruptions of course. Every time Sally had to go back to school there would be scenes. She would cling to me and beg me … and then Joan would get angry.

How could I have been lulled into thinking it had all been resolved? To stand up for Sally against Joan was like stirring a hornet's nest, my wife buzzing and furious and so …

Like my decision when we went on holiday in the Lake District, I had done nothing. What an idiot, I thought. How could I have been so stupid?

I switched off the light. I couldn't read, I just needed to lie there and think. It was a pity because I used to like reading, once upon a time when all was calm.

I would sit in an armchair back then with my book and Joan would be sprawled on the couch with hers. In the early days, when she was pregnant for the first time, I would read aloud to her. We used to sit by the fire while she knitted or sewed little things, either listening to the radio or with me reading to her. A favourite was Charles Dickens. We laughed over *The Pickwick*

Papers, while I honed the voices with suggestions from Joan – No, make him more like Archie Blades! Yes of course, who else could Nathaniel Winkle be except … We filled the book with the voices of the people around us.

I was a natural mimic. I don't know where it came from, but it had stood me in good stead all my life, particularly in the army. As a shy man it seemed to make up for my lack of conviviality, and my ability to take off superior officers, in particular Visiting Dignitaries, was a source of great amusement in the Mess. My favourite, and theirs, was a maddeningly obscure Polish doctor who had come to talk to the men about hygiene and either because of his accent or his refusal to call a spade a spade, left them all totally mystified. Thereafter this became the voice for any sort of elaborate explanation where a complete lack of clarity was essential.

When Joan became pregnant again, this time with Jack, we started on *Great Expectations*, where Miss Haversham somehow became the voice of our friend Oliver and when 'Miss Haversham' accidentally discovered this, he came tottering around with his knitting to listen as well. Oh my, how we used to laugh. When did that joy I used to get from books, that fun, those gales of merriment cease?

Cease it all did though. Maybe when we got a television? Did we start to read less because of it? I had an uneasy feeling that I was trying to fix blame on an inanimate object and that was not where the trouble lay.

And in the middle of that thought I fell asleep – which was odd because I was expecting to lie there and worry about Sally all night.

Eight

The next thing I knew, daylight was coming through the window and I was still lying propped up at a slightly stiff angle. I got up and stretched awkwardly, pulled back the shutters and looked out over the city. What was I going to do? How in fact could I do anything? When I was so far away with no money. All I could really do was pray and my knees were already worn out from this activity. I remembered when I had uncharacteristically asked God to help me – was this the punishment? A reminder that however bad you thought the situation, there is no guarantee it isn't going to get worse?

And now Joan, who I had blamed in the past for indulging our daughter, would have to stay, give up a course for a while … None of this would have happened, I thought, if she had kept to her promise. Again I returned to her promise, the fact that when I had planned this trip I had received a cast iron confirmation before doing so that Joan would be looking after Sally. Jack would go to the continent as usual. And I would be free of all responsibility for the space of two weeks. That was the agreement. But of course, one can never be free of one's children. Did anyone else have this frightful conundrum in family life? A youngest child who was so focused on being allowed to do whatever her older siblings were doing that the entire life of the family descended into everyone retreating behind barricades? Like in a war zone?

I gave up on my tortured examination of the past and went down to breakfast.

I talked about the situation with Gregory and Bob. 'Jack thinks she's probably gone to France. She's always been jealous of him going away in the summer. At first we thought she was missing him, but that seemed odd, the age difference being what it was. In the end it was more likely that she saw it as some treat that she was excluded from. It's always been like that, whatever the boys have, she wants too.'

But even as I was saying it, it didn't sound right. It wasn't that I thought she'd completely grown out of her previous behaviour, but I knew somehow that things had moved on, though I wasn't sure how.

My friends were concerned. They offered to lend me the money to get back to England, but I refused for the moment. My wife was urgent with me to go back not so we could better deal with the crisis together but so she could return to her studies – that had really galled me. Again my anger rose about the broken promise.

Not being able to find Jack, I nevertheless managed, with the help of someone at the conference centre, to first send a telegram to my wife at the university reiterating that Jack thought Sally had gone to France and secondly to get through to the British Embassy in Spain. I reported that my daughter, who had just turned thirteen, had forged my signature on a passport application and how run away and was now probably in France, and I gave the likely town she would be attempting to get to. I asked them to contact the French authorities. I also gave them my brother-in-law's phone number, although I felt that Don had probably done enough already.

Drained by this activity I then went to a Bible meditation at the Purisima Church, thinking that maybe meditation was what I required to soothe all the frayed ends. However, I concluded that mass meditation was like trying to fill a teacup at a considerable distance with a fireman's hose. I hoped that other people benefited, but I myself came away with a mental cup that was dry and dusty and nerves still frayed as before.

Perhaps that was because of my situation. I wondered how much money Sally had. Joan gave her pocket money, that had been the arrangement, but I didn't know how much. I was certain that as Joan was a bit of a tightwad it would be minimal. It suddenly struck me that the finances of the family, instead of being the joint enterprise they'd been when mine was the only income, had somehow fractured, and that I didn't know what Joan was doing with the bulk of her salary. I didn't even know how much she was earning. As a result, and this disturbed me, Sally might have more ready money than I did. I felt both vulnerable and impotent, knowing that if I was to take an active part in helping look for her, I would have to borrow money.

How had I got to this position? I hadn't demurred at my wife's new financial independence over the last few years, and in fact during our courtship I had admired her competence and energy. But I had shared my income when she was raising children; our decisions had been made jointly. Now it seemed I was excluded, and although I had been uneasy about this for some time, it had suddenly come into sharp focus. Again the realisation that I had less than £20 in cash.

I had never thought about money before. Or only in the sense of whether we had enough to cover the electricity, the gas, and day-to-day living expenses. My half of the school fees was a heavy impost on my stipend, but we had never lived extravagantly, never taken expensive holidays; this was the first time I had been abroad since the war. And now, quite suddenly, money did matter. Was this another step back down the road away from Damascus?

I rejoined my discussion group because I couldn't think of

anything else to do. I could walk up and down and mope in the heat, but I couldn't see how that would be of use to anyone. Then again, I also thought I wouldn't be of any use to my group due to my preoccupation, but this proved to be wrong. The discussion went extremely well, and I became so completely engaged in it that I forgot everything else. I noticed that a rather prickly lady Salvationist who had been a bit of a pain the day before had become very mellow, amenable and ecumenical. Our discussion centred on the work of the Holy Spirit, and I felt my own spirits rising as we proceeded.

At lunch, I sat opposite a fire-eating Venezuelan, a man with a highly revolutionary agenda. This again distracted me. The only other political table talk I could recall at Salamanca was when someone trotted out the 'women problem', the question being: 'How are women regarded in Spain?' The answer was, 'Ver-y pretty!' Hmmm. This did not make the American nuns gasp with delight.

I then went to another unity service (Methodist), which would have been fine if done with the aid of a guitar and a harmonium in a downtown church hall. But alas, it wasn't, and the grand organ, with its horizontal as well as vertical pipes, simply wasn't suitable. I again felt unsettled and depressed.

Instead of attending the Annual General Meeting, I went window shopping. I felt somewhat soothed by being alone and being able to wander aimlessly. I discovered I liked Salamanca. It was hot, dusty and slummy in places, which suited my mood, but I also came across cosy squares like the one I went to with Jack, where perhaps a fountain was playing and people were sitting around with their children. After a while I found I was slightly lost and got out my map to locate myself. As I stood there, I was hailed and saw that Bob was waving at me – he also had been shopping. He led me to the square where we had first met Manuel and family, and we sat down at a café table and had coffee. We talked about the fact that Spain was a police state – in fact there had been discussion earlier on as to whether it was appropriate to hold a liberal religious conference in such a place. From what I could observe, it was now relatively benign whatever the savagery in the past. My trouble, I noted, was that thirty years on from the savagery of my own war, the horror had somehow faded, and I was glad in some ways to let it go. I didn't want to live any more in those grim years; I was more interested in the present. Looking around me, I wanted to take what I saw on face value, and being optimistic and judging from the construction work, the Spanish economy was far from stagnant.

Bob was too young to remember much about the Second World War and wasn't even born when the Spanish Civil War was being fought, but he somehow evinced a greater degree of outrage than I did about the suffering, the massacres, the horror of that Spanish conflict. Also, he didn't like the beggars, who he thought were a sign that the economy *wasn't* working that well. Bob said it took him a while to get to a point where he could ignore them, and even then he felt guilty and unchristian. I didn't feel guilty because there was nothing I could do for them; I was only just managing to get by myself.

But in the square, although down at heel, there was an appearance of homeliness, of people gathered together at the surrounding tables for recreation and pleasure. On the table next to us three old men were playing cards.

Bob said, 'One of the downsides to our American adventure, for me anyway, was that Becky, the woman we met in Baton Rouge, taught Barb how to play poker, and Barb insisted we play for nickels and dimes all the way around America on the bus. She became fiendishly good at it and was always cleaning me out. In fact, if the worst came to the worst, she could probably make a living from it.'

I was surprised. I thought it was a game of chance you won by not showing any emotion. But no, according to Bob there was a lot of statistical calculation in it, weighing up the possibilities, which Barb was good at.

'You seem to have had a very productive few days in Baton Rouge,' I said.

Yes and no, said Bob. When during some conversation the origins of Becky acquiring her mansion came up, she'd said, 'Barb. Always keep your eye on where the money is so when your marriage goes down the gurgler you can snatch it up and run for the hills.'

Bob said, 'Of course we thought it hilarious because neither of us had a penny and if either of us did it was more likely to be Barb. Especially once she got to learn poker. But she quite often writes to Becky. I think they became friends over their joint plan to do me down!'

I laughed. I marvelled, as I sipped my drink, at how things could amuse you – even in the middle of a crisis when I felt nothing should be able to break into my worry.

As we sat there, other conference attendees (refugees from the AGM) came past and joined us. Soon there was quite a group and conversation was lively, with much laughter. As we got up to go to dinner, I noticed that Jack had at some point appeared with his gang of young girls but as usual had been snaffled by the nuns.

When we got back to the conference centre, my son detached himself as we were milling before going into the dining room and came over to me. 'Has she sent a reply?'

'Oh, damn,' I said with a jump. 'I didn't go and look.' I had spent most of the day in a worried state and had prayed earnestly on my knees that morning that my daughter would be found and everything would be all right but now, after a day spent in miserable worry, I hadn't even thought to go and check if my wife had sent a return telegram.

'Shall I nick down and see?' said Jack.

'Oh, would you?'

Jack was gone for about fifteen minutes, and in that time the doors opened and people started moving into the dining area. I wasn't quite sure what to do, whether to wait, which in the end I did, hovering near the doorway. When Jack came back it was clear there was nothing. 'So I conclude no news is bad news. She's still out there,' he said.

Well, there was nothing to be done by us, so we looked around to find seats. There weren't any together, but Sister Carol waved at Jack – she had kept one for him – and I saw another not far away.

I was near enough to my son to realise that he was telling his friend something important, which I assumed from a couple of words I managed to catch was about his missing sister. I was perturbed, in fact distressed, that this matter should become common property. However, as I watched the two heads together bent over the problem, with Jack talking and Carol listening, I suddenly thought that my son had not talked to me like that for a long time. I felt a powerful sadness that I was not the recipient of these confidences; nor was I being asked for advice and counselling, which clearly Sister Carol was giving. Where had it gone so wrong?

The first time I had noticed there was something really badly wrong was on Jack's twelfth birthday. It was the bike. Jack had outgrown the bicycle he had been using, plus its age and various faults had made it virtually unrideable, so Joan and I decided to buy him a new one for his birthday. Joan had gone off into York with Sally to buy it and they had hidden it somewhere, so I myself hadn't seen it either. So when it was handed over with great fanfare it was a surprise to me as well as to Jack and Pete.

It was a girl's bike.

Not only was it girl's bike but it was a magenta colour that was only just on the right side of pink.

I remember the two boys standing there and Pete reaching out and putting his hand round Jack's neck and patting him as if to say, *there, there.* Joan was standing holding the bicycle and Sally was jumping up and down and clapping. And Jack didn't move. Didn't go forward to take it. Didn't react at all, not even disappointment, as if he had it been expecting such a result. He just said the obvious: 'It's a girl's bike.'

Joan said, 'It's a bicycle. What's the difference? It doesn't have a bar at the top but how does that make it a boy's bike? It means when you outgrow this one, it will be easier for Sally to ride it.'

'Yippee,' cried Sally, cavorting around and clapping.

At that moment Tony rode up and Jack sighed and went over and climbed onto his crossbar.

'What! Didn't you get a bike?' Tony said.

'No, Sally did,' Jack said. And they rode off.

Sally immediately went over and took the bicycle out of her mother's hands but before she could do anything, like put a ding in it, scrape it along the gravel, whatever she usually did, I rushed over and grabbed it. 'Get off the bike.'

'Jack's gone! I can ride it.'

'Yes, let her ride it, if Jack's going to act like that,' said Joan.

'Get off the bike!' I screamed, as I was now nearly foaming with anger.

I took the bicycle away into the garage, put it into the boot of my car, locked it then went into the house, trying to contain my rage. I found the invoice in Joan's handbag, got my cheque book and went back out and drove into York. The shop assistant was quite pleasant, he remembered the purchase, how the young girl had picked it out, but it was a second-hand bicycle with no returns. After some persuasion, however, he allowed me a reduction on the boy's bike I subsequently bought.

I drove home with the new bike and went straight to the Barkers' place, a largish farm about a mile from the vicarage. Janet Barker was in the poultry yard and waved to me.

'Jack's not here?' I asked.

'I think they're down in the bottom meadow helping Rick.'

'Can I leave Jack's new bike here for him?'

'Is that the one …?'

'That was a mistake. I went and got another one.'

'Good.' She came and looked. 'Yes. That bike is quite suitable. Not flash, just what the rest of them have. Boys that age, they spend all their time trying to fit in.'

Exactly. I put it in the shed with Tony's bike. 'He can leave it here,' said Janet. She thought for a moment as if wondering whether to say anything further. 'He leaves a few things here,' she said quietly.

That was the first I knew of it and afterwards I was constantly on alert. Previously I had merely thought that Sally was clumsy, but I had been increasingly concerned that Joan did not seem to take the destruction of the boys' possessions seriously enough and when they tried to protect their things, chided them for not sharing. Now I understood Jack's quiet resistance and Pete's, well, definitely not quiet reaction.

But this knowledge, learned so casually, was now the source of more discord with my wife.

'Where's Jack's guitar?' she asked one day.

Jack had bought it himself with money he'd saved, and I responded, 'I expect he's keeping it at Tony's, where Sally can't break it.'

That was ridiculous, Joan had said, he had to bring it back, Sally wanted to try it. He needed to learn to share his things.

'That's something you teach a five-year-old, not someone who's nearly an adult and who's bought it with his own money. And Sally needs to learn she doesn't have any rights to anybody's property apart from her own. So if she wants to find out how to break a guitar, she'd better start saving up for one.'

'You always take the side of the boys,' she said furiously.

'Because you never do.'

And so on. It wasn't good. And it just seemed to be getting worse.

Someone next to me at the table was saying, 'Things can't go on.' The context was lost on me as I had been pretending to concentrate on the meal. But it was true, things couldn't go on.

———

After dinner I walked back with Jack. 'Are you going to have a nightcap with Manuel and the girls?'

'No, they're going to visit relatives tonight. Anyway, I'm a bit tired. I managed to get through to Antoine. The funeral was yesterday and he was feeling quite low. So it was good to talk to him. They'll be in Switzerland for at least another week, probably longer. He's not enjoying it. I told him about Sally, and he thought immediately the same as me. His father is going back today, just overnight to check everything is okay, and he'll ask him to ring the police chief and put out an alert that a young girl might be in the district with an illegal passport.'

Well that at least was something positive being done. 'What did Sister Carol have to say about it?' I asked.

'She's trained in psychology, which is all about how the brain works. We talked about sibling rivalry, but the thing is, I don't feel any rivalry. Or I don't think I do. But maybe just existing is a form of rivalry in some situations.'

We came into the hall of residence. 'I'll just ring reverse charges again,' I said. 'If she's not there, I presume she'll have got the telegram.'

Jack organised it for me and then departed.

Joan picked up immediately and I heard her voice agreeing to the charges. We talked over the top of each other, me saying 'You *are* still there?', and her saying 'About time, why haven't you rung before?

'I sent you a telegram. To Oxford.'

'Why did you send it there?'

'Because you said you were going back.'

'Going back! How can I go back? With Sally still missing. You don't seem to be taking this seriously.'

'Of course I'm taking it seriously.'

'No, I don't think you are. You're still over there, making no effort to help.'

I waited. I couldn't be bothered going through the same routine I'd gone through the previous night.

'I've been rushing around, the police, everything.'

'Jack is sure she has gone to France, to Pontarlier. Monsieur Berger is going to contact the police there today when he gets back.'

'I don't know why you keep saying that,' said Joan sharply. 'She couldn't possibly get over there.'

'Did she have access to any money?'

'Only her pocket money, two-and-six a week, and whatever she gets at birthdays.'

'Is there any money lying around she could have taken?'

'No, not lying around.'

'Well, any money anywhere in the flat?'

'Just coins for the power. And the money I put away every week for other bills such as for the car insurance, rent and so on. But that's in the desk and I keep it locked.'

'Could you go and see if it's still there?'

'Oh for heaven's sake,' she muttered, 'this is costing a fortune.' But I heard the footsteps going away from me and a short while later much slower footsteps coming back. 'It's gone.'

'How much was there?'

'I'm not really sure, probably about ten pounds.'

'Enough for the boat train then.'

She was silent for a moment. It was sinking in. 'You really think she's gone to France? But ten pounds – she'd never get across France on that.'

'Not unless she's stolen money elsewhere. You'd better ask your brother.'

She sucked in her breath, and I thought I knew what she was thinking. Sally was her Golden Girl; she would never hear anything against her. To ask a brother whether she had stolen his money would be too humiliating, too awful; I knew she wouldn't do it. But instead of that it then came out that they weren't speaking to each other. Don had refused to accept any responsibility for Sally's disappearance and they'd had words.

So we didn't know what other money she might have, and if all she had was £10 the only alternative was: 'She must be hitching.' My wife said the unsayable, nothing worse was in our lexicon. Now she was becoming hysterical, I must come home immediately. I listened to the torrent and then said, 'If she's there in France, hopefully the police will pick her up. And march her back to England. I'll ring again tomorrow.' And wearily hung up the phone.

I didn't think she would hitch; in fact I was sure of it. She didn't like strangers, and she hated it when I picked up hitchhikers. This only left the possibility of her having stolen money elsewhere.

My weariness increased when I went over to the lift and found it was temporalmente lacking in servicio. Four flights of stairs. When did I start getting old, I wondered, after I'd trudged up the first two flights. It was insidiously gradual and I resented that. I felt there should be a midpoint which you reach to a blare of trumpets and then they present you with a golden wristband which dispenses into your bloodstream a mixture of pain relief and anti-inflammatories for your war-wounded leg and all your other aching joints. After that, with such a golden gift, you could go forward more easily. I wouldn't mind getting old if I could get round the pain and maybe get a shot of invigorating steroids at the same time. So you didn't have to climb stairs with your knees creaking and sighing *ooof* sounds.

I arrived at my room in a gloomy frame of mind and climbed into bed. I didn't bother propping myself up, I just lay there expecting to be miserable.

And went straight to sleep.

Nine

I awoke much lighter and more hopeful. I didn't exactly bound out of bed, but I got up with more enthusiasm than I would have thought possible the night before. The day was overcast, hot and sticky. After breakfast it was Pentecostalism in force at the Purisima Church. Yes, a plane-load of Pentecostal persons had dropped in on us the day before. Jack and Bob accompanied me to the service, and I explained that Pentecostals believed in the Holy Spirit in the same way that the Wright brothers believed in aeroplanes; except that they didn't so much invent as discover.

Anyhow, it hadn't long got underway when I began regretting my decision to come as the preacher told of his first ecstatic encounter with the Religious, in his case a Catholic nun. Torrents of words, hyper-neologisms swooping through the surreal, tautologies doing a lush waltz with metaphor. Then one of those jolly happy-clapping hymns. With more torrents of words in prospect, I decided I'd had enough and departed, leaving Jack and Bob behind looking highly entertained.

I felt rather uncharitable; I was sure I would be much more patient if they weren't Christians. But they were, and everyone else had developed a hunted look. I supposed they wouldn't be so bad if they didn't, within two minutes of learning your name, demand to know if you'd been reborn. They hadn't managed to corral me yet, but it had already happened to Gregory who'd replied, yes – about a month after being born the first time.

Bob, on the other hand, was one of the few not fleeing from this inquisition. How could he know, he said, whether his baptism 'took' at the time? He was just a baby. So he would be quite happy for them – using an expression from the sermon just given – to take his spiritual temperature. I admired his openness to these experiences, without it dimming in any way my own determination to get as far away as possible.

I was not the only one. The American monk in my group walked out at the same time saying, 'That voice – like hail on a tin roof.'

I felt depressed again and returned to the hall of residence to wash my smalls and a couple of shirts which were getting quite pongy with the heat. I noticed that Jack had been hanging his washing on the railing outside his window and as it was a windless day I managed to attach several underpants to a hanger in such a way that hopefully they wouldn't astound the local population by blowing away.

In the past Joan had always bought my underclothes, but I realised that this hadn't happened for some time. They were grey and dispirited-looking, rather how I felt. It suddenly struck me that maybe Bob wasn't giving up cotton briefs for Aertex Y-fronts but was going the other way. Embracing the new fashion, living in the moment. Maybe I too should give it a try.

I hung a shirt on either side of the open window. They were also worn and past their best. I wondered again why we were going backwards. I'd always thought that when Joan returned to work we'd have a lot more money for everything, such as holidays together, mini breaks, things like that. But instead I was perennially short of money, even for the charities I supported. Well of course Joan had expenses, she'd had to get her own car, the flat in York and then, looming large, the school fees. But even so, should life be such a struggle?

I sat down at the desk in my room intending at first to have another go at my diary, but decided that would make me feel even worse and instead turned my mind to writing up a provisional report for my discussion group. Concentrating on spiritual matters in this way, I managed to put off for a while something which was starting to oppress me. Perhaps it had been triggered by the service that morning.

Had I been reborn in Normandy? And if I had, could I be unborn again? Those days of certainty surrounded by exploding shells, was that what I was lacking now? Was my faith, let alone my ministry, now a slim version of what it had been? Had I turned into a mere entertainer, not preparing my flock for the next life but instead merely bolstering their desire to appear good, by showing them the way to live with grace in this life? I felt shaken by the possibility that I had taken a wrong turning and that I was subjecting my parishioners to the pale approximation of a parson, a fraudulent copy of what they could be getting, a simulacrum.

In fact, however strong his faith, could any middle-aged man with family problems really lead a flock? Maybe the Catholics had it right, single men without entanglements. Or better still – I remembered the discussion we'd had about wisdom – maybe women as priests was the way forward. Nowadays women seemed keen to reconnect with the world when their children were grown, and they seemed to reach middle age with a burst of energy and at least some form of ambition. I felt I had neither.

I went off to lunch in a subdued mood. However, the final session of the discussion group went very well. My provisional report as acting secretary was well received and, thanks to the American monk, we changed its ending into a series of questions rather than statements and suggestions.

I then attended a very good talk by a German theologian who translated it himself into two other languages as he went along. This gave the talk a feeling of immediacy which was lacking when they were translated by someone else. It was about belief, strange how everything was coming down to that. The synchronicity.

I sat next to Bob at dinner and after a couple of glasses of wine wondered aloud to him whether I was in the right profession. Bob looked at me with concern and said that he hoped, if I was having a crisis of faith, that this hadn't been brought on by the conference, which he was sure was not its intention!

I laughed. Or rather chuckled. I didn't feel like doing so but the irrelevancy of that remark struck me. Yes, come on a pilgrimage to Holy Spain and lose your vocation.

After dinner several of the group were going with Jack to have a nightcap in the square with his friends there. 'I just have to go and make a phone call,' I said.

I now managed on my own, with a script from Jack, to ring reverse charges. I was hoping there would have been some result, but I also felt immensely tired, tired of all of it.

The glad tidings were that Sally had been picked up by the police in eastern France. Jack had been right! In that instant I was so relieved I could barely express my joy. I felt a great weight departing, a stone rolled from the cave, a freedom to breathe. Joan's voice as she transmitted this news, however, was tight, as if a wedge of anger was being contained.

She had got a phone call from the local police asking whether she was going to go and pick Sally up or whether she wanted the French police to escort her back to the border where she would be deported. 'I told them we would pick her up.'

'So, you're going to go and get her.'

'No! You are.'

I was astounded, shocked. 'Don't be daft! How can I!'

Joan's anger exploded down the line, but I suddenly realised it meant nothing to me. It was just background noise, the scrape of munition across a distant horizon, one you're not travelling towards. I didn't care if she was angry. And I realised that was a change in our relationship, because in the past I had been afraid of rousing her fury, always trying to appease such moods before they arose. Now it was nothing but a jumble of shouted words, none of which were hitting home.

When she gave me space, I pointed out that where I was at the moment was further away from where Sally was than where she was in England, and I had no direct route. Going cross country would take days and Sally would be stuck at the police station in the meantime. 'Plus, I keep telling you, I have Jack with me and I have practically no money. You don't have the care of any of our children at the moment so if you want her picked up, it's up to you to do so.'

Joan's voice, when she replied, was frosty. 'So you are going to leave it all up to me as usual. And what are you going to do?'

I breathed in. Suddenly I knew what I was going to do. I said slowly, 'I'm going to see the archdeacon as soon as I get back as a prelude for possibly giving up the living and leaving the priesthood. I'm going to look into what training I need to do to go back to being a solicitor.' She was silent on the other side of the phone. 'And as far as Sally is concerned,' I said after a moment, 'I want her to go to the local grammar school next school year. Where I can keep an eye on her.'

She spoke angrily again, defending the school she was at, refuting any connection, blaming Jack and Pete for the current problem, if they weren't so mean to her—

I broke in, aware, despite my effort to control myself, of the anger in my voice. 'Don't blame Jack. Don't blame the son you apparently forget you've got. He's done nothing to bring this on.'

The words were there at the brink, behind the dam, words that I was doing my best to stop from cascading over.

There was silence for a moment, but with the way my heart was thudding the crackle was as loud as pile drivers. When she spoke again her voice now sounded even more frozen and remote. 'I hadn't forgotten Jack. I had a lot on my mind. I wasn't paying full attention to what you were saying when you told me back then. I'm sorry, it sounded terrible the way it came out.'

I breathed in and held my breath tightly to keep control of myself. I said, 'Hopefully things will come right. I'm ringing off, this has been a terrible few days but at least she's been found. Goodbye for now.'

I had been standing at the phone in the lobby and I now sat down. I felt drained and hollow and shaky. Was that relief? Or something else. There were so many things that were unsaid in the conversation I'd just had. When did conversations with my wife start being a series of gaps intermediated by tension?

But at least Sally had been found. Now things had to go on differently, and that meant I had to do things differently. I was determined she wouldn't go back to the boarding school. I realised that I had probably only agreed to it because Joan was so adamant, laying things on the line, this was how it was going to be. And so I had gone along with it, despite all my daughter's subsequent pleas … I had absconded from the parenting role to avoid more unpleasantness with my wife and that had to stop. Especially as it was clear that Sally wasn't thriving there.

I thought back to what Jack had divulged. Tony's cousin was at the same school and had told him they were trying to expel Sally because of her behaviour. Expel was probably not the right word – suggest that she would be better elsewhere. One of the girls had been waiting outside and had overheard some of the headmistress's conversation with Joan, so naturally the whole school knew. Apparently Joan had pleaded with them to give Sally another chance, so she was being allowed back for the autumn term on sufferance.

I had never been told, and my anger with my wife swirled up again. Plus I realised that if gossip was coming in that direction, it could also go the other way and those at the school very likely knew about the incident at Christmas. I had no doubt that Jack told his friends everything. In fact, now I was sitting there doing a bit of soul-searching, I concluded that Jack's equanimity and general cheerfulness was the result of his ability to talk through all these matters with his friends. I felt a stab of distress that I did not seem to be able to do that.

I thought once I did have that ability and did have those sorts of friends, but in marrying I had made the unspoken contract to confide my inner worries and concerns to Joan, my soul mate. I expected my marriage and family would be a site of comfort and consolation and for the first few years that was how it had worked out. But now … Now it seemed to be just the opposite, that my marriage and family were the source of my greatest woes.

I thought of Sally. Her behaviour might glorify her as a rebel or 'bad girl' but it wouldn't help her develop into a happy person. I wanted her to be happy, to have friends, to do well in life and to fit in. But I couldn't see that happening unless she could learn to be a different person to the one she was or the one she was turning into. But then, who was I to decide how a person should be? I just wished that Joan and I had had a better agreement on her upbringing.

There was another thing I was going to do when I got back. Get some professional help for my daughter. I didn't think what was going on was normal, even for a teenager. I needed advice, I needed counselling. Perhaps Joan and I needed counselling as a couple, marriage guidance, but I wondered if that was too late. And I couldn't for a moment imagine that Joan would agree to it.

I continued sitting there for a while, feeling hollowed out and flat. I felt I should be more euphoric about the news that she'd been found, and that the background thread of worry that had been pursuing me should now diminish. But I didn't feel euphoric. I felt angry. All I had wanted was a two-week holiday free of tension and complaint, and it had been taken away from me.

But I had to carry on. There were a few days left of the trip and I needed to go through the motions. If I couldn't enjoy it myself, I would try to ensure that my companions' enjoyment of it was not affected by my own mood.

Ten

THERE WAS THUNDER IN THE night; I heard it rumbling aimlessly. When I got up, I looked out at showers drumming on the red rooftops. It cleared the air – it hadn't rained in Salamanca for five weeks. When I went out, the temperature was a mild seventy-two degrees according to a thermometer in the main square – and this was well below normal which (according to the same thermometer) was usually about ninety degrees. I felt reinvigorated and alive, my depression lifted.

I decided to miss the Bible meditation and instead went with Bob to try and buy a petrol cap, as ours had gone missing from the Viva. Jack would have been useful but was not an early riser, plus the family he was friendly with had some plans to entertain him on his final day.

Bob's phrasebook was no help; the only sort of cap we could find in it was the sort worn by the landed gentry on the Glorious Twelfth. Gregory's Spanish dictionary wasn't much better, giving several words for it but with no explanation, so presumably knee, percussion and yellow breasted black-cap. No matter – by mentioning gasolina, and going through the motions of burgling a safe, we managed to make our meaning clear – but there was no cap, or tapon, to fit the Viva, as continental cars seemed to be different.

It struck Bob during this exercise that none of us were the least bit handy with cars, and he hoped that if anything mechanical went wrong with the Viva it would at least have the decency to break down in France where he supposed Jack's French would be up to translating the bad news.

Strangely enough, I said, my eldest son, who had shown no especial interest in cars or machinery while younger, had turned into a very handy mechanic.

I had decided to buy Pete a second-hand car after he left school and intended it to last him throughout university and into his first job, but I had made the mistake of taking him in to look at the one I had in mind, a three-year-old Cortina with reasonably low mileage.

Unfortunately, sitting in the corner of the caryard was an Austin-Healey Sprite with a lot of miles on the clock, incipient rust underneath and possible problems with both its CV joints and its gearbox. Pete wouldn't even look at the Cortina after he'd seen it and despite the arguments of both myself and the salesman he had to have it. I gave in, I explained, because I thought it might be a good lesson for the future, after it broke down and became undrivable, on the advantage of choosing reliability over looks.

But it hadn't turned out that way. Pete's practical nature made him capable of fixing it and keeping it running and, far from tiring of the endless maintenance required, his love for this vehicle seemed to grow over time rather than diminish. He would return home at intervals and spend the whole weekend happily tinkering with it.

Yes, said Bob, one of his friends at university had an old Fiat, horrible to travel in in winter, cold, draughty, noisy, plus the hood leaked. 'But on the rare summer's day when it was possible to take the hood down, ah, well then look at us! Yes, weren't we the thing, wearing sunglasses and Hawaiian shirts and Clive's double bass lobbed casually in the back – the epitome of cool. When you're young you'd put up with any discomfort for just one moment like that in the sun.'

Bob had no doubt, as Pete became more firmly ensconced in adulthood, he would look back on his little sports car as the concentrated embodiment of youth.

———

We went back to the hall to listen to the group secretaries' reports. I was pleased with my group and thought that ours was the best.

At lunch I saw a vacant chair next to Sister Angela and went to join her. I found her company engaging, a lightness breaking through the cerebral wall of worry I was carrying with me.

'Tell me some more country stories, tales from your rural idyll,' she said. She recalled that I'd told her what I did in the morning, but what else did I do about the parish?

I said that in the afternoon I engaged in pastoral work. A lot of old agricultural workers and elderly single women had been left behind by the demographic shift and were now paying small rents for rural slums.

'You Americans would love those cottages,' I said. 'Limestone terraces with ancient slate roofs and climbing roses over the door.' Two up, two down, with a precipitous staircase which someone with dodgy knees could only negotiate safely by coming down backwards. There was a lean-to scullery behind with an even more cobbled-together bath house behind that and even further behind, an outside lavatory. The houses smelt of chamber pots and mice and overwhelmingly of damp.

I kept pushing the council to do something about such places, which were completely inappropriate for old people and in some cases should be condemned. The trouble was that they were so picturesque, and the landlord had said that if they were condemned he would pull them down. The council couldn't bear the thought of the gap in the chocolate-box facade if that happened, even if it meant the early death of the tenants through mould. 'I keep pressuring the council to build suitable bungalow units for the elderly in the village, but they tell me that would alter the character of the place!' The character of the place being one where people died early of preventable diseases. These elderly people would be much better off in a council flat where they could stay in their own home, but the only ones available were in the local town and none of them wanted to move there, so what happened, inevitably, was that they would end up in a nursing home because they could no longer manage the stairs.

'You're a crusading vicar,' said Sister Angela.

'Lifting up the poor is part of our job description.'

Of course, by no means all of my parish were poor and at Harvest Festival, Mothering Sunday, Christmas and Easter there was standing room only in church. And then of course there were christenings, weddings and funerals. Though not so many weddings or christenings; young people didn't tend to hang around; they wanted to go to the cities. Or at least somewhere with a decent bus service. Funerals were still plentiful, however.

'So the population is declining?'

'Yes, but that's inevitable. The farms are getting bigger. It's flat and fertile and ideal for mechanisation. And the only way most people could afford a farm now in such an area is to inherit it. Otherwise, they are bought by companies. The two smaller churches are rarely used so one day soon I imagine they will be sold.'

'How do you feel about that?'

'Well to be frank …' I explained that I was thinking about my future and whether or not my time in the ministry was, or should be, coming to a close. Even though I was only in my early fifties, I felt that the initial surge of enthusiasm for my calling was waning.

Not that my faith was waning, just my mission in life to spread it to others. I felt maybe there was a time limit to these things and that twenty years was enough, not only for me, but for my congregation. They needed someone new and dynamic because otherwise, well, it was all too comfortable.

Sister Angela demurred. It seemed to her that I was still fighting the good fight.

'Yes,' I said. 'But a younger man would shout louder, demand more, not be distracted by problems in his family.'

Plus I dreamed of working and living in modern buildings with central heating just like hers. There. It sounded superficial but I'd said it aloud.

After lunch, I went sightseeing with Gregory, taking in some of Salamanca's churches. The nearest one to the hall of residence was the Church of Saint Thomas of Canterbury. It was pleasingly unpretentious and uncluttered. Then on to the new cathedral, which was very magnificent but reminiscent of a zoo in places – so much of it caged and locked up. The side aisles, however, were clear and airy with hefty columns shooting to the intricately decorated vaulting.

Next door was the old cathedral – a gem. Why the ecclesiastical authorities wanted a new cathedral in the sixteenth century was not at all clear to me, as the old one was in perfect working order and had a wonderful strip-cartoon behind the altar – the life of Christ in pictures.

We then visited the Diocesan Museum, after which we'd both had had enough of sightseeing. We came across Sister Carol trailing behind a uniformed guide, and she informed us of two new diseases – Madonna migraine, and campanile crick.

As we came out into the hot sun from the cool interior, Carol said, 'I have to sit down. Sightseeing is so exhausting.'

There was a bench seat in the shade and we followed her over. It was certainly pleasant to sit after standing for so long. 'Sister Angela is very fond of *The Canterbury Tales* and refers to this as a pilgrimage,' she said, 'so I feel duty-bound to seek out all the blessings on offer, although I have to say we came on a plane and will go back on a plane, so the amount of effort to get here wasn't really what Chaucer had in mind.'

'I don't think in Chaucer's day you had much option. Horseback, or muleback for ladies, was the deluxe method of travel,' I said. I was sure they would have flown by preference if they could.

'Yes, and no clean little individual cells en route or when you got there,' said Gregory. 'I hear that the pilgrims' inns back then were pretty torrid spots.' Disease central, where you would take all sorts of vermin and diseases back home with you, including the plague.

The plague. Imagine coming to be blessed, receiving absolution and bottles of holy water and then returning home with the seeds of destruction, black death, seething through your system.

'There's someone in my discussion group,' said Gregory, 'who coughs all the time. He'll open his mouth to speak, but before the end of the first sentence he's coughing like a man possessed. I hope he's not contagious but I'm too polite to ask.'

Afraid of taking the seeds of destruction back to his community? Carol asked.

No, Gregory liked to talk and he didn't want to end up like *that*.

She laughed. 'So I gather you've been enjoying your time here?'

'Oh yes,' said Gregory, 'rather too much, I fear.'

'Enjoying it too much! That's a psychological condition you don't come across much in my line of work. Do explain.'

'I was raring to get away. The excitement of packing and gathering provisions from the store. Then travelling down here and the fun of engaging in conversation with so many people. It makes the thought of going home tomorrow rather dull.'

'It makes it sound like a holiday you mean. Or holy day, to remember its derivation.'

'When I took orders, I chose a contemplative life. The monastery. I thought I would be serene and untroubled there. But when the term is over, I can't wait to pack my bags and go somewhere.'

'And you don't think that's what you should be doing?'

'Not really. I thought once teaching was over I should be rejoining my community.'

'And is the community happy for you to go on holiday?'

'Well, yes. Although I didn't exactly describe this trip to them as a holiday.'

'Good for them though, they could see you needed a break even if you can't. What do you teach?'

Gregory taught maths from third year up to A level. He was also a reserve teacher for English literature, mainly for the junior school.

Carol looked surprised. 'It's a bit of a strange combination, isn't it?'

But no, not according to Gregory. He was interested in the history of mathematical speculation and the strange and weird things mathematicians came up with. So long as they could prove it mathematically, it didn't have to be real. You could speculate about whether time was curved in the same way you could speculate about whether Elizabeth Bennett would marry Mr Darcy. They were real on the page even if they were both made-up entities.

'So which is easier to teach?' asked Carol.

'Oh, maths by a long shot. Getting teenage boys to read a book, a whole book … Most of them can't do it in other than small chapters. More than ten pages and they start squirming around and kicking each other.'

Carol laughed. And there was the reason he needed a holiday, she said. 'Otherwise you'll burn out. Although I'm intrigued by the notion of enjoying yourself too much. Maybe that feeling requires a little bit of guilt. Yes, I can see it, having a lot of fun when you think you should be doing something else which is not nearly as much fun.'

I could see that too. 'You're a practising psychologist?' I asked.

'Not as such,' said Carol. That's how she'd started out, but she'd been led by a trail of circumstances to specialising in the needs of women in the workforce, one of those digressions you often found on life's journey. She currently ran workshops and training courses, mainly in the public sector, trying to maximise opportunities for female workers. Gregory would be interested in this, she said. Because one of the tools she used was a speech out of her favourite play, *The Taming of the Shrew*, which went:

> I am ashamed that women are so simple
> to offer war where they should kneel for peace
> or seek for rule, supremacy, and sway,
> when they are bound to serve, love, and obey.

'What do you think of those lines?' she asked.

I thought they sounded a bit craven.

Nice word; Carol looked pleased. 'Now,' she said, 'how about if I say it differently.' She said it again, putting emphasis on the word 'bound' and holding her arms tight against her side while rolling her eyes. So what did we think of the lines now?

'Subversive,' said Gregory.

Another good word. She ran workshops in which she got the women to say these lines in many different ways and she would point out that words only had the meaning that was imputed by the person saying them and women should weigh words, giving them their own meaning, and not allow themselves to be brain-washed into accepting the kind of idiotic and ludicrous things told to women in the workforce, which if told to a man would have him die laughing.

She had set up a mentoring and training group called Rule Supremacy & Sway, which had now over fifty consultants in New York and was growing all the time. Times were a-changing and even men of goodwill were finding themselves wrongfooted, so all sorts of companies were now asking the group to run courses for them – banks, finance corporations, even the defence force.

Equal employment opportunity. 'Coming, somewhat reluctantly, to an organisation near you,' she said, tapping my arm.

'I can't wait,' I said.

'Good for you. Although I think half of the General Synod will have to die before you get female priests ordained in England.'

'Maybe we could put something in their sherry,' I said.

On this happy note, we got up to walk towards the Purisima church and the final unity service – Lutheran – which went very well compared with the others. I noticed that Jack had come in with some of the girls, and during a candlelit procession there was some spirited Spanish singing – including from the young people and also from the local congregation who had come in to watch.

Afterwards Jack came over to where the three of us were sitting and said his Spanish family had asked us all for a meal, so we gathered up Bob, who was very pleased to think he would be eating something Spanish. With the addition of Sister Angela, we returned to our accommodation to freshen up and then made our way into the square we had been to on previous occasions. We were led by Jack up a passage beside one of the shops and emerged around the back where a giant frying pan – that was the best way I can describe it – was sitting over a barbecue of red-hot coals, with Manuel's wife slowly stirring a steaming mass of rice and prawns and seafood. Lights were strung out between two poles, and a long table with chairs stretched up a narrow garden.

'Oh,' said Sister Angela, conscience-stricken. 'Maybe we should have brought some wine.'

Jack turned to translate this to the eldest of the girls, who I noticed all of a sudden was very pretty, although perhaps a little younger than my son. She immediately laughed, all merry white teeth; clearly the answer was no, not necessary. Manuel, her father, appeared out of the back door of the house clutching several bottles of wine, some red and some white. We were invited to sit down, bottles of water were produced, many different sorts of appetiser, bowls of salad, and then finally a luscious paella, probably spicier than I would have liked but still very tasty, real Spanish food.

I was sitting opposite Angela, who later in the meal announced that she had been voted onto the organising committee for the next conference because so many people had absented themselves from the AGM – she looked severely around the table. But now she was going to harass all the absentees by going round and demanding that they make suggestions on topics they would like for the next conference.

I happened to have on me the page of criticism I had written on the unity services which I gave her. 'Yes, this is good stuff for organisation. But any topics you'd like to see on the program?'

'How about a discussion on goodness?'

'In what context?' she wanted to know.

Perhaps the changing nature of it. I said that I didn't know what 'goodness' was anymore. I had expected goodness and mercy to follow me all the days of my life, but if I didn't know what goodness was in the modern age, then that expectation became worthless.

'Yes,' agreed Carol. 'People tell me they've been "good". What they mean is, they didn't have a second slice of cake. I'm not sure how that is relevant to their immortal soul.'

Ah, we all concurred, like a serial killer saying he had been good that day. Meaning there was no body in a pool of blood out there at the moment to be discovered. It was more about discipline and abstemiousness than traditional notions of goodness.

'I don't even think that people who abide by the Ten Commandments and who steer clear of the Seven Deadly Sins are necessarily good, either,' I said. 'There have been some deeply flawed good men and women in the world, some of whom have committed adultery and some of whom have coveted their neighbour's Range Rover.'

The way the world was set up now, coveting your neighbour's goods was part of the capitalist plan, said Bob. And as for adultery, people lived so much longer now. Too long to put up with an unhappy marriage, so new laws were needed with easier provisions. Very controversial of course. But if churches were to keep up with society's expectations, not to do so would result in huge churches designed for big congregations being attended by smaller numbers and then eventually just smatterings.

Jack was translating as far as he was able, and Manuel pointed out that the Catholics filled their churches still, as divorce was not possible.

Yes, they do at the moment, the others agreed. But is the Church in tune with what young people want, is it still relevant to them? If not, as the old people die out and the young people turn away, will those congregations still be there?

It was a very pleasant evening with lots of good discussion and rich Spanish food, but comparatively early, around midnight, we had to give our thanks and depart, as we had to make an early start the following morning. Much lamentation from the family and hugging of Jack and the presentation of a small gift, presumably from the shop. I was pleased with the family and pleased with the fact that my son had clearly enjoyed and made good use of his time in Salamanca.

As we walked back, I reflected that I had also made a number of good friends there. I had the addresses of the American monk, as well as Sister Angela and the lady Salvationist. I suspected that Jack's address book was bulging with dozens of names, and I was proud of his helpfulness and sociability. I didn't mind the reason that I myself had made my mark in Salamanca – as the father of Jack!

3

Homeward Bound

Eleven

GREGORY WANTED TO SAY MASS next morning before leaving for home, and as we planned to be off in good time it was set for 6:45 a.m. Bob and I thought we would be the only congregation and we were both surprised when Jack appeared, having made the effort to get up. All that was needed was a vacant chapel. The seminary (where meals were served) and the college (where we slept) were riddled with chapels, but they were all booked. However, as we stood somewhat confounded, another party turned up: a monk and two nuns. The nuns immediately smiled at Jack and began talking to him in French, and it turned out they had a booking. The upshot was that with very little fuss there was a concelebration. I read the epistle very slowly and distinctly for the benefit of the French speakers and was very heartened afterwards by the general goodwill across religions and language groups. This was truly ecumenical.

We were off by eight thirty. Jack, no doubt exhausted by his early morning rise, fell asleep immediately. I was driving, with Gregory in the front seat, and I raised something which had been on my mind since the previous day. 'Sister Carol talked about bolstering the confidence of women and making the workplace more female-friendly. I'm wondering if that's the right place to start. Or whether schools, particularly same-sex schools, may be the problem.'

'I've always thought that women, that is girls, came out of all-girls schools with more confidence than if they were at a co-ed,' said Gregory.

'But maybe the problem is that boys come out of all-boys school knowing nothing of the capabilities of women. They think that they're the masters of the universe and therefore women should serve them. If they went to a co-educational school and put forward that proposition, no doubt they would be met by a look of blank amazement followed by howls of derisive laughter.'

Gregory was thoughtful. 'Yes, it's talked of, even at my school. Who knows what the future may hold. But your own daughter is going to an all-girls school.'

'Maybe that's a mistake. Instead of help to empower her, she needs help to deal with reality.'

'Still, at least she's been found. What's going to happen?'

'I don't actually know. I tried to ring my wife again last night, but it seems she must have left the flat. I was somewhat relieved because of her unrealistic expectations about my involvement in Sally's repatriation, which have led to some pretty frosty conversations. She's dealing with it. Well, she promised back in March that she would look after Sally. So I am trying very hard not to feel any guilt.'

Gregory sighed. Yes, those little nagging spurts of guilt. He had liked Sister Carol's explanation of why he thought he was having too much fun. We discussed guilt in its many manifestations on the fairly fast road to Burgos, where we stopped at noon.

Gregory went shopping with Jack for lunch stuff while Bob and I had a look at the cathedral. It was supposed to be famous but neither of us was particularly sure why.

We had lunch in a park beside the River Sewer – I have forgotten its real name but by any name it was still the same smell.

However, the wind changed from time to time and (as always) we had a very agreeable picnic meal.

Then on eastwards towards Pamplona – an impressive walled city.

Franco had done much to widen and straighten the roads, but we saw the results of two or three accidents – car wrecks beside the road. According to Jack they all had French numberplates. Too much panache and élan, we all agreed.

We started talking about death and the afterlife, and I was amused to discover that my son thought of the afterlife as a bit like Waterloo Station, with people standing around waiting for their preferred destination to click up on the departure boards.

'You think you get to choose?' said Gregory.

'Oh yes,' said Jack confidently. 'Otherwise think what would happen if Dad got put on the train to Pentecostal heaven. I'm sure God couldn't be so unkind.'

We all laughed and perhaps Gregory, who was now driving, got distracted. Which went to show that people in glass houses … On the brow of a hill he overtook a slow-moving tractor which had partly pulled into the side to let him pass, and although it wasn't a near-miss situation, it was still a rather dangerous thing to do in a left-hand drive car, and the result was flashing red-and-blue lights in our rearview mirror. Fortunately the police officers were in an understanding mood, perhaps because Gregory was a monk or because Jack said something pleasant and placatory to them in Spanish. We were waved on.

Phew, we all said, and Jack wondered whether a police cell would be better or worse than a monastery cell. 'And whether the food would be better,' said Gregory.

As a result of this, Bob recommended that we all focused on what destination we were going to choose at post-death Waterloo Station, so that we were prepared. Because the somewhat uncommitted, like himself, might be standing around too long trying to decide and get shovelled onto the wrong train. He definitely needed to have a plan with Barb so they ended up in the same place.

Perhaps, I suggested, anybody planning to meet up with someone on the other side should choose a very small religion. Much less chance of missing each other.

We pulled off the highway and found a pleasant grassy bank and over afternoon tea, tried to come up with suggestions for the smallest religion we could think of. Gregory was drawn to St Chad, who was a spiritual leader in the seventh century, just at the start of the time when the Benedictines were starting to spread through England.

Would there still be a train going in his direction though? Jack wondered. He thought with the small number of people likely to be travelling, Beeching had probably axed it.

'Plus isn't he a bit austere?' I queried. I didn't think there was any likelihood of yoghurt in Chad heaven. And, I added, wouldn't people choosing such a niche sort of heaven likely have a good smattering of odd types?

Possibly a train for card-carrying crackpots?

Bob, however, was starting to warm to St Chad. A heaven heavy with eccentrics – would it be hell or actually quite interesting and perhaps as good a way as any of surviving eternity?

We drove on, Bob and I still in the back, and I now broached a subject that I had been thinking about for a couple of days: how difficult it would be to turn back time and for me to become a solicitor again.

Bob didn't know, because his own training had been different, through university. But he assumed that once you became qualified in a profession you would stay qualified, though the problem was whether I could actually work at something I hadn't done for thirty years.

'Well, twenty-five,' I said. 'I did a bit during the war. They made me Adjutant, mainly trying to sort out failing marriages, more a social worker than a solicitor. Bigamy was quite popular as well as adultery. And then there was larceny, especially when it concerned adapting army property for the greater profit and utility of the general population. I defended quite a few courts martial and prosecuted at a couple as well, but none of them were particularly interesting or onerous.' Since then I had kept up a subscription to the *Solicitors' Journal*, mainly to stay in touch with changes to laws that might affect the parish land holdings, but I also regularly read articles of a general nature out of interest. So although I hadn't practised for twenty-five years, my knowledge of property, trusts and company law was still fairly strong.

'As those are the main money-earners that come through the door, I should think you should be able to catch up quite easily. But then you're probably asking the wrong person. I'm thinking of jacking private practice in for a bit.'

'Really!'

'It's clear that they're not going to make me a partner, and I don't think I've got enough business nous to go out on my own. So I'm looking for a nice cosy legal department in a government organisation. Or a company. Something like that.'

'Is there a problem in the practice you're in? You've been there a number of years.'

'Nearly seven. But I don't rank on the social scale, so I'll never progress. Not highborn enough for them.'

I was outraged. 'Surely they don't think like that still! It's 1970.'

'Of course they still think like that. Old Mr Bentley is married to a Hon. And young Mr Bentley's wife is a double-barrelled showjumper. Meanwhile, Barb and I are only just on the verge of being presentable, barely scraping into the middle class.'

'I've never come across any attitudes like that in my parish.'

'No, of course not, you wouldn't. It would be very poor form to criticise a man of God for not being of quite the right stock. But for the rest of us, it's a blood sport.'

Jack turned round to Bob from the front seat. 'Mr Barker, Tony's father, reckons you're the only one that knows anything in that practice. He said he'd gone in there one market day and got old Mr Bentley because you were in court and young Mr Bentley must have been somewhere else. You had to ring him up next day to sort it out.'

Bob laughed. 'I have learnt a great deal from old Mr Bentley. He doesn't know any law, well he probably did once but he's forgotten it all. But the thing is, people don't go to him because they want to know what the law is. They wouldn't understand it anyway. They go to him for reassurance, that they're going to be all right. So we always make sure there's a clerk in with him, taking notes. And this is the learning experience. Either through education, or comfortable circumstances, or possibly in old Mr Bentley's case even through wisdom, he has the gravitas and manner to give that reassurance. And Rick Barker would have gone home relaxed and unworried and the next morning, like a genie out of a bottle, I ring him up and tell him how we're going to solve his problem.'

'Have you ever been given any problems you *couldn't* solve?' asked Jack.

'No, not really. A man once came into my office with a shotgun in relation to a family matter I was dealing with and said he was going to shoot me and then he was going to go and shoot Mr Sonley. I said that in the interests of procedural fairness he should shoot Mr Sonley first. By the time he got over there I'd rung Harold, who's a lay preacher, and apparently they both got down on their knees praying for enlightenment. Or forgiveness. Or something.'

'I can't believe that they wouldn't want to hang on to you!' I cried. 'With sangfroid like that! But surely if you know how to solve people's problems, you wouldn't need an old Mr Bentley. You could set up in private practice yourself.'

'Like I said, I don't think I've got enough business sense. Do you know what's coming in? Something called "billable hours". That's where you apportion every moment of your time, like a slave in chains, towards what you can charge. Whereas me, I go up to a moorland farm to sort out a new will which would take an hour tops, all of which I can charge for of course. But then I sit there for another hour having afternoon tea and talking about the price of wool and government subsidies in New Zealand and what the new choirmaster has in mind for Christmas, none of which are even remotely billable. I'd never make a go of it, I enjoy chatting too much.'

'Some people need to chat,' I said. 'Especially people in isolated locations. I often find on pastoral visits to lonely people that letting them tell you all their problems and what they think is wrong with the world is as good for their state of mind, or better even, than any prayer or biblical quotation. In any case, rushing off after the will is signed might be bad for a lawyer's business. Obviously they wouldn't be making wills every day, but farmers seem to be as prone to getting into legal stoushes as anyone else. Sitting around having afternoon tea would be forming a relationship.'

'Yes, wisely said,' said Bob.

Maybe his employers would see the error of their ways if he started making a move to leave, suggested Gregory.

Not according to Bob, who thought they would probably be quite relieved if he took himself off. He had been getting above his station. He wrote articles for the *Solicitors' Journal*, mainly about historical legal matters that he was interested in. Of course no one in his small market town would read such an article, except perhaps the younger Mr Bentley, but even that was unlikely. So imagine his surprise, walking across the marketplace one day, when he was hailed by a member of the local aristocracy – he wouldn't say who in case they thought he was namedropping which he'd been told was 'common'. Anyway, this titled gentleman demanded that Bob come out to his estate and look at some historical legal documents he had. Bob thought that the man, who was not a client of his firm but of some big posh lot in London, was probably looking for some free legal advice but went anyway. To his surprise he was shown a bulky chunk of history called the *Manor of Little Hamptonby Court Book*, quite fascinating, all about Court Leets and Court Barons and offences like skittle playing and keeping greyhounds and conspiring to sell victuals at unreasonable profits.

He had written rather a jolly article about it and when returning the documents had left a copy of the proof. So suddenly, to the alarm of the partners, the local lord started popping into Bob's office from time to time to tell him about other things he'd discovered. 'Well, you can't have that can you, him mingling with someone with an uncouth Glaswegian accent like me, whose father worked on the railways. What if I committed some faux pas or didn't treat him with the correct degree of reverence? It could all rebound against the practice. And what if he brought our firm some work and chose me instead of old Mr Bentley?'

Ridiculous, we all agreed.

'Hasten the day when you get another job,' I said.

'Yes, because now I have to put my nose to the wheel on account of … Well you'll find out soon enough, she can't hide it much longer, but Barb is pregnant again. I had a few quiet prayers in Salamanca on that front I can tell you. But it's over five months and no miscarriage yet.'

Everyone opened their mouths but nothing came out except a gentle murmur of encouragement. Two miscarriages and a stillbirth. No one wanted to be the one to jinx the latest pregnancy by offering congratulations.

Towards Jaca, the scenery became more and more impressive. Eventually, by turning northwards off the main east–west road and climbing steadily for two miles or so, we reached our destination – the Royal Monastery of Leyre. It was a building that couldn't be anything else, it was so perfect in its representation of a monastery. It sat on the side of a mountain with a jagged edge of dolomite above and in every other direction, mile after mile of Spain: mountains, valleys and, beneath, a great lake. The lake was a magnificent afterthought; it was in fact a reservoir, perhaps ten miles long and, in the stretch of water immediately overlooked by the monastery, well over a mile in width.

We had some difficulty in penetrating the building, and when eventually the Reverend Porter arrived, he was besieged by a minibus-load of Cistercians who had been crawling up the track behind us. Gregory later wondered what happened to them – they were on their way to Pamplona and were relying on the Benedictine rule of hospitality. He thought possibly they were all pushed over a precipice, but that was judging only by the Reverend Porter's facial expression ('bloody Cistercians') and the fact that there was no sign of them the following morning.

When eventually the guest master arrived, all was kindness. Fortunately he spoke good French and, with Jack translating from time to time, told us something of the history of the place. It was 'Real', or Royal, because the ancient kings of Navarre would hold court there – many of them were buried there, too.

And disinterred – for in anticlerical times more than a century ago, the building was abandoned and its royal tombs despoiled. However, there were many bits of the original eleventh-century building still to be seen.

We were accommodated within the monastery but were then too late to join the community for the evening meal. Instead, we had a most enjoyable dinner at the restaurant used by the occupants of the adjoining guesthouse. The guest master brought along a young man from Colombia to join us – an Episcopalian studying for the ministry. We were all rather shocked by his views, even Bob who I thought of as being the most radical among my Christian friends. The young man foresaw a revolution in South America and thought of it as both necessary and inevitable. He said colonialism had been succeeded by American imperialism, which represented a form of capitalism in which the rich grew richer and the poor poorer. He was not concerned with poverty, some of which was inevitable, but with utter misery, which wasn't. He was prepared for this revolution to be by force and yet he was a dedicated Christian. It was a disturbing to me because he didn't look like a revolutionary. In fact he looked like someone who voted Liberal.

I wondered if it shouldn't be made mandatory for people to adjust their appearance to their politics so they didn't turn up at dinner clean-shaven in a blazer and neatly pressed slacks when really they should have been wildly hirsute and wearing a leather jacket.

After dinner, having managed to find a phone, I again rang the flat, but it rang out – no answer. And then I remembered what day it was, Saturday, so of course Joan wouldn't be there. I tried my home number but no answer either – she must have gone back to the university. I rejoined the others and with all the talk it was quite late, so we went into the abbey church and said Compline and so to bed.

Twelve

Up betimes as it was Sunday, and I was going to celebrate Holy Communion which was done in the 'primitive' church in the crypt. I put on the vestments lent to me by the Benedictines – I was travelling light – and was able, in some fashion, to explain to the brother in charge what was to take place. The brother, having deduced apparently that Bob was to be the server, insisted on giving him a small box of incense. Bob accepted it placidly; his Presbyterian hackles didn't rise. I wondered whether Bob even had any hackles: I thought he would probably be quite happy to accept anything that was for the greater glory of whichever Christian God happened to be in the room at the time.

We had our service, the congregation being the brother, Bob, and the young Colombian. Later we were joined, unobtrusively, by the Prior. He had been impressed (he later told the Colombian) by the service, and particularly by the resistance of non-Romans to genuflection. As far as could be gathered, he approved.

Gregory, meanwhile, was at a service in the main church. When I finished my own service, we all went in for the latter part of the proceedings but failed to find our way through the Latin.

After breakfast we talked with the Prior, who regretted that we were not able to stay until after the midday meal. He would not hear of us paying for our board – as at Belloc, Gregory's guests were regarded as honorary Benedictines. We were all solemnly hugged when saying our goodbyes.

As we drove away, the first few miles were along the shores of the newly formed reservoir. 'Farndale simply doesn't know what it's missed,' I said.

'Yes,' said Jack. 'You were all criticising posh people yesterday but if it wasn't for Sir Something Something Somebody-or-other, our lovely daffodil valley would look just like this.'

'Sir Samuel Knox-Cunningham,' supplied Bob. 'But that's the thing about toffs. They sit quietly behind closed doors while the hoi polloi go out and protest against the flooding of a beautiful valley and march and block access roads and wave banners saying Save Farndale, none of which has any effect. So when everyone else thinks the reservoir is a done deal and the cause is lost, this upper-class toff quietly blindsides the parliamentary select committee and scuppers the whole thing.' He laughed. 'Ten thousand peasants marching up and down and it has no effect whatsoever, but one titled bloke puts a red pencil through it behind closed doors and voila, no more lake.'

'And here was me thinking how nice this looked,' said Gregory. 'Clearly I will have to recalibrate my thoughts.'

We drove on to Jaca, where we stopped for provisions and looked briefly into the cathedral. Being Sunday, there was a full congregation including many babes in arms, and centre stage a small boy confessing his sins, in full view, to a partly seen confessor in an ecclesiastical sedan chair. Jack later translated it as 'Father, I have nothing to confess, so far as I can remember, and seek forgiveness for wasting your time.' The priest placed his hand on the little boy's head – 'That's alright, my chiquito' – and told him to come back next week and see if he could do a little better.

From Jaca we set off eastwards, and Jack commented that he did quite like the idea of confession. The only problem for him would be working out what thoughts and actions were a sin.

'You don't think following the Ten Commandments might be a start?' said Gregory.

'I think I'm a bit young for them, all that adultery and coveting.'

'And anyway,' said Bob, 'as I'm sure I've said already, there are so many civil issues with the Commandments and the Seven Deadly Sins. For instance, if the government encourages you to invest in the stock market, you are indulging your greed. Can that be a sin if it results in ICI raising capital to expand? Or is ICI greedy for wanting to make more product? And if so, why don't *they* confess, instead of the investors?'

Different world these days.

'So, why do you think you might want to confess?' Gregory asked Jack. 'And to what?'

Jack thought about it. 'My friend Sean has got a much better miracle medal than the one I bought. His family is actually Catholic, and they got it in Rome, blessed by the Pope or by someone high up. So we decided to try and see if it worked. We would all hold it together and pray really hard that we got trifle for school dinner, three prayers being stronger than one according to Sean. But you see, I don't like trifle, or not the trifle they make at school which is a bit slimy. And I found I was praying instead for treacle tart and custard. Mainly we didn't get either, we'd get something none of us liked like spotted dick. But then occasionally we would get treacle tart, and I'd feel guilty and feel I wanted to confess. But I'm not sure it would be a sin, not about the treacle tart, but the secret bad faith, not joining in the joint enterprise to try and get trifle.'

Gregory laughed long and loud until he had to get out his handkerchief and mop his face. 'I am doubly encouraged in my decision not to become a priest and hear confessions.'

We went merrily northwards into the high Pyrenees, talking about the boundaries of sin and the best recipe for custard.

As we got higher and higher we became silent as the view entranced us all. It was tremendous.

After climbing for miles we reached a village and stopped briefly to fill up the water container. Then on and up for many more miles until the tree-filled gorges were left behind. There were man-made scars – water pipelines and an occasional ski centre with ski lifts – but the scenery was on such a grand scale that one forgave the engineers. And in any case, the road itself was an engineering feat in places, with precipices undercut or tunnels constructed where there was no other toehold.

The Spanish and French frontier posts waved us through and, shortly after passing the summit of the pass, we stopped for lunch. There, in a perfect Arcadia among short grass, autumn crocuses in profusion (and another thistle which Gregory uprooted for the garden) we arranged ourselves in the warm sunshine, with an ice-cold stream from a nearby spring to keep the drinks cool. The menu, announced Gregory like a waiter in a grand hotel, was to be sardines Portugaises, imported from his monastery; jambon de Jaca; fromage de Normandie; gateaux Aragonais; various fruits de Burgos; limonada gaseosa and red plonk du pays.

I was completely revived and felt that the world was an amazing place and that I should throw off my doubts and inhibitions and my fear of the future. Here I was in one of the most beautiful places I had ever been, and everything seemed to be urging me on. Even a hawk landed on a nearby rock to see if it could be of assistance, and when it flew off I imagined it was because the bird could see I was about to make the right decision.

When we set off again, with Bob driving, I felt almost giddy with excitement over the new possibilities that lay before me. Or maybe I was giddy from the glass of wine, which I didn't usually drink at midday. For whatever reason, I felt happy to be riding a rollercoaster as we began a long descent into a deep gorge followed by another great climb way up beyond the fleecy clouds.

We passed Lourdes (Gregory would have liked to stop but we had a deadline to make) and finally came to Tournay and to a quiet, newish monastery.

There were only about a dozen monks but quite an active lot. We were just in time for the evening meal, so I put on my clerical collar, Bob a tie, and Gregory got into his habit. Jack was a little underdressed for the occasion, but that was allowable in a boy.

Afterwards, while we were still in the dining room, the Prior, a zestful charismatic type of about my age or possibly younger, gave us an account in French of what was going on. The monastery was only half finished, and he had decided to make the cloisters open on one side – U-shaped instead of an enclosed square, so that the monk's life was clearly seen not to be shut off from the world. They were trying to appeal to a younger cohort.

Jack translated some of it when the concepts got beyond us, and the Prior congratulated him on his good French and asked him what subjects he was doing at school.

French, maths and music were his main subjects, with German as an add-on even though he didn't have a German teacher, and Spanish as a minor subject.

What instruments did he play for music, the Prior wanted to know.

The piano and the guitar, he replied. He had started on the cello, borrowed from his school, but his sister had broken it and they wouldn't give him any more instruments to take home.

I had been following this conversation as well as I could with my more basic vocabulary and verb tenses. Again the exposure of my daughter's misbehaviour distressed me, although I noted the neutral way that my son imparted the information. I reflected on Sally's early efforts to destroy our piano as well, but she was caught in flagrante and given a good hard smack by Joan, who also liked to play it occasionally. Thus preserving at least one instrument for Jack to use.

The Prior then asked Jack what his hobbies were and he replied, chess and listening to music. But he added that they made up their own rules for chess in which each player had two minutes to make a move, and during that time the opponent could make as much distracting noise as they wanted including making disparaging remarks and whistling.

The Prior laughed and said he didn't think they would be introducing that in his community. Then he asked what music Jack listened to and expressed astonishment when he said his favourite music was by The Rolling Stones – the Prior thinking he would have liked classical music in light of his other interests. He asked Jack to explain what he saw in this music.

'It's based on the blues. It's all about loss and longing.'

'I've always been given to believe that it was about sex and the devil,' replied the Prior.

In response, without the slightest self-consciousness, Jack broke into a slow, halting song in English. Until his voice had broken a couple of years before, he had been the leading light of our choir. It seemed his voice had now stabilised into a sweet, light tenor, and he sang sadly about being taken to the station with no expectation of ever coming back. He translated the words and said, 'That's one of their songs and you see, all it's about loss and longing. It's not even clear who he's leaving, it could be a lover, it could be parents, it could just be a way of life he's saying goodbye to.'

Some other monks, who had been in the dining room clearing up, stopped what they were doing to listen to him, and I saw them bow their heads and look thoughtful.

'Are young people sad like that?' asked the Prior.

'Yes, they are sad sometimes, I suppose. They spend their teenage years saying goodbye to things. Goodbye to school, goodbye to their classmates and, as they head out into the world, goodbye to their home, goodbye to everything they've known. Some of those things you can never go back to. Going away from safety, out into the world with all its dangers and promise is sad and frightening. But it's exciting too.'

The Prior then surprised us all by putting his hand on Jack's head and blessing him.

I actually felt shocked. I couldn't explain it, it was as if a small discharge of electricity, like a whisper, had tingled me from head to foot in an instant. And in that instant, the world had stopped.

And in that instant, when everyone was looking at him, Jack seemed for a moment to give out an inner glow. A sort of warmth which enclosed us all.

It was then time to attend Vigil but perhaps because we were thinking of other things Bob and I lost ourselves hopelessly in the psalms.

Afterwards I lay flat on my back in the austere room allocated to me and thought about my marriage. Jack's song could be about me. I had little expectation that we could go back to where we started out.

Joan and I had married in the spring of 1943, when the world was a pretty dark place. I had no idea what the future held, but sometimes you just had to take life with both hands and hope for the best. Of course we couldn't live together at that time; my unit was constantly on the move and Joan was still teaching and wanted to keep doing so. But those infrequent weekends when we managed to meet were wonderful; they filled a lack in me that

I never knew was there. All the difficulties associated with finding a place to stay, writing ahead with my ration card and her ration card, and then finding my way through blackouts and bombing to some dreary cold room in an unprepossessing hotel, all that was as nothing when I stood on the station platform and saw Joan's jaunty little hat coming down from the train to meet me.

Even after the war, when Joan had got an exemption to keep teaching while I went to theological college, meeting up for the weekends was still wonderful. When I was given a ministry in 'darkest Yorkshire' we had no idea what to expect, and we set off northward with no preconceived ideas except that there would be 'furnished accommodation' provided – our first permanent home together. The fact that there was accommodation was important because housing was incredibly scarce after the war, and just as important was the fact that it was furnished, because all the requirements for setting up house together – furniture, manchester, housewares – were rationed. Multigenerational households had become the norm, and older family members were having to cull their effects to help out the newly forming families of their younger kin. Fortunately, in our case they didn't have to.

However, we had no idea what the house would be like. So when the taxi pulled up in front of the vicarage, we gawped in open-mouthed astonishment and thought there must have been some mistake. We got out with our meagre possessions in two suitcases and just stared. A substantial stone dwelling stared back, Georgian with mid-Victorian additions, set within an established garden behind stone walls.

The churchwarden and other members of the parish council were there to greet us, and there was a wonderful spread set out on the dining room table – scones and home-made jam and local cream and all sorts of sandwiches and cakes. Speeches were made, and when everyone had left and when we looked around, we just couldn't believe our luck. The vicarage seemed huge to us: five stately bedrooms, several smaller attic rooms (for servants, which of course we couldn't afford), a formal dining room, expansive drawing room, the music room with French doors leading out into the garden, and a beautiful study lined with books. There was also a recently installed modern kitchen and adjoining breakfast room on the ground floor, with the basement service area now consigned to storage. And outside, a large garden with a vegetable plot and orchard. It all seemed too good to be true.

We were happy. It's hard to put a finger on what happiness consists of, but whatever definition you use we were happy then. We got out of bed in the morning with a swing and a zip and a clatter. The Rayburn would be shaken awake, blue-and-white plates laid crisply on the breakfast-room table, the crunch of toast, cups moving in saucers – happiness has a soundtrack. Cheerful voices. Laughter, singing, humming. Slow kisses and the sound of hair and fabric moving.

When did it start to change? I wasn't sure; maybe it was too gradual. And perhaps it had started to change earlier for Joan than for me. But it had something to do with Sally.

Joan had only had older brothers and always wanted a sister. She felt shortchanged as the only girl and believed her brothers had had an easy path into adulthood whereas she had had to fight for everything.

When the first two of our children were born, she was a fond and loving mother. But when Sally was born, it was as if all her wishes had come true at last. Any pretence of not having a favourite child went out the window. Sally could do no wrong. She was the most beautiful baby. She was the most precocious toddler. She was the brightest star in the firmament.

And yes, she was a beautiful child. Pushing her in her pram through the local market town, you could see heads turn. A princess travelling among them, her face wreathed in smiles. Sally revelled in a pool of adulation in public but was becoming less and less admirable in private.

Sally's birthday was the least contentious time of the year. She would sit like a queen in full possession of the birthday cake and all her presents. However, on Pete and Jack's birthdays – as at any time the focus of attention was on them – Sally became uncontrollably jealous. When presents were given to her brothers and not to her she rampaged around, trying to grab them and throwing them down when reprimanded. Not unexpectedly with this behaviour, things got broken.

'She's just a baby,' Joan would say placatingly.

The boys quickly got tired of all this and wanted their own share of attention. Soon Sally wasn't a baby, and what had been excusable and even amusing in a tiny tot was neither cute nor funny in a child with range and aim and accuracy. The family dynamic changed, and despite my best efforts to rein Sally in, I was constantly frustrated by her mother's refusal to join in the discipline. To my distress and annoyance, Joan often told the boys off for not sharing their things. Pete, especially, pushed back – Pete had been the golden one up until then and the birth of Jack had not changed this. It was like living in a war zone, but the war was not between Pete and Sally but between Pete and Joan. Joan grew increasingly sharp and peremptory with her eldest son, while Pete became ever more rebellious and angry with his mother.

I tried to focus on what I saw as the real problem. Sally was not learning to respect boundaries. 'You're turning her into a monster,' I said to Joan after an incident in which she had been reluctant to criticise her daughter. She dismissed my criticism as playing favourites, preferring boys to girls.

So nothing was resolved.

I now realised, as I lay there thinking back, that peacemakers were only trying to preserve their *own* peace. The appeasers, the diplomats – the showy jetting in and out of high-profile mediators was only about what was in it for them. 'Peace in our time' was just 'Don't muck up our comfortable existence'. I had tried to play the peacemaker, but shouting, crying, and angry scenes offstage had become a constant background to my life.

I felt suddenly that I had spent the last ten years under constraint, not able to say what needed to be said, or do what needed to be done, because the semblance of an orderly family life was part of the job. Every day that I didn't act was a day in which the situation just got worse.

I wanted to lie there and sort through all the incidents over the last year, including Christmas, to try and get them into some form of clarity which would illuminate the current situation. But I couldn't. I just couldn't. It had all become too much, too painful. Too fraught with my own failure.

Even as I tried to force the thoughts from my head, Easter came unbidden. I resolutely shut it down but … it was there already. Another explosion. This one so quiet and deep it felt less like an explosion and more like the moving of tectonic plates.

Jack had announced that he was going to Germany during the Easter holidays, as he had been invited to stay with Antoine's cousins to improve his German. Sally had immediately become upset that he should get such an offer, and Joan also protested: he would miss Sally's birthday. But fortunately Joan's aunt invited them to use her holiday cottage in Wales; Joan gladly accepted and Jack departed without further remark.

When he came back he brought Sally a birthday present – it was a record. He gave it to her in the breakfast room the next morning and she eagerly pulled off the wrapping paper. She then gave a cry of disgust, holding her arm away from her as if she'd touched something nasty, and it fell from her hand on to the ground – causing the disc inside to fly out and shatter on the hearth. I looked down. The record cover featured a rather fanatical-looking man with a beard, and the title was in French. *On me recherche*, it said and then at the bottom, *Jesus Christ*.

What did it mean? Was it some religious thing, finding Jesus? I didn't know.

Jack didn't react. None of us did. Joan, standing near the doorway, seemed to go rigid with shock, staring at Sally as if she'd seen some strange magical apparition sliding out of the ether and into the body of her daughter. I was shocked too, not only at Sally's gesture but at my own inability to move or do anything. Sally left the room but I wasn't looking at her, I was looking at Jack and realised I had my arm around his shoulders and was patting him in very much the same way as Pete had done during the bike incident. 'I'm sorry,' I whispered.

Jack said, 'It's okay, Dad. I don't like Johnny Hallyday either. Antoine's sister is crazy about him and was sure that Sally would love this, but I think he's just a pale imitation of the rock stars he covers.' And with that he departed.

I remember the scene as if it'd been branded into my brain. I was standing there near the broken record. Joan had moved a few paces forward and was standing near me. Out in the hall Sally was standing halfway up the stairs, where she had stopped when Jack was explaining why he'd bought the record. We were all looking at the front door closing behind him. It was like a tableau, a living portrait of some tragedy not explainable to the viewer. The only clue for the viewer was the look of despair on each of our faces.

So that was the image I had as I eventually went off to sleep – everyone looking at Jack. It was no good praying for guidance about the past. The past was the past and how would you know even in the light of hindsight what should have been the right course of action?

Things would change and change again to a soundtrack of sad songs, with no expectations that you could ever go back.

Thirteen

Next day before breakfast, I knocked on Jack's door and, getting a muttered grunt, went in. He was still in bed of course, curled up under the rather sparse blanket provided.

'Sorry, you're going to have to get up soon anyway, but I just wanted to have a talk with you. I saw a phone box near the entrance, although I'm not sure it's going to be worth ringing the flat again, your mother seems to have gone.'

Jack propped himself up. 'Ring Uncle Don, he may know something.'

I hesitated. I had already worked that out, but the problem was … Before I could say anything, however, Jack said, 'I'll do it if you like. And let me pay for any expenses today, it's not right that you're not letting me contribute. I've got the money that I saved for France and that may not come off.' For a moment I was flooded with relief, because I wasn't sure how much the phone call would cost and I didn't really want to discuss it with my son, but Jack's unexpected addition to the trip had stretched my budget so there was even less leeway for emergencies or unforeseen extras. But then I caught myself. Jack was only sixteen and had worked so hard to get that money. I couldn't accept it. Before I could say this, however, Jack had bounded out of bed in his underpants, saying, 'We'll go and call him now. It's early so he's bound to still be at home.' He put on his shorts and T-shirt and thrust his feet into sandals in a few economical moves.

I followed him out of the room feeling that the determination to do the right thing is sometimes overwhelmed by events. And also wondering when was the last time I myself had got out of bed and been ready for the day in under fifteen seconds.

We went together into the cool of the morning. The sun was up and the vegetation smelt fresh and robust, and there was the pleasant sound of a river running nearby. The call box was only fifteen minutes' walk away, and Jack got through quite easily. I heard him say, 'Hello, good morning Uncle Don. It's Jack.' Yes, he said, Dad was with him. Dad hadn't been able to reach Mum. 'Oh, is she!' (There was then a pause.) 'Wait, I'll tell him.'

He turned to me. 'Sally is there but she's still in bed. The police delivered her yesterday evening. Apparently she's been threatened with juvenile detention so he's fairly certain she'll stay this time.' He handed me the phone. I had a short conversation with my brother-in-law during which I realised to my shock and horror that when Joan had complained that everything was being left to her, the sum total of her actions had been to request the authorities to repatriate Sally and then, before this even happened, to go back to Oxford, job done. Why? I couldn't even imagine. To punish Sally for disappointing her? To punish me!

Don seemed resigned to the situation. Joan had accused him of precipitating Sally's disappearance, and he was no longer talking to her. The question remained as to what was to be done with Sally, as Joan seemed to have washed her hands of the whole matter. She had told him that I would pick Sally up from his place as we went north.

I was silent for a moment. Even this, I couldn't do. I said, 'Don, there is barely room in the car for the four of us, it would be simply impossible.' I breathed out in distress. 'It's alright, they can drop me at your place and I'll take her up by train.' I had no idea how I would pay for it or what I would do when we got to York, the bus service being sketchy at best. 'Don, I'm sorry you got landed with this.'

My brother-in-law was philosophical. He had agreed to look after her for the two weeks while I was away and that's what he was doing. It was not an arrangement he would ever agree to again. His adult daughter, Naomi, was coming that afternoon. He hoped that would work for the next couple of days. The pips went and I rang off, saying I would call again.

'What a situation,' I muttered to myself. There was no way in the world that my brother-in-law, a widower, should be having to put up with a sulky, resentful thirteen-year-old. What on earth was my wife thinking, leaving an innocent bystander to pick up the pieces.

I walked back, leaving Jack at the call box engaged in ringing Antoine. I was in time for a self-service breakfast in the refectory and, the coffee dispenser being recalcitrant, it took me some time to get together the big bowl of café au lait which I now enjoyed in the mornings. I felt unsettled, upset, angry.

We were taken off to be shown over the pottery department, and the monk in charge insisted on handing out four unglazed specimens. Well, at least I supposed I had some sort of gift to take back.

Then to Mass in the plain and pleasant church where, after an effort, I felt comparatively calm again. Things were what they were and would be sorted out as and when it was possible. I noticed that Bob and I had been promoted to the monks' stalls for the concelebration. When the monks moved up to range themselves around the altar, we held ourselves apart but nevertheless felt very much at one with the service. The bread was actual rye bread, and the wine was poured from an earthenware jug into an earthenware drinking vessel. Consecration to make the commonplace wonderful. It was a reminder as to the importance of a spiritual life even in the midst of confusion and despair.

When we were ready to depart, Jack came up smiling. As we drove, he told us Antoine was having a horrible time in Switzerland; the will had been published and everyone was now arguing with everyone else. Even his parents were bickering. On an impulse, Jack had invited him to England to go youth hostelling for the rest of the summer. It would be good for his English.

Youth hostelling. 'Ah,' cried Bob. 'To be young again. Your youth hostel card, a sleeping sheet and a packet of crisps.'

'Processed cheese, Ryvitas and a tin of sardines,' hooted Gregory.

'A battered rucksack, a pair of boots and a few tattered maps.' Ah yes, to go anywhere and all summer in front of you. They both sighed, oh for the open road, the limitless possibilities of moorland tracks.

Endless rain, I contributed in my turn. Sloppy bogs. Midges.

Not much of an outdoorsy person then Martin, they commented.

I replied that I had lived outdoors in a tent for long stretches of the war and would be very happy never to do it again.

'Oh, come on,' said Bob. 'You were an officer. Only the best for people like you.'

I pointed out that a second lieutenant was an immaterial speck in the queue clamouring for scarce resources. Although life was pretty bloody for everyone having to live in a tent in England, even when it was theoretically summer.

More evidence. Tell the story, they all said.

'Okay, if I must,' I said resignedly.

My home-away-from-home had been a bell tent shared with one other man, who in the summer of 1943 was Barry Kendall, an auctioneer from Grimsby. The furniture consisted of two camp beds, two bed rolls, a suitcase (Barry's), a number of open petrol tins (acting as a chest of drawers) and chunks of equipment of various sorts cast here and there. The conversation in the morning largely consisted of 'Where the hell is so-and-so?' as we searched for our PT kit buried somewhere under the wreckage.

As well as a human, I also shared the tent with various other creatures, some of which were friendly and some not. Sometimes a worm would stalk me across the room and then disappear down a hole in the carpet, the carpet being well-trodden and rather damp grass. But mainly the domestic pets were large black beetles and spiders. 'Did you know beetles could bite?' I asked. They crawled everywhere; a big one once climbed into my trouser pocket and we were both surprised next morning when I put my hand on it. But I didn't mind them, it was the millipedes that made me stiffen with horror. Nor did I much like shiny black slugs exploring the carpet. I wouldn't have that – messy pets, not nearly as cuddlesome as the beetles. So I would push them out into the rain.

Then one night while I was writing a letter to Joan on my bed I was interrupted by a mole – the first I had ever seen alive. It wandered over the carpet, sniffed at my boots (which were Dubbined) and then retired behind my chest of drawers (the petrol tins).

Barry and I discussed what to call our new pet. I wanted to call it Mole like out of *The Wind in the Willows*. My tent mate wanted to call it Daphne, which was what we called our regimental sergeant major (out of earshot). I thought that was a bit mean, because Mole was a rather quiet, thoughtful creature. But Barry pointed out that Daphne the mole, like our regimental sergeant major, liked digging, which was illustrated by many of our exercises involving hacking trenches out of bullet-riddled hillsides.

'What, real bullets?' exclaimed Jack.

No, not real, just imagined. Preparing for war was all about imagination. That was the trouble with a real war, when you were actually there and surrounded by dead people it was nothing like the exercises. In fact, I thought that all wars were started through a failure in imagination. Nobody could imagine, nobody, the true concentrated horror of modern warfare, the noise, the blood, the smell, the way the ground shook, the way the trees burned, the zipping past of bits of metal intent on sinking into flesh.

So, to move on from the tent to describing the surrounding environs. The countryside where we were camped was very desolate – great stretches of heather or swamp, with occasional rocky outcrops. It seemed to rain all the time and the camp was very primitive. The water supply, for instance, was drawn from a local bog and chlorinated, which gave it a faint flavour of TCP disinfectant. It also had the appearance of TCP – a cloudy lime juice colour – but that was doubtless due to its boggy origin. Hot water existed only for making tea; shaving was carried out in an open field with the aid of the dilute TCP mixture.

What did I do most of the time?

Most of my time was spent in getting wet. Usually at night. We would be withdrawn from the pretend firing line to a pretend reserve position. The reserve position could be well over the thousand-foot contour line, on a cloud-swept hill. Wet heather to lie on though occasionally I had a groundsheet to keep off the drizzle, but it wasn't very efficient, so many miserable nights with already wet feet from splodging through streams, curled up in the cold trying to sleep. Then off we would go again and march about all night. At 2 a.m., the night drizzling and as black as pitch, I would want to stop and lie down in the lee of a hedge but I couldn't – I had to follow the man ahead. Often I couldn't see the man ahead – just a black shape against an inky sky. Sometimes the man ahead appeared to stop, so I would stop and then find that the man ahead had disappeared.

Finally I might arrive in an open field, get half a pint of cocoa, and be allowed to sleep. No blankets, no greatcoat, not even a groundsheet. At 6 a.m. I would be glad to get up and stop shivering. And then coming back in the morning stinking like the public baths after sloshing on bleach cream to remove our camouflage. Even after a reasonably thorough washing, my hands smelled of it. My batman did sometimes manage to scrounge some hot water and we would try to get a bit less muddied by having a bath in half a gallon of water – well not really a bath but it effectively loosened the dirt, although my towel would turn brown in consequence. Meanwhile the tent looked like a jumble sale, with our muddy kit mixed in with everything else as we changed from our wet clothes into only slightly less damp ones.

Everything got damp. One by one, my three grey blankets got damp. Everything felt damp anyway in a bell tent which could be only partially laced up, leaving gaps where the wind howled through, lashed by intermittent heavy rainstorms when the surrounding hills were lost in cloud. And just when you thought the weather could get no worse, they'd send you out on yet more exercises.

———•———

I had been recounting these experiences to the great amusement of my fellow travellers as we proceeded northwards with the windows down, the warm breeze blowing in, the smell of hay drying lazily in the sun, the whole countryside blazing with summer.

'I've found a new way to keep cool!' exclaimed Bob. 'Have you seen these cars now with air-conditioning? Not needed. If you want to stay cool, just install Martin and get him to tell you what he did in the war.'

'I suppose it was even worse for the ordinary soldiers,' said Gregory.

'I'm not sure it was. They had barrack-like tents and it was all pretty orderly. Our tent wasn't orderly. Maybe the problem was with us.' Yes, I suddenly realised, two men in their mid-twenties who had both been living at home before the war and had never done a stroke of housework between them in their lives.

'How did you get to be an officer?'

'Yes,' said Bob. 'When the war started, how did they decide?'

'I think it's a bit like drafting cattle. Only based on age and occupation instead of size. Both of you would have been sent down the officer chute.'

'Never!' said Bob. 'A tough like me with bolshie attitudes.'

'But with a law degree. They'd never let you in the ranks, polluting the men's minds with their legal rights.'

'Some of the parents want us to instil a more military sort of discipline in the school,' said Gregory. Yes, two wars down and preparing for the next one. 'They think our standards are sliding. They can't believe we actually want the boys to say what they think about issues. And involving them in art. And drama.'

I said that the drama bits would come in very handy in wartime. And I told them about one of the exercises we'd been sent out into the rain to do. In that particular one, we fought another company who had kidnapped the Mayor of Fishguard's daughter – as played by a lance corporal in a dress borrowed from the Padre. Yes apparently the Padre kept a collection of frocks, presumably just for such wartime eventualities.

After it was over, and the lady was no longer in mortal danger from 'B' company, we escorted her back to our mess in triumph and celebrated the successful conclusion to our mission. But then the next morning we were in turn attacked by 'C' company, who seemed to think we had captured the young lady and she was again being held against her will. It was all silly. But sleeping in wet ditches, that was one thing that did prepare you for real war. I used to think, when I was on those exercises, that I would catch my death. But I later realised in Normandy that on the contrary a wet ditch, any sort of ditch in wartime, was a lovely place to be. Twenty-five years later though, my enthusiasm for ditches of any sort was zero. So gaily squelching through a scenic peat bog was extremely low on my list of holiday choices. In fact, when I thought of purgatory it wasn't hellfires I thought of but Welsh moorland in July.

'Well there you are,' said Bob. 'I thought all you in the army ever did was march up and down in lines.'

'You know what?' I reflected. 'That's all young people see. Veterans wearing their medals marching on VE Day and everyone applauding. We should stop the marching, the commemoration of war, applauding the spectacle. It's the wrong message.'

'But wouldn't you feel resentful if people turned away and ignored you after the sacrifices you'd made?' asked Gregory.

'I didn't make any greater sacrifice than those living in the East End of London or those around the docks in Hull and Liverpool. Where are the cenotaphs for them? And I don't want young people thinking that any of it was glorious. It wasn't.'

We were travelling northwards, with Gregory driving, and we all became immersed in a discussion about the causes and solutions for war and as a result became distracted from something that suddenly lurched into importance. We were short of petrol and, because we were going by minor roads, once we realised this we couldn't find a petrol station anywhere and eventually the inevitable happened and we came to a halt just outside a farm.

The farmer happened to be there and benevolently drove Gregory to the next village with a can while the rest of us got out of the hot car and stood in the shade. Jack passed the time by chatting with the farmer's ragamuffin son and was taken off to scratch the head of a friendly cow.

Gregory came back with enough petrol to get us to the next village, where we filled up completely. Not much more than an hour behind time and off we set again.

'So what did the farmer's son have to say?' asked Bob.

Family dramas. Huge family dramas. Jack told us that the lad's eldest sister had unfortunately fallen in love with a most unsuitable young man. He had no land, none. Not a skerrick. Nor any hope of acquiring any or inheriting any. He just drove a van delivering cattle feed and was showing all the signs of becoming a rogue, giving discounts if his customers bought larger amounts, delivering any time of the day or night, and worst of all, sometimes even delivering on Sunday.

'Sacrilege!' cried Gregory.

'A rogue indeed,' I said.

'Sounds like a bloody good catch to me,' said Bob.

The daughter was determined however, even if it meant getting married in a civil ceremony at the mayor's office, and that created a crack in the parental facade as her mother wanted her to be married in church 'like a Christian'. But would that entail her mother making the dress? And what about inviting the family? If the family came then there would have to be a marquee. All very upsetting.

'But the father overstepped the mark by telling his daughter that if she left to marry this no-hoper then her cow, which is a gentle soul but ageing, would be sent to the knackery. Young Pierre told me with glee that the explosion that followed made the Paris riots look like a junior school outing.'

It seemed the most excitement you would ever get in a French farming family was when you threatened someone's favourite cow.

⸺

We had another splendid picnic in a sunny field. Looking around him at the agricultural landscape, Gregory commented on the old farming conundrum, sentimentality versus practicality and the dangers of giving animals names and getting attached to them.

Apart from Bob, we had all grown up in rural or semi-rural areas and had stories from our own families or those of our friends of how chickens, or geese, or bunny rabbits would mysteriously disappear and no one among the adults seemed to know where they'd gone and we would sadly mourn the strange disappearance of these familiars while having roast fowl or rabbit stew for dinner.

Gregory then told us that coming back from the village the farmer had expressed curiosity to know why three adult men were on the loose together and what we'd done with our wives.

Gregory could be excused the omission and as for Bob, well Barb was in no condition. Mainly the pregnancy but she also had a problem with her heart which had been diagnosed some years ago after the first miscarriage and which was exacerbated by pregnancy. Bob had stopped wanting to try for children after the stillbirth because of the toll it was taking on her health, both physical and mental. But now there they were again, well into the second trimester. If it didn't work this time, Bob said he would only contemplate adoption in future. That is, if Barb was well enough even for that.

What a situation. I prayed earnestly for the pair of them.

I wondered if I should also pray for Joan as an act of Christian charity. But I didn't know what to pray for. What would make her happy? Clearly I didn't. What it was about myself that she was no longer satisfied with I couldn't quite put my finger on. Perhaps my lack of ambition? Joan demanded more than I seemed able to give, and she was restlessly focused on a future that was planned. She would have hated this free-form peregrination, shattering to a stop in the middle of nowhere and sitting in a field brewing tea.

I suddenly remembered – why were these memories surfacing all of a sudden? – the trip back from the Lake District.

The plan had been to call into a roadhouse halfway and fill up with petrol and have lunch, some chip-heavy meal to satisfy the kids and then maybe some cheap treats to keep them quiet for the rest of the trip. I had a £5 note carefully put aside for this purpose. By the time I pulled in the kids were well and truly ready for something to eat and were bouncing with anticipation. I opened my wallet before we all trooped in – just as well! – and started back in horror. Wait, I cried. The money had gone. 'The five-pound note. Someone's taken it.'

Joan looked at me sharply. 'Was that all you had?'

Yes of course that was all I had. It was gone!

And then Pete piped up, 'Mum took it.' I gaped as the boy continued, 'I saw her.' On the day his mother had got up early and dressed to go walking, he watched her take the wallet from among my clothes.

When I looked at her, she merely shrugged and said she needed some things and then started attacking me – she couldn't believe that was the only money I'd brought. I would have to use my cheque book.

How could I use my cheque book, I said. She knew very well we'd spent all our money on this trip.

Well why hadn't I been to see the bank manager to get an overdraft like she'd been telling me?

Why would I need to do that? I had put £5 aside which was more than enough money to get us home, why on earth had she taken it without discussing it with me …?

The row. One of the first really bitter rows we'd ever had, in a roadhouse car park on the A1.

So that was that. No lunch, no treats, every spare coin had to be gathered up, four gallons of petrol later and we were on our way with Sally screaming in thwarted outrage and the two boys fractious and my wife withdrawn into lock-toothed mutiny. Was there ever such a long trip? Was four gallons going to be enough? With my eyes constantly on the petrol gauge, I had nursed the car over mile after frightful mile until it finally shuddered to a halt turning into our driveway.

Joan immediately got out of the car and walked off without a word or a backwards look, got the key, opened the door, went in and slammed it shut. I just sat there slumped and feeling numb. I became aware after a while that the kids were still sitting there and the car was quiet, no one saying anything – it was as if the end of the world had come and they had a front-seat view of it. With enormous effort I clawed my way back up to a semblance of normality. I told Pete to get the shopping bag and run down to the village shop (where we had an account) and get bread and butter and two pounds of sausages. And three small packets of crisps. And three small KitKats.

The kids were out of the car and gone in a blur of stripey T-shirts, the apocalypse over.

Why had I found it so difficult to move forward? From then on the landscape seemed to be altered and the ground I walked on seemed riven by sinkholes and craters.

Moving forward fearfully, under fire.

Meanwhile Gregory was laughing; he assumed the farmer had asked the question about the absence of our womenfolk not as if he was wondering about our morals, but as if wondering how to do it himself.

'Yes,' said Bob, 'We'd better keep quiet about this or who knows how many Vivas full of men escaping their wives will be taking to the highways and byways of France.'

I suddenly saw with clarity that was exactly what I was doing – escaping Joan. Perhaps my anger after the recent phone conversation was because despite all my efforts I hadn't succeeded. And the depressing thought now, the dark impossibility of ever doing so.

—◦—

Apart from the stop for petrol, things went well and we began to congratulate themselves on reaching our destination in such good time – there it was, Aubazine Station. Aubazine itself was up a hill, just a few miles away. So we would be at the hermitage in half an hour or so.

At the small, resort-like town we were given directions: the hermitage was just beyond the school, we couldn't mistake it.

We proceeded beyond the school, on and on, and up and up, until a farmer at the next village gave us fresh directions. We went back the way we had come, still congratulating ourselves on arriving in daylight. Still no sign of a hermitage, but fortunately Bob noticed gate posts at either side of a narrow track. This must be the barrière we'd been directed to. The track wound up steeply and the Viva responded dutifully to start with, ploughing up and up in first gear until the ascent became so acute that it gave up, as well it might. We got out in the gathering dusk and wondered what to do, surrounded by trees and tall bracken on a steep hillside. While Bob carefully backed the car downhill with my help, Gregory and Jack continued upwards on foot. Finally Bob and I, now in complete darkness, heard voices and were joined by the other two and a genuine bearded hermit. Despite our expectation, the hermitage didn't really have accommodation except of a very limited kind; it was more of a mountain retreat and so the hermit took us down into Aubazine and introduced us to a local hotelier.

The Hotel St. Etienne at Aubazine was licensed as fourth class, and after ordering dinner, we were shown to rooms which were equally as austere as those we were used to. After freshening up, we returned downstairs to wait until our dinner was ready.

'Pity about the mountain retreat,' Jack remarked. 'I would like to have stayed in a hermitage. Arthur and his Knights of the Round Table – they were always staying in hermitages.'

'It seems that the accommodation for guests was mere proleptic eschatology,' said Gregory.

Jack looked mystified. Bob said to him, 'There you are, that must be a lightbulb moment. The fruits of a privileged fee-paying education mean longer and more difficult words.'

Gregory laughed. His education was by no means privileged but theology was full of long words, and Jack's state school education would set him up just fine unless that's what he wanted to study. He had just meant that the literature about the hermitage was being overly optimistic about what was offered in the end.

We were called into the dining room and were expecting, as it was by then well after nine o'clock, the same sort of simple fare that we would have received at a monastery if we'd arrived after the community meal was over. Some bread, some cheese, a platter of processed meat perhaps, and if we were lucky some hot soup. It didn't matter because by the time we sat down we were so hungry that even this would have been quite acceptable.

So we were pleased when a huge tureen of potage du ménage arrived and we helped each other to it with enthusiasm. This augured well but we shortly realised the meal had barely begun. It was followed by a heaped-up dish of coleslaw with spiced beet-root. Then tunny fish covered in an unimaginably delicious sauce with accompanying salad. In Gregory's view, even by that stage the hotel could add the words 'honorary first-class, with laurels'.

'Stupendous,' I said, letting out my belt as we waited for the next course. It truly was a slap-up meal.

'Yes,' said Bob. 'Make the most of this, young Jack. Macaroni cheese for you for the rest of the summer.'

We had barely had a chance to draw breath and sip from the local wine, when a great assiette of chicken appeared before us with all the vegetables rising in well-ordered ranks above the noble gravy.

'Ah,' sighed Bob, finally coming to a halt. He put aside his serviette and patted his stomach. 'The one downside from this trip has been all the institutional food we've been eating. It'll be very hard to make Barb envious of most of the meals we've had, though I don't count the picnics, some of which have been magnificent. But now I've got at least three fantastically good dinners that I can describe in detail.'

'You don't think describing a meal like this to her might make her a bit cross that she missed out?' said Gregory.

'Oh no, quite the opposite. Because of her condition she has a very restricted menu and she gets so bored with it. She specifically told me to come back and describe my gourmet adventures.'

'What's the third meal?' I asked. 'This would be one and Manuel's would have to be another.' The only other one I could think of was the picnic up on the high Pyrenees.

'The night we delivered the package for the lady Jack met in the church. That meal.'

'I thought it was just some vegetables and meat.'

'Well it started with soup and bread cut off fresh baguettes while Jack told his tale as to how he met the woman. And then there was the aubergines and the beans in tomato sauce but by then other relatives and friends had come in to hear the news and Jack had to keep going through it all again.' The chaos of tables being added to tables, chairs coming from everywhere, plates and cutlery, and at the calm centre of it all was Jack lit by the westering sun as he recounted the story and everyone else scrambled to make a tableau around him like the Last Supper. 'The auntie brought a dish of fresh sardines with herbs and oil, and the cousin brought the meat and the niece the salad. All home-cooked, simple food but it was like a fiesta, everyone talking and eating and exclaiming. And then Grandma brought one of those upside-down apple tarts. And so on and so forth until the house was full. And I was full. And then when we realised the time, they all walked with us up to the monastery gates, practically the whole village. I love events like that, they're somehow as memorable as the food.'

'So what was in the package? I don't think I ever heard you tell.'

'Well it wasn't anything important,' said Jack. 'Just a family Bible and some other documents. But her sister had lost track of her. She'd had some mental health problems because of events which happened during the war. And now, it seemed, also physical problems. When she said she was going to go and get the things for me to take to her sister, I asked where she lived and she said at the hotel. When she came back I asked her if she meant the hospital and she said yes, she was getting treatment, she didn't say for what. I saw she was wearing some sort of plastic bracelet with her name on it, so I was able to tell them the name she was going by. Her sister was overjoyed to find out where she was but also worried that she'd send these things, it didn't bode well. An end of days feel to it. She was going up there on the train the next day to locate her.'

It was a blessed thing, Gregory mused, that this woman should find them in the church conducting a service in English and in the process be herself found by her family.

On this philosophical note, having tried and rather splendidly failed to finish the ice cream, we went to bed.

Fourteen

WE'D BEEN INVITED THE NEXT day to go up to the hermitage for a Mass according to the Eastern rite and to stay for breakfast. I very much wanted to go but worried about my ability to get up such a steep hill. 'I'll push you,' said Jack.

I wasn't sure how that would work but anyway we set off. When we got to the steep bits, we found the best way to manage it was for me to lean back slightly while Jack leaned forward behind me, arms outstretched with his hands in the small of my back.

'This is how we push Jenny into the horse float when she's scheduled to go and see Brian.'

Jenny being? Oh yes of course, the Barkers' prize pig. And Brian being her paramour.

'Mr Barker thinks she's trying to appear blushing and modest, but we've been doing it for some years and it doesn't appear she is getting any less modest. Mrs Barker finds the whole thing hilarious.'

Yes we could all see how it might appear funny. But I didn't mind so long as I got up to the hermitage. And with the other two helping, this was finally achieved.

The building that the hermit lived in, high up the slope, was accessed by a steep winding footpath from behind the main square or a slightly less steep 'vehicle' track which they had tried the previous night and which in Bob's view could probably only be accessed by tractor.

The building took in magnificent views of the surrounding mountains. The hermit had built a good deal of it himself, with rough-cut stone up to the first floor and the second storey of wood. It made a very pleasant mountain retreat in summer but what it was like in winter I couldn't imagine. I thought it would probably be completely cut off.

Next to it was a tiny chapel built in a small clearing, like a small folly in a fairy dell. Very Orthodox in feeling; no sculptures but various icons, some of which were home-made.

We were surprised to discover over a dozen other people crammed into the tiny space – a couple of whom we recognised as fellow guests at the hotel. Clearly the service attracted a certain following.

Afterwards we got a little tour of the hermitage and were invited to sit at a long hand-planed plank trestle table while the hermit cut slices of bread from a huge round loaf, to which chewy cherry conserve made a good accompaniment. We drank dried nettle tea out of home-made earthenware mugs while the hermit gave us, in answer to our questions, some idea of his way of life.

We could see he was not an unsophisticated believer – witnessed by his extensive library. He was also by no means a recluse, though he found his vocation in solitude. Two others 'shared' the solitude, though they normally met socially only once a day, at the midday meal. The other two had their own dwellings elsewhere.

As we were preparing to leave and walk back down to the car, a thin shy creature appeared almost from nowhere. It was another hermit – an English monk with a calling for the life. I assumed he was probably middle-aged but he kept his eyes and face averted, so it was hard to be sure. He spoke softly and slowly and held on to a young birch tree as if he was afraid his instincts would make him turn and run away. He clearly wanted to be friendly but at the same time it was also clearly an effort. I also in the past had suffered in my quest to overcome my own shyness so appreciated the lacerating effect on the man of such an invasion of privacy, especially by four people speaking a language which he had obviously not used for many years.

Fortunately we were already running late and the poor man's ordeal was soon over.

The hermit very kindly lent me a stout stick and so I was able to get down the path without too much damage to my wounded leg.

As we drove on, we spoke much of 'vocations' and what it meant to other people if one was called to live the life of solitude.

'I always thought to be a hermit, you had to live alone,' said Bob. 'I've never heard of a group of hermits. It sounds like a non sequitur.'

'I wonder how you get to be one?' said Jack. 'I'm all for it.'

'You want to be a hermit?' I said in surprise.

'What could be nicer! Your own little house. I presume the food comes from somewhere. Nothing to do all day. If you advertised it you'd probably get thousands of takers.'

'And a lot of them would be very weird,' said Gregory. 'The retreats we run always have a sprinkling of mad people.'

Bob then recalled Jack's religious instruction teacher who went mad. 'How did that manifest itself?'

'Well not at school,' said Jack. 'It was during the holidays. He took off his clothes and sat on the roof. That's a bit of an indication I think.'

'Well I'm glad you weren't there,' I said. 'Madness can be distressing.'

'Danny Woodhouse who's in my class went mad at school. He was in the common room and he got stressed about something, apparently he has anxiety attacks. And he started walking round and round this central table, saying the same thing over and over, I can't remember what it was now. And all the teachers seemed frozen, saying stupid things like, 'Stop that now,' when you could see that he couldn't. So Tony and I just came up on either side of him and took an arm each and walked round the table with him, trying to slow him down. Then his mother came and gave him a sedative and spoke very soothingly to him and we helped her to get him out to her car. A couple of days later he was back at school, right as rain.'

Gregory exclaimed that he wouldn't have had a clue what to do, and I hoped that Jack hadn't been upset by the experience, while Bob wanted to know how the boy had fared afterwards.

Jack seemed to view it all very casually. He said that Danny had thanked them later but suggested that in future it might be good if, when they grabbed him, they pretended they were practising some dance routine, so it would all look a bit more with-it than it actually was.

Bob said cautiously, 'So was he aware what was going on?'

He was but was powerless to stop it, as if he could see from the outside how it looked but he had no control at all, and in fact his relentless movements around the table felt as if they were being directed from the outside, like a robot being programmed. 'He talked about it quite openly, which was interesting as mainly madness seems to be some horrible dark secret that you hide away.'

'And he's recovered?'

'Yes, same old Danny. He's very bright, maybe it's brought on by him being too hard on himself, he wants top marks every time. At least there's no chance of *me* going mad like that!'

At Bourges we went round the cathedral, which was airy and had brilliant glass; the pillars were beautiful and functional and devoid of curliwurlies and whigmaleeries according to Bob, who liked his architecture plain. And with that fairly brief visit we had to be satisfied as we were now really running late – partly due to the long talk with the hermit, partly due to the twists and turns of the second-class roads north of Tulle.

We had a fast run in the late afternoon to Sully, but we were still just too late for the community meal at the monastery at St Benoit-sur-Loire. I was disappointed, I loved the community meals in these monasteries, the few that we had managed to get to – I loved eating in silence while being read to, even if I didn't understand most of the reading.

Bob thought there was a commercial opportunity right there! Find some big square stone building, get in large quantities of Spam, have someone with a sonorous voice read something pious and uplifting and the punters would come in droves. 'We'll call it Abbey Mortadella and charge them bucketloads for a seat at the table. I bet it would make millions, probably even enough to keep the place in repair.'

Yes, we wondered, who paid for these huge ancient places? Who banished the damp, who drilled electric wires into the ancient walls, who piped water and brought the twentieth century into a fifth-century building? Because the monks weren't brought up in hovels and would probably not thrive spiritually or in any other way if asked to revert to 640 AD.

We put our overnight things in the small guestrooms. Enclosed in stone, I thought. I wasn't worried about the meal situation, the weight of history in the place made hunger bearable. But not for Gregory who had gone off and found, as he seemed to find in every place we stopped at, some acquaintance or friend of a friend, and he returned to say he'd got us fixed up with a good plain late meal.

There was even yoghurt on the menu, which the rest of us realised was Gregory's weakness – a weakness he had indulged at every breakfast in Salamanca.

'You can't get yoghurt at home?' I queried.

No, he was guarded from temptation by the catering gentlemen at his monastery.

'It's funny having a weakness for something that's healthy,' said Bob. 'My weaknesses are all for things which are definitely unhealthy.'

'I'm not sure our catering people think of it as healthy,' said Gregory. 'It's foreign. So by its very nature it must be suspect.'

'You can make it yourself, you know,' said Bob. 'In fact, I think we've got the thermos equipment for it somewhere lying around at home. You can have it if you like. Barb has to eat low-fat so we're not using it now, yoghurt made out of skim milk tastes like very bland junket.' He sighed. 'You don't realise how nice fatty and salty foods are until you're not allowed to eat them anymore.'

Gregory was much struck by the thought of being able to make it on his own and said he would check out the possibility when he got back. But was Bob sure he wouldn't need it in the future, to make yoghurt for himself for instance?

No, said Bob, he'd never eat anything at home that Barb couldn't eat, 'It's one for all and all for one with us.'

We attended Vigil and I was distracted by wondering about the communal life and whether Gregory making yoghurt for himself was a good idea in that context. Maybe, I thought, it might be better to introduce all of Gregory's fellow monks to yoghurt as a choice so that Gregory could with a clear conscience eat something he enjoyed.

When we retired for the night, I was exhausted as usual. Long days travelling would, at the start of the trip, have sent me straight to sleep in whatever was provided in the way of a bed. But although I had joined in with the conversations in the car, although I had visited sites of interest with my fellow travellers, I had been weighed down all day, a stone of worry as dense as the ones that surrounded me now.

I couldn't stop myself lying there and going through everything again. It was now four years since the bicycle incident and things had not been getting better. Gradually over those four years I had realised there was more at stake than just somehow keeping my family out of the limelight, avoiding the possibility of being a spectacle in the parish.

I remember suddenly the day Joan had come barging into my study a month or so previously and launched into an attack on Jack's friend Tony. 'The whole neighbourhood is laughing at Sally.'

When she had calmed down, she explained the situation as some sort of art project that Tony had done. He had called it *Malice through the Looking Glass* and it supposedly showed Sally in Jack's bedroom scratching a record.

'Scratching it deliberately?' I asked.

'Everyone in the district is talking about it,' she complained.

'Scratching it deliberately?' I said again. 'Is that what they're saying?'

'Are you listening?' Joan asked angrily.

'Are *you* listening?' I responded, getting angry in my turn.

The story I had been told about the Christmas incident … I didn't want to think about the Christmas incident. But the story had been that Pete and Sally had been fighting as usual and that Jack's record, which had been a present from Pete, became collateral damage, was accidentally dropped and as a result got scratched. That was the story Joan told me. It wasn't Sally's fault, she just wanted to play the record and the boys would never share their things with her. After the accident, Pete had stormed into Sally's room and destroyed the present he'd just given her. So somehow, in the telling, Sally became the victim.

It now appeared that the story in the neighbourhood was that Sally had deliberately scratched the record to enrage Pete and he had reacted in kind. When I then turned to Jack for an explanation one way or the other, Jack just shrugged his shoulders. What did it matter. He didn't mind about the record, he minded that Pete had gone.

But to settle things in my own mind, I had gone with Jack to the opening of the exhibition where the artwork was displayed. It had been selected to be hung in a gallery in York as a representative of the best art submitted from the local schools in the district and when I looked around, I thought that Tony's work (in comparison to the others) showed real talent.

A new art teacher had arrived at their school at the beginning of the last school year. As well as teaching painting and drawing, this teacher had introduced the older pupils to photography and had managed to get the funds for quite a sophisticated darkroom.

Tony's work consisted of a triptych of three large black-and-white photos overlain with a collage of actual objects. It showed scenes in the mirror of a bedroom. On the bed in the reflection lay a record cover collaged in bright shiny cardboard and on the floor lay shards of a record. Scattered around the corners of the room were other broken and torn items. Each of the photos was from a negative which had been scratched, the lines jaggedly scarring the image.

But as for the story which was circulating, it seemed to me that there was nothing in the art, not even the title of the piece, that gave credence to the neighbourhood's interpretation as reported by Joan. There was nothing in it about Sally at all. But it still grieved me that this had become common gossip in the district. If it did refer to the incident, then maybe there *was* some other undercurrent to the story I hadn't been told, embodied by the tensions of moody desolation in the work.

There in my stone cell, with its austere geometry and chisel-cut scars, I fell asleep. And the last thing I thought of before I drifted off was of Jack in the gallery in animated conversation with his friend Tony. However despondent the work, Jack himself appeared unaffected.

Fifteen

The next day we were up in good time for Mass in the crypt, at an altar behind which stood a reliquary containing the bones of St Benedict, which had been pinched from another monastery. I wasn't quite sure how I felt about this; I supposed I couldn't call it thievery, this reallocation of possession. What was very relevant was the intense fellowship of that Mass and if the presence of St Benedict facilitated this, all the better.

Before setting off for home, we were shown over the abbey and had agreeable discussions with the Prior and a couple of the monks, with Jack translating. The story of the monastery was much like all the others we visited, the clash and jingle of armies, the march and retreat of orthodoxy and new ideas, the greed of monarchs and carpetbaggers. Stone was put on stone, levered off stone, taken away, brought back, built again, sacked again, as history marched on through.

In its latest re-creation, the monastery was making leadlight windows for sale throughout Europe and confectionery, for sale locally, of which we were given a sample to try. In view of the conversation we'd had the previous day, I didn't think either of these pursuits would come even close to meeting the everyday costs of running such a huge establishment. I could only imagine that the two things which couldn't be ransacked – from mediaeval France to the present – were the land and the faith. And so, with money from the faithful, the monasteries kept rising phoenix-like from the ruins.

Driving north, we called in at Chartres and had a look round the cathedral. We thought Bourges was better although Chartres was very impressive in a way meant to impress (i.e. by a kind of heaviness). In any event, there was a general feeling among us all that we'd had enough of mediaeval monuments. Bob even made the scandalous suggestion that maybe the experience would be improved if all the cathedrals had little cafés where you could lie back and look roofwards in comfortable chairs, thus avoiding campanile crick. After all, if you could break bread and drink wine at Communion, then why couldn't you drink coffee with Christ, and what was wrong with a nice brioche instead of a tasteless wafer?

Jack and I left the others, who went off to stock up for the last time with bread and cheese and fruit (and yoghurt), so that I could ring Don again. I was pleasantly surprised when Naomi, my niece, answered the phone. She was a bubbly twenty-one-year-old studying singing at a conservatorium. She immediately told me that there was no reason for us to stop there and to ring and let her know once we were home, and she would drive Sally up.

I was immensely relieved. I couldn't thank her enough and invited her to come and stay for a while, to which she happily agreed. Sally was currently out shopping with Don but 'We're all getting on fine,' she assured me. 'Sally's been a bit subdued, I don't think she's had a very good time and I don't think the French police treated her very well, or the local cops for that matter. And I know Auntie Joan has been under strain with this diploma she's doing – she's only rung once, and Sally was in tears after a few minutes and wouldn't talk to her. Dad told her not to ring again – I think she and Dad have fallen out. But I'm sure Sally will get through it. That's what growing up is all about.'

I fervently hoped that was the case.

We had a picnic lunch in a deserted grove of apple trees some-where in Normandy. I wondered if I had been there before, it felt vaguely familiar but then it had been over twenty-five years since the war.

As I stood holding the kettle I felt a flashback of memory again, walking forward buoyed by faith and the poor man I saw quaking beside the road. I suddenly thought, maybe he wasn't quaking with fear, maybe he was actually physically ill, left behind not through cowardice but through infirmity. I'd just assumed, with my newfound valour papering over the cracks of my own terror, that this man was in need of my own spiritual solvency. Maybe what he was really in need of was a medic. I hadn't asked, I had just assumed. In the flush of superiority perhaps?

But in the end did it matter? Whatever was the reality for that man, I had felt something great in that moment and that feeling had translated into a desire to be of service to my fellow soldiers.

Now, I wondered aloud whether I had come full circle. From the dark days that had inspired me to take up the ministry to the current trip, which had made me think maybe it was time to step aside. Gregory thought it was a lifetime's commitment, but I thought that the faith could last a lifetime but there was temptation for the actual work of the ministry to turn into just another job, that wonderful seed of commitment deadened by the day-to-day need to pay the bills. We discussed, with some amusement, a recent 'scandal' in the district when a priest and a nun, drawn together for ecumenical purposes, suddenly decided that they wanted to stay together and instead of the horrible consequences for Eloise and Abelard, they merrily threw off their habits and got married. No dark romance, just a sunny change of purpose. Yes, everything changes, we all agreed.

Driving on, we had a hellish route through Rouen and a final brew-up of tea somewhere in a lay-by on the road to Le Havre. Gregory and Jack had been discussing the choice of A-level subjects in small schools. Gregory said it was a balancing act, what was offered, sometimes teetering on the edge of disaster when a teacher went sick. Finding a replacement when you were miles from anywhere was horrendous.

Jack had reverted again to his astounding discovery that universities taught all sorts of subjects which were not offered and not even heard of at his school. 'Philosophy, for instance. How could I put down to study that when I don't know what it is!'

Surely he must have done something about the Roman philosophers in O-level Latin, suggested Gregory.

No, according to Jack all they had to do was to get Caesar across the Rubicon with the words in the right order and the verb in the right tense. No discussion ever eventuated as to why he was crossing the Rubicon.

'What about religious studies?' asked Bob. 'Nothing philosophical there?'

Only the possibility of proving God existed.

'Ah well,' said Bob. 'I think I know a thing or two about philosophy. Listen and learn, it goes like this. Unknown forces exist. God is an unknown force. Therefore God exists.'

'How does that work?'

'In the same way as the proposition: All crows are black. That bird,' he said pointing to a blackbird in a hedge, 'is black. Therefore that bird is a crow.'

'That's ridiculous,' said Jack.

Da-dum. There you are. All you need to know about philosophy.

Gregory suggested that maybe Jack was already following his interests in the subjects he had chosen.

Jack said he didn't really know if these *were* his interests, because he had chosen his subjects from a narrow range of possibilities. And even that had been difficult, as the German teacher left after O levels. Antoine lived not far from the Swiss border and when he went to school there he was learning German taught in French! He got a good mark for it at O level and as a result he was being allowed to continue because his French mistress had agreed to facilitate. Antoine and his German cousins were also sending him material. He didn't know how he'd go because he was hardly likely to sail through maths and needed to work a bit harder on that.

'What was the plan behind choosing maths and music as well as languages?'

Jack said they seemed to all go together, different sorts of languages. Equations and musical notations. Anyone from any background who'd studied maths and music could generally read what somebody else had written, whatever language they spoke.

'But what about European history,' queried Bob. 'Don't you think that's a useful accompaniment to languages? After all the wars that have been fought between people with different languages intent on killing an enemy that they can't really understand. What do they say about history? That those people who don't learn lessons from it, keep on repeating the same mistakes.'

Gregory said he didn't really believe that. One thing he did believe was the saying by Heraclitus that you can't enter the same river twice. The mistakes people made in the past were in relation to situations which can't be reproduced. You can't make the same mistake twice, because everything has moved on and everything is different. Every mistake you make is unique.

We all thought this was an interesting proposition and it led to much discussion until we got to the outskirts of Le Havre, after which a tense hour's driving ensued, through the darkness and the ever-decreasing arcs and squares, until we eventually found the car ferry.

We were all exhausted and somewhat subdued. We had a compline-a-trois in the deserted lounge – the ship was only half full – before retiring to our couchettes.

Sixteen

DESPITE MY RELIEF AFTER TALKING to Naomi, I didn't sleep well. I kept waking up and going over and over, round and round things. I thought again about the incident with the bicycle, it kept gnawing away at me like a dog with a bone, crunching the fabric apart.

When I had returned from delivering the new bike to the Barkers' farm, I was met by a cold and reproachful wife and a resentful daughter. For once, I had not given ground or even agreed to discuss my actions, apart from stating what I thought of as the obvious, that you don't give a girl's bike to an adolescent boy. My wife's constant carping and my daughter's constant whingeing were just a new background noise which I firmly blotted out. How stupid. I should've said than what needed to be said, laid down rules and this time taken a more pro-active role in child rearing. Instead, my refusal to talk about it further incensed my wife and the gap between the two of us seemed to widen.

Plus all of the incendiary material was still present. Pete mutinous and increasingly hostile with Joan but solicitous of Jack, Sally beady-eyed and lump-jawed with jealousy, and Jack quietly withdrawing from the conflict.

For some reason when Pete went off to university, things shifted again. I thought everything would be easier because the arguments between Pete and Sally were the main focus of all the acrimony.

However, things didn't get better although they were different. Jack worked Saturdays at the printing works and usually spent most of Sunday working for Tony's father around the farm, all to raise money for his trips to France.

This became another bone of contention. Sally, when she was home from school, now constantly complained that she was bored. Joan said that she was lonely and told Jack she wanted him to stay home more at the weekend, but Jack was now of an age when making him fit in with his mother's wishes was not an option. He just quietly ignored her.

And as for me, well, my response to Joan's demand was bemusement. 'Why would you expect him to do that?' I asked. 'Sally behaves so badly towards him I don't blame him for putting as much space as possible between them. Even if she was the perfect little sister, Jack's nearly four years older, so of course he's not going to hang around with her.'

Bemused. Was that the opposite of amused? I didn't know where Joan was coming from anymore, we had somehow lost touch with each other. And as for Sally, I knew she needed to find friends of her own in the district, but this was more difficult with her being away at school. The girls at her school were mostly other boarders and some didn't live in the district, plus she never talked about any of them with any particularity. Perhaps Jack was right, and she didn't know how to make friends.

I needed to get help. I should have done it years ago. Whatever Joan said, the first thing I would do when I got home was ring our local doctor and find out how to go about it. Joan's constant rejoinder that Sally was normal and would grow out of it, no, that was rubbish.

———

None of the others slept particularly well either. The end of a holiday is always like this, we agreed the next morning. A bit grey, a bit dusty, a bit wishing we were home already.

The advertisements from the shipping company had said that we could get off at 7 a.m. but, as with the trip over, it was clear that the boat crew were eager to disgorge us all as early as possible. In this case, unlike the trip over, there was no need to even think of breakfast, as we would call again at Bob's sister and brother-in-law's in Gosport. I hoped they would be up, but Bob said with two young children there was no likelihood of it being a problem.

We rolled up to the neat semi-detached before seven and Bob was right; before we'd even got out of the car the front door was thrown open and the family spilled out in welcome.

Before long we were crammed round the dining table having an excellent breakfast of scrambled egg, bacon, fried tomatoes and, my favourite, fried bread. Toast and home-made marmalade. Percolated coffee in a proper cup.

'First eggs in over a fortnight,' Bob said appreciatively.

After breakfast, Bob distributed small, rather garish presents to his nieces, the theme of all of them being bullfights. Before long Jack was out on the back lawn with the cover from the sofa swing, pretending to be a matador while the young girls, their fingers pointing out of their foreheads as horns, charged the impromptu cape and shrieked with laughter.

The rest of us sat in the dining room looking out. 'How has it been?' asked Bob's sister Sue. 'Taking a teenage boy with you on your big manly pilgrimage?'

Bob answered immediately with a laugh. He couldn't imagine it would have turned out anything like as good without Jack along. Not only was Jack a magnet for females of all ages wherever he went, but his fluent French and his ability to speak some Spanish had opened up possibilities which would never have been there otherwise. He had spent an evening with a French family. He had met a Spanish family and had had a wonderful evening meal with them.

Gregory agreed. He had listened to a most wonderful dingdong argument or discussion between two nuns, one American and the other French Swiss, about the trials and benefits of either going out into the world to teach or bringing the world into the convent to school there. All of which was simultaneously translated by Jack, including the many amusing asides made by these nuns as they tussled with the problem. It was definitely the best exchange of the whole week and when he got back to his monastery he was going to write it up for the benefit of his community.

'I remember that discussion too,' I said. Sister Angela had been asked why she had become a nun. She replied that she wanted the dramatic value of the status. She'd said, 'If I was walking in the woods and was attacked and eaten by a bear, in my previous life I would have been Woman, 52, Eaten by Bear. Or, possibly, Middle-Aged Academic Eaten by Bear. Neither heading would create much commotion. On the other hand, Bear Eats Nun, well that's the jackpot, that's international, that shifts everything else off the front page.'

'Yes,' cried Gregory, 'and then she turned to me and said, sadly it doesn't work for monks.'

We all laughed but then Sue said, 'I suppose it's true. What was the last time a monk got in the media?'

'Quite,' said Bob. 'The nuns are out there saving the wretched of the earth. Plus they have that mystique, especially if they're handsome women like many nuns are, where they fill some sort of gender vacancy, is that the right expression? What I mean is, you listen to them without any other social overlay, and everything they say seems wise and irrefutable. Whereas it doesn't work for monks because why would you pay attention to what a monk said as supposed to any other man – men are always laying down the law.'

'So true,' said Sue, looking at her husband fondly. 'So there were some handsome nuns were there?'

Yes there were, we all agreed. In Bob's discussion group there had been a lovely Russian-born nun with thick dark hair gathered to one side who looked like an antique painting of the Madonna, serene and autumn-coloured, and would drop pearls of wisdom that felt like real pearls.

'And Sister Angela and Sister Carol were particular favourites of ours,' said Gregory. Handsome, energetic women with lots to say and a spirit of fun.

'So it sounds like you had a good time,' said Bob's brother-in-law. 'I'm glad. It sounded like a bit of a dry old outing when we saw you off.'

No, we all agreed, it hadn't been dry.

It hadn't been dry and it hadn't been dull, and it was borne in on me that the last-minute addition of Jack did not result in the friction I had worried might happen at the time. I now realised that my two companions hadn't wanted to be either scholarly or serious. Gregory needed to be refreshed from the stress of teaching and Bob need to be diverted from life-or-death problems far beyond any that I had to deal with. Clearly they had found the presence of Jack enjoyable, and also of immense value on many levels.

And that was also the case for me. I wasn't sure what I had expected from these two weeks, probably nothing more than relief from the increasing domestic strain and some agreeable companionship. Instead it turned into something else, a pilgrimage certainly, but one in which I had ended up questioning every facet of my life. If I changed direction, should I stay in the district? Probably, until Jack had finished A levels. And what then? Well, I had to think about Sally even if Pete and then eventually

Jack went to Australia. What would happen when Sally was old enough to leave school I didn't know. But I did know that there might be further huge disruptions in my life, just as I was getting to an age when others were slowing down and looking forward to retirement. I wasn't even sure, if I upgraded my qualifications in the law, whether that would be enough to get me employment. I might have to think about some new career entirely. Maybe I could look into the some of the possibilities that I had heard Sister Angela discussing with Jack. I was pretty sure I could do social work. After all, over twenty years in holy orders, it involved a lot of that sort of thing.

Meanwhile, Bob was saying, 'I've decided that whether we manage a child or not, from now on I'm going to save up the money every year so that we can go somewhere sunny and have a good laugh. No more bed-and-breakfast in Skegness or Blackpool, gazing out at the drizzle. No, every year we're going to go south to somewhere warm with crisp loaves of bread and ripe tomatoes and nice bottles of wine. Gathering together in the evening in fellowship and cheer. That's the plan for the future. I might even trade in the Viva and get a Dormobile.'

It was a good plan, we all agreed.

———

We extricated Jack from the little girls and continued on our long journey home. Jack, after his play with Bob's nieces, had become incensed about the so-called sport of bullfighting. He thought that if the bulls just got to run about a bit and have a good time, like the little girls, it would probably be quite a nice thing to watch. Rushing towards the cape, *whish*, missed him, what fun. But the fact that they tortured them by sticking darts in their necks and then eventually killed them made it one of the darkest of sports.

We discussed all sports involving animals. Sheepdog trials featured fairly high on our list of sports where animals appeared to be enjoying it. Dressage possibly, although Bob thought some of the horses looked like they might fall asleep through boredom. Horse racing on the flat would be okay, after all it was pretty much the same as people racing except for the whips. Some of the tricks that dolphins did at zoos seem to keep them merrily occupied. Plus they got fish.

I recounted our rather disastrous decision to get a dog, or rather get a sheltie instead of a common or garden mutt. Sally had got a hula hoop for Christmas and was determined to get the dog to jump through it like at the circus. Many a time I saw the dog with a great grin on its face and the hula hoop in its mouth, running away from my daughter who would end up down on the lawn having a tantrum. A doggy version of Comedy Playhouse.

Fortunately, or unfortunately, these gales of tears came to an end when the dog started getting in among the local sheep – which wasn't funny at all. Despite our best efforts there seemed no way of keeping it within the vicarage grounds and so a new home had to be found for it and to our relief, Sally accepted its departure.

———

We bowled up the motorways stopping only a couple of times for toilet breaks and to have lunch beside a river where we stretched our legs along its banks for a while – so much better than churches, we all agreed!

Onwards again, and Gregory did a mathematical calculation and estimated the length of the journey, or pilgrimage as he referred to it, as 2,800 miles.

I wondered about the concept of a pilgrimage, which in the

literature was the struggle in getting to a certain place in order to be blessed. 'Nobody talks about the journey back, as if it's an anti-climax.' Perhaps that would be the case if they just flew back like Sister Carol and Sister Angela but in my view, the struggle to get home was just as important as the rest of it. Think of all we would have missed!

'I certainly learnt a lot about the way religious people live,' said Jack. 'I had thought of the religious life as more like the hermit we visited, everyone in their cells just coming together for meals, not very social at all. Then Sister Carol told me about where she lived, which she said was more like a nun-collective, and she said that every month they go out as a group to the theatre and they take it in turns to choose. She usually chooses Shakespeare but Sister Angela always chooses musicals. Musicals. In New York! What luxury!'

Bob remembered something. Luxury in New York. 'Did I tell you about the brother of the old woman we met in Baton Rouge?'

No, as usual we'd got distracted and he never finished the story.

Bob and Barb arrived in New York at the end of their trip very weary and almost completely broke, not enough even for a hostel, and the only options open to them were to get back on the bus and mindlessly travel up and down until it was time for their plane to depart, or to go to the airport and spend two days lying around with their luggage. Before they did either, however, they thought they'd give the brother a ring. Who knows, they might get a free meal out of it, they thought, remembering the afternoon tea.

So Bob rang, using some of their few remaining coins, and got a very suave voice on the other end. Unfortunately Mr Campbell was away. What business was he wanting to have with him? So his heart sank but he answered that he'd met Mr Campbell's sister in Baton Rouge, who had asked him to ring when he and his wife got to New York. 'Ah yes,' said the voice. 'The Railway Children. We've been expecting you. I'll send a car to pick you up.'

So, said Bob. 'What is the swankiest apartment you can imagine? Imagine that then double it. No, triple it. And then imagine arriving in this glittering gold-encrusted Shangri-La with dirty backpacks full of grubby clothes. And then imagine a maid showing you into a bedroom as big as a normal house with a bath that's ten feet wide and taking your clothes away to be washed in a proper washing machine and bringing out silken Japanese robes for you to wrap yourself in. And then when you emerge, the butler is there to converse with you about the menu for that evening. Hoo hoo hoo! And all because I grew up on a station platform!'

The whole car sighed with satisfaction – what could be a more excellent end to a road trip than a deep hot bath, a splendid meal and New York, the glittering lights of New York, New York spread out before them? And just think, Sister Carol and Sister Angela lived there all the time, going to musicals, going to plays…

Sister Carol had also told Jack that, while she usually chose Shakespeare when it was her turn, in the previous winter the only Shakespeare on offer was *Coriolanus*, which was a bit too brutal, so instead she had plunged forward two hundred years and taken her household to see *She Stoops to Conquer* by Oliver Goldsmith, a play which Samuel Johnson said reintroduced hilarity to the London stage. They had all laughed themselves silly and felt all the better for it. There was something in such concentrated laughter which set them all up for the winter – while walking down the freezing grey streets of New York suddenly scenes from the play would come back to lighten the grey. She said that only humans had been created with the ability to laugh, and it was a gift no one should underestimate.

Yes laughter, I thought. We all need laughter. I definitely needed laughter.

Meanwhile Jack was saying that one of the nuns in the house originally trained as a chef and one reason they all fasted on Sunday was because otherwise they would get vastly overweight.

Gregory could barely contain himself at the enchanting prospect of becoming overweight feasting on good things. 'Should I feel this envious? I do try and fight against it, I try and persuade myself it's only food. But when I have to go into the city on business I go to Betty's Café afterwards and it feels so wonderfully sinful having something to eat that's actually delicious. I can taste the sugary depravity in my mouth all the way home.'

'There's a bit of money left in the kitty,' Bob said. 'We could stop in York if they're still open, and buy you some cakes to take back to the monastery with you.'

'No, no, no,' cried Gregory holding up his hand. 'No, that would be disastrous. I bought a big round of French cheese for them which is sweating nicely in the boot. Some will like it and some won't, but even those that don't will dab a bit on a piece of bread and thank me most heartily. But if I brought back cakes that had to be shared … It's much easier to divide what people don't particularly want than something which they all do want. Unchristian thoughts will seep in, Father Thomas got a bigger piece than me, I got the raspberry one when I really wanted the strawberry. Sharing in a community, in a family – I had six siblings, and it was a nightmare. Better by far to give up everything desirable, nothing but bread and butter and peace. But preferably nice bread and proper butter.'

'It was a bunfight in our family too,' Bob said. 'My mother had the solution though. When she finished her shift at the bakery, she would come in with the broken and burnt bits all in paper bags and you had to choose, without being able to see what was inside the bags. Luck of the draw. Then after that, you negotiated if you wanted what someone else had. You learnt that if you don't give ground and share your spoils when you're ahead, it comes back to bite you when you're not so lucky. It certainly honed my skills as a mediator!'

I had nothing to add to these tales of sibling rivalry. 'There were only two of us, my older sister and me. My father came back from France damaged, and like a lot of marriages it didn't survive, couldn't survive. My sister had a scar on her cheek which no one would talk about … I can't remember the two of us arguing about things, maybe we did, it all got forgotten because when she was killed in the Blitz I felt as if the sun had gone out.'

—·—

I'd had a forty-eight-hour pass to go and visit my sister and her family in Hull where her in-laws lived. I'd acquired, I can't remember how, a small bag of liquorice allsorts, an almost unimaginable treat during the war. As I struggled cross-country on the train, on many occasions I was tempted to break into the crackling paper bag in my breast pocket but I couldn't do it – I liked them too much and I was worried that if I took one I wouldn't be able to stop and then I would never be able to share them with my nephew and niece. I thought of their excitement seeing me. I thought of my pleasure in unfurling the paper bag lip and holding them out, I thought of them poised there making their choices and their gummy liquorice smiles after. So the bag stayed in my pocket and in the evening, after many stops and delays en route, I finally reached Hull where we were immediately disembarked into an air raid shelter as the sirens went. All night the bombs fell as I wrapped myself in my great coat and tried to sleep with my head on my overnight bag. In the morning, I set off through the burning streets towards where my sister lived. When I got there, from a distance I could see a lot of activity and then I saw that where her house had been there was now a hole in the terrace. No flames, no smoke, just nothing. A hole. Three houses taken out as neatly as anything. Of course I wasn't worried, she would have gone to the nearest bomb shelter with her children and their grandparents.

But she hadn't. Being heavily pregnant she had of late been electing to go down into the cellar to shelter. And that's where they'd all been …

As I sat there on the edge of the crater, I remembered the sweets and got them out and spent an age just staring at them – my brain unable to move forward, staring down at those bright spots of colour among the grey devastation. I've never been able to eat them since, or in fact any brightly coloured confectionery … So there it was, suddenly I was an only child when I very much didn't want to be. Suddenly I didn't have to share when I very much wanted to.

My mood of melancholy seemed to affect the others. As landmarks that we recognised gradually started appearing, and the homecoming bulk of York Minster could be seen massing on the horizon, gradually we started easing back into discussion of the here and now for the next few days.

'Back at work tomorrow,' said Bob. 'There'll be a pile on my desk … I bet no one's even looked at my files in the last two weeks.'

'Similarly,' I said, 'there'll be a tangle of admin waiting for me I'm sure. And a sermon to write.'

'The syllabus for next year will be out,' said Gregory. 'I'm worried I'm going to be getting 4B for English – they gave Mrs Pearson such a hard time in third form she may demand that I take them for O level, oh horror.'

Jack, we all agreed, had no worries at all in the world. Apart from how many blister plasters to put in his pack.

What we had chosen to call a pilgrimage was over. Two weeks of scenery, companionship, mirth and serious discussion, all the stories we had told, the stories *I* had told … Now I needed all my faith and resolution as I realised that the pilgrimage I'd been on had merely shaken me loose from my old supports and had done nothing to resolve the central issue which loomed like an almost insurmountable barrier to any way forward. Although the cavalcade, the pilgrimage, the caravan of souls went on, there was nothing smooth in the progress. Was this the experience of times gone by? Camels plunging, horses getting cranky or lame, pilgrims falling off and shouting, blaspheming, everything lurching and the whole purpose of the event losing meaning with everyone demoralised?

I envied Bob his stoicism as he adjusted to the possibility of a family and the likelihood of Barb's worsening health – his panacea of a trip south to the sun every year seemed a simple and wholesome outcome from the trip.

And Gregory too was taking away from the pilgrimage the necessity for some changes. He was returning to his community, already determined to exercise more but also to go somewhere every year, such as the pilgrimage we'd just been on, where people would tell stories and he'd laugh and laugh and in the process set himself up for the year ahead.

So both of my adult companions had taken from the pilgrimage the need for small but important adjustments to their lives. For myself, the more the pilgrimage went on, the greater the changes I foresaw in my own life. And yet all of these changes seemed somehow cosmetic and all of them were skirting the real issue.

———

We arrived outside the vicarage just as the church clock struck six. We were happy to be home and all very tired. Everyone helped carry stuff into the cool dark of the vicarage interior and I shook hands with my companions, and Jack and I stood on the drive waving the red Viva on its way.

When we went back inside, nothing appeared to have been disturbed since we left. As ordered, the milkman had delivered that morning, but in collecting the bottle from the back door I noticed no sign of any other bottles there or in the refrigerator, so unless the curate who had come to take the services was a person of incredible neatness and didn't eat or drink, it would appear he hadn't needed to stay. As a result, the house felt rather cold and unforgiving.

I knew that any house that had been left unused for a couple of weeks would probably feel the same, and yet its lack of welcome was depressing. Even the cat barely raised its head and went back to sleep. And the dark wood of the central staircase with its faint whiff of polish and the hard clacky tiles of the hallway felt somehow alien. As I sorted and put things away I was struck by the fact that after half a lifetime of working as a vicar, I owned virtually nothing.

While engaged in this I heard the cheerful ring of a bicycle bell and went through to find Tony outside. I was surprised to see him, as was Jack. The two boys both exclaimed at each other. Tony had gone down to Devon for the summer but that plan had crashed and burned in the same way as Jack's had. Except his had literally burned. A barn fire had got into the eaves of his relatives' old farmhouse and although the house had been saved, smoke damage meant that it was uninhabitable. Half his relatives were up the road staying with his mum and dad until repairs had been made.

'All is not lost,' said Jack. 'I'm hoping Antoine is going to come over and we're going youth hostelling. Do you want to be in on that?'

'Oh yeah,' said Tony, looking delighted at the thought of getting away. 'Where are you thinking of going?'

'No idea,' said Jack. 'Get a few maps and decide on the day I suppose.'

Tony turned to me. 'Mum sent me down, as she heard you would be back today and wanted to know if you would like any bread and butter and stuff.' He indicated the contents of a satchel he had across his shoulders.

The goodies were brought gratefully into the kitchen, and I made a pot of tea while they sat at the kitchen table and Jack told Tony of his exploits and Tony reciprocated, before they went out and Tony zoomed off home on his bike.

When Jack came back in I was reconnoitring the food situation. There was no shortage of eggs: a couple of dozen with a note from the neighbours, who had been looking after the chickens and cat, saying they couldn't use any more.

'Looks like it's going to be eggs again,' I said. 'How about baked beans on toast with a fried egg on top?' We both agreed this was haute cuisine of the sort the continent was not able to provide.

As we ate, I asked Jack as casually as I could how he felt about Sally's imminent arrival.

Jack's response surprised and depressed me. He didn't mind Sally on her own, and especially not if Naomi was going to stay. He said, 'If I'd been in France and she'd found us, it wouldn't have worried me. So long as Mum didn't turn up. Sally can be a bit of a pain but she would probably have been all right without Mum.'

I didn't know what to say. I had always thought that both Pete and Jack had a real problem with Sally's behaviour. And now it was revealed, as far as Jack was prepared to say anything, that the problem was actually Joan, his mother.

I could see how that might happen. Joan always believed Sally and took her part in the children's squabbles. It must've been demoralising for the two boys, year after year, to not be believed. No wonder Pete had got angrier and angrier and Jack had withdrawn.

But Joan's attitude had changed in the last few months. Maybe the defection of Pete had hit home to her: she'd lost a son. And Sally must have seen the change, the slipping of her position, the gradual disappearance of total parental support for everything she did, demonstrated by the criticisms which were now coming her way.

That was the result of Christmas. I tried not to think of it but here in the kitchen it all flooded back. It was then, out of nowhere it seemed, that things had come to a head.

Christmas. The festival of peace, the birth of the Saviour, everything that should be good in the world, the highlight of the Christian calendar. And a battleground on the domestic front.

Pete had not been coming home that often from university, as he now had a serious girlfriend. But he had come for Christmas and so we were all there, for Midnight Mass on Christmas Eve, Christmas breakfast together and the opening of the presents.

After breakfast I went off to prepare for the morning service. I had written a good sermon and the small rituals in the church always soothed me. It went well; it was well attended though not as well as the previous night. The midnight service was traditionally held in the very old church in my parish, originally eighth century with some additions, and a lovely place in spring and summer, popular for Mothering Sunday and Easter services when all the daffodils were out but fiendishly expensive to heat in winter, so it was only used occasionally. Nevertheless, its location and sheer antiquity pulled in the crowds for the midnight service and on this occasion, as everyone came out, an added bonus – it was snowing. Great big flakes falling slowly against the ancient fir trees and lit by the floodlights lining the path! It had people gasping as they streamed back up to the gate in the first hours of Christmas morning, while I stood in the porch farewelling people in my glittering white vestments embroidered in gold. It was so gorgeous, so chocolate box! Surely after such an auspicious start, this Christmas had to be all tinsel and gilt.

The morning service was not so spectacular but a great deal more comfortable. As I was bidding my congregation farewell and Christmas greetings after the service, I noticed to my surprise that none of my own family were there. Jack was pretty regular in accompanying me, even when his voice broke and he could no longer sing in the choir. I didn't think he was particularly religious, but he didn't seem to mind sitting there. That's what he'd once said: 'I don't mind it.' Which was heartening for a religious person to hear, that his son could put up with an hour-long service.

When I got home, having closed the church, it was nearly noon and to my surprise the house was still and silent. In some alarm, I went through to the kitchen and found my wife sitting at the kitchen table with her head in her hands, looking dolefully at a heap of vegetables. In the oven the roasting goose hissed and spat softly but there was no sign of any other preparations.

What happened? She didn't know, she'd been in the kitchen just putting the bird in the oven after stuffing it and she'd suddenly heard angry shouting, Sally screaming at the top of her lungs and the slamming of a door upstairs followed by muffled crying. When she'd got her hands clean and gone upstairs and tried to find out from Pete what was going on, he'd said some very nasty things to her and declared he was leaving and never coming back, and the next thing he was actually going down the stairs with his bag packed. And Sally had locked her door and when she tried to find out from Jack what had happened, he'd just shrugged and said, 'The usual', and then he'd gone off too.

I was shocked and upset but that was the only information

to be gleaned; my wife seemed sunk in an immobile depression. I went up to the boys' rooms to see if anything gave a clue. In Jack's room, the Christmas paper he'd unwrapped that morning was lying about on his bed, and also a brightly coloured LP cover that Pete had given him. The record itself was on the floor. His other presents were piled on his desk. In Pete's room, a few pieces of wrapping paper. And nothing else.

The door to Sally's room was shut and I could hear a snuffling within. I knocked and found the door was locked. 'Sally,' I called.

The only answer I got was a wail and to leave her alone, everyone was so mean et cetera.

After standing indecisively for a moment I went back down to the kitchen, but my wife was nowhere to be seen, so I put on an apron and started preparing the vegetables.

I put the carrots and parsnips and potatoes on to parboil. I shelled the peas and put them aside in a pan then took the goose out of the oven to drain some of the juices to make gravy with. I put the half-cooked vegetables into the pan and returned it to the oven. Once the pan juices had separated I made some gravy, carefully stirring in cornflour and a steady stream of liquid from the vegetables. All of this activity helped to balance me somehow.

I went into the dining room and cleared away all the breakfast detritus. I then got out the best placemats and cutlery, put out glasses, found some Christmassy table decorations and decanted a bottle of wine which I had been keeping for a special occasion. If it was just going to be the two of us, we might at least try and celebrate. Or at least *I* would. It was Christmas, Christ's birth, supposedly a time of hope and renewal. Although later I wondered if my dogged continuance of a past tradition wasn't just obfuscating the situation. Maybe we should all just have had a cheese sandwich and recognised the reality. But at the time, I was trying for a normality which didn't exist.

While the vegetables were roasting, I washed up and put everything away. I put in serving dishes and plates to warm, set the peas to boil, re-warmed the gravy and then went and put on the new sweater that my wife had bought me, carefully brushed my hair, and then banged the gong in a no-nonsense manner.

'Dinner time,' I said to empty air and went and put the vegetables into serving dishes and took them and the bird through to the dining table where I started to sharpen the bone-handled carving knife against the bone-handled sharpener, another soothing ritual. I then bent over the bird, carefully slicing it into portions, spooning the stuffing into a separate dish.

My wife came in, looked at what I was doing and then went out again. 'Oh well,' I thought to myself. But she came back with serving spoons and sat down next to me.

I served her some roast goose and stuffing and then myself.

'What about Sally?' Joan asked.

'She can come down if she wants some,' I said. I said it firmly, brooking no arguments. Those who wanted to celebrate Christ's birth with me came to the table or not at all.

Then I poured some wine into her glass and into my own. I sat down and sniffed it, hmmm, nice. Very nice. A bottle that Jack had bought back from France.

Joan lifted her glass and took a tentative sip. 'Oh yes,' she said. She started serving vegetables for us both and then to my surprise and relief Jack slipped in beside us at the table. I said nothing but just served him some goose and stuffing. 'This is a nice wine,' I said.

Jack smiled and said he was glad we liked it and so, with a certain degree of civility, we ate Christmas dinner together.

I hadn't made any provision for the Christmas pudding, so there was only one course. By the time we had washed up it was nearly three o'clock, and Jack said that Tony's family had invited us over for afternoon tea. Joan declined, saying she would wait until Sally came down, so Jack and I walked over to the farm, the cold turning our faces red as we walked through fields scattered with snow. I felt an extra level of cold, as if my chest was encased in ice. I tried several times to ask my son what had happened but when I opened my mouth my lungs refused to operate and nothing came out.

I still remember the warm welcome we received at the Barkers', the feeling of coming from the outside into a family gathered happily together and feeling a pang that my own was not like this.

Back in the present, I watched my son contentedly shovelling up beans with his fork. Despite the challenges of the past few years, he had an equanimity I wasn't even close to emulating. All I seemed to do was wallow in regrets.

I knew I should have done things differently at Christmas. I should have insisted on being allowed into Sally's bedroom to talk to her about what had happened. I should have overcome my stultifying weakness, somehow forced myself to question Jack at the time. I was wrong to have been focusing on the bricks and mortar of household tradition. What was a Christmas dinner with all the trimmings if no one eating it was happy? But that was the trouble with peacemaking; you never actually got to the heart of the problem. At the end of the war, all over Europe people were persuaded to lay down their arms, but no one persuaded them to stop hating each other.

The months after Christmas had passed with no communication from our eldest son, and Joan became much more sharp and critical than usual, not only with me but surprisingly also with Sally. I saw the shake of surprise around the bottom part of Sally's face when Joan launched into her, the sudden welling of shocked tears. But mostly there was a sort of peace. Sally at school, Joan in York during the week and coming home at weekends. Jack at home during the week but mainly absent at weekends. And no Pete.

My mind went forward again to when Sally had thrown down the record Jack gave her for her birthday and my fear of a future without either of my sons. But Joan had come in from the next room and seen it – she'd never been a direct witness before. I thought again of that tableau, us all standing there with the record lying broken in the hearth. For once, Joan wasn't looking at Sally, she was looking at Jack. And Jack moved through the hall and out the front door without looking back.

What did that feel like for Joan? Suddenly wondering if it was too late, that she'd lost both her sons. Yes, I now realised, Jack absented himself at the weekend whether Sally was there or not, when only Joan was at home. I hadn't thought of it before.

And for Sally, why this trip to France? You could explain it as something Jack had that she wanted, but this seemed too bizarre, too unhinged to be the true explanation. What did she think would happen? Maybe it hadn't anything to do with Joan or Jack, maybe it was to do with me. Maybe in trying to ameliorate what I saw as injustices to my two sons, I had given the impression of being against her, of not caring for her. It was, I realised, years since we'd walked arm in arm like we used to do, me telling stories about Edmund the cat (long dead and replaced). Years since there'd been hugs and kisses. Of course, those signs of affection tapered off, but still …

The bad behaviour Jack had alerted me to at her school, her constant entreaties not to be sent back there, and now the running away. Was it all aimed at me? Forcing me at last to act and do something?

Shells bursting around me again.

And then here was Jack's surprising admission.

I fiddled with the salt cellar, somewhat at a loss. 'I hope you didn't suppose that I …' I didn't know how to finish the sentence or what in fact I wanted to say. I had launched into a minefield and now didn't know how to retreat. It meant saying aloud the unsayable, that Joan and I were divided, the distance between us ever growing.

'Oh no, Dad, you've always been good,' Jack said, reaching out to pat my arm. 'But it's a pity she's driven Pete away. I do miss him.'

It didn't matter who the 'she' was. Yes, I missed him too.

'He's just written.' Jack took out a letter. I assumed he had got it off the large pile of correspondence lying on the hall floor, but saw that it was in a blank envelope with just 'Jack' written on it. 'Did he drop it in?' I asked in surprise.

'No. I told you, he's sending letters to me through Tony. He won't write here direct anymore. I didn't know before, but apparently Mum tried to get hold of his new address by going into the university and telling them a whole lot of lies. Pete gets so mad about things, he goes over the top. Anyway, you're included.'

He read it aloud. It was a cheery letter with an address in Inverness where Pete would be for a while. He was enjoying his summer surveying job. He sent his love to me and said he had been getting my letters which were appreciated. His plans for going to Australia were now firming, with one company having made him a job offer when he completed his degree. It would mean working at the back of beyond, hundreds of miles from the nearest town or city.

'It's not sounding that attractive,' said Jack. 'I've heard it's very hot in those places and full of killer snakes. I don't think I'll be rushing out there.'

I agreed, trying to hide, I hoped, my relief.

That night I sank to my knees by my bed, exhausted. I thanked God for our safe journey and I prayed for guidance. I longed, as I prayed, for that reassuring hand on my shoulder that I'd once felt, that feeling that God was walking beside me. But as I knelt there it didn't come. Perhaps I was seeking a generosity which only came once in a lifetime, and I was lucky to have received that benediction in Normandy. Now I must make my way forward as best I could, using my own judgement to skate craters and find my own path. It was a daunting and lonely feeling.

I climbed into bed and wondered whether to take up my writing pad. I felt like starting a letter to Sister Angela but then thought, while our trip was still fresh in my mind, maybe I should turn again to my diary which had sunk into desuetude after the first couple of nights, barely even a list of places and events. Also I needed to write down the stories we had told each other on our way to and from Salamanca – our own version of *The Canterbury Tales*. Plus my own emotional journey through a strange land.

I thought of the mountains and the sun shining on crocuses and the cool of thick monastery walls and the heat hitting as you walked out of churches and the balm of shady squares. I thought of drinking tea in the late evening surrounded by laughter and discussion. I thought of the intellectual exercise called forth by my discussion group, the people I met, the interesting topics of conversation. And the bird who visited in the high Pyrenees and the tingling feeling I got looking at it.

I thought of Sister Carol's examination of the concept of too much enjoyment. Had I enjoyed it too much myself? And if I had, what did that tell me about my current life? Yes, it was time to move out of this tiny village, find something larger to do in the world.

I was just going to turn out the light when the phone rang. I slipped back into my slippers and dressing gown and went down into the chilly hall where the phone was located. It was Joan.

'Ah, hello,' I said cautiously.

'You're back.'

Yes, we'd got back at six, I was just in bed and Jack was having a bath. 'Jack, our son,' I added.

'And what's Sally doing?'

'She's coming up tomorrow with Naomi, who's going to spend a few days here.'

'I thought you were supposed to go and pick her up.'

'No, that was just another of your completely impractical suggestions.'

I heard a slight chirrup of annoyance and then there was a pause during which she seemed to be waiting for me to explain. But I didn't feel there was anything to explain that hadn't been explained before. She said, 'Don won't speak to me.'

'No, I understand that you've stuffed up that relationship by blaming him for Sally's little escapade.'

She was still willing to fix the blame on him, clearly it was something he'd done. But I cut in. 'Sally's obviously been planning this for weeks. Starting with forging my signature to get a passport. If it was her that is. She's told the police it was you but that's obviously a lie. I can't believe you would do that, because for one thing, if they prosecuted you it would stuff your job prospects, I imagine.' I waited for a moment but there was silence on the phone, as if of shock. 'Then there's stealing money from you and stealing money from Don, yes another ten quid,' I added. 'Naomi is on top of it all though. It's all going to be paid back, there is no likelihood that anyone is going to be allowed to sweep it under the carpet.' This was an oblique statement of intent – I could have been more assertive but I didn't feel I needed to spell it out. I continued, 'And when she ran away, she didn't run to you, she didn't turn up at your university, did she! No, she was clearly intending to take off the moment my back was turned. You were supporting her in her previous bid to get to France, and she probably thought it would be okay with you but she knew that it wouldn't be okay with me. Poor Don had no blame in the matter whatsoever, he just got stuck with the mess.'

'I can't believe she'd do that. I just don't believe it.'

I wasn't quite sure which of the previous statements that referred to, but she didn't elaborate so I went on. 'I think she's beginning to realise she's got to grow up and learn to start acting differently or she won't make friends or live a happy life. That's Naomi's take on it anyway, she's been having long talks with her.'

'Why is she talking to Naomi? What's Naomi got to do with it?' Her complaints were now shrill on that score, turning Naomi from a concerned outsider into a troublemaker.

I said nothing because I felt there was nothing I could contribute. Naomi's take on what had been going on hadn't spared me either, but I wasn't going to shoot the messenger. The conversation seemed to be going nowhere. Instead I changed the topic. 'What are your plans?'

'I'll drive up Saturday evening. I have a major assignment which is due in, and I need to spend Saturday in the library.'

The next day was Friday, and Naomi had thought they would arrive early afternoon. That left a day and a half before Joan could be expected. I was slightly relieved at the delay; at the moment I could see no way out of a hysterical and possibly unpleasant reunion in which poor Naomi was going to get involved.

I changed the topic again to something that was less gratingly immediate. I asked her what she had thought about my plans to leave the ministry.

She responded, after a pause, that she hadn't been sure I was serious. But then she hadn't thought me serious back in 1944 when I first proposed going into it. The difference was that I wasn't young anymore and had dependent children. It was a big step, and she hoped I'd thought it through financially. She also hoped I would bear in mind that she didn't intend to give up teaching, in fact the whole point of the university course was that it would increase her chances of obtaining a more senior position. And as she knew of one that was coming up in the area in the next year, she didn't intend to leave York.

So, she would keep renting the flat? I only put the question because I was trying to think of ways of cutting back on our expenses in the coming year – this holiday had brought into focus the need for economies.

Instead of answering straight away, there was an odd pause as if she hadn't heard me; then she cleared her throat slightly as if judging whether to say something. Eventually she said, 'I'm going to buy a house.' When I didn't say anything she continued with more confidence. 'I've seen one I like, that I can afford, it will save paying rent.'

It came at me like the sudden unheralded arrival of a missile, a white plume out of a clear blue sky and the smack of earth. My teeth rattled from the blast. I said nothing because some part of my brain stopped working. She continued more and more assertively that it would be a good investment, that it wasn't far from the school, in good condition and so on but I wasn't listening. All I could think of was, that's why we had no money. Or rather that's why *I* had no money. She had been diverting all her extra cash for some other purpose. A purpose that we hadn't discussed and in which I'd had no say and presumably in which I would have no share.

Eventually there was silence from the other side of the phone as she waited for me to reply. I felt I was standing on a black battlefield, blind and helpless. I gathered myself to stay on top of my distress and not give way to a hot gush of anger. 'How nice that you have the money for that. While I've been having to borrow money off Jack. I'm glad to hear that you at least will be nicely set up, with a house you bought at the expense of the rest of us – even though I can't see how you will ever be able to manage a school and treat schoolchildren in a fair and equal way when you can't even manage that with your own family. I'm putting the phone down now. I'm too tired to hear any more about this.'

I had intended to answer as remotely as possible, to hold back from the dam wall as usual, but somehow as I started to talk it was no longer possible to leave unsaid the unsayable.

I climbed the stairs in a bitter frame of mind. Whatever our differences and the increasing strain in our relationship, I had always felt that we at least were joined in a common enterprise and that we would have each other's best interests at heart. I had trusted her, relied on her, and now I felt betrayed, completely betrayed.

As I got back into bed the phone went again, and I swung my legs back round reluctantly and sat there for a minute. If she was ringing to continue the conversation I had abruptly ended, I didn't know if I had the heart or the courage to speak to her again without this cup of bitterness spilling out further in a scalding volcano of recrimination and accusation. Presumably though, it wasn't all one-sided. I didn't know which of my failings she would blame our distance on, but I was just too tired at the moment to find out.

I heard Jack coming out of his room and clattering down the stairs. If it was Joan I would have to go down again, I couldn't use Jack to send messages.

But when I opened my door, I could hear Jack's chirpy voice talking in French. Antoine. Thank God. I left the door open and got back into bed. Eventually I heard Jack coming back up. 'When's he coming?' I called out.

Jack came to my door and looked in. 'Tomorrow. Probably mid-afternoon. He'll ring from King's Cross when he knows his train. He's all set, he'll even be wearing his walking boots! But I said Tony was coming so he should come here first so we can make some plans and leave the day after.'

So they were all coming the next day, meaning food to be cooked, beds to be made up, shopping to be done, extra milk from the milkman. Suddenly as we discussed this, I stopped with a feeling of unease and foreboding. 'This is going to be difficult, maybe,' I said. 'Sally's coming home in disgrace, I suppose you could call it that. And here you all will be, milling around in excitement, ready to set out and have a wonderful time. It could make it worse than it already is.'

Jack's response astounded me. 'Well if Naomi is with her, why can't they both come too, I mean youth hostelling. I don't know what it is that Sally wants, but if she went to all the effort to try and track me down in France, let her come walking until she gets sick of it.'

For a moment I was so astonished I didn't know what to say. 'But wouldn't that put a dampener on it for you?' I said eventually.

'No, not necessarily. Unless Mum got involved. I think Sally might give up after the first rainy day. But if Naomi came too I don't see why it would ruin it. They could both walk together. And anyway, Naomi's fun.'

Yes, Naomi was fun. She would break into snatches of operatic aria at a moment's notice. She had given one of her goals in life as delivering the Queen of the Night's 'Der Holle Rache' from the highest mountain she could manage. Yes, it was possible Sally might give up early, having achieved what she seemed to have wanted, being included in the activities of her older siblings, having a share of what they had. Or maybe she wouldn't, it was hard to know. 'I can come and pick them up, wherever they are, when they've had enough. Or when you've had enough of them. So long as it's not a Sunday. But I mean, they may not want to go.' I would ring them both in the morning and see what they thought of the idea.

That was settled. I was astonished and humbled by Jack's generosity in suggesting it, but now I thought about it, steering Sally out into the landscape away from her mother might be the circuit breaker. If she wanted to join in with what her brother was doing, then let her get blisters and carry a pack and sleep in damp dormitories smelling of sweat-curdled wool and packet-food farts.

I would be left behind and I was aware that that wouldn't be easy, worrying about whether it would work. I got out of bed and knelt on my prayer cushion and humbly prayed to God to watch over these young people and if it was at all possible to let them all have fun. After that, I knelt there for a while thinking of myself and of the things I needed to do the next day. It suddenly also struck me that I needed a sermon for Sunday. I wondered if I should move off my comfortable cushion and onto the hard floor in order to try communing with God about it, because I always felt that if I was going to ask God for a favour I should make myself suffer for it. But then I realised I didn't need to: I had the sermon right there based on Luke 5:39. I would deconstruct the saying 'you can't teach an old dog new tricks' and show conclusively how wrong that was. Whoever had come up with that adage had never seen an 80-year-old Yorkshire farmer looking speculatively at a field with a brand-new seed catalogue in one hand and a brand-new calculator in the other.

Or worse still, according to Bob, going into a lawyer's office with a calculator and a shiny share prospectus. Doing the calculations longhand with an ageing brain led naturally and properly to caution. But when you could lay your hands cheaply on a wonder tool, one that you could hold in your hand and carry around with you, well throw caution to the winds! Percentages were right there at your fingertips, profits appearing weirdly real because they were lit up and instant.

You can't teach a *dead* dog new tricks, I thought, but while there was still life, there was still the ability to learn and more importantly to make new and interesting mistakes – all of which I knew I was going to find out for myself in the next little while.

I got back into bed, took my notepad off the bedside table and started to map the whole thing out, chuckling to myself as I thought of a few examples my congregation would enjoy.

When I was done, I switched out the light and my last thought before I went to sleep was, I must send Sister Angela a copy.

4

The Cavalcade Goes On

Seventeen

I STOOD IN MY GARDEN shed, stricken. The days, which previously had been separate and come in formal procession, were now suddenly jumbled and clumped together. Friday had been a day I couldn't bear to think of, so shocked was I by events as the morning unfolded.

Then in the afternoon the young people arrived and I tried so very hard not to let my distress be visible. Had Jack noticed? I hoped not.

As for Sally ... I had meant to have a serious talk with her. About how terribly worried I'd been. A rebuke, and a stern admonition along the lines that there was only so much to go around in this world and she couldn't have everything she wanted and she couldn't do whatever she pleased, because everything has consequences as she had just found out. And so on and so forth and people would turn against her and she would have no friends.

But I didn't have that talk. Because my heart was no longer in it and the moment I saw her drawn, anxious face ... I wound her in a hug, holding her tightly to me and gave thanks for her safe return.

Today it was Saturday, and earlier that morning they had all packed into Naomi's car, the three boys at the back, laughing and elbowing each other, holding maps, excited. Sally was sitting at the front next to Naomi and as she looked at me, I could see the anxiety still in her eyes and I reached over and kissed her. I meant to say 'Be good', but instead said 'Have a good time.'

And they drove off, making as much noise as possible.

So now there was peace of a sort. The constant clatter of young and importunate voices, like thin echoes around the back of my head, had faded. But to some extent I was still with them in the car. I hoped against hope that Sally would be able to rise to some form of companionship with Naomi and the boys, that she would be able to find a way to fit in and that they would all come back hardy, suntanned, and happy. They were small things to pray for but however much I longed to do it, I found last night that even when on my knees nothing would turn my thoughts to God, I was so overwhelmed by my own shock and misery.

I turned my mind from that to focus on things that I could actually deal with. Why was I in the potting shed? Ah yes, I was on my way to my lettuces. I needed to protect those that had managed to survive the onslaught of slugs and snails while I was away.

My dislike of slugs and snails would usually be enough to kickstart me into activity. I had once given quite a contentious sermon on the subject. Yes, a sermon on snails. I should write to Sister Angela and tell her about it. It was funny how often in the last couple of days I had thought of writing to Sister Angela. I needed some wisdom, a wise woman in my life, because my own attempts at wisdom were snail-slimed and withered.

I thought about my grandmother, who knew what to do about snails, who had known what to do about pretty much everything. There was a great joke in the family after I, when probably around three years old, had misheard something she was saying to one of her cronies about the facts of women at war. I had heard it as fat women at war which had apparently delighted me and when I repeated it back she was equally delighted with it, yes that's what they were, fat women at war. Because she was determined that none of us should starve.

We had lived permanently with her after my father's mental health deteriorated. She had been called to the boarding house where my mother was lying battered and semi-conscious and my three-year-old sister was found hiding in the wardrobe clutching me to her in terror while blood from a hole in her cheek dripped on my head. That was the aftermath of war, the trauma …

I was just a baby, of course I didn't remember any of this. I had pieced it together later from what an aunt told me because it was never discussed at home. I never saw my father again, nor ever wanted to. I was quite happy with a household of women and the crowded landscape of my maternal extended family.

I remember my grandmother's large garden, which was crammed to the boundaries with produce. Every year in winter there were cartloads of muck from the surrounding farms to be dug in and raked flat, the beds laid out in lines. Then as the ground warmed in spring came the grand planting with myself and my sister roped in after school and sometimes even before school. Squatting over the rows, I remember my total concentration as the peas were counted off in lines like a regiment of soldiers and the fine dusting of carrots and celery and parsnips shaping up behind them. And then there were the potatoes, carefully spaced, rows and rows of them so that we would all always be fat. I still have her planting plan for 1925; I had it framed and hung there on the wall of the shed. There was something about its drive towards plenty, that struggle to grow and prosper, which always filled me with resolve. If I could only maintain the level of focus and dedication in that planting guide, life would be a honeyed Eden featuring basket-loads of produce, a never-ending cornucopia of crisp delicious vegetables and fruit.

An exploratory mutter, like a violin-string tuning, came from the doorway. Fancypants, my favourite Rhode Island Red, was standing there looking at me. 'You've been fed,' I told her severely. Well, she responded, with a shrewd change of key to a higher register, if that is so, why are you in the shed?

I threw a handful of corn out onto the grass and watched the rest of the flock gather up their feather bloomers and start running splay-legged towards the unexpected treat. The less fluffy feathers you have, I thought, the faster you can run. It seemed an obvious thing but then, these chickens were handsome and good layers and running was not a survival necessity.

I sat down on the mended chair beside my potting-up bench and looked at the old planting guide for potatoes.

I was seven years old, there was a warm spring wind and I was in the east side of the garden, over on the other side of the hen-house where a mixed gaggle of Rhode Island Reds and Sussex Greys were watching me help dig the furrows with murmurs of disappointment, come on lad, let us out, there'd be big fat worms in there. What were their names, Poopy, Poppy, Petunia and … or were they a later lot? Grandma had no sentimentality – if you don't lay then you're dinner, was her attitude.

On 15 May 1925, we planted one row of Arran Comrade, two rows of The Bishop, one row of Sutton Early Favourite, three rows of Come to Stay, two rows of Recorder, two rows of Roder-ick-Du, seven rows of King Edward and one row of Kerrs' Pink. On the west side of the garden on May 16 we planted one row of Divernon, two rows of Great Scot, one row of Railway, two rows of Canadian, three rows of British Queen and two rows of Catriona. Then nothing happened on May 17, was it a Sunday? It must've been a Sunday, nothing else would stop my grandmother.

Going to church for her was part of her indefatigable effort to stay fat, where you prayed for benign intervention, for the sun to shine, for the wind to blow soft from the south, for the rain to fall sweetly, for the nights to be warm and for frosts to depart. To get through to God and his bounty she wasn't fussed which church she went to; she believed in spreading her crop so that if one row failed through bad seed or insect ravages, there were always plenty more to come of a different sort. So she would be popping off to the Methodists, the Congregationalists, the Presbyterians – a promiscuousness which my mother disapproved of.

My mother had been training as a nurse when the war started, and after her short-lived attempt to revive her hasty and imprudent wartime marriage, she had worked as an assistant and apprentice to her great-uncle in his chemist shop. By the end of the twenties she was herself a qualified pharmacist. During the course of this scientific progress she had lost faith in those hedgerow simples beloved of her mother and so every Sunday me and my sister were dressed in our best clothes and taken to the Anglicans where we prayed for world peace and progress and political stability – I don't remember the vicar ever praying for potatoes.

These recollections were getting me nowhere. The calm and order of my grandmother's regime was from a day long past. I had thought once upon a time I could replicate it here but that too was from a day long past. I needed to get to my garden beds. Maybe I should give thanks for whatever lettuces survived my two-week absence. That was always the resilient position, wasn't it, thanking God for what you have. Or had. Because giving thanks was always in the past, a historic gratitude. Even if a tidal wave had swept it all away and left you with nothing, perhaps you should still give thanks for the blessings you once received.

For what you once had.

I needed to do something else. I got up and went back into the kitchen and started sieving flour into a bowl. Soon there was a soothing slap and turn of dough beneath my hands, there was a lively symphony on the radio and the worrisome buzz of my thoughts had calmed. I didn't hear Joan come in.

She was standing at the kitchen door looking at me. I stopped what I was doing and stood there, dough on my hands, flour all over my arms, saying nothing and looking back. I didn't know what I was looking at: twenty-five years we'd been married, and she'd become an amalgam of all our joint experiences over that time. Now, in light of my current knowledge, I looked at this once familiar woman willing her to be what I had always imagined her to be. But all the imagination in the world couldn't separate me from my current shocks – she was a stranger.

She went over and turned down the radio. 'Where's Sally?' There was no preamble, no questions about how I was or how my trip had gone; no, it was accusatory like a commanding officer requiring me to explain myself. 'I thought you said she was coming yesterday.'

So the first thing she had done, obviously, was go up to Sally's room before ever looking for me or acknowledging my presence. Once upon a time we would have celebrated each other's return, once upon a time we would have kissed each other with relief to be back together again. How long since that had happened? Years, I thought.

Now, the moment she spoke, the way she spoke … everything was resolved. I had been anxious, undecided, fearful, reluctant as usual to engage, but all that was over. This was not the woman who had once fluttered my heart and sent heat racing to all my extremities so I was almost overcome with longing. Nor was this the woman who had lately terrorised me with fears of what she might do, making me miserable. Now I knew the worst of it and I felt something like relief, as if I had been locked up or clogged, held to ransom by the requirements of my position.

'Been and gone,' I replied, going back to my kneading. 'She's gone youth hostelling with Jack and Antoine and Tony. Naomi's driving them.'

Was it too early to start worrying how they were going? But

I needed to concentrate. Joan was shrieking questions. What were their plans? Where had they gone?

I had no idea. I very carefully had no idea. 'If you don't want your mother turning up, don't tell me where you're going,' I'd said to Jack. Ignorance is indeed bliss, there are no lies to sprout even innocently among the cracks in the interrogation, no guilt. I knew nothing.

She changed tack. 'When will she be back?'

I had no idea of that either. But that wasn't intentional because how could anyone know. A day. A week. Two weeks. Who knows how long she would stick it out for.

Joan was shrieking again. Why hadn't she been told? She'd rung last night but no one had answered. Who was looking after her? How could I possibly let her go, she would go this minute and get her back.

During this harangue, I had finished kneading and put the dough back into the bowl. I covered the bowl with a tea towel and sat down at the table with my arms around it. It was a real breadmaking bowl, glazed earthenware, solid and functional. I suddenly thought, this may be the last bread I make in it, and felt a short pang of loss, one more thing I would be leaving.

'Jack organised the trip for Antoine's benefit who arrived yesterday. He didn't mind Sally coming, so long as you didn't get involved. When I put it to Sally, she immediately said she didn't want you turning up either. So they've gone who knows where with the proviso that although Naomi may ring from time to time and tell me how Sally is going, she doesn't ever tell me where they are. Until Sally has had enough, when I can drive out and take them both back to Naomi's car, wherever that is. So that's the arrangement.' I got up, turning my back to wash the flour off my hands, and when I looked round she was gone. Had she even been listening?

I got my kitchen scissors and the basket from where it hung beside the scullery door. I knew I was upset, I had known I would be upset, but I also knew it would be better if things went slowly, at a pace I could cope with.

Returning to the garden, I walked along the path we had made many years ago. The previous way to get to the vegetable garden had been out the front and through an ancient studded wooden door in the wall to the left. With help from the men in my group, I had made a more direct route from the back door (which previously only gave onto the garages and a dreary covered hedged-in area for dustbins and washing line). We had cut through the hedge and built steps and a path using the bricks from a derelict outhouse.

I smiled to myself at the memory. I would miss the easy companionship of that group of men and the sense of achievement when we managed to fix something in the community which needed fixing. As a man who was not particularly outgoing, it was hard to say goodbye to this ready-made source of sociability, so as I walked along the path I felt another small shard of grief.

I arrived at the lettuces. My battle with slugs and snails had been mainly successful. Before I left for the continent, I had surrounded my tender plants with a palisade of chemical weapons, knowing full well that the battalion of gastropods would throw themselves on my defences with kamikaze enthusiasm. Those at the front would give their lives so that those at the back could sail over the top and devour the greenery.

Often, while singing 'Onward Christian Soldiers Going as to War', rather than fighting the conventional devil I would visualise the enemy as a giant snail, with horns and a tail of slime. I was focusing now on this as the enemy, anything rather than visualising another enemy looming large.

Looking down, I saw that most of the lettuces were reasonably perky and there were enough larger leaves to make a picking.

Good. So, lettuce for tea with some young radishes, boil and slice some beetroots, grate a carrot. There was a bit of salad cream left and then there were the eggs of course – a herb omelette with salad. Plus my newly made bread. The kids, like locusts, had gone through everything else and what they couldn't eat had been packed up and taken. The pantry was down to its bare bones and so was my wallet.

I got my fork and started turning over the potato patch, six or seven medium ones slid into my basket, nice. There was no butter and the last of the margarine had disappeared into someone's rucksack. Still, a minted potato with or without any addition was quite acceptable.

Joan appeared out of the house, walking quickly down the path towards me, determination in every fibre of her body. It was a warm day and she was wearing a sprigged white blouse and dark green skirt and her greying hair was cut into a helmet – in a style which I thought was new. It suddenly struck me that her shoes also looked new, in fact she looked new all over, perhaps I hadn't noticed before.

'I've rung several hostels, none of them have got a reservation. I've told them to ring me if Sally turns up, the moment she turns up. I shall go and collect her as soon as I know where she is.'

I stared at her for a moment. What was this? She'd shown no interest in rushing to Sally's side when she was found, and even when she was brought back from France she'd been with Don several days without Joan going there to see her. So now, what was the tearing hurry now?

'I couldn't leave the course before, we were doing presentations … Now I need to see her, to talk to her about everything she's been doing.'

'Well she doesn't seem very keen on talking to you, after you made very clear what your priorities were.' I picked up the basket.

'Oh my giddy aunt!' I exclaimed. 'This has got something to do with what she told the police.'

Joan seemed to me like a firecracker about to go off and her heels clacked on the paving stones behind me as I walked back to the house.

'What did she tell the police?'

'Just to remind you, I was travelling back from Spain. With no money or opportunity to get here any sooner or to be there when she was interviewed. Unlike yourself who was here on the spot, even if you did have something better to do. Why don't you ask the police what she told them.' I put my basket down on a stool near the sink. 'That will save them the trouble of coming out here to try and find you again.' I was astonished at my own calm. 'I told them you wouldn't be here till this evening, late this evening I thought from what you'd said. But here you are' – I looked at the clock – 'barely afternoon. Full of surprises.'

The footsteps had stopped behind me but I continued on filling the sink with cold water and putting in the potatoes, carrots and beetroot to be washed.

She pulled out a chair and sat, her demeanour subtly altered. 'I had nothing to do with Sally getting a passport.'

'I know,' I said carefully, rubbing the soil off the vegetables. 'Naomi went with her when they interviewed her and got to the bottom of the matter of the passport. She had found a way to unlock your desk and there got the idea of forging my signature. I don't think they'll take it any further, I hope not anyway.'

'There was no reason for you to go raising it in the first place,' said Joan tightly.

'Yes I thought you'd think that.' My voice was caustic as I dried my hands. 'You'd rather she was still out there wandering around in France, thirteen years old with no money and not much of a grasp of the language. A runaway girl, they're ten a penny I suppose. But forging a passport, forging anything, now that's a crime, something the police have to deal with. So they gathered her up with admirable efficiency. I think she had a fairly unpleasant time once they found her but that's the reality of the world. She's been behaving badly for years and never had to face the consequences because you've always been there in the background, telling her there was someone else to blame. Her brothers. Or her father. Or her uncle.'

Joan looked nonplussed by the energy and aggression of my response and said nothing for a moment. 'So how is she now?'

'She's come back very subdued,' I said. Naomi had told me some of the trauma Sally had described to her. When they had finally got her to a police station in England and were wanting to interview her, her uncle had refused to come to the station and told them to contact 'the mother', and Sally had spent long hours in an empty cell while the police had tried without success to contact Joan. In the end they gave up and drove Sally to Don's house, telling her they would interview her when some responsible adult was willing to be in the room with her. Don had not been exactly overjoyed to see her, but his anger over the situation was directed firmly at his sister. He told Sally he definitely wasn't going to be entertaining her this time and went back to his marking, leaving her to her own devices.

Enter Naomi, a sympathetic older cousin but one not intending to abstain from judgement. I suspected that Naomi drilling into all Sally's bad deeds was even more traumatic than her experience with the police. But perhaps holding her actions up for examination one by one, the forgery, the stealing from her mother, her uncle, her classmates, yes her classmates too, would bring home to her the reality: you behave badly in the real world and there are consequences, including short sharp spells of lonely cell time, and if you don't lift your game, down the track even worse.

I was looking at my wife, we were both looking at each other now, strangers separating at the speed of light, the cosmos between us ever expanding. Joan had a strange expression on her face, something apprehensive in her manner. But I couldn't look any more; I was starting to feel sick in my stomach and to divert myself I got a cloth to scrub the breadmaking off the kitchen table. The kitchen table where so many of life's chores and pleasures had taken place.

'The reason I'm here now instead of later tonight,' she said, speaking the words crisply but I noticed with a slight crackle of nervousness, 'was because I couldn't contact you. You didn't answer the phone last night. And I tried again this morning and still no answer.'

'This morning I went into York to the archdeacon's. And last night we all went down to the Barkers for tea because the alternative was baked beans on toast. I had no money for anything else, look' – I took a coin out of my pocket – 'that's all I have, one shilling. I haven't been able to pay the monthly bill at the shop because you withdrew everything out of our account, and I couldn't buy food for the house elsewhere because you even took the overdraft. Why was that?'

She started tugging and turning at her rings. 'I have to pay for my share of the phone at the flat. You kept ringing reverse charges. It came to nearly forty pounds ...'

I stared at her for a long minute. Suddenly, the dam wall broke. 'What a paltry, piddling, mean-spirited thing to do. That was the housekeeping account, you cleaned out the entire housekeeping account and left me and our children to starve. In what way was the phone bill at your flat anything to do with the housekeeping here? And why was it so urgent that you did it without even discussing it with me? When you've already indicated you've got enough money to buy yourself a house!'

She jerked back in shock, I had never spoken to her like that before, ever. I had always kept the words walled up. Even after my fury at the bike incident, I had said mildly enough, 'Don't get Sally to choose presents for Jack, she's not old enough to understand it has to be something he wants, not something she wants.'

Joan meanwhile was calibrating the change in my attitude, the words no longer mild but sharp and critical, unfriendly. 'If you're going to be so nasty about it,' she said getting up, 'I shall leave.'

What should I say? 'Please do' and then possibly regret it? Should I add, 'And don't bother trying to get me to come and bail you out because I won't be doing that.'? I didn't say that either. The problem with the future … well you were never exactly sure what it was that you actually wanted. So I was back behind my wall.

Then the previous day came into focus and I was ready to break it down again, smash through and say things … But she had already gone.

<hr>

Friday morning had started in an ordinary sort of way. I woke about seven and had a bath. As I lay there, I could hear Jack playing the piano in the music room, a pleasant relaxing sound. It wasn't always thus. Sally, having failed to get away with destroying the instrument, then decided that she wanted Jack to teach her how to play it. Joan had supported her to start with until I had pointed out that Jack was only twelve, was still learning himself and was not qualified to teach any subject let alone music. Would she be happy with a twelve-year-old teaching Sally at primary school? When she conceded the point, I said that Sally should go to Mrs Blades in town who was a qualified music teacher and where Jack and all the other children in the district went to learn.

Sally had duly gone to Mrs Blades but only, I suspected, to promulgate an ongoing war as to practising rights on the piano which I then had to mediate. Surprisingly, during the course of this war, Sally actually became quite good. Sometimes in moments of truce she and Jack used to play duets together and I held my breath and hoped that maybe they could become friends. But as Jack had pointed out, Sally didn't know how to be friends. And the war would start again, with Jack usually withdrawing and practising on the church organ (to the greater glory of God) or on the piano in the church hall, an inferior, badly tuned instrument where he played (to quote Bill Wilson) honky-tonk and the devil's music.

After my bath, I dressed in a leisurely way and then rang Woking where Naomi and Sally, after their initial surprise, had immediately agreed to the youth-hostelling plan. After that I set out for town, leaving Jack in charge of preparing the sleeping arrangements for Naomi and Antoine. When I reached town, before going to the butcher or anywhere else, before ever getting out my cheque book thank God, I went to the bank to get cash. If Sally was going to go walking, I would need to buy her some things and get some money to give Naomi to cover their expenses. After our disastrous Lake District holiday I had arranged with the bank for a small overdraft of £30 on our joint account and this, with what was in the account, would be sufficient.

To my surprise and dismay there was nothing in the account. All the money which had been in there when I went on holiday had gone. There hadn't been much, possibly only £10, but enough to get by in the normal course of things until my stipend went in the following week. But now there was nothing.

I was puzzled and alarmed by this. It was an account for our housekeeping and although Joan would use the account when buying for the household, she hadn't done that sort of shopping for weeks. So why would she need to use that money while she was not even at home?

To my even greater puzzlement and alarm, Joan had used up

the buffer of the overdraft as well. There was something strange and odd about that. I thought again how little I knew about my wife's finances. Possibly something had come up in Oxford … But to clean out the whole lot meant that I was to all intents and purposes penniless.

Fortunately, that was not my only reason for going to the bank. The local car-dealership had been keeping a lookout for a suitable car for Jack when he turned seventeen and had sent a postcard saying something had come in which I might be interested in. The car the dealership was proposing, a late-model Hillman Husky, sounded like a good buy – I'd decided after the experience with Pete not to allow Jack too much of a choice and to go purely on quality and reliability. I planned to take £400 from a trust account, holding money from my mother's estate, which was to help the kids with educational and other expenses as they went out into the world. Or not 'the kids' exactly …

It was also a way of getting over my current short-term financial difficulty, as I could borrow some of it until my stipend arrived.

I'd never had a cheque book for the trust account; it had never seemed necessary. I transferred money monthly into Pete's account and doled out cash occasionally for school or university expenses to both Pete and Jack. And anyway, the car yard would only accept cash or a bank cheque in payment.

So I innocently filled out a withdrawal slip, unaware of what was to come. When I presented it to the teller, however, I was confounded, astounded almost beyond words, when told there was not enough money in that account to cover the withdrawal. Not enough money! What were they talking about! I immediately asked to see the bank manager, where had that money gone? I knew exactly how much should be in the account, why was I being told it wasn't there anymore? Very concerned, the bank manager then showed me a withdrawal slip purporting to withdraw nearly all of the money except for £200. It was withdrawn the day after I left England and it wasn't my signature. 'That's nothing like my signature!' I cried. Someone had stolen my money.

It was a forgery and not a particularly good one. But mine was a very hard signature to forge. During the war I had defended a charming man who was also an out-and-out bounder, a subaltern like myself who had a hobby if not a livelihood of forging signatures. As they were good forgeries, very good forgeries in fact, it had struck me at the time that this facility might be of use in wartime and made enquiries. The result was that the charges were dropped and the man disappeared into a secret lair somewhere where hopefully he helped the war effort without defrauding too many people in passing. But before he did so, out of gratitude, he had given me some tips on how to sign a forge-proof signature. As a result, I had obtained a particular fountain pen with a particular nib and particular ink and had thereafter always signed my name in the same way. I always carried the pen with me, another suggestion by my forger friend, and always secreted the ink elsewhere (in a drawer in the church vestry) and this signature was not with that nib and not with that ink and the down strokes were not thick enough or strong enough. The bank manager could see it straight away.

The result at the bank was universal dismay. It was a small branch in a small town and nothing as terrible (or as exciting) had ever happened to it before. A bank robbery. And the teller who had signed off on the transaction had just got married and was currently on her honeymoon. The police were called, local bobbies who had also never dealt with a bank robbery before. Reinforcements were called for from York.

For nearly two hours the ramifications swirled around me as I got more and more upset. Eventually I went to see Bob, who in the process of giving me legal advice also obtained confirmation from the bank that they would honour my cheques drawn on the housekeeping account until the matter had been sorted out.

Leaving the whole matter in Bob's hands I had somehow got through the rest of the day, but it had been a huge strain. Naomi and Sally arrived, I ferried them all into York to an outdoor shop where I bought things for Sally while Jack went to the station to pick up Antoine. After that, we went to a supermarket where every sort of hostelling food was purchased and then back home where after some excitable settling in, the young people walked down the road to the Barkers' farm to plan the trip.

At last, the space of silence. It settled around me and I knew I had to ring Bob and yet something was catching at me, something that made me want to put it off. But I rang. And Bob told me … something I desperately didn't want to hear.

After I'd talked to Bob, I rang the archdeacon's office and asked for an urgent appointment the following day.

And then I walked down the road to join the others, trying to breathe deeply, and it was only when I was sure I was completely under control that I went in and had a pleasant evening meal. Hopefully nobody noticed anything amiss.

———

So now I was in the kitchen still and I needed to move on, any activity I could find to do would keep me more on an even keel, I thought. Tomorrow was Sunday and I should be writing my sermon. Thank God for the notes I'd made in bed, at least I had some sort of shape.

I went wearily up the stairs to fetch them. I had hardly slept the previous night and had spent much time on my knees trying to pray, hoping for guidance but unable somehow to channel my thoughts.

To my surprise Joan was sitting on her side of the bed, looking blankly out of the window. I stopped in the doorway, 'I thought you'd gone.'

'Why do the police need to see me?'

I sat down on the chair on my side of the bed where I used to fold my clothes at night and leaned my head back against the wall. Did she not guess? Or did she just want me to say it out loud …

I sorted it through in my mind. 'This is what I've been told. Two weeks ago, the day after I'd left for Spain, someone went into our branch of Barclay's with a withdrawal slip and took most of the money out of the trust account that had been set up to honour my mother's wishes.'

I left that thought hanging. My mother had always had a jaundiced view of my change in career, especially as she and my grandmother had supported me for many years while I did my articles. Over time, however, she had come to enjoy her visits to the vicarage and had become very fond of Pete and Jack. She saw in them the potential which she believed I myself had squandered and had directed that part of the money from her estate be deposited to be used for the education and advancement of her grandsons.

This had been a shock to us both, that Sally was so specifically excluded, and it had created a lot of friction when Sally's school fees became such a large part of our financial lives. But I had always been true to my mother's wishes as expressed in her will.

'The police eventually managed to track down and interview the teller who had accepted the withdrawal slip. The withdrawal slip was forged. Quite obviously forged. Clearly there's blame on the bank and the teller.'

And the teller had identified Joan as the woman who had withdrawn the money.

I continued. 'The poor woman, apparently she was outraged at being taken in, outraged that you, a vicar's wife, could smile and smile and be a liar.' I couldn't bring myself to say villain.

Joan sat there saying nothing.

'Bob has been dealing with it for me, as I couldn't deal with it myself.' The breach of trust was too great. Bob had said we would demand full reimbursement from the bank. 'Do not,' he had warned, 'at any point allow them to persuade you that this is a domestic matter.'

We both sat there, the silence as heavy and cold as a wet curtain. After some moments I continued. 'Bob assumes, as he does a lot of matrimonial matters, that someone, some lowlife in the legal profession, has advised you to strip all the communal assets so that you will be in a better bargaining position when it comes to divorce. Pretty well everyone involved from the police to the bank assumes. Because otherwise why would you do that … take money from that account, a trust account, an account which has nothing to do with you …?'

I couldn't say any more, couldn't go on, the betrayal was written in my voice. I got up and took my notebook from my bedside drawer and went back down to the kitchen.

I sat at the table and put my head in my hands. The compounded weight of loss was bearing down on my lungs, squashing the air out. I breathed back in with difficulty, the smell of yeast coming to me from my hands, all the bread I had made and broken in this place.

I remembered the first time we sat at this table the night we arrived. After the welcoming committee had gone, we'd sat here with the kettle boiling on the hob, sipping from china cups and eating the last of the cucumber sandwiches. What a turn up for the books, I'd said, or she'd said, and we'd laughed. Two imposters, two ordinary people suddenly by the grace of God living in a mansion. How we'd laughed!

But that was then, and things hadn't been like that of late. I'd been skating along for ages trying to avoid reality, the peacemaker in the unending battle that family life had turned into. Skating along – where did that phrase come from? The smooth crisp sound of skates over ice was nothing like the bumpy journey I'd been negotiating over the last few years. Perhaps it was appropriate though, because in the end, when the skates slide from under you, you come crashing down in an undignified heap.

Once when I was a boy, a cold snap had frozen over a local pond and my mother and grandmother had decided we would all go skating and my sister and I staggered drunkenly onto the ice and promptly fell over. Once we got precariously back to our feet, we saw to our alarm that our aged kinfolk were advancing on the ice on their own skates and hot embarrassment had swept through us, no, no, there are other people here, they'll see you! The spectre of these two geriatric mortals crumpled in full view, their skirts spilling up, was a horror too great to contemplate. But then a different horror unfolded. Mum pushed off from the side in a graceful movement and travelled towards the centre of the pond, where she whipped to a stop and waited for her mother, who glided after. They then linked arms and proceeded with complete insouciance to whirl and cavort around the ice.

What a shock! They were skaters, dancers, purveyors of surprise when all they should have been was a dowdy old parent and grandmother.

Never assume. It was a lesson I thought I'd learnt then but over the years I'd had to learn it over and over again. That everyone, and everything, has some core which is hidden and even in families where you think you know everything, there are layers within layers within layers like infinite Russian dolls. Never assume.

I needed to keep moving, I couldn't afford to shilly-shally any longer. I divided the bread, patting the dough down into the greased baking tins and put them aside to rise while I turned on the stove.

I was in my study at my desk when she came slowly down the stairs and stood at the doorway. I was aware of her presence like some pressure on my skin. In the past, unless invited to assist, she had avoided disturbing me when she could see I was writing a sermon, bible and books propped up around me. But not of late – I suspected that not only did she no longer want to assist but that she no longer regarded what I was doing as important.

She came in slowly and sat in my visitor's chair looking out the window. 'What's it about this time?' she asked.

I answered after a pause, 'I started out negating the saying "You can't teach an old dog new tricks." Now I'm moving on to a new proposition, that sometimes it's difficult to teach a young dog old tricks.'

I had been taking a last look at the complex leases, like a patchwork of old parchment, knitting the agricultural lands in the district together. All the riverfront leases forbade the plough and this of course was an affront to modern farming methods. Who heard of anything so stupid, you must improve pasture.

Old farmers who had been through a few floods would understand it; the new ways were not necessarily best. After inundation, the old pastures would grow up through the mud sweeter than ever.

What was needed was not modern farming practices but humility, knowing that the land on these floodplains had everything they needed to survive. So, I had written, the young should learn from the old and the old should learn from the young. Wisdom was something that you must strive for and in the end you could only find it within yourself. And the words in my sermon, as Joan sat there, seemed prophetic. When you turn that first sod there is no going back. Whatever was there can't be repaired, once gone it's gone forever. Rare plants undisturbed since before the monasteries – gone. The threads of life beneath the soil, the microorganisms, all the adaptive structures across the riverine plains, gone.

My heart quaked within me: was I myself about to destroy everything around me?

But this was not the same, there were no lush pastures to be safeguarded. And it was all too late, the frosty wind had blown away the soil.

In any case, she wasn't interested in my sermon. She would no doubt say again, 'This is all about yourself', my interests, my life. Yes, it was always about myself, what other stories could I tell, what other advice could I give? All my sermons, over the last twenty years, were part of my personal journey. They were part of my determination to make Christianity relevant to my congregation and to the district. Not just a homily that you could snooze through on a Sunday morning but something with real relevance where they could prick up their ears and think, I know that person, I've done that action, I've thought that thought.

The basis for the second sermon, because already the two together were too long to be one, was my experience earlier that morning when I had gone into York for an urgent appointment.

I had talked to the archdeacon's secretary, John Williams, an elderly Welshman with whom I'd always had a good rapport. I'd sat with him many times before, trying to ease for the older man the complexity of some of the issues that constantly seemed to be coming up in my parish. Williams was about to retire, and they had started talking about finding a replacement who was going to have to start from the beginning again – all the more unfortunate because they already had the same problem with the archdiocesan lawyers. What needed to be understood, when dealing with some of the complex agricultural leases in the parish inherited from the dissolution of the monasteries, was not so much the archaic English, the occasional Latin, and the dense flowery language of these documents. It was more the issues. The monastery, after farming these lands for four hundred years, had come up with farming methods which suited the area. The Archbishop of York, who had taken delivery of these lands, decided that the leasehold farmers who would now farm the area would follow the perceived wisdom of that time.

And so that had been followed for the next four hundred years with no record of dissent as far as I could see. But in the last few years new and urgent arguments were being raised, young farmers were pushing back against the terms of their leases, battle lines were drawn. And I, having had twenty years talking to the older farmers, was not giving way.

There had to be a warrior, someone to hold up a Stop sign to 'progress' and say no, in this case you're wrong. But now, suddenly, that warrior was not going to be me.

Williams was aghast when I told him I was leaving. Not phasing out, not giving them time to train a replacement, but leaving as soon as I could. It was urgent. Scandal was on its way.

In the process of explaining what was about to transpire and how it would affect the parish, I became as upset as Williams. We sat there in silence for a minute and then I said, 'I'd been thinking of leaving, going back to the law, but not like this. As it is, I'm leaving with nothing. Barely a penny. If I'd stayed in my previous profession I would in the course of twenty years presumably have had a house with or without mortgage, furniture, my own car. I have nothing.'

But now as I sat at my desk with my sermon in front of me, I realised that I did have something. I had carefully kept all of my sermons and although I had nothing much of a material nature to take with me, I did have those. If the spiritual could be valued like the material, they would be priceless to me at least. But now I put that aside as Joan was talking.

Joan said she had snapped after Christmas; after what happened my calm demeanour had depressed and infuriated her, I never stood up for her, never. Pete had said nasty things to her and I had just floated on as if it hadn't happened. It all got too much to bear, she was sure the whole thing would circulate as it always did and that the neighbourhood would be judging us, would be judging her. And then the chance came up for her to upgrade her skills but I wouldn't even think of giving up my holiday for her, this jaunt, this trip away with my pals, how could it even compare with the importance of what she wanted to do – she waved her hands to demonstrate the delinquency of that decision.

She was sick of it, she no longer wanted to live at the vicarage, she wanted to live full-time in York and only visit occasionally. But it would be impossible to live full-time in the flat, it was only for four days a week. Plus in any case, sharing had become difficult whenever the school suspended Sally …

What! I was unaware that Sally had ever been suspended!

Joan wasn't listening. To start with she had been looking for a flat on her own to rent but then it struck her that it would be much more financially sensible to buy a place. There were terrace houses out a little from the centre which were reasonably priced.

She had never thought … She believed that I would be fixed in the parish, stuck here in the middle of nowhere for the rest of my life, happy to slowly decompose. Whereas she felt she had a lot of life left and she wanted to live it away from judgemental eyes, nasty comments, little village mentality. She couldn't shift me or so she thought, but she could shift herself and she was horrified to find that the bank wouldn't let her raise a loan without me going as guarantor, because she was a woman, infantilising her, treating her like a child even though she had a full-time job; she was so angry.

The anger fizzed off her and enveloped me, as if as a man I must also shoulder the blame.

She rushed on. She had forged my signature as guarantor and

the bank had agreed to a loan but just based on my stipend. Her own income was of no account because she was a woman and instead of paying the mortgage she might fritter it away on a diamond necklace.

Now I could see why she was angry at that! I thought of my mother, who was a businesswoman from the tip of her heels to the top of her head. And my grandmother, who wasn't. Lumping fifty per cent of the population into one category, one capacity ... I remembered the archdeacon who interviewed me all those years ago saying watch out when hemlines started going up. An indication of growing heat? Freeing themselves of constrictions in order to better express their rage?

And I could see that with women's rising expectations, even men of goodwill would not always be able to respond appropriately. But did freeing themselves of constrictions mean the abandonment of probity, the trampling over everything in their way? What had I done which was so bad that I deserved to be treated like this?

Joan meanwhile twisted and fidgeted around in her explanations. The loan would have been just enough to cover the cheapest house she saw, a mid-terrace two up two down which had barely been modernised, basically a Victorian slum. But then a house had come up belonging to someone she knew, lovely condition, new bathroom, right near the castle, a fantastic investment. Of course it cost a lot more, more than twice as much, but still easily manageable on her wage. But the bank refused despite ... Anyway she had to move fast or she'd lose it, so she took that money, what of it, money for the boys who would get on in life because that's how the world was set up, ignoring females who had to scrape what they could from what was left. Money for Jack's trips abroad but nothing for Sally, the whole thing was as unfair as could be. She was only borrowing it, I wasn't using it at the moment ...

I sat there wordless. When I could speak again I pointed out that I *was* using it at the moment, for Pete as she very well knew, helping him out with his books and living expenses – money transferred into his account every month. Suddenly I twigged – so that's why she hadn't taken all of it, so it wouldn't be discovered for some time. What a calculating … I was going to say 'act of thievery', but I couldn't.

What she'd meant, she said, was the majority of the money was just sitting there. They were her sons too, they should be happy that she was making use of it. And she would pay it back.

How would she pay it back? How would she pay it back in time for it to be any good to them? The reason I had discovered the theft, yes I called it that, was because I would shortly be using some of it to buy a car for Jack. In case she had forgotten, he was turning seventeen in a month. How much was she going to be able to pay back by then?

A car, she said impatiently, a car! He could do without a car! At least until she persuaded a bank to give her a loan to cover what was owed.

My indignation rose even more. What if there was no such bank? And also, why hadn't she told me any of this before. Only now when it was too late. Words words words. Whatever was hidden, was still hidden from me.

Words. Like those used in her phone call the day before I departed, to make sure I was actually going? Because then she must have taken a day off, driven all the way back up to Yorkshire, despite constantly going on about how important the course was and how she hadn't had time to go and visit Sally …

And the words were not there that could describe how difficult the last twenty-four hours had been for me, with the young people swirling around, the three boys so excited that their atoms seemed to combine and coalesce in one big fizzing bar of anticipation. Normally I would have loved to have watched my quiet son expanding outwards into this dance of joy. Instead there was I, as watchful and quiet as Jack had ever been, trying to pretend everything was normal. Funnily enough it was Sally who had seen through me, who kept looking at me with increasing concern and as we walked back last night from dinner at the Barkers' with her arm through mine, had seemed to cling to me, like when she was a child. At that moment I had wanted to cry but fortunately Naomi had come up and taken my other arm, and so we had walked together back to the vicarage with Antoine and Jack ahead of us also arm in arm and prancing down the road.

I had spent a long time on my knees the previous night trying with all my might … The effort, the sheer effort to act my part, joking with them over their early breakfast, waving them off. Please God let everything go all right for them, please God let them have fun.

Because this was absolute hell for me.

I began, 'On the first day of my trip—'

'Your trip. I note you haven't asked anything about the course I've been doing!'

I paused. 'I don't think we're very interested in each other anymore.' I said it sadly. 'Anyway as I was saying, on the first day of my trip I started thinking about what normal was. I kept thinking about it all that fortnight, and in the end I thought if this is normal, this life we lead here, this relationship we have the two of us, then I don't want it any more than you do. But I didn't know how to get out of it, apart from the decision to change my employment. Because even if I did that it would still leave the two of us unresolved.' When I'd found out she'd stolen the money, suddenly the conventional bonds were rent asunder. Now I realised I could move forward, no guilt, no blame, just an obvious parting of the ways. 'After what's happened, I've decided I want a divorce, and I've instructed Bob to start proceedings. I'm getting out of the priesthood, I'm getting out of this house, and I'm getting out of this marriage as soon as I can.'

I needed to get it over with, I needed to say it, I couldn't let it go on slipping. And so out it came, spilling over the dam wall in a rush, washing everything before it.

I looked at her; she was looking out the window again. 'I presume you are already getting your own advice in relation to a divorce.'

'Why do you presume that?' She was hunched forward now over her gripped hands, almost like a contorted attitude of prayer.

'Because you've just been telling me in effect that we're separating, that you're going to live your own life in York.' Separation, the lesser more socially accepted form of parting, where nothing needed to be ever actually explained. What had she expected I would do about that? That I wouldn't protest, that I would go along, not rock the boat, that I would just let her get her way as I'd been doing? Peacemaking I'd called it, but now I saw it was just the fear of what she might do if I did stand up to her – fear that she might publicly leave, publicly complain that she never wanted to be a vicar's wife, that she was sick of being in a position not of her own choosing and that it was all my fault in any number of ways.

But that wasn't going to happen anymore. Now I was telling her, yes I agreed we were separating but not into some unacknowledged form but out where everyone could see it – I was leaving her and we would divorce. The worm had turned. Or was that the point of it all, that she would push me and push me until out of desperation I pulled the plug?

She looked down at her hands. 'So what of the money, what are you going to do about that?'

'Do about it? What can I do about it?'

I really hated the look on her face after I said this, that small told-you-so smile – that I would let her get away with it. With shock, I realised that was the same expression I used to see on Sally's face when, with Joan's connivance, she emerged triumphant. It wasn't nice to be confronted with the knowledge that I could be manipulated; that family life was a war game for the redistribution of spoils and that what I thought was mediation was in fact no more than puppetry.

I gathered myself and continued, 'Bob's pretty sure they'll admit negligence and return the money. After that, it's their problem.' Then I felt ashamed at the vindictive pleasure I got when I saw her face change.

Return it! What did that mean?

'You know,' I said, 'when I set that account up, I thought my mother had worded her wishes like that because she had never warmed to Sally. But now I realise it was to protect the money from you. That it was you she didn't warm to. Because if she had left it in a more general way, so it included Sally, you would have insisted that all Sally's school fees came out of the account and over the years, by the time she finished school, it would all be gone and the boys would have received nothing. And you would be perfectly okay with that.'

Yes, they would have got nothing, as they would get now if Bob was not successful. But if Bob was successful, as was most likely, it meant that the money would reappear in the trust account and I would continue using it for the purposes it was intended.

Joan had stood up suddenly. 'But where does that leave me?' she cried. 'What have you done?'

What had I done? Nothing. Then I suddenly realised why she was suddenly strident. 'How could I have done anything? When I found the money had gone, you were the last person on the planet I suspected of having stolen it.' Which was true; in the shock of finding the money gone I assumed it was a charming ne'er-do-well like that subaltern. Glib excuses, confident demeanour, shiny presentation. What happened to that man, I wondered.

But there was Joan walking up and down wringing her hands. By the time it became clear that it was Joan, everyone was involved – bank officials, police from York, lawyers. 'It was too late. You forged my signature, what on earth were you thinking of? It stopped being something that you could rearrange within a family, it meant you were stealing from a bank. They'll crucify you! All of them. And it put me in a terrible position too. I wasn't in any rush to leave before, but now I am. Precipitated by … Can you imagine when the press gets hold of it? "Vicar's Wife Robs Bank".'

Although, I considered soberly, if I hadn't changed professions it would have been just as bad, worse probably. 'Solicitor's Wife Robs Bank' somehow moved out of the realm of cosy crime into something a bit more evil.

For that and for everything else yes it was all too late. Everything comes crashing down, reputations, livelihoods … What would the bank do? Perhaps the bank would come to an arrangement with her over the money she'd taken, roll it into a loan perhaps. Would they do that? Would that satisfy them? Probably not. They're a bank, a hard-surfaced entity, rhymes with tank. Would she still have a job? How would her employers view the situation? A reputation for lies and deceit was not a good advertisement for future promotion and the dark art of forgery even less so. As for theft … How would she maintain the loan if she didn't have a job?

Those were the issues but the solutions … that was up to her. I was walking away. I still cared for her but I could and would walk away – to another life where I would have enough of my own problems to deal with.

I sat at my desk, she sat back down in the chair. We were waiting for something to happen, both of us stranded there, perhaps waiting for the police to arrive.

After a while I said, 'It's funny, now I'm leaving here, how many topics for good sermons keep popping into my head, on betrayal and forgiveness and pride and assumptions.'

I paused but she said nothing. I left it for a few moments and then said, 'We have to talk about Sally.'

Joan appeared to pull herself together. 'She'll live with me.'

'And where will that be?'

Joan was in denial, she'd still get the house, she'd still keep her job, and then of course Sally would be at school …

'I've made an appointment to go and see the headmistress at the school next week. I seem to have been kept completely in the dark about what's been going on. But in any case, I won't have a job after next week so there goes my half of the fees.'

'You could use the money from the—' She stopped.

'From the account you stole from? No, face facts, she's not going back to that school. From the second-hand intelligence passed on to me through third parties, they don't want her back and she doesn't want to go back. No doubt I'll find out everything you've been hiding from me when I go.'

'You never seem that interested in her. You're always criticising her.'

'Yes, because her behaviour is so bad, and you seem incapable of even seeing it let alone correcting it.'

'I was standing up for her. Which you never did. I can see how the world works, boys get the best of everything and if you don't stand up for your daughters they get the rotten end of the stick. The behaviour you criticise, that was just Sally trying to get her fair share.'

'You only see it like that because you could never accept that most of the time she was lying. And that encouraged her to keep on lying. And that's eventually going to destroy her. Is it true the school wants to expel her because she's been stealing money and lying? But maybe you see that sort of behaviour as normal, as okay, things you would do yourself?'

She sat crunched not looking at me, her mouth clenched, fists crossed on her chest. I was aware of her breathing, as if she was dragging air through a misty swamp. Finally she said, 'Well you take her then. If you think you can do any better.' She collapsed her arms and bent forward, head towards her knees. 'I'll take Jack.'

I was genuinely startled. Jack! Did she mean her son Jack? Who was standing in the hall when I'd told her Jack was coming with us to Spain? Who was standing beside me in Spain when it became clear that she had thought I was talking about Jack Halsted? The son who on neither occasion she'd asked to speak to, to console with him for not going to France, or to apologise for insultingly mixing him up with a Methodist minister, was that the Jack she meant? Was that the Jack she thought would want to live with her?

She got up suddenly and rushed through the hall and out the door without saying another word. I stood and watched her drive off.

Have Jack. I wanted to tumble to the floor and start praying, *please God however things turn out, please don't let me lose Jack.* But it was ridiculous to even think of asking for such a thing. Jack was nearly seventeen; he would have his driving licence and his own car soon. Where he lived, where he went, would be his decision.

Having Jack … I suddenly thought of the French family and Jack arriving, a pal for their isolated son. A gang. As Bob said, if you're in a gang you can avoid bullying, especially if you've got something the others want. Like Jack. Something even better than Dundee cake to share. No wonder the family had been looking to move to somewhere less isolated for their daughter, the result for Antoine must have been instantaneously beneficial.

Time stretched and slumped, gathered itself up and stretched again, like the waves of pain I sometimes got in my leg. The last few years passed in review; I wished I could have them all back so I could examine them more minutely as they passed. Loss and longing, another good subject for a sermon.

I sat back down in front of my writing pad, in front of my current unfinished sermon. I felt everything was unfinished and in that state it was going to be rolled up and put out of the way in the box room and left there for the silverfish, the moths, to chew on.

I took up a sheet of letter-writing paper instead and tentatively started a letter.

Dear Sister Angela,

By the time this letter gets to you you'll be back in New York, I can't imagine what that would be like, a big city, cars everywhere, guns going off if it's anything like the police dramas we get on TV. In contrast it's so quiet here I can hear Rick Barker's cows a mile or so down the road mooing that they're ready to be milked. I understand that when their udders are full it's unpleasant for them and being milked is a release. But they also get a rich cattle cake for their trouble which makes them swoon with desire, a bit like Father Gregory swooning over some buttery, orange-soaked seed cake as sold in one of the best cafés in York (old York that is).

The cows walk up morning and afternoon to the milking shed from their summer field by the river, along a partly paved road which runs past a few dilapidated cottages and one very fine new brick house full of pretensions to comfort. In this house there is a cloakroom downstairs, a family bathroom upstairs and another bathroom off the main bedroom. Three toilets! The vicarage only has two, and one of those is outside. Anyway, the reason I am adding this detail is that the cottagers who only have outside toilets, and bathrooms if they're lucky, used to complain to me about the cowpats from Rick Barker's cows disfiguring their route to church in their good clothes on Sunday. However, Mrs Hanley-Watson, the owner of the new house, is starting a garden and is to be found nearly every day in her wellies walking the road with a bucket and shovel gathering in the cow manure with cries of wonder that this free resource is so bountifully being left to her alone.

The grumbling has stopped, I suspect in surprise. I'm not sure whether it's going to start again but now about how 'some people' always get more than their fair share of things. Or whether they will all go and get their buckets and shovels and join in the feast.

A lot of things have happened since I got back, some of which I won't describe in this letter. As you know, I was thinking that I might leave the priesthood and go back to my original occupation. This is actually going to happen. I didn't want to put pressure on the archdiocese, but something's happened over the last few days which meant that I am now going to leave faster than I was intending.

When I went to talk to them about it this morning, it was all quite clear in my head before I went, but when I got there it was a lot harder to put into words than I thought. Somewhat pathetically, the greatest problem for me was that I would be walking away with literally nothing. Somehow, despite the great weight of other intervening reasons, this was the matter which caused me the greatest distress. No one joins the ministry

to grow rich so why it should suddenly flood all my
sensibilities I don't know.

The vicarage was fully furnished when we came and
with that heavy Victorian furniture which you can bash
quite a lot without it breaking, as having three children
living here has demonstrated. So nothing has had to
be replaced, and it will all stay when we leave. And the
thing is, I wouldn't want to take it with me anyway, it's
the kind of heavy musty stuff you find in heavy musty
buildings, and I would really like to live somewhere lighter
and more modern. I have had a few grieved moments
over some individual items and of course leaving behind
an extensive library will be hard. But as the kind of books
I will need in future will be law books, it wouldn't have
been much help to me anyway.

Fortunately what I had to tell them about my general
reasons for leaving seemed to focus their attention very
much. A scandal is brewing in which I had no part but the
way the world works, in particular the kind of newspapers
which I don't read, means it is to everyone's benefit that
I move as soon as possible.

Interestingly, being quite upset because a life of
penury was harder to face than I was expecting, the
archdeacon's secretary, who I have always got on very
well with, went off and after some discussions further
up the line came back with a pack of filing cards which
he told me were all properties that they were currently
seeking to offload. The archdiocese has a number of
church properties which are superfluous to their current
requirements. As I think I told you, in my own parish a
couple of the churches will probably be sold, and the
accompanying dwellings in the meantime have been

leased. The motor car has made a great difference to how parishes are run.

He told me that a lot of the ones on the surplus list were quite big, unrenovated vicarages in country locations, which would be quite hard to sell because most of them were in medium to poor repair. However, he showed me one which was a bit of an oddity, a newish three-bedroomed bungalow in a town not far from York and on the railway line. It was built for a minister who'd had twin children, both with a disability and both eventually confined to wheelchairs. It appears to have been cheaper to build something from scratch than to adapt and renovate the vicarage. Times move on and the new vicar has chosen to move back into the original vicarage.

John suggested maybe I should have a look and see what I thought and if it suited me they would transfer the title to me in exchange for me giving up any future rights to a pension. I think on paper it will suit me very well. It's a reasonably easy run for Jack to get to his current school, under his own steam hopefully, because he will be 17 in a month. And would give me scope to try and find legal work in a number of larger centres such as York and Hull. I immediately agreed to go and view it and so I may be moving soon – I'm not sure when as the kids are out tramping somewhere in England, or Scotland, who knows where, Jack and his sister (now found and restored to us), his cousin, his best friend and his French pal. I hope so much they are having fun. I am not having fun but when planning a big change of life, fun doesn't usually come into it.

I do reflect though on how lucky I have been in life

so far. And how things never turn out quite as badly
as you imagine in the dead of night. The archdeacon
himself rang me later and somewhat astonished me by
expressing the anxiety they had been feeling for some
time at the amount of complex administrative work
required by my parish and by the fact they had no Plan B
for when I got sick of it and left. He asked me if I would
consider continuing to do this work as a paid part-time
position, including taking on some other knotty leases
in other parishes. I immediately said yes of course. Not
only to help them out but also to keep a connection to
the district. And for myself, because even a part-time
position is a godsend and one I have thanked Him most
humbly for.

I sat looking down at what I'd written. I noted with vague
satisfaction that I was not bleeding out onto the page. Mentioning the cows coming down to milking gave the letter an air of
whimsy. I doubted I'd send it but at least I seemed to be moving
forward somewhat. Although I wasn't any further forward with
my sermon – I needed time to recapture its tone. I was waiting
in a blank sort of way for this to happen when a small car pulled
up outside.

It was Gregory, redistributing the money left over from the
kitty and a piece of Jack's clothing which had been left in Bob's
car. I wasn't sure I could rise to the effort of being hospitable,
but Bob must have said something to him about my situation
because I found I didn't have to.

Later that night, I continued my letter to Sister Angela.

I'm very lucky with my friends. Bob has been a tower of
strength and hugely helpful to me. And Father Gregory

too. He came round on some matter to do with the trip and found me sitting in a shellshocked way after my wife left me (I wasn't going to tell you but now I suppose I should, we are going to be divorced). He immediately made himself useful, putting two loaves I had made in the oven, and gathering together food to make a meal out of. I told him I hadn't had a chance to get to the shops, which wasn't quite true because I had been to a supermarket with the young people, but I have been too despondent to get food for myself.

So anyway, we managed to put together quite a nice salad and boil some freshly dug potatoes, by which time the bread had come out of the oven. We also found some home-made butter which I'd forgotten about from the farm I was describing earlier. So we made some herb omelettes and it really turned into a nice meal after all. I asked Father Gregory what he would have been eating back at his monastery and he said 'shepherd's pie' in a tone which evinced no enthusiasm at all. We both got to thinking about you and Sister Carol who we've heard eat so well, a fact which fills poor Father Gregory with envy!

I think he is going to write to Sister Carol for her advice. He has found that he is going to have to teach English literature to a rather disruptive fourth-year class preparing for O levels (I'm not sure what your equivalent is) and one of the plays he is going to have to teach is *The Taming of the Shrew* which we know is a favourite with Sister Carol. It fills him with dread, teaching a play about the control of women to a set of stroppy adolescent boys.

He then spent the rest of the meal recounting in detail

another play, a mediaeval drama called *Everyman* which his Young Farmers branch had adapted before he went to university. It eventually won first prize for the best Young Farmers production in England. No, sorry, in the United Kingdom, I mustn't sell them short. It was just like one of those films where a band of unlikelies pip the favourites at the post. In the last heat before they got into the finals, the van which was carrying their props – coffins which they carried on stage to make the set and all their cowled monkish robes – broke down! When finally the props arrived, in the nick of time, it was at the front door of the theatre and with no time to do anything else they went in that way and through the audience which worked so well they did it in the final.

Gregory then went through the play, acting out all the different voices and personalities in a very amusing way which so engaged me it completely restored me to equilibrium. Eventually he departed when there was no food left, having eaten nearly a loaf of bread and most of the butter. I can't tell you how glad of this visit I was. How lucky you are, surrounded by a pleasant group of nuns. I think when you are at a low point, the communal life definitely attracts.

Bolstered by Gregory's visit, I was able to finish the sermon, which I thought rather a good one. And the next day, I was able to gather myself enough to deliver it without, I hoped, showing that I was under strain, and was encouraged when my congregation seemed to find it at least entertaining, discerning a lot of knowing looks and the occasional chuckle. At that time, I was fairly sure that no one knew yet about my situation, even though the 'bush telegraph' was extremely fast (though not necessarily extremely accurate), one of the things Joan hated about the place.

All of that changed very quickly.

Eighteen

On Monday and after another sleepless night, I rang John Williams's office and told him I simply couldn't go on, that things had completely got on top of me. I was aware to my shame that my voice was cracking up over the phone and one part of me was furious at how pathetic I sounded. They agreed that I would go off on sick leave for the rest of the month. The curate who had run the parish during my recent absence would be asked to come back and carry on with services.

On Tuesday, I started a second letter.

> Dear Don
>
> After my brief phone call on Saturday I am writing to you rather than ringing you again because I'm not sure that I would go any better explaining things over the phone. Firstly, the good news. Naomi rang me this morning and they are getting on very well on their hike, no suggestion of Sally giving up yet. They stopped the first two nights at a farm belonging to one of Tony's relatives and did a day walk to see how everyone's boots and fitness levels coped with going up a large hill

(or small mountain). Apparently everyone coped quite well, so they have set off to do part of the Pennine Way. Originally, the plan was that Naomi wouldn't tell me where they were going, but this is no longer necessary. Before I turn to that, Naomi has been teaching Sally the harmonies for some songs as they walk along, and the hostel last night had a piano, so they tried them out to great success. It sounds like they are all having fun and the weather has been kind, so I feel as if my prayers have been answered as far as the kids are concerned.

Now I have to turn to other matters which, as you know, are deeply distressing to me. So to recap, on Saturday evening I received a frantic phone call from Mandy, Joan's flatmate in York, asking what was going on because the flat had been 'raided' by police who had opened Joan's desk and gone through her drawers and taken some things away. I said that the police had also been to the vicarage trying to find her and that I didn't know where she was, and I had assumed she had gone to the flat. Mandy is engaged, in a stately and non-urgent way, to an engineer with the East Riding Council who stays at the weekend in the room Joan uses during the week, and therefore of course Joan couldn't have gone there. I was immediately concerned, some horrible possibilities presented themselves to me ... But then it appeared that Joan has formed a friendship with another teacher at her school and has stayed overnight at her house on a number of occasions. So that at least soothed my fears that she might have thrown herself in the river. Instead it was much more likely that she had gone to this friend to throw herself on her sympathy and complain about me, or men in general, or possibly bank managers.

The next day on Sunday when I set off for Morning Service, I locked the house but then, possibly in a confused state through lack of sleep, I took the key with me rather than leaving it under the potted azalea to the left of the porch. After church my verger, Bill Wilson, invited me back for Sunday lunch and I was very glad to be distracted and have a nice meal as it's pretty slim pickings at the vicarage. Coming back at about 3 p.m. with still plenty of time to prepare for evening service, I found a very strange sight. A stoutish middle-aged woman in a lumpy green suit (maybe it hadn't been lumpy before but was as a result of her sitting on the doorstep for some hours) greeted me in a belligerent manner and demanded entry 'to get Joan's things'. I was not happy about either her manner or her request and told her I had no intention of doing that. She then told me it was against the law to refuse to let a person have their property back, that was theft. I answered civilly that I wasn't stopping Joan getting her property back, and she could come anytime, but I wasn't having strangers appearing out of the blue. At this point she started screaming at me in a most intimidating way and I went inside, firmly shut the door and bolted it and left the woman outside still screaming and banging on the door. I then rang the police.

It appears that Joan was arrested on Saturday night and a bail hearing has not yet been held, as the police in York are trying to get to the bottom of where the money is. Why, if she was in the lock-up, would she urgently need her things, I asked them. The officer in charge thought it over. 'Would she have known that you weren't there, when this friend of hers came over?' he asked.

Of course. I'm a vicar and it's Sunday.

He then said they would like to come and do a search for evidence and take another statement from me, which upset me greatly, I don't know why. A woman outside creating a scene and police coming to the house to do a search. But I managed a semblance of calm and when they came I sat in the study, diligently pretending I was working on preparing for the evening service. While one of them was looking in our bedroom and going through Joan's cupboard in the dining room, the sergeant sat down to take a statement. Joan has told them some story ... That taking the money was all part of a plan we had cooked up between us to get out of the terms of my mother's bequest so that the money could be used for something else, and I had in fact signed the withdrawal slip and we planned to buy a house in York for when I gave up the ministry, but then when I came back from Spain I had demanded a divorce and was now pretending that the withdrawal slip was forged. She told them that she didn't know where the money was because I had it.

I said I didn't even know where to start with that scenario. It was all lies. I was wanting a divorce because she had stolen the money from my sons and I could see that the marriage was over. Then I told him what she'd told me about the house she was going to buy ...

I came to a halt. It was another letter I probably wouldn't send. Although Don wasn't talking to his sister at the moment, I assumed that blood would overcome and in the end her brother would stick with her.

What I could have gone on to say was that the police had carried off a box with presumably something in it, I didn't know what, the last fragments of our life together perhaps, the scrapings of a marriage gone sour.

What dreadful lies. Scandal on top of scandal. Women screaming at my door. Police coming and going, the village no doubt riven with speculation and gossip. I had to escape while I still had my sanity. Evening Service was a nightmare; I kept having to stop in my tracks to remember where I was and had to concentrate on the words of the hymns with all my might in order to stop bursting into tears. I had barely the strength to get through it and I was pretty sure my congregation, even if they weren't privy to that afternoon's disturbances, could see that something was wrong.

Shortly after I'd put the letter to Don aside, the police sergeant came round again – keeping me in the loop, he said. They had now managed to follow the money trail to the house that Joan was going to buy. This had proved difficult because Joan had been uncooperative, but from material they had obtained through the two search warrants, they'd become aware of further facts and after ringing round a few conveyancing clerks, had located the house. It was being bought for herself using her maiden name. They also had proof that Joan and/or the other woman had been practising forging my signature. They were checking fingerprints and might also charge the other woman with conspiracy to defraud.

The upshot was that my wife, on legal advice, was now going to plead guilty. The sergeant said this as if he felt I should be relieved. But I didn't feel relief, just an overriding horror. What I felt, though it was hard to put into language, was that my wife had robbed me as part of a conspiracy. Not a solo spontaneously reckless act with a misapprehension of its seriousness, no, rather as a planned and executed scheme, setting out deliberately to defraud her own sons and implicate me in the blame.

This upset me even more. And what upset me the most was an

uneasy feeling that I *should* be shouldering some of the blame. For what and why I didn't know, but how else could my wife of more than twenty-five years have undertaken such an action, such a breach of trust, of love, of support, of everything that is promised in marriage, if I myself hadn't done something to precipitate it?

The sergeant left, warning me not to talk to the papers about the matter while it was still in front of the court. What papers? Yes, the papers were sniffing around and even with my limited acquaintanceship of tabloid newspapers, I could understand they were going to have a field day. Joan had wanted to be charged under her maiden name but that was not the name she was generally known under, and the police prosecutors had refused. Pity, said the sergeant. That sort of press were like rats devouring everything in their path.

At midday, to my surprise, Jack Halsted dropped round. He brought an egg-and-bacon pie which one of his parishioners had given him and some of his own home-grown hothouse tomatoes. He had seen Bob in town and Bob had suggested he visit, that I might need some company.

Yes, actually I did need some company. I told him over lunch that while we were in Spain I had started to seriously question whether it was time for me to move on from the ministry and now it was going to happen.

'Yes,' said Halstead. 'Going on holiday, putting some distance between you and your problems, often has that effect. In fact it was the reason I *joined* the ministry. I went on a walking tour through Provence after my wife died, and I was sitting on a bank eating my lunch when a flock of sheep went past below with wooden bells, plonk clonk plonk and a little shepherd boy wearing his father's shirt and a pair of sandals. They all stopped and looked at me attentively, and I had an almost overwhelming urge to start preaching to them like Jesus on the Mount. So I declaimed Psalm 23 and at the end the little boy said Amen, and the sheep said something that sounded like Amen though it could just have been baaa. And then I thought, do I really want to go back to being a civil servant? It all came to a head.'

I wondered if going to war had the same effect.

Well, it was a change of scenery, said Halstead. New places, new experiences, and an endless number of new people trying to kill you. It was a concentrated way of looking at what was important. 'You go away to war and become changed utterly and then you go home to people who haven't changed at all. And who don't, after the leeway of the first few weeks, want to keep hearing about it. That little group you started was a lifeline for some of the men around here. Remember back then those awful funerals with the word "accidental" in the death certificate? They all stopped, thank God. Of course Dr Boyes got all the kudos, getting the government to fund similar groups, but everyone knows it was you who started it.'

Had I started it? Can just sitting there and listening start things?

'Yes. They'll really miss you round here,' said Halstead.

Nineteen

THE NEXT DAY, I WENT to look at the house suggested by the archdeacon's office. From the outside it looked like a rather undistinguished modern bungalow in a fairly new estate. On the inside, Oh Lord! I could see why the new vicar wanted to go back to the vicarage. And why it was still on John Williams's books, unleased unsold and unloved – the interior looked like a better type of hospital.

Fortunately I took Jack Halstead with me for support, and he thought there was nothing there that couldn't be fixed fairly easily with the help of the men's group; it was all just cosmetic. The wet room could be remodelled into a conventional bathroom and the large disabled toilet into a separate cloak room. Apart from that, some nice carpet instead of the brown linoleum, paint the shiny green walls and Bob's your uncle. It had quite a useful-sized garden area, currently concrete at the front but 'the lads will get stuck into that,' Jack assured me. Plus it was quite a pleasant neighbourhood with easy access by train and bus to many surrounding centres.

In fact Jack thought it was rather splendid, and I recollected that the manse he lived in was smaller but equally as inconvenient as the vicarage. Look, Halstead said, pointing in wonder at the radiators. Central heating!

How did it work? A manual sat on the mantlepiece above the gas fire and we stood reading it. You could set it automatically, we learned, so it came on early in the morning, and you got up to a warm house. There was something rather thrilling about this prospect. And for me it was the clincher.

Perhaps ministers of religion should always have been living in places like this among the common people, enjoying the common wonders of modern life. Maybe they were wrong to live in those palatial vicarages as if to the manner born. I remembered what Bob had said about the snobbery in his law firm – which I had not experienced even though my family came from the same strata in society as Bob's. But that might have less to do with social mores and more to do with the fact that I lived in a bigger house than many of those double-barrelled county folk. My vicarage was originally built by a man who, even before he'd been given the rich living of the parish, was wealthy in his own right. And in case anyone in the surrounding gentry doubted it, he made sure his home was as grand as theirs if not grander.

I rang Bob when I got back and said I wanted to take up the archdeacon's offer and wondered how I should go about it. I would like to move as soon as practicable, but I had no furniture, no crockery, no kitchen things. Even most of the linen and bedding which was at the vicarage when we arrived all those years ago was still in use. My entire worldly possessions could be transported by a couple of trips in my parish-provided car.

Bob was impressed. He and Barb dreamed of living in a more minimalist way but once you had a house, it somehow on its own filled up with stuff. His brother was an insurance assessor who came into possession, legitimately of course, of vast quantities of written-off goods which he doled out among his friends and relations with admirable impartiality, whether they wanted them or not. Barb was a dab hand with fabrics and Bob was pretty handy with a drill and plane, so what they couldn't use themselves they did up and gave to the Prisoners' Aid Society. But all they had at the moment was an armchair which Barb was reupholstering. However, his brother had a house-lot of good quality carpet if I didn't object to teal as a colour.

Then Bob said he'd approach the archdiocesan movers and fixers to find out what they could do for me. 'I'll tell them you don't want stuff out of their second-hand charity shop.'

'I don't mind second-hand things,' I said.

'No, you'll have a newish house which will immediately start looking higgledy-piggledy because it's impossible to get stuff to match from those sorts of places. Leave it to me. And I'll start the process of transferring the title.'

Twenty

AT THE END OF THE week, I took up my neglected diary intent on describing something momentous, but in the end found I couldn't. All I could do was write about the lead-up but when it came to the point, the event that I was trying to capture, somehow words were too small, too insignificant, too breakable.

Friday Trip to York. Bob came round this morning to take me shopping for furniture. To my surprise Barb came with him. She was looking glowingly fruitful, her skin almost translucent, and she was surrounded by a brightness as if the pregnancy was the best thing in the world for her body instead of the worst.

She had told her boss on Monday that she was 5½ months pregnant and was immediately given two weeks' notice. No, she'd said, if you're sacking me I'm leaving now, and she did.

I was outraged. I said, 'I'm appalled how they treat women, like disposable commodities, as if their skills and experience are infinitely interchangeable with any other woman they can get off the street.'

But Barb just laughed. 'They did exactly what I expected them to do, so I didn't tell them until I was ready to go.'

And Bob laughed too. 'They know she's had miscarriages, and they don't want anything messy like women weeping on work time.'

But I couldn't see the humour in it, and as we drove along I kept returning to the unfairness of it. 'Was what you did there so unimportant to the organisation that you could be shown the door without a second thought? I don't get it, I thought you were a senior accountant.'

Barb said, 'If you're asking whether they're going to miss me, well not necessarily this week or next week, but by the end of next month they're really going to miss me when the project I've just been doing percolates through to their head office.' She laughed again. 'Sod them. I'm sick of working for organisations set up to convenience men's careers. I'm going to set up my own business, accountancy for women. Bob and I have been trying to think of a business name. He thinks it should have the word "pink" in it.'

I then suggested that what she really needed to start was a bank, a pink bank, one that was only for women and who treated women as rational beings and who extended loans to them based on rational calculations. Barb thought it was a fabulously good idea and if only she had a few million to spare she'd start one in an instant. She had thought, before their surprise defeat in June, that Barbara Castle and the Labour Party might be persuaded to bring in an anti-discrimination bill because although equal pay was a good start, it still didn't fix the inequality rampant in many other spheres of life. Money, as always, was the problem and it was also the solution.

'Hurray for one small pay packet,' said Bob. 'Cuts the complications in half!'

They laugh a lot, the two of them. And I noticed as they drove along and she turned from the front seat to speak to me, she was always touching Bob. I felt envious and sad, I remembered the time when we were like that. When did it stop? Maybe it was after that dreadful Lake District holiday, Joan seemed to bristle with fury. 'Don't I even get a single day off?' she'd said at one point. Jack asked why we didn't just go home. Why didn't we? Money again, we didn't have a fallback position, we'd done all our dough on sleeping bags. Plus, all the packing to get there, all the packing up to get home, extricating the boys from their band of ruffians. We took the easy course. I took the easy course ...

I found the furniture warehouse we went to overwhelming. I was not used to shopping and wasn't aware that these conglomerations on the outskirts of York even existed. It was a place the size of an aircraft hangar, full of noise and crowds. Barb forged ahead and Bob and I followed.

'How much have we got to spend?' I asked.

A nebulous figure, apparently. An account had been opened for me so that I could spend a 'reasonable amount' on furnishing the bungalow. Apparently the archdiocese had a relationship with this store, having negotiated a discount arrangement while sourcing large numbers of stackable chairs. Out with the old pews, worship in the round was the new buzzword.

I tried to imagine my own church without pews and instead of the serried ranks of attentive faces turned towards me, some jumble of individual chairs, each occupant uncomfortably aware of their neighbour. I felt fractured by this thought and the huge jangling range of choices all around me. But Bob put a hand on my shoulder, warm and steadying, to comfort me, and I felt calmed.

I turned to say …

But Bob was over to the side looking at bedside tables. There was no one near me, no one and yet …

And yet I had felt that light touch again.

Not going into battle, not when danger threatened, no bullets, no shells, but in a vast commercial building among bedding and white goods, with carpets in the basement.

Now I was truly undone, tears sprang to my eyes, tears of gratitude. There was nowhere to kneel and give thanks, I would have to do it later. Just like in France I had to keep moving forward. My heart wobbled within me, fluttering with joy and I wanted to cry out to the noisy crowds around me, I AM NOT ALONE!

But instead I was gathered up by Barb and chose my first bookcase.

Twenty-one

On Sunday morning I was sitting at the kitchen table plucking a couple of pheasants. It felt a strange thing to be doing on Sunday, not to be at church, but I'd held a small service earlier for my verger and the new curate and now, with nothing official to do, I was making myself useful. Young Jamie the new curate (yes, he'd asked to be called Jamie) was running the service for me, and I hoped very much that it went well.

The pheasants were a gift from the new owners of the Manor. I thought Oliver was the reason.

Poor old Oliver had been carted off by his family to a nursing home 'in the middle of nowhere', he'd said. 'Nothing to look at, just bloody fields. Why couldn't I have gone to the council one in town, at least there'd be company. So what if it smells a bit of piss.'

The home he was 'incarcerated in' had once been a vicarage and the ground floor extended to accommodate twelve guests. It was surrounded by pleasant gardens and fields, and everyone agreed it was probably the best nursing home in the area. Everyone except Oliver. 'No one will come and visit me here,' he'd said sadly.

How wrong he was. He'd remained a waspish gossip with a hair-raisingly accurate gift for prediction and his fears of being left to moulder like a mushroom were unfounded; he still held presidential court among the ladies of the district.

I also visited him often and we engaged in our favourite activity, which was me reading from Dickens while the old man sat at his tapestry or with his knitting. We had been three quarters of the way through *The Old Curiosity Shop*, with me experimenting by making the voice of Little Nell whiny, demanding and bad-tempered (in counterpoint to the banal goodygoody of Dickens). Yes, more like a real girl, encouraged Oliver with glee.

We were also both in complete agreement about the voice for Daniel Quilp.

The previous year, after a long time on the market, Oliver's ancient, dilapidated pile had been bought by city folks as their country bolt hole. The new people had grand ambitions for the manor and estate, and also the money to achieve them. Joan and I had been invited to dinner once and had returned the invitation once and that I hoped was as far as it went.

'What do you think of them?' asked Oliver.

I responded that I had little interest in the social ambitions of this couple and their worship of money. Fortunately they had joined the local hunt and so become on good terms with the county aristocracy and went to shooting parties on their estates. And having risen to these dizzying heights they had no further need to socialise locally.

Oliver had also met them. He had gone for the day, before the place was sold, to do some gentle rose-pruning along with some lady friends, and the couple had been there for a viewing and had come up to him and, addressing him by his title, had shaken his hand. 'The moment I saw them I knew they were going to be the best scandal ever. One that would even eclipse your scandal.'

'My scandal!'

'Yes, because anything a vicar does outside the etiquette book is a scandal. You are in a straitjacket of respectability and any deviation … look out! Newspaper headlines.'

At the time it seemed an odd thing to say as I had no intention, or in fact means, of breaking out of my 'straitjacket'. But there was no question that Quilp in *The Old Curiosity Shop* should have the ingratiating transatlantic tones of the new owner of the Manor, a man about six foot six inches tall but who, in both our views, was perfectly acceptable as an evil dwarf.

We proceeded with this enjoyable pastime on each visit. One afternoon, a cold day in March when leaves were only reluctantly starting to bud on the trees, I noticed Oliver had a slight sniffle, nothing more.

They rang me the next morning. Oliver had died in his sleep.

And now, just as he had predicted, I was caught up in a scandal.

Perhaps the new owner of the Manor would be too; I'd seen in the *Times* that some regulatory body was looking into his company's pension fund. But even if they found something untoward, it probably wouldn't be much of a scandal. People like that would just brazen it out and blame the overly complicated regulations.

They were there at Oliver's funeral, to my surprise, sitting in the front row along with Oliver's nephew who had inherited the title. Perhaps they wanted the reflected glory of propinquity. When I announced the hymn 'Abide with Me', which I said Oliver loved 'because it's so wonderfully gloomy,' I hadn't meant to mimic him but it just came out like that. Oliver's nephew let out a laugh which startled the new owners of the Manor.

After the service they'd been most pressing that I and my good lady come and dine with them again. I had been somewhat dismayed by this re-engagement, which I suspected arose through my friendship with an old baronet and my being on joking terms with a new one.

In the meantime the couple maintained their rising social trajectory, and now it seemed they had started raising pheasants on their estate, so it wouldn't be long before the poor birds were being slaughtered in the vicinity.

Hence the gift. Unfortunately. Because they were not a delicacy I was particularly fond of. I knew that they hadn't been hung for long enough, but I didn't like the gamy taste when they were.

———

As I was thinking all this, the back door opened and Joan walked in. For some reason I'd been expecting her. When would she come and pick up her stuff, I had wondered, and the most obvious time was when I was, or when she thought I was, at church.

I had a great desire to talk to her normally, to say something like, I've just been thinking about Oliver and how he always seemed able to predict things. But I didn't say that; those days were gone.

She stopped when she saw me at the table. I noticed she was carrying her suitcase, which she put down. 'I wasn't expecting …' Her manner was hesitant, so different to her arrival on her last visit.

'Jamie Robinson is taking the service. The curate,' I said. 'I'm officially on sick leave. It was all too much for me.' Especially since the papers … But I didn't have to say that.

She stood there uncertainly, and I looked behind her. But no sign of that awful woman. 'Didn't bring your friend,' I said.

'You could have let her in.'

Yes, I could have left her in and avoided a scene. I had always been adept at avoiding scenes, anything embarrassing, anything off-kilter. A scene, like a French woman acting oddly. A scene, like Jack and Bob being dragged into a French family to tell their tale while eating a meal surrounded by excitability and drama. A scene. Something memorable, a life lived vividly, which I'd thought I wanted and now seemed suddenly to have achieved.

No doubt Joan, knowing me as she did, had told her friend, 'Just create a scene.' Because in the past that would have done it.

'It was Coleen's idea to say you were involved. She thought, well I thought too, you might save me.' She had sat down on the opposite side of the table, the two of us at the table like so often in the past. She wasn't looking at me though, she was playing with the charms on her bracelet. Save her! I stared at her for a while, not comprehending. Then I realised.

Save her. By agreeing that I too was also a liar and a cheat, and had joined with her to steal the money from our sons.

'How would that have helped?' I said in exasperation. 'Plus it's stupid. I could have just gone in, signed a withdrawal slip and taken the money legitimately. No need for a whole lot of lies and a forged signature. Why would anybody believe such an idiotic story?'

Clearly they hadn't. And now it was so much worse for her. If she had just said she needed it until she could persuade a bank to give her a loan, after which she had intended to pay it all back, the story would have been much more believable and the blame lighter.

And as for saving her. 'There was a time,' I said, 'when I would have laid down my life for you, offered up all my worldly possessions for you.'

'But not the ministry.'

'No, but then I never demanded that you gave up teaching. We do the work we're called to do and at that point in time I wasn't called to work in the law.' I paused. 'I've been thinking in the last couple of weeks about when our relationship changed. I think as close as I can put a finger on, it would have been that holiday in the Lake District.'

'That dreadful place.'

Dreadful place then. But by Easter the following year it had all been done up, central heating, games room, kitchens with all mod cons. Dotty had made it clear to Uncle Peter that no one, not even a young person, would want to stay in it as it was. And the wider family had been invited again to take part in the 'After' part of the exercise, hopefully forgetting the 'Before' part. But our family hadn't gone. Or rather, it had been privately put to me that Joan was not welcome and nor was Sally. Obviously I couldn't go without Joan, but my mother had taken the two boys and had made no bones about the exclusion. 'You both behaved so badly last time, you're not invited.'

Sally was too young to remember her previous behaviour and had a monster temper tantrum. 'There she goes again,' said my mother. 'And what are you going to do?' she said to Joan. 'Find a café somewhere and sit at your ease until she stops?'

Because one of the aunts, alerted by my wife's suspicious dryness, had raided her raincoat pockets and discovered very good evidence that Joan's hike had not included climbing the dark brow of the mighty Helvelyn but instead consisted of catching a bus into Penrith and watching a film at the cinema there, followed by a leisurely three course meal at a hotel, a visit to a bookshop and then a toasted teacake in the High Street. Five quid's worth of recreation and pleasure. And bugger the rest of us.

It had lain there like a sore which never healed. Joan's attitude to her fellow holidaymakers had hardened, and socialising with my extended family became something I did alone or just with the kids. And it was worse when my mother's will was read.

I was fond of my uncles and aunts, my cousins and their children, and this tension had taken its toll on my marriage. The happy, thoughtless hugs, affectionate kisses, the reaching out and casual touching of our previous relationship, all gone. It became a partnership for the raising of the children, nothing more. And even that was now broken and gone as well.

—✦—

'They've been hounding me,' she said.

I knew what she was talking about, flashbulbs going off when you least expected it. Yes, I agreed, they were outside the vicarage day and night. I expected that the reason they weren't outside at that moment was because they were down at the church, thinking that I would be there. 'Jamie's moved in, he's in the spare room. He fends them off. As he fends off all the well-wishers who come bearing food.' (And who distressed me almost as much.)

'I don't get any well-wishers,' she said. 'Not even my own family.'

No. Don had offloaded his extreme disappointment in his sister on Naomi when she'd rung him. He'd said it was typical of Joan when she was growing up, always complaining she'd got the smaller slice, always determined to get more than her share. And now, look where that kind of attitude takes you! In his disgust he exaggerated her crimes and committed her to a lengthy jail sentence.

Naomi had rung me immediately after. What should she tell the others?

I had toned down my brother-in-law's view of the situation and then left it up to her what she told her cousins but suggested that maybe she wait until they were heading back to the car so as not to put a dampener on the trip for them.

She had subsequently rung me and said that both Jack and Sally had picked up there was something wrong. In the end she had told Sally that her mother and father were separating. Was it because of her, Sally had asked, and then Naomi felt she really had to tell her all of it, which was that her mother had stolen quite a large amount of money from a trust account set up for her brothers. Sally had then asked what had happened to her mother and Naomi admitted that she'd been arrested. Sally then became very fearful that she herself would be arrested for stealing and Naomi said no, she was sure that wouldn't happen now but as for the future it could be a different story. She'd given her a big hug and made her promise never to do it again.

In Jack's case, she hadn't told him about the theft but would do so later. Just that his parents were separating, and that his father was leaving the ministry. Jack seemed to know about the second outcome and didn't seem surprised about the first. She had repeated my wish that he continue on with whatever plans he and Antoine had made.

I summarised the conversation for Joan: that both Sally and Jack knew that we were separating. 'Naomi and Sally will be here in a couple of days,' I said. They were taking the bus the next day and returning to Tony's relatives, so they would be back on Tuesday or Wednesday. Apparently they'd all been having a wonderful time; Antoine's repertoire of English now extended to a wide variety of slang and Naomi had met a nice oboe player.

The boys were also going back on the bus with Naomi but afterwards they were going south to Tony's uncle in Devon, to live in a tent outside his smoke-damaged farmhouse and help with the harvest and do some walks on Dartmoor.

As for me? I was moving out by the end of the week. The archdiocese had found me a house to live in and I would continue to do some work in the parish. The electricity and gas for the new house would be put in my name on Monday and the phone was due to be connected soon. My Methodist friend had swung into action, and yesterday a team of volunteers had started painting over the grief-stricken greenish gloss of my predecessor. 'White ceilings and cream-coloured walls, keep it neutral,' Jack Halstead had said because no one knew how lairy the carpet was going to be. Bob's brother had brought it down that weekend and a carpet layer would lay it on Wednesday. The bathrooms would take more planning but were usable as they stood. In any event the furniture would arrive on Thursday. Hopefully Sally would help me arrange it, and after that I could move in.

Joan said nothing for a while. I continued plucking feathers and she reached over and took the second bird and started plucking too. Pluck, pluck, pluck, fast and assured.

'I have nowhere to live.' It came out of the blue. Her flatmate in York had asked her to leave and in fact been quite horrible to her about it and the press had somehow found Coleen's address and had been laying siege. Coleen was now fed up with standing next to a scandal and possibly being involved in it.

I paused. I'd finished plucking. I looked at the scrawny bird in front of me and experienced not even the slightest urge of generosity. 'I'm sorry to hear that,' was all I said.

'There's no point going back to Oxford, I've missed too much time and …' She didn't finish the sentence. Plus they'd frozen the house sale; she couldn't even get her deposit back.

I felt nothing, not even sympathy. Perhaps I would in the future, but at that moment I felt scarred and wounded and unable to treat with the enemy. I remembered again her smile of triumph when I'd said I wasn't going to do anything about the money she'd taken. This image reared up now and my rage returned just as her suitcase near the door swam into focus. More forcefully than I intended, I said, 'If you're asking to stay here, the answer is no. If you're asking to move in with me at any point, the answer is no.' I calmed and looked at her. 'I want our divorce to be as painless as possible and I want us still to be on speaking terms at least as far as the children are concerned. But when I said I wanted a divorce, I meant a real divorce, not a piece of legal paper. I don't want you in my life anymore. I feel used, done over, and cheated. As I said before, I want out of this house, the ministry, and the marriage as soon as possible.' I reached out to a packet of pills beside my coffee cup. 'Look at these,' I said. 'Jack Halsted suggested I go to the doctor and get some. He could see, everyone could see, I wasn't coping.'

She picked up the packet. Valium. 'Can I have one?'

'Be my guest. But take it later, you're not supposed to drive.'

'Where can I go?'

Why was she asking me? Why was her problem now suddenly my problem? After a moment of blank resentment I suddenly thought, what about her aunt's holiday cottage, that might be vacant. No one would find her, it was so remote.

She nodded. Sally had liked it there.

Well, good. If Sally preferred that arrangement … With her boots and her new equipment, there were plenty of walks she could do in the area.

Before she went back to school.

That hung for a while. 'She's not going back to that school,' I said. 'I should never have agreed to it in the first place. I don't believe you started thinking of separating at Christmas, I think you've been planning it for some time and this school was part of the plan. You in York, Sally in York, then you buy a house and you both stay in York, whether Sally wants that or not.' I paused but she said nothing. 'I think it should be clear, even to you, that she doesn't want it. Of course she's been telling me right from the start that she doesn't like the school, that she doesn't like being there, but then you always said "She's settled now." Why did I listen to you? No wonder she thought I'd abandoned her.'

She'd told Naomi she'd been talking to Pete about running away to his share house in Sheffield, but he'd described in detail his unforgivably unwashed housemates and the insalubrious, vermin-ridden and anarchic nature of the household, such that only a twenty-year-old male student could possibly call it home. The entry of her own brand of anarchy into such a place would barely be remarked on but as for breaking people's things in one of her tantrums they'd probably respond by going and peeing on her bed and he didn't think she was up to that level of warfare yet. Instead he'd advised her to up the ante at the school. He told her she was an expert at introducing chaos into her environment and it would be a very stoical institution who could put up with her when she really set her mind to it.

But the problem was, Joan had manoeuvred the school so that all the communication was being directed through her. I never found out about Sally's subsequent delinquencies.

Sally had realised, when she got into her mother's desk, that her mother had been forging my signature, and also realised that she could do that too and that once she had a passport she could run away to join Jack instead. She didn't appear to have thought beyond that. Perhaps the Berger family would invite her to stay and go to school with Antoine's sister like Jack had done. Her main plan seemed only to be about getting away, to escape from a mother who smothered her and a father who …

… Who had abandoned her in favour of peace.

Peace from all the discord, peace from the fighting …

A father who for all that was not a peacemaker, just a coward.

'When you said on the phone that Sally tells you everything, what you really meant was that you believe what she tells you. It must be clear to you now that that *isn't* everything, because a lot of the time what she tells you are lies. You ignored what she was saying about hating the school because you were so bound up in your own plan of escape. Just like hers, only escaping from different things. I went and talked to the school during the week because I wanted to hear their side. They said that as a result of our entreaties, they were willing to give her the benefit of the doubt and allow her to stay there for another term to see if her behaviour improved. I told them I had had no indications from them that her behaviour required any entreaties. They then showed me some letters they said they'd sent me and replies I was supposed to have signed and I in turn showed them, from among their records, which was my signature and which were the ones you'd forged. And then it turned out that the whole discussion about Sally staying on was in relation to her returning as a day girl! A day girl! That knocked me flat!'

Joan kept her head down and continued plucking. 'Did you say anything else?'

'What, did I say you'd stolen money from your sons? No. For one thing, they seemed to know that already and anyway it wasn't relevant. I assume that bank robbers still send their children to school. I told them I was very dissatisfied with the school in allowing themselves to be manipulated despite the clear indications that the child involved was not happy. I was appalled when I saw her reports, her real reports …' I paused to gather myself. 'I think they are now as appalled as I am so you can forget about her going back there. In any case, I will shortly be only semi-employed.'

Again there was a pause while Joan gathered up the feathers. 'You're not destitute,' she said. 'The church seems to be taking care of you. Plus your mother's money, you could have spent it any way you liked really, who's to know?'

I sighed impatiently. I had tried many times to explain to her that when a will left money to a named person, such as myself, for the benefit of other named persons, such as Pete and Jack, it was in fact setting up a trust and the money was not left to me to do as I liked with. And as a trustee – but I couldn't be bothered trying to explain it again, I was fed up with the whole thing. 'I'm going to have a talk with the boys. Now that you're out of the picture …' Of course she wasn't out of the picture as far as the children were concerned, but what I meant was, her voice no longer had weight in my decisions. I decided not to elucidate what I'd just said, I needed to keep ramming home to her the change in the situation. I was going to divorce her and we would be two separate people in two separate families. 'I'll talk to Pete and Jack about the money. They may be happy for me to spend some of it on Sally's education, the interest for instance. But it certainly won't be at that school.'

Joan handed me her pheasant. 'How are you going to talk to Pete?'

I arranged the birds on the baking pan and started layering bacon rashers over them.

'I wrote to him last weekend – he'd written to Jack with his address in Scotland. I didn't want him to learn what had happened by reading things in a newspaper. He rang during the week and he's coming on Thursday.'

Joan said nothing. I began placing forcemeat balls around the pheasants. 'He's going to help me set up the new place. I told him Sally would be back by then and he said he was fine with that. Sally has never been the problem.' I looked at her as I said it and she was looking out of the window as if searching for something. 'He told me that at Christmas you'd come and angrily demanded to know what he'd done to Sally this time. Assuming as usual that Sally was the victim. The truth of the matter was that the fight had nothing to do with the record. Pete was moving in with his girlfriend and Sally wanted to run away and live with them. Pete said that she was already breaking up *our* relationship and he wasn't having her breaking up his. That's when she scratched the record. It's always more complicated … Sally isn't always the victim and she doesn't always tell the truth, but you don't seem capable of understanding that and Pete said he won't put up with it anymore, always being blamed by you. I said to him that maybe he *was* partly to blame in this instance and that Sally had nothing to do with breaking up our relationship. I said that at some point in the past we'd just stop loving each other and if it wasn't for the fact I was a vicar we would probably have separated some time ago. So he agreed that yes he had gone too far. That's why he's coming back.'

She still said nothing, her face a frozen gargoyle caught in a stone-framed grimace of desperation. I couldn't look and turned to put the roasting dish in the oven. When I straightened up and turned back round, she was gone. I heard her in the hall talking on the phone.

I busied myself between the kitchen and the dining room, keep occupied the doctor had said. I was aware with relief that Joan was packing and suitcases and boxes were making their way through the house to her car.

I was shelling peas at the kitchen table when Jamie came in, cheery and excited. The church had been packed and he had initially detected a ripple of dismay when it was clear that he was running the service. When he went up into the pulpit he'd said, as we'd agreed, that I was withdrawing from the ministry. However, good news, instead of worthy topics straight from theological college, for the next little while he would be giving sermons written by me. So today's sermon, following on from last week's proposition disproving the adage that you can't teach an old dog new tricks, was going to be from Job 12:12 on the proposition that sometimes it's hard to teach a young dog old tricks. And he'd cheerfully added that next week's sermon would be on bricks.

The shuffling leaf-litter noise of suppressed laughter. How seductive, how irresistible. He had always thought if he hadn't been called to God's work, he would have liked to have been an actor.

I said, 'My Catholic friend, Father Gregory, is coming to lunch. He is also an actor manqué. And Jack Halsted, our local Methodist minister, is coming too. I think he's more of a stand-up comedian.'

Jamie told me that while standing at the church door farewelling the congregation (who emerged buzzing and humming like a beehive), one old man with a weatherbeaten face had greeted him and said, 'Eee Vicar that were a powerful sermon. If me and the lads don't go home to our dinner and have an all-out flaming row, you're not earning your keep!'

I laughed. I hadn't laughed for a week and it shook out of me, taking me by surprise. The satisfaction expressed by the old farmer showed that I had managed to poke the hornet's nest again. And they'd be back next week for more, oh yes, for a sermon on bricks there'd be standing room only.

Jamie went off to the study to prepare for Evensong, clearly buoyed by his experience at Morning Service. Thank God, I thought and joined my hands and bowed my head at the table. Thank you, God, for sending a young man with a cheerful disposition and a sense of humour to do your work here. Yes, he's a wee bit young with not a lot of life experience and who knows if they'll make him permanent. But at the moment, just at the right time, he's a breath of fresh air.

When I opened my eyes I saw Joan standing in the doorway looking at me. 'Praying again?'

'All the time. My knees are killing me.' Night and day, praying that things would come right, praying all the time for each of my family in turn, praying to God to grant them happiness as it was clear to me that no one in the family was happy. Only Pete had been overt, rattling sabres and saying what he felt. Jack had camouflaged it by withdrawing, and Sally had referred it sideways into increasingly bad behaviour and finally running away. And the two of us, we had let it drift and accumulate by not discussing things anymore until we were like atoms pinging in from outer space and I had to deduce our joint unhappiness not from direct evidence but from consequences.

She smiled, a forlorn smile, perhaps acknowledging the analogy, and then to my surprise came over and patted my shoulder and, ducking quickly, kissed me on the top of the head. 'Don't get up. I'm off. I've taken most of the suitcases I'm afraid, I'm going to store everything in Coleen's garage and go and visit my aunt as you suggested.' She turned at the back door. 'Keep praying.'

The gesture and the words were sad and affectionate, out of context for what had gone before. I got up and limped to the door but she was already in her car and driving off. I waved, did she see me? I wasn't sure.

I suddenly thought, was that smile she gave which had so infuriated me with regard to the return of the money, was it possible that it was not in fact a smile of triumph but a grimace of frustration? My response to her query, what was I going to do, was 'what can I do?' A positioning of myself as powerless, like on that holiday when she had demanded we all go home. We're here now, let's just put up with it.

Nothing was ever resolved …

Keep on praying.

I thought of my sudden spontaneous cry for help, *Help me, God*, in the bare room in Salamanca when I was looking down the dark tunnel into the future and could see no way forward. God moves in mysterious ways and I wondered if this wasn't to some extent an answer to my prayer. Because there was no going back; this was the end of things. I had said to Oliver that faithfulness was the most admirable of all virtues and was worth suffering for. And Oliver had said, 'You won't always feel like that.' I had misunderstood. I thought, as we had been talking about Oliver's life partner, that Oliver had meant I wouldn't be able to stand up to the disapproval of the Anglican church for such relationships. Now I saw that Oliver was predicting the end of my own faithfulness. To my marriage, to my wife. And in that ending, in my situation … what else but scandal!

The end of one journey and the beginning of another. I had been thinking again about Jack's comment in the cathedral, 'Is this normal?' I remembered how I had reacted against the question, as anyone probably would when questioned on their own version of normality. Maybe that was the question I needed to resolve, not goodness but normality. Unless you knew what was normal, how could you construct goodness or any of the other virtues? It seemed the one issue I needed to grapple with, and I had been striving to define it ever since because I knew by then that the normality I'd been trapped in was not one where I wanted to remain.

I remembered Bob's uncertain reaction to Jack's question in the cathedral and how the two of them had resolved it: Let's go and join in, what are friends for. Thus entering a new normal, the work of a moment. That flexibility they found so easy.

How long does something take to become normal when you *don't* find that flexibility easy? You were married and now you're not. You were a minister of religion and now you're not. You lived in one of the biggest houses in the district, and now you live in an unprepossessing bungalow. The entire landscape was different.

Then I thought of the trade-offs. I'd lived a life, of late, of walking on eggshells, trying to appease my wife. And now I didn't have to do that anymore. I'd been worrying about where the money was going, but now my income would be all accounted for and I could embrace poverty in comfort. I'd lost my eldest son, but now that son was back. And my youngest son who had been so quiet and restrained before, maybe he would now be able to dance down the road and act like a rowdy teenager.

Perhaps that was the thing about accepting a new normal – being thankful for new benefits, concentrating on the positives. I resolved to give that a go. Perhaps with the help of a counsellor I could learn to understand and accept my daughter's aberrant behaviour. Perhaps I too could change. I would certainly pray for that.

In the meantime, there were things to do, jobs to complete, the constant small actions of everyday life. I turned back to the sink and started on the potatoes.